WILLOW BROOK ROAD

Center Point
Large Print

Also by Sherryl Woods and available from
Center Point Large Print:

The Summer Garden
After Tex
Angel Mine
A Seaside Christmas
The Christmas Bouquet
Dogwood Hill

**This Large Print Book carries the
Seal of Approval of N.A.V.H.**

WILLOW BROOK ROAD

Sherryl Woods

CENTER POINT LARGE PRINT
THORNDIKE, MAINE

This Center Point Large Print edition is published in the year 2016 by arrangement with Harlequin Books S.A.

The text of this Large Print edition is unabridged. In other aspects, this book may vary from the original edition. Printed in the United States of America on permanent paper. Set in 16-point Times New Roman type.

ISBN: 978-1-62899-816-0

Library of Congress Cataloging-in-Publication Data

Names: Woods, Sherryl, author.
Title: Willow Brook Road / Sherryl Woods.
Description: Center Point Large Print edition. | Thorndike, Maine : Center Point Large Print, 2016. | ©2015
Identifiers: LCCN 2015042186 | ISBN 9781628998160
  (hardcover : alk. paper)
Subjects: LCSH: Large type books. | GSAFD: Love stories.
Classification: LCC PS3573.O6418 W557 2016 | DDC 813/.54—dc23
LC record available at http://lccn.loc.gov/2015042186

Dear Friends,

I usually use this space to give you a little background on the story you're about to read. This time I hope you'll indulge me as I thank some folks who've made it possible for me to write the many, many books you've read through the years.

Almost from the very beginning I have worked with the very savvy Denise Marcil, whose dedication as my agent has made her an incredible business partner. She had faith when mine flagged and a calming influence when I was on the edge of some writing cliff. No one could have worked harder or made this long career as much fun.

I've been blessed with so many fabulous editors through the years as well, women who've gently nudged me to create better and better stories. Lucia Macro started my career with Silhouette way back in the '80s. Joan Golan guided me through literally dozens of books. Now I have the absolute pleasure of working with Margaret O'Neill Marbury for the second time. I'm a better writer because of them and too many others to name (there have been 140-plus books, after all).

Once a book is polished to perfection—or as near to that as we ever get—it's in the hands of the publisher and sales team. I've worked with several, but no sales force could be more determined or enthusiastic than the men and women at Harlequin. Getting these books where you can find them is a tough job, and they're the very best at it. They have my undying gratitude!

There are dozens of others I'd like to thank, including family and friends, but I'll use this last little bit of space to thank you! Your emails and letters mean the world to me. And I've always tried to keep you in mind with every page I write. Bless you for the support and love you've shown.

All best as always,

Sherryl

1

The original Mick O'Brien–designed cottage on Willow Brook Road had been built with weathered gray shingles, white trim and a tiny back porch barely big enough for two rockers side by side. They faced Willow Brook, which fed into the Chesapeake Bay. The backyard sloped gently to the brook, with the graceful branches of a trademark weeping willow touching the lawn at the water's edge. The peaceful setting was just right for quiet conversation or relaxing with a good book.

In front the cottage featured a small yard with an actual white picket fence and a climbing yellow rosebush that tumbled over it with a profusion of fragrant blooms. Bright red and hot-pink geraniums filled pots on the stoop in a vibrant display of clashing colors. The property oozed picturesque charm.

With three cozy bedrooms and a fireplace in the living room and a surprisingly large eat-in kitchen, it was the perfect Chesapeake Shores vacation getaway or a starter home for a small family, but Carrie Winters had been living there alone and at loose ends for almost six months now. The only personal touch she'd added beyond the mismatched furniture she'd acquired from various family attics was the portrait of the whole O'Brien family taken at the Christmas wedding of her twin, Caitlyn.

These days, sitting in one of those rockers for more than a minute or two made her antsy. After two years in a pressure-cooker public relations job at which she'd excelled, being idle was a new experience, and one she didn't particularly like. She was too distracted for reading anything deeper than the local weekly newspaper. And though she loved to cook, making fancy meals for one person just left her feeling lonely.

Worst of all, she seemed incapable of motivating herself to get out of this funk she'd been in ever since coming home. Chesapeake Shores might be where she wanted—or even *needed*—to be as she tried to piece her life back together and reevaluate her priorities, but it had created its own sort of pressure.

While the rest of the O'Brien clan was unmistakably worried about her, her grandfather Mick was bordering on frantic. O'Briens did not waste time or wallow in self-pity, which was exactly what Carrie had been doing ever since the breakup of her last relationship. Timed to coincide with the crash-and-burn demolition of her career in the fashion industry, the combination had sent her fleeing from Paris and straight back to her loving family.

Carrie sighed and took a first sip of the one

glass of wine she allowed herself at the end of the day. Wallowing was one thing. Getting tipsy all alone was something else entirely. Even she was wise enough to see that.

An image of Marc Reynolds, the fashion-world icon she'd thought she loved, crept into her head, as it did about a hundred times a day. That was down from about a million when she'd first flown home from Europe after the breakup. If it could even be called that, she thought wryly. Truthfully, she'd finally realized that Marc thought of her more as a convenient bed partner and workhorse whose public relations efforts for his fashion empire had helped to put it on the fast track to international acclaim. Unbeknownst to her, his heart apparently belonged to a she-devil, self-absorbed model who treated him like dirt. Carrie could relate, since Marc had pretty much done the same to her. She was still struggling to understand how her judgment could possibly have been so clouded that she hadn't seen that sooner. Surely the signs had been there. Had she been so besotted she'd missed them? If so, how could she possibly trust her instincts about a man again?

Not that she was going to let *that* be an issue anytime soon. She was swearing off the male of the species until she figured out who she was and what she truly wanted. At the rate she was progressing on that front, it could take years.

Enough! she told herself firmly, carrying her almost-full glass inside and stepping over a scattering of toys as she went. She smiled as she picked up a floppy-eared bunny and set it gently in a chair. A stack of children's picture books sat on a nearby table.

Taking care of her twin sister's little boy, Jackson McIlroy, was about the only thing that gave her a sense of fulfillment these days. With Caitlyn serving a medical internship at Johns Hopkins, and Caitlyn's husband, Noah, running an increasingly busy family medicine practice here in town, Carrie had volunteered for day-care duty whenever they needed her. More and more often they'd come to rely on her, which suited her just fine, but seemed to be making everyone else in her driven family a little crazy. Babysitting wasn't considered a suitable career goal for the granddaughter of the town's founder.

She picked up a few more toys, put them in the brightly colored toy box she'd painted herself one particularly dreary winter day, then grabbed her purse and walked into town. Ten minutes later she was at O'Brien's, the Irish pub her second cousin Luke had opened a few years back. She knew she'd find a good meal there, even if it came with a serving of family meddling from whichever O'Brien happened to be around.

When she walked in the door, she was startled to find it mostly empty.

"Hey, Carrie," Luke said, automatically pouring a glass of white wine for her.

"Where is everybody?" she asked, as she settled on a stool in front of the magnificent old bar that Luke had found in Ireland and shipped home to be the centerpiece of his pub.

"It's barely five o'clock," he pointed out. "We'll be filling up soon."

Carrie glanced at her watch and groaned. Today—a day without the baby to watch—had been endless. Apparently it wasn't close to being over, either.

"Can I ask you a question?" she said, as Luke polished glassware and readied the bar for this evening's business.

He studied her face for a moment, then came around the bar and sat down beside her, giving her his full attention. "What's on your mind?"

"You were the youngest in my mom's generation, right?"

"Oh, yeah," he confirmed.

"Did you feel pressured to accomplish something?"

He laughed. "Are you kidding me?"

"Not even a little bit," she said seriously.

"You know all this, but let me remind you. By the time I finished college, your mom was a financial success story on Wall Street. Kevin had served in the military, then jumped onto the bandwagon to preserve the bay with Uncle

11

Thomas. Connor was a hotshot divorce lawyer in Baltimore. Bree had opened a successful flower shop, then a local theater, where she's now writing and directing to critical acclaim. And Jess was barely into her twenties and already turning the Inn at Eagle Point into a successful regional destination."

He allowed that to sink in, then added, "That's what I was up against. On top of that, my brother started working with Uncle Mick as an architect straight out of college, and my sister is all but running the real estate business here in town with my dad. O'Briens seemed to know what they wanted in the womb, all of them except me."

"And me," Carrie lamented. "Funny how you were the youngest and felt lost. Cait and I are the oldest in our generation. She recognized her destiny even before she got out of high school. She's determined to be a doctor and save the world. Not even marriage and a baby have derailed her plans."

Luke grinned. "And your goals aren't that lofty?"

"I'm not sure I even have goals," she admitted. "I thought I did. I enjoyed PR work well enough. I was good at it, too. And I liked being in the fashion industry, but that was more about being with Marc than the work. It didn't break my heart when another job in fashion didn't materialize right away. Working with him is what I miss most, so that must be telling me something."

Luke studied her with a commiserating look. "Have you figured out the message?"

She shrugged. "Nope. All I know is that I hate being at loose ends."

"What about that trip you took with Uncle Mick to Africa? Any inspiration there?"

Her grandparents had gone to Africa to check out several villages in dire need of medical help, especially since the outbreak of Ebola had had such a devastating impact. Mick had been drafted by Cait and a doctor in Baltimore into designing small medical facilities for the villages to provide the care they so desperately needed. It had been an eye-opening trip with an idealistic mission she admired.

"Sure. It made me realize how lucky we've all been. I've donated a ton of money from my trust fund to the cause because I've seen firsthand how worthwhile it is, but I don't want to return, not the way Cait's chomping at the bit to go. She was so envious that I got to go with Grandpa Mick and Grandma Megan. Me?" She shook her head. "I could hardly wait to get back home."

"The States?"

"Not just the States, but here, back in Chesapeake Shores. I thought once I got here everything would magically become clear to me."

Luke gave her a long, considering look. "Have you thought about staying here, Carrie? Really thought about it? I always knew this town was right for me. It was just about the only thing I did know, but you've lived in a lot of exciting cities—New York, Milan, Paris. Are you absolutely certain Chesapeake Shores is big enough for you?"

She frowned at the question, which seemed to suggest a shallowness she didn't appreciate. She didn't need glitz and glamour. She really didn't. She'd had a taste of it. That had been enough.

"What do you mean?" she challenged. "This is home for me, Luke, the same as it is for you."

"If you say so," he said, his doubts still evident.

"I do say so."

"You were born in New York," he reminded her. "You went to college there, too, and traveled all over the world when you were working in fashion. I've only been to Ireland, where things were pretty laid-back, especially in the smaller villages, but I imagine the lifestyle here is very different from the glamorous places you've seen in France and Italy. It's definitely a world away from the hustle and bustle of New York."

Though her instinct was to counter Luke's obvious skepticism with complete certainty, she took a sip of her wine and actually gave the question some thought.

"It is different, but in a good way," she replied slowly, trying to put her gut feelings into words. "The pace is slower. The values are different.

Family really counts for something. Mom saw that. She left New York and brought me and Caitlyn back here."

"Because she was in love with Trace," Luke said.

Carrie sighed. "Yes, Trace did play a big part in her decision, but she's been happy being home. She'd tell you that. She's figured out how to balance the career she loves and the family she loves even more."

"Balance is important," Luke agreed, then gave her another of his annoying long looks. "What do you envision doing with your life here? I know the ambition gene can't possibly have skipped over you completely. All O'Briens have it."

"Not me," she admitted as if it were a crime. Luke was right about one thing—O'Briens were expected to be excellent multitaskers, and, despite her last name being Winters, she was an O'Brien through and through. Luke had brought the conversation full circle, right back to those goals that seemed to be eluding her. She'd been so blasted lucky her entire life. What right did she have to complain about an unexpected bump in the road?

"All I ever really wanted was to be a wife and mom," she told her cousin. She made the admission in a hushed voice, as if it were some sort of crime to want so little for herself.

When Luke didn't react as if she were crazy,

she continued, "Gram was my role model. Nell made a real home for Mom and her siblings after Grandpa Mick and Grandma Megan split up. I always saw myself doing that same thing—cooking, baking, nurturing my kids—right here, surrounded by family. All through college I kept expecting to meet someone and fall in love. I practically made a career out of dating. I thought for sure I'd get a marriage license fifteen minutes after I picked up my diploma."

She sighed again. "That was the plan, but it never happened. Then I met Marc and thought he was the one. Of course, he was the last man on earth who'd ever be happy in a small town, so I have no idea how I expected him to fit into my dream."

"Ever heard of compromise?" Luke asked with a smile.

"From Marc? Not likely."

"How about you?"

"For the right man, sure," she said glibly, then wondered. "Okay, you're right. I can't settle. It would never work. I want what Mom and Trace have, what Bree has with Jake and Grandpa Mick has found with Grandma Megan now that they're back together. I want the whole happily-ever-after thing."

"So you can't settle and you claim you don't care about a career," Luke summed up. "You have yourself a real dilemma."

"Isn't that what I've been trying to tell you?" she said in frustration.

"Maybe you need to focus, pick the area of your life that matters the most to you, the one over which you have some control."

She smiled at that. O'Briens did love to control things. Her grandfather was a master at that and he'd instilled that stubborn, we're-capable-of-anything streak in all of them.

"We've already concluded that I can't control when or if the right man might come along, and I have no career goals, at least not the kind I'm passionate about," she reminded him yet again.

"I think you're making this too complicated," Luke suggested. "Stop fretting about a career, if that's not what you care about. Put it on the back burner. Get out there and start dating. There are single men in here every night of the week. I'll fix you up. When was the last time you went on a date? The path to marriage generally starts with a first date."

"So I've heard," she said, though random dating didn't appeal to her. She'd done that all through college to no avail. Besides, she'd sworn off men until she figured out how she'd been so wrong about Marc, how she'd misjudged his values and his feelings.

But Luke was right about one thing. She did need some sort of social life before she went completely stir-crazy. "How about this? I don't want to be fixed up, but the next time I'm in here, if there's a nice guy around, introduce us. Women and men can be friends, right? That's not a bad starting point."

"I have my doubts about men and women being pals, but it's definitely a start," Luke said. "I predict you'll be married in no time, with a half dozen kids underfoot."

As alluring as that image was, Carrie could see the downside. "Can you picture what Grandpa Mick will have to say about that? He loves all his grandchildren and great-grandchildren, but he expects more from us."

"Forget your grandfather. This is about what you want. You know Nell will be on your side."

Carrie smiled. "Sure she will, but she'll be standing there all alone. Grandpa Mick will be horrified. So will just about everyone else. Even Mom and Trace will think I'm wasting my potential."

"This is about you, though," Luke argued. "And about what will make you happy. When it comes down to it, I think that's what they truly want for all of us. As appalled as my dad was by the idea of this pub, he got on board when he saw how much it meant to me. Treat the whole marriage thing as if it were a job hunt. Interview applicants on a daily basis."

Carrie gave him a chiding look. "You say that

as if it's perfectly simple to pluck the perfect man out of thin air or to identify him by getting him to answer a list of questions. Trust me, it's not. Besides, where's the magic in that?"

Her cousin chuckled. "Ah, so you want the magic, too?"

"Of course. And until I find it, I can't very well sit around and do nothing. I still need a goal. Being idle isn't all it's cracked up to be. I'm not suited for that, either."

Luke's expression turned thoughtful. While he pondered whatever he was pondering, Carrie sipped her wine.

"You're babysitting for half the kids in the family, aren't you?" he said eventually.

"Yes, but what's your point? That's not exactly a job."

He gave her a long look. "Make it one."

She frowned at the seemingly offhand suggestion, though it was evident Luke was warming to the idea. "What do you mean?" she pressed.

"You love kids. You don't have any of your own on the immediate horizon." He stared at her as if willing her to reach the same conclusion he had. When she remained silent, he added with a touch of impatience, "Consider opening a day care."

Carrie immediately waved off the idea. "Come on, Luke. I can't charge family for keeping an eye on their kids."

"Why not? If you weren't around, they'd be

paying somebody else. I certainly charge them for their pints of ale when they come in here."

"Not the same thing," she insisted. "This is a business. We all understand that."

He laughed. "And the day care could be your business," he said. "Just something to think about. The town could use one. Moira was saying that to me not twenty-four hours ago. She said if we're ever going to have kids, given our busy schedules and her traveling with her photography exhibits, we'll need someone we trust to care for them. She flatly refuses to put a playpen in the corner and see our child raised in a bar."

Carrie could just imagine Moira making that point very clear. From her very first introduction to the O'Briens in her native Ireland, Moira had never hesitated to express an opinion. It had earned her the nickname of Maddening Moira, until Luke had pleaded with all of them to drop it.

Luke gave her a grin. "Maybe when you're totally focused on starting a business for yourself, the right man will suddenly appear. By then you may be so busy, you won't even have time for him."

"The way you were when Moira came along?" she said, recalling how he'd expected Moira to sit by patiently while he got the pub up and running. She'd taken exception to that.

"Exactly," he admitted with a grimace. "Moira tried to get some sense through my hard head, but it was Nell who finally set me straight about waiting."

"How? I never heard the story."

"After Gram fell ill during the trip she and Dillon took to New York, she called Moira and me into her room at the hospital and told us to stop wasting time. She reminded us that we should never put off the things in life that really matter, that there's never a perfect time for falling in love. I swear, even lying there in that hospital bed looking so blasted tiny and frail, she was a force to be reckoned with."

"She still is," Carrie said, then admitted, "It scares me to think what will happen when we lose her. She's the bedrock of this family."

"And to hear her tell it, she's not going anywhere till she's satisfied we're all settled and content," Luke replied. "With a whole slew of great-grandchildren around now, I think she's planning on being with us for a while."

"I hope so," Carrie said softly.

Luke patted her shoulder as he stood up. "I need to get back to work. Just think about what I said. Maybe day care is the right fit for you, maybe not, but you won't know until you've explored the possibility, the same as I figured out a pub was the right fit for me the first time I walked into one in Ireland and realized it could be the heart of a community. I found my true calling on that trip."

"And Moira," she said, smiling.

"And Moira," he agreed.

After he'd gone into the kitchen to check in with his chef, Carrie sighed. Was there any merit to Luke's idea? Or would it feel as if she was giving up on her own dream of having a family by surrounding herself with other people's children? She was a great babysitter, a terrific aunt, but there was a whole lot more to running a day care, including more regulations than she'd ever had to deal with. Of course, she had taken a couple of early childhood development and child psychology classes in school. She'd been fascinated by the topics and she'd aced them. She might even have pursued more classes back then, if she hadn't gotten a PR internship and gravitated in that direction.

She thought of all the O'Brien kids who were underfoot on a regular basis and smiled. They were the best part of her life, no question about that. Could she turn that into a career?

Just as Luke had suggested, it was something worth considering. She certainly didn't have an alternative in mind and she needed to do something before her family lost patience and she lost her mind wrestling with all this indecisiveness.

Sam glanced in the rearview mirror and saw that his nephew had finally fallen asleep. He breathed a sigh of relief. He wasn't sure which was worse, the long silences when Bobby said nothing at all or the string of unanswerable questions that had been thrown at Sam ever since his sister and brother-in-law had been killed in an accident two weeks earlier. The discovery that Bobby was being placed in his care had shocked *him* into silence, for sure. It was little wonder it had left the six-year-old thoroughly confused.

And now, here they were driving into Chesapeake Shores, a town where Sam hadn't even had time to get himself settled before learning about the tragedy that had taken Bobby's parents. He'd left his new job as a grieving brother, his only thoughts focused on getting through the funeral. Now he was returning as a single parent with so many thoughts and fears swirling in his head, he had no idea which needed to be tackled first. He'd put his own grief on the back burner so he could stay focused on the scared little boy suddenly in his care.

"Dinner," he muttered under his breath. Whenever Bobby awakened, he'd be starving. The one thing Sam did know was that he couldn't go on feeding the boy nothing but fast food, the only thing that seemed to tempt Bobby to eat. Fortunately fast food was in short supply in Chesapeake Shores, which didn't have a chain restaurant in town. The closest McDonald's or Burger King was miles away.

Instead of heading straight to the Inn at Eagle

Point, where he'd been staying since his arrival in town, Sam turned onto Shore Road and found a parking spot across from several local restaurants, including O'Brien's, a pub that specialized in traditional Irish comfort food. Wasn't that exactly what he and Bobby both needed? Something comforting and filling?

Exiting the car, he hesitated. Did he have to wake Bobby just so he could run in, order some food and run back across the street? It was early enough that the street was mostly deserted. The shops had closed, so few tourists were lingering along the waterfront, and it was too early for most people to be heading out for dinner. And it was, after all, Chesapeake Shores, a town without any significant crime except for the occasional high school prank.

Even as Sam opened the back door of the car, he could hear Bobby's soft snores. The boy looked so peaceful; it seemed a shame to wake him. Convincing himself his nephew would never be out of sight, he jogged across the street and went inside, grabbing a menu off the bar, then moving back to the doorway while he glanced through the offerings. Irish stew was the day's special. That sounded healthy and filling. And how long could it possibly take to dish it into a container so Sam could be on his way?

After one more glance to reassure himself that Bobby hadn't awakened, he returned to the bar, only to find no one there to take his order. In fact, the only person in the place was a young woman, her expression glum as she stared into a glass of wine she'd barely touched.

"What's a man have to do to get some service in here?" he asked irritably.

The woman's responding frown was likely justified, but Sam couldn't worry about the impression he might be making. He had a child outside and way too much on his mind.

"Sorry," she said in a cool, polite tone. "My cousin had to go in back to speak to the chef. He'll be right out, I'm sure."

"You don't work here?"

"No, but if you're in a hurry, I can get Luke."

Sam nodded. "Please. Or can you just tell him I'd like two orders of the Irish stew to go?" He hesitated. "Do you think a six-year-old would like that?"

Her expression brightened. "Sure. It's great. All the kids in our family love it. I'll give Luke your order. He'll fix you right up."

Sam couldn't help noticing the sexy high heels she was wearing when she slid off her bar stool. Those shoes drew attention to long, shapely legs. He didn't know a lot about fashion, but he had a feeling she hadn't bought them at the discount store out on the main highway. In fact, her entire outfit, as casual as it was, seemed to shout that it had come from a designer, not off the rack. A rich tourist, perhaps, though she did seem to be totally comfortable in here. And hadn't she referred to the owner or the bartender as her cousin?

Sam didn't have time to try to put the puzzle pieces together. He sure as heck didn't have time to allow his curiosity to be stirred by a beautiful woman. His life had recently gotten more complicated than he could ever have imagined. Right now, he needed to get his food and get back to Bobby.

Once more, he went back to the door and glanced across the street. There was no sign that Bobby was stirring and nobody was standing beside the car looking alarmed that a child had been left alone inside. That didn't mean Sam could be gone for much longer. The last thing he wanted was for Bobby to awaken, find himself alone and panic.

Pacing impatiently, he was startled when the woman appeared at his side, obviously on her way out.

"Your food's on the way," she said as she opened the door.

A light floral scent that reminded him of summer nights was left in her wake as she passed him, then headed across the street.

Sam saw the exact moment when she spotted Bobby. She stopped beside the car, did a double take, then turned back to give Sam a look that could have melted steel. She whirled around on those spike heels of hers and marched straight back in his direction.

The pub's door slammed open and she stood before him.

"That's your car?"

Sam nodded, a flush crawling up his face.

"You left your son in the car all alone? What were you thinking?" she demanded indignantly. "This may be a safe town, but no place is 100 percent safe. Plus it can get hot inside in practically no time, especially on a sunny day like this."

Even though he knew she was probably justified in her indignation, Sam stared her down.

"Why is this your business?"

"Because innocent children need to be protected from irresponsible parents."

"I'm not his parent," Sam retorted, though not only was that not entirely true, he knew it was also hardly the point. He'd been a parent for about a nanosecond. He was still getting the hang of it. "He's my nephew."

Since her harsh stare didn't waver at that, he found himself explaining. "His parents died in an accident two weeks ago. I'm just bringing him here to live with me. You'll have to forgive me if I thought letting him finally get some rest was more important than dragging him over here to wait with me while I get some food. He was never out of my sight, was he? And the windows are all cracked, so there's air circulating. Didn't you see me standing right here by the door keeping an eye on him?"

"I suppose," she said, backing down, but sparks still flashed in her eyes. "You can't take chances with a child's safety. Things can happen in the blink of an eye."

"I'm well aware of that, probably more so than you are," he said. "That's what happened to my sister and brother-in-law. They were gone in the blink of an eye. Nobody could have anticipated that. And I sure as heck didn't anticipate becoming a dad overnight."

She faltered at that, her cheeks turning pink. "I'm sorry. Look, just go back to the car, okay? I'll bring your food out as soon as it's ready. It'll make us both feel better if he's not over there alone."

Sam started to argue, then gave in. He pulled a couple of twenties from his wallet and gave them to her. "I'm not sure how much the bill will be, but this should cover it."

She handed back one of the twenties. "This will do. I'm going to have Luke put some chocolate-chip cookies in with your order. They're not on the menu, but he keeps them on hand for the kids in our family. They're my great-grandmother's recipe. She bakes once a week and brings them over here. She leaves a supply at my house, too, since most of the kids are in and out of there, too."

The thought of home-baked cookies triggered a longing in Sam, one he hadn't even realized he'd buried deep inside. "My grandmother used to do the same thing. She baked for the whole family. She's been gone for years, but I still remember the way her kitchen smelled."

A smile spread across the woman's face at last. "There's nothing like it, is there? Don't ever tell Nell, if you happen to meet her, but I bake, too, just so my house will smell like that when the kids come by. I want to be the go-to aunt or cousin or neighbor when it comes to cookies."

She shooed him toward the door. "Go. I'll be over with your food in just a minute."

Sam dutifully left the pub and crossed the street. He stood beside the car and waited for the woman to emerge with his order. At least he told himself his gaze was so intense because his stomach was rumbling, but the truth was, he wanted another glimpse of her. She was a mass of contradictions with her fancy clothes and home-baked cookies, the lost expression he'd caught on her face when he first noticed her sitting at the bar, and her fiery indignation when she'd found Bobby alone in the car.

Contradictions like that, though, usually meant trouble. And these days Sam had more of that than he could possibly handle.

❧ 2 ❧

Through the pub's window, Carrie studied the man as he waited beside the car. He looked bone-weary. Little wonder after just suffering a tragic loss and then finding out he was responsible for his nephew. No longer furious about finding the boy alone in the car, she was able to cut the man some slack, but just this once. She'd be keeping an eye on him, and not because he was handsome as sin with his tousled hair, deep blue eyes and firm jaw, but because that child was likely in need of an advocate who knew something about kids.

When Luke emerged from the kitchen with the take-out order, Carrie held out her hand. "I'll take it to him."

Luke frowned. "Since when did we offer curbside service and how'd you get roped into it?"

"Just give me the bag. Did you put in some of Nell's cookies?"

"You told me to, didn't you? Of course I did. Are you picking up the check, too?"

"Very funny. His money's by the register. Keep the change."

She was about to open the door, when Luke called out.

"Carrie!"

She stopped, but didn't turn around.

"Come back here after you've delivered that," he said.

"I was going to head home."

"Not just yet," he said firmly.

A few years ago she might have reminded him he wasn't the boss of her, but she was more mature now. "Fine," she said grudgingly.

She crossed the street and handed over the bag. The aroma of the stew made her stomach rumble. Maybe returning to the pub was a good idea, after all. She could use some of that stew herself.

"Here, take this quick, before I decide to dive in and eat it myself," she said, handing him the bag.

He reached for the bag, took a sniff and sighed. "It does smell good. I hope Bobby will eat it."

"Is he a picky eater?"

"It's hard to tell. He's shown little interest in anything the past couple of weeks, but that could be because of the circumstances. The only thing I've been able to coax him to eat are burgers and French fries, but I know I need to break that habit."

"Now you're talking like a responsible parent," she told him approvingly.

He gave her a wry look. "If only it were that easy. Make sure he eats healthy meals and all will be right in his world."

"Are you staying here in Chesapeake Shores or just passing through?" When he didn't immediately respond, she added, "I'm Carrie Winters, by the way."

He held out his hand. "Sam Winslow. I gather you're a local."

"Absolutely. My cousin Luke owns the pub. I think I mentioned that. My grandfather, Mick O'Brien, designed the whole town."

He regarded her with amusement. "Is that what entitles you to dig into the lives of everyone you meet?"

"That's just natural curiosity," she said, trying to keep a defensive note from her voice. "And friendliness. Chesapeake Shores is known for being a very friendly town. We roll out the welcome mat for strangers. You'd know that if you'd spent any time here, which must mean you're passing through."

For a moment she thought he wasn't going to answer, but then he sighed heavily. "Actually I moved here about two weeks before my sister's accident. I'm the new web designer and tech expert for the local paper."

Carrie's mood immediately improved. She beamed at him. "Then you're working for Mack Franklin. That makes you practically family. He's married to my cousin Susie—well, my second cousin, actually—she's Luke's sister."

He shook his head, amazement written on his

face. "There really are O'Briens everywhere in this town, aren't there?"

She gestured toward the carved gold letters on a dark green background on the front of the pub. "We don't try to hide it," she said. "And there are a lot of us, especially when you take into account extended family. And it's a close-knit community in general. You're going to love it here, and it will be a great place for your nephew to grow up."

Exhaustion and defeat seemed to settle on his face once more. "I hope so. His parents dying so suddenly, moving to a new place plus adapting to having me as, well, whatever I'm supposed to be now." He shook his head. "It's a lot for a six-year-old to handle."

Carrie could only imagine how difficult it must be, and not just for a little boy, but for this man, as well. "If you ever want to talk to someone, my aunt Jess, who owns the Inn at Eagle Point, is married to a shrink."

"Will Lincoln?" he said, looking surprised.

"You've met him?"

"I'm still staying at the inn till I can find a place to buy or rent. I've had a couple of conversations with Will. He invited me to join some of the guys to shoot hoops. He never mentioned what he does for a living."

"He's a great guy. Or if you just need somebody to listen, Luke's not bad. He lives up to the stereotype of a bartender who can listen without passing judgment. That's why I was in there tonight spilling my guts to him. I have a slew of people in my family who'd happily listen, but not without telling me what to do. Luke just threw out suggestions. He gave me some interesting food for thought."

Sam looked her over skeptically, apparently leaping to conclusions based on her designer clothes, the ridiculously expensive shoes she loved and the flawless makeup she'd learned to apply working in fashion, where looks mattered. Being in the world of cover models required that she pay a lot of attention to her own appearance if she hoped to compete. Was it too much for Chesapeake Shores? So what if it was? It was hardly something she needed to apologize for. Since when was looking presentable in public a crime?

"You have problems?" he asked, proving she'd read his disdain correctly.

"Everybody has problems," she said. "Some are worse than others, but that doesn't mean they don't matter to the people trying to get through them."

"Tell me about yours," he said. "Did you have trouble deciding what to wear tonight? Perhaps your Porsche wouldn't start? Or maybe you accepted a date with a guy and are trying to figure out how to get out of it?"

The comments suggesting that she was so

shallow stung, especially coming from a man who couldn't possibly know anything about her.

She backed off at once, no longer trying to hide her annoyance. "Look, I was just trying to help. That's what we do in this town. I don't deserve to be judged or insulted."

He turned and faced her then, and she could clearly see the despair in his dark, shadowed eyes along with what was perhaps just a hint of guilt.

"I'm sorry," he said. "Truly. I don't know what got into me. I usually have better manners than that."

"You obviously have a lot on your mind," she said, deciding yet again to make allowances. It seemed she was being called on to make a lot of allowances, something she rarely did. "Sometimes sharing a burden helps. If you don't want to talk to me or Luke, just about anyone in Chesapeake Shores would be eager to listen and lend a helping hand."

"I'm not sure there's a well-meaning person on earth who can fix this," he told her.

"Well, as difficult as it might be, time usually takes care of most problems." She gave him a rueful look. "And just so you know, I don't have the patience for waiting for that to happen, either. I'm just told that it's true."

He smiled as she'd intended.

"I'm pretty sure this test was designed to try mine, too," he admitted. "They do say karma has a way of getting you. A couple of weeks ago I was a pretty carefree guy. Now I'm tense and capable of biting off the head of someone who's only trying to be nice."

"You're probably entitled, but fair warning," she said lightly. "I won't let you get away with it again."

"Thank you." He looked away. "The grief, that's one thing. You're right. I'll get over that in time. But becoming a dad to a boy I've only seen a few times before . . ." He shook his head. "I have no idea how to do that." He gave her another doubtful look. "Any thoughts on that?"

"One day at a time," she said at once. "I know it sounds glib, but that's the only way to do anything that's difficult, at least that's what my family is always saying. And ask for help when you need it."

"I've always relied on myself. My parents are long gone and my sister and I, well, we'd had our differences. We hadn't been all that close the past few years, which is another reason this custody arrangement came as such a shock." Sorrow darkened his eyes. "Now I get to live with regret for not doing more to mend fences. We always think we have all the time in the world to fix things."

"I've found that regrets are usually pointless," she told him. "The situation is what it is. You have a child to consider now. If you do right by him, I'm sure that's all that would really matter to your sister. And trust me, when word gets around about what you're going through, you'll have all the support you could possibly need."

She hesitated, tried to talk herself out of making an impulsive offer, but then made it, anyway. "In fact, if you need any help with day care, I can probably help out. I don't run a day care, but I watch my sister's baby a few days a week. Several of my younger cousins stop by from time to time to hang out. Your nephew would be welcome. I have an endless supply of cookies on hand and a lot of the coolest toys."

For the first time since they'd met, Sam smiled, and it actually reached his eyes. Carrie's heart did a sudden and entirely predictable flip, something that hadn't happened to her in all the months since she'd been away from Europe and Marc. It was disconcerting—and very untimely, given her recent resolution to avoid jumping into another relationship anytime soon.

"I'd better get back to the pub," she said hurriedly. "Luke's waiting for me. And I hear a bowl of that stew calling my name."

"Sure," Sam said and held up the bag. "Thanks for bringing this to me, and for the cookies."

"No problem. And remember what I said, if you need help, ask. You can always get my cell phone number or address from Luke or Mack or Susie."

She turned and crossed the street quickly. She

hesitated for just an instant, trying to assure that there was a perfectly neutral expression on her face before she saw Luke. She was careful not to glance over her shoulder to see if Sam had left or even waved. He was just a guy, after all, a customer. She didn't need her cousin going all protective on her.

"You took long enough," Luke said, frowning when she finally went inside.

"You're lucky I came back at all," she retorted. "You know how we all dislike being ordered to do anything. And I'm only here for some of that Irish stew, not for one of your lectures."

Luke's scowl deepened. "I just want to know why you were waiting on that guy. It's not as if you work here. And he was rude. I might have been in the kitchen, but I'm not deaf. I heard the way he talked to you when he first came in."

"There were extenuating circumstances," she said.

"Really? Tell me."

She debated doing just that, but decided it wasn't her story to tell. "I'm sure you'll be seeing him around. He's working for Mack. Get your sister to fill you in. Forget about the stew. I'm going home."

"Please just tell me you have no interest in him beyond being nice to one of my customers," her cousin said.

"What if I can't say that?"

38

"Carrie, come on. That guy has issues."

"No question about it," she agreed.

"Don't you have enough issues of your own without taking on his?"

"I'm not taking on anything. I'm being friendly. That's what we do around here. Ask Mick."

Luke groaned. "Blast it all! I leave you alone in here for five minutes and you manage to get tangled up in trouble."

She laughed at the exaggeration. "Stop fretting. I'm not tangled up in anything," she said, waving as she went out the door.

Not yet, anyway.

Mick watched his granddaughter walk away from O'Brien's as if she were in a big hurry to get somewhere. She didn't even turn around when he called out to her.

"What's going on with her?" he grumbled to his wife as he held open the door to the pub. "Since when does she ignore her own grandfather?"

"When she doesn't want to talk about whatever's on her mind," Megan said. "Ever since she came home, you've been all over her to make some decisions about her future. Maybe she's tired of it."

"Well, she needs to stop wasting time," he replied. "You can't tell me she's still brokenhearted over the jerk in Europe. He obviously wasn't good enough for her."

"Not your call," Megan reminded him. "It's not about whether he was or wasn't good enough for her, or about how long it should take her to get over him."

Mick just scowled at his wife. He hated it when Megan got all reasonable and pointed out that he couldn't control everything around him, especially when it came to his own family. Okay, she was usually right, but that didn't mean he should stop trying to make sure things worked out the way they were supposed to.

"Hey, Uncle Mick," Luke said. "Aunt Megan. Do you all want a table or are you going to sit at the bar?"

"We'll sit at the bar," Mick told him. "Then you can fill us in on why Carrie was in such a state when she left here."

"Mick!" Megan protested. "Don't involve Luke in this."

Luke regarded them with an innocent expression that Mick wasn't buying for a second.

"Was she in some kind of a state?" Luke inquired, as if he hadn't noticed a thing out of the ordinary about her mood.

Mick frowned at him. "Did all you kids make a pact to keep me in the dark about things?"

His nephew laughed. "No pact," he insisted. "But I did take an oath to protect my customers' privacy."

"Carrie's not a customer. She's family."

"Then march right on over to her house and ask her yourself," Luke suggested, setting a pint of ale in front of Mick and a glass of red wine in front of Megan, who was trying hard to bite back a smile.

"Ungrateful wretch," Mick mumbled.

"Watch it or I'll tell Gram you were calling me names," Luke retorted.

"Ma doesn't scare me," Mick said.

"Well, she ought to," Megan said. "Now hush. Let's have a nice dinner and then go home."

Mick sighed as Luke beat a hasty retreat, leaving him to stew over the lack of information. "You're both acting as if I'm in the wrong for being concerned about my own granddaughter," he told Megan.

"Not wrong," she soothed. "Just misguided. Carrie's a grown woman. She'll figure things out for herself. And to be honest, Mick, the more you push, the harder you'll make that for her. Stubbornness is a family trait. You, of all people, ought to know that."

He scowled at his wife. "You saying I'm stubborn?"

She gave him an incredulous look. "You are the king of stubborn!" she declared. "But you're also caring and thoughtful and I wouldn't have you any other way. Just, please, this once, stop your meddling. It was partly because of your good intentions that our Caitlyn barely made it down the aisle before her baby was born. Learn from past mistakes."

"Caitlyn's married now, isn't she? And every one of our kids and my brother Jeff's are settled and happy, in some measure due to my so-called good intentions."

"In spite of," Megan corrected. She called out to Luke, who was hovering just out of view in the kitchen doorway. "Luke, bring us some of that stew, and hurry, please. Maybe if Mick's stomach is full of some good old-fashioned Irish food, he'll take a break from fretting about Carrie."

Mick frowned at the suggestion. "I'm perfectly capable of doing two things at once," he told her.

She leaned over and kissed his cheek. "I know," she said quietly. "More's the pity. If you need something else to chew on, how about this?"

The suggestion she whispered in his ear for how they might spend the rest of the evening pretty much wiped all thoughts of his granddaughter and her problems right out of his head. He grinned at his wife.

"Clever woman," he murmured approvingly.

"You haven't loved me all these years for no reason," she said smugly.

Mick sighed. That was true enough. Even during all the years they'd been apart, he'd loved her to pieces. It had just taken getting past his hurt pride to give him the courage to fight to win her back. Now that he had, maybe he shouldn't be wasting quite so much time on fixing everybody else's lives.

"I'll make you a deal," he offered.

"What's that?"

"For the rest of tonight you have my full attention."

"And then?" she asked.

"You run your art gallery during the day, and I'll do the things I need to do."

"Of course you will," she said with a sigh. "But if that's the best I can hope for, at least Carrie will have the night off from your interference."

Mick gave a nod of satisfaction. He doubted Carrie's problem would resolve itself overnight. He'd make it his priority first thing in the morning.

Carrie wandered around the cottage, half expecting her grandfather to appear any minute with more of his questions and disappointed looks when she had no answers for him. When he never appeared, she knew she probably had Grandma Megan and maybe even Luke to thank.

Oddly enough, she would have welcomed the distraction of one of Grandpa Mick's cross-examinations. Images of Sam Winslow were a little too enticing for her comfort, especially when counterpointed against the disdain she'd felt radiating from him during their conversation. Add in his boneheaded move of leaving his nephew alone in the car, no matter how he'd justified it, and he definitely wasn't someone she should be giving the time of day. Luke had probably been right about that. She wasn't crazy about acknowledging that, either.

When her phone rang, she seized it, grateful for the excuse to escape her conflicted reaction to the man.

"Who was the guy?" her twin asked the second Carrie answered.

"Excuse me?"

"The guy at the pub," Caitlyn said. "The one who got you all tied up in knots."

"There was no guy," Carrie said, then amended, "Well, there was a man who came in. We had words. I actually yelled at him."

"You yelled at him," Cait repeated, sounding shocked. "Why would you do that?"

"He left a child alone in his parked car. I discovered the boy sound asleep in the back-seat when I was leaving the pub."

"So this guy left a sleeping child in a car, then came into the pub to drink?"

"Not to drink," Carrie said hurriedly. "To order takeout. And to be fair, he was keeping an eye on the boy the whole time, but I freaked out just the same."

"I don't blame you. But the second you realized the guy was an irresponsible jerk, why'd you hang out with him?"

"I didn't hang out with him," Carrie replied impatiently. "How'd you hear about this, anyway?"

"Noah stopped by the pub after work with Jackson. He and Luke got to talking. Luke was worried. He thought he detected some sparks flying between the two of you."

"Luke never even saw us in the same room," Carrie argued. "He doesn't know anything."

"Okay, he has his suspicions," Caitlyn said with exaggerated patience. "He shared them with Noah."

"Please tell me Grandpa Mick was nowhere around when they had this conversation."

"Noah didn't mention our grandfather. Why would you think he was there?"

"Because he and Grandma Megan were going in just after I left. He called out to me, but I pretended not to hear him and kept on walking."

"Oh, boy!" Cait said. "I'm sure that went over well. Don't you know by now that just makes Grandpa Mick more determined to find out what's going on?"

"I know," Carrie said with a sigh. "I've been expecting him to turn up here ever since I got home."

"So you apparently got a reprieve till morning," Cait concluded. "Now tell me more about this guy who's a jerk. What's his name?"

"Sam Winslow. He's the new web designer and tech expert for Mack at the paper. You know how much Mack depends on whoever's in that position. He says the paper's web presence is what's saving it from failure. The guy can't be a total flake if Mack trusts him."

"And the boy? Is Sam a single dad?"

Carrie told her what she knew of how the boy had come to be with Sam. The story was met with an uncomfortable silence.

"Come on," she said, resigned to the inevitable. "Say something. I know you want to."

"Oh, sweetie, you already know what I'm going to tell you," Caitlyn said, sounding worried. "Stay far, far away from this situation. You'll get sucked in. I know you will, and there's a very good chance you'll get your heart broken."

"How can you say that? He obviously needs help."

"Not from you," Cait insisted. "You're vulnerable. You want a family too much. He'll take advantage of that."

"Nobody's going to take advantage of me," Carrie replied irritably.

"Marc did," Cait reminded her gently.

"That was different."

"It was," her sister agreed. "He didn't have a child to sweeten the appeal."

"You're wrong," Carrie said. "I'm going to bed. Good night."

"Don't hang up angry," Cait pleaded. "Just be careful, that's all I'm saying."

No, Carrie thought with a sigh. She was saying so much more. Worse, just like Luke, she was probably right.

Sam put the dinner he'd ordered at O'Brien's into the backseat of his SUV next to Bobby. The boy had been sleeping while he was talking to Carrie Winters, but he was wide-awake now and looking around with a curious expression.

"Are we home yet?" he asked Sam, his tone plaintive.

"Just about, buddy. We'll be home in a couple of minutes. I stopped long enough to pick up some dinner for us."

"Where? I don't see McDonald's."

Sam pointed to O'Brien's. "See the restaurant right across the street? Dinner came from there and it's going to be delicious. I'm told there might even be some homemade cookies in the bag for dessert."

"How come you didn't take me with you?"

"You were sleeping."

Bobby's expression turned serious. "Mommy never left me alone in the car. She said it was too dangerous, even when I told her I was big enough to take care of myself."

Once again, all of his shortcomings as a prospective father slapped Sam in the face. He'd discovered that no one could induce guilt quite like a six-year-old . . . except, perhaps, an indignant, red-haired stranger.

"Your mom was absolutely right, but you were just a few yards away and right where I could see you the whole time I was inside the restaurant," Sam said in his own defense. He wondered if that sounded as hollow to Bobby as it obviously had to Carrie Winters?

"And Chesapeake Shores is a lot safer than the city, even one as safe as Louisville," he added for good measure.

"Does that mean I can play outside by myself?" Bobby asked hopefully. "Mommy never let me do that. She said I always had to be with a grown-up."

That sounded just like Laurel, Sam thought. As far back as he could remember she'd been making up rules and issuing orders. As a kid he'd resented it, but with the hindsight of maturity, he could see that she'd been trying to make up for the chaos of their family life. It had been her self-assigned task to protect him. Recalling how often they'd butted heads and recognizing now how good her intentions had been brought the sting of tears to his eyes. How had he let some stupid argument come between them?

"We'll have to work that out," Sam hedged, fighting tears as he drove along the curving, waterfront road to the Inn at Eagle Point. He'd vowed not to show any sign of weakness in front of his nephew. Bobby needed to believe in him.

"First we need to get you enrolled in school, so you can make lots of new friends this fall," Sam continued, injecting an upbeat note into his voice. "And we need to find a real house so you can have your own room and maybe even a big yard to play in."

Bobby's eyes widened. "You don't live in a house?"

"Not yet. I just moved here, remember? I'm staying at an inn. It looks just like a great big house, though."

"I went to a hotel once. Is it like that?" His eyes brightened with excitement. "Does it have room service?"

"I haven't tried it, but I imagine it does. We can check that out in the morning. I know it has a dining room with lots of windows so you can see the bay and all the big birds like osprey and eagles. I can say for a fact that the pancakes are really, really good."

The last hint of Bobby's uncertainty vanished completely. "I love pancakes," he said with a sigh of satisfaction. "Mommy only made them on Sundays, though."

"Well, here you can have them any day you

want them," Sam promised. "At least as long as we're at the inn."

His nephew fell silent until they pulled into the parking lot of the inn. "Wow! It's the biggest house ever! Can I play in the yard? Can we go swimming?" His eyes grew even bigger. "It even has a pool. I never, ever want to leave here."

Sam chuckled at his sudden burst of enthusiasm. It had been in short supply for the past couple of weeks as Sam had dealt with the details of the funeral, putting his sister's house up for sale, and facing the shocking news that he'd been named Bobby's guardian. His sister's in-laws had threatened to fight him for custody until the lawyer had convinced them the will was airtight and that Sam had the energy to cope with an inquisitive, lively six-year-old, something a retired couple in their sixties and living on a fixed income might not be able to handle.

"I'm afraid we can't stay here forever," he told Bobby. "It costs a lot of money, but I promise you we'll pick a house that you're going to love just as much. You can help me decide on the right one."

A familiar frown settled on Bobby's face and Sam's stomach tied itself into knots. He could feel the disappointment radiating from the backseat. How many times was he destined to let this boy down before everyone realized what a mistake had been made in giving him custody?

"Sam?" Bobby whispered hesitantly.

Sam turned and saw tears dampening Bobby's round cheeks and realized this was about more than staying at the inn. "What, buddy?"

"If we keep moving, how are Mommy and Daddy going to find us?"

Sam's heart twisted. "We talked about that, remember? Your mommy and daddy can't come back. They're in heaven."

"But you said that even in heaven, they'd always be looking out for me. How are they going to find me?" he asked, his expression way too serious and worried for a child his age.

Sam had never felt more out of his depth in his life. "That's the thing about heaven," he said eventually, praying he was getting it right. "The people we love who live there can see us wherever we are. Your mom and dad will always know exactly where you are and when they asked me to take care of you, they knew I was in Chesapeake Shores."

"Have they been here?"

"No, but I'll bet they have this amazing GPS thing in heaven and it's already guided them right here."

"Really?"

Sam nodded, though he was certain of no such thing. He wanted to believe. He really did. But what sort of god took away a little boy's parents and left him all alone with an uncle who didn't have a clue about how to raise himself, much less a child? Even as those words crossed his mind, he remembered Laurel saying much the same thing, telling him it was time to stop his restless roaming and grow up. He'd accused her—yet, again—of trying to control him. The heated exchange, one of many in a similar vein, had occurred months ago, but it had been the last straw. After that he'd simply avoided taking his sister's calls, leaving messages when he'd known she wouldn't be home so she wouldn't worry, but not wanting to risk another lecture on his flaws. Despite the distance that had grown between them, she'd never stopped texting pictures of Bobby or sending notes on special occasions. To her credit, she'd done all she could to keep the lines of communication open, while he'd behaved like a spoiled jerk. He'd live with that regret the rest of his life.

Sam climbed out of the car, then opened the back door to help Bobby out of his booster seat, but the boy had already scrambled free. He raced across the wide expanse of green lawn toward the water, then turned back just as Sam feared he might go toppling straight over the edge of the cliff overlooking the bay. He had to remember just how fast a six-year-old could move and do a better job of staying on his toes at all times.

"Come on, kid. Let's go in and eat dinner before

it gets cold. Then we can get you settled down for the night. We've had a long day. Tomorrow's soon enough to deal with all the complicated stuff."

And maybe by tomorrow, he'd have some clue about how to do that. Surprisingly, it was the memory of Carrie Winters's impulsive offer to help out with day care that centered him enough to get through one more night. Even if he never took her up on it, just knowing backup was around seemed to ease his panic.

Carrie knew that the odds of getting through the morning without a visit from her grandfather were between slim and none. To at least postpone the inevitable, she headed to the café on Main Street for breakfast. There was a very good chance there would be lots of family around since many of her aunts had stores nearby, and her grandmother's art gallery was right around the corner. They tended to start their day at Sally's with coffee, raspberry croissants and conversation. Carrie could catch up on the town gossip and avoid her grandfather at the same time. Then she could go by Noah's and pick up Jackson for the day since Noah had office hours from early morning until dinnertime on Wednesdays.

Sure enough, at Sally's she found her aunts Bree, Shanna and Heather already on their second cups of coffee, telltale crumbs from their croissants still on their plates. Two raspberry and one chocolate, from the look of it.

"Did you leave any of those croissants for me?" she demanded as she slid into the booth beside Bree.

"I put a chocolate one aside for you," Sally told her with a wink as she poured a cup of coffee. "And there's a raspberry for your grandmother when she gets here, too."

"Thank you," Carrie said gratefully. "You're the best."

"I just know my customers. I hear a lot of talk about carbs and dieting when you all are in here, but there's not a morning that goes by that my tray of fresh croissants doesn't magically disappear."

After Sally left to get her croissant, Carrie glanced around the table and noted all the expectant looks. "So, what's up?"

"Maybe you should tell us," Bree suggested slyly. "Word on the family grapevine is that you had a little tiff with a man at the pub last night. Luke swears he saw sparks. He may be a lot of things, but he's not usually attuned to those kind of undercurrents, so I'm guessing they had to be more like fireworks for him to notice."

Carrie took a deep breath as she tried to avoid the sea of curious stares. She needed a strategy to get out of this conversation. She gazed at each woman intently, then began innocently,

"Out of my deep respect for you as my elders . . ."

Before she could complete the sentence, her words drew the expected horrified gasps. She barely managed to contain a chuckle at their predictable reaction.

"And because of my deep understanding of what each of you went through with too much meddling in your lives," she continued, then beamed at Bree, "I'm going to ignore that line of conversation."

Heather was the first to recover. "Nicely played," she said, a note of grudging approval in her voice.

"But we don't have to like it," Shanna added.

"And I'm gonna tell your mother you called us old," Bree claimed, looking thoroughly disgruntled. "Since she's older than any of us, I doubt she'll appreciate it."

Carrie laughed. "I didn't call you old. I said you were my elders. That's an undeniable truth. And I do respect each and every one of you. Be sure to tell Mom I said that, too."

"So we're not going to get a thing out of you about the man?" Heather asked, clearly disappointed.

"Nothing to tell," Carrie insisted. "You could always ask Susie about him. The guy's working for Mack at the paper. They're bound to have crossed paths."

All three women promptly looked dismayed.

Carrie studied their faces, then asked, "What? Has something happened with Susie? I ran into her a couple of days ago. She seemed fine then."

"You know she and Mack want a baby in the worst way," Bree said.

"Sure," Carrie said. "They finally decided to adopt. I thought Uncle Connor was trying to help with a private adoption through his old law firm in Baltimore. Susie was practically bursting with excitement when I saw her. She said the baby was due any minute." A horrifying thought occurred to her. "Nothing happened to the baby, did it?"

"Not exactly," Heather responded. "Not the way you mean."

"Then what?" Carrie asked.

"Connor kept cautioning them that things could go wrong, but Susie was so sure this was it. If you saw her, you know how she was floating on air, making all these plans. And then, at the very last minute, the mother got together with her boyfriend and they decided to keep the baby."

"Oh, no," Carrie whispered.

"Susie's devastated. Connor said the look on her face when he broke the news was something he hoped never to see again. Nothing Mack said or did could console her. She says she can't go through that again."

"She's giving up?" Carrie asked, genuinely shocked. O'Briens didn't give up that easily, not when something truly mattered as much as a baby mattered to Susie.

"That's what she told Connor," Heather confirmed. "Mack thinks she'll come around once she gets over this latest disappointment, but I don't know. I spoke to her last night for about two minutes. She sounded terrible, but the one thing she seemed certain about was her decision that this was it. I offered to go over so she could vent, but she said she wasn't in the mood for company, that there was nothing more to be said, anyway."

"And she's not here this morning," Shanna added. "The last time they got close and the adoption fell apart, she didn't leave the house for a week. This time could be worse. She really thought a private adoption was the answer, a guarantee of some kind, despite all Connor's warnings that things could go wrong."

"She'd actually painted the nursery this time, because she knew it was going to be a girl," Bree said. "I was over there just last week and she had drawers filled with frilly little outfits for the baby."

"That's so sad," Carrie said, unable to imagine the depth of Susie's disappointment. She'd been so brave all through her bout with ovarian cancer, even after finding out she'd never have children of her own. Now this.

"Is there anything I can do?" Carrie asked.

"She has to come to us," Bree said. "She'll do that when she's ready. I'm hoping she'll talk to Jess. For being such rivals when they were kids, they formed a really close bond during Susie's cancer treatments. Maybe she'll open up to her."

"And if she doesn't?" Carrie asked, not liking the idea of Susie going through this alone. Families were supposed to stick together in times of crisis, even when the person pushed them away. That was another of the lessons Nell had taught all of them.

"Then we'll go to her in a few days," Heather assured her. "You, too, if you want to come." She sighed. "Although right now I have a new baby at home. I'm not sure how she feels about that. She says all the right things, but I've seen the stricken look on her face when she has to be around the baby."

"So have I," Shanna said. She and Carrie's uncle Kevin had just had another child, as well. "She skipped the whole christening and the party afterward. She had an excuse, but it was pretty flimsy."

"It must just about kill her to be around all these babies in our family," Bree said. "But we can't feel guilty about it. All we can do is try to be understanding and supportive."

Carrie sat back in her seat and sighed, thinking of Sam and how he'd become a dad when he least expected it. Did he appreciate what a gift that was? Maybe in time he would, but right now there was little question that he was struggling with it. And there was Susie, desperate to hold a child of her own, but running out of options. Life sometimes truly was unfair. Nell would assure them all that God had a plan, but Carrie sure wished He'd let them all in on it.

Mack was at his wit's end. Susie had been sitting on the deck of their home on Beach Lane for hours, staring out at the bay and clutching the handmade baby quilt she'd bought at Heather's shop.

He'd known when she'd brought it home that the quilt was a bad idea and that painting the nursery and buying a boatload of baby clothes were even worse ideas, but Susie hadn't been deterred. She'd believed with every fiber of her being that this time they were going to get their child, a daughter, according to Connor's former associate in Baltimore, the lawyer handling the arrangements.

"Babe, come inside," he begged. "You need some sleep."

She shook her head. "Not yet."

"You were out here all night." He knew because he'd awakened to an empty bed. He'd checked on her half a dozen times during the night, but she'd refused to come back to bed.

Heaving a resigned sigh, Mack brought his

coffee and joined her on the deck, ignoring the look that told him she'd prefer to go right on being alone.

He set the coffee aside, then pulled his chair close enough to reach for her hand. Even though it was a warm morning, her hand was like ice and trembled in his, but at least she didn't pull away.

Susie was the bravest, most courageous woman he'd ever known. He'd never seen her this defeated, not even when she'd been battling cancer and sickened by chemo and radiation. She'd had her share of down moments, her doubts about her future, but this was different. There was a steely resolve behind her decision to give up, one that left little room for argument or hope.

"I love you," he told her, holding on tight, willing her to draw on his strength.

She turned and gave him a vague smile. "I know."

"Are you ready to talk about this?"

Once again she shook her head. "What is there to talk about?"

"What we're going to do next," he suggested.

"Nothing," she said flatly. "It's over."

"It's only over if we give up."

"Well, that's what I'm doing. I'm giving up." She turned and gave him an earnest look. "I can't go through this again, Mack. Now I have some idea of how women feel after miscarriages. They carry this little baby inside of them, inside their hearts, even if only for a few weeks, and then it's over. There's no baby to hold."

"The right baby will come along," he insisted, though he knew no such thing. "Or we could look into an older child adoption. Think of all the children who need loving families, kids who've bounced around in foster care. We could open our hearts and our home to them. Maybe that's what we're meant to do."

Susie closed her eyes and, he suspected, her ears, to block out his words. "I can't do it, Mack. Please don't hate me, but I can't."

Mack wasn't sure what to say. Susie had always been more certain about parenthood than he was. It had been her dream and, because he loved her so blasted deeply, he'd wanted to give her that, no matter how the child came into their lives. He could accept her decision and move on, but he knew in his heart the day would come when she'd regret it. Maybe he needed to accept her decision for now, then bring this up again when this latest wound wasn't so fresh.

She glanced his way. "Have you heard from Sam? How's he coping with losing his sister?"

"He's doing okay, I think," Mack said, relieved to have her show an interest in something, even if she was only doing it to change the subject. "The accident came as a terrible shock, but there's more. He's reeling, in fact."

Real interest sparked in her eyes. "Why? What else happened?"

"His sister and brother-in-law named him guardian of their son, a six-year-old boy."

Shock spread across her face. "Sam's a dad? Just like that?"

Mack hesitated, sensing that the news had stirred envy as much as surprise. He should have considered that and kept quiet, but it was out there now.

"It was a shock to him, too," Mack reported. "He said he'd tell me more when he got back to town. I think he was hoping to make it by last night. I imagine he'll check in later today. I told him to take as long as he needs. We can manage okay at the paper for another week, if he needs that long to deal with the situation. Even longer, if need be."

That vacant stare returned to Susie's eyes. "Sam has a son," she murmured. "Of all people."

"Hey," Mack protested. "Sam's a good guy."

"I suppose so. He's a talented web designer, for sure, and a tech genius to hear you tell it, but come on, Mack, do you really see him as dad material?"

"I'm the last person to ask about that. I don't know what it takes to be a good father."

"Reliability's a good place to start," she said.

"Sam is reliable."

"He left you in the lurch right after he started

on the job," she said, a critical note in her voice.

"Babe, his sister and brother-in-law were killed. Did you expect him not to attend the funeral?"

"Well, he hasn't exactly settled down, has he? He's still living at the inn."

Mack suspected she was uttering these judgments for a reason, one he didn't particularly like. "He'd only been here a couple of weeks, hardly enough time to find a house or even an apartment," he said, defending Sam. "Where are you going with this, Suze?"

"How many jobs has he held over the past few years? Three? Four? What kind of man does that?" she asked without responding to his question about her motives.

"Someone who's talented and very much in demand in a new field," Mack replied, not sure why he was so ardently defending a man he barely knew himself, but having the feeling that he needed to make his position clear. Susie seemed to be heading in a worrisome direction. She'd liked Sam well enough when they'd had him over for dinner. This had to be about the boy, though Mack hoped he was wrong about that.

"We should go over to the inn and see how they're doing," she said out of the blue, standing up and proving that Mack's instincts had been right on target.

"This morning? You haven't slept a wink. You

need rest more than you need to be running around paying social calls."

She frowned at him. "I want to see for myself how Sam's coping with a child to care for."

Since Mack had been praying for a distraction for Susie, even one as misguided as he was sure this one was, he told himself he could control the situation and gave in.

"While you take a shower, I'll call Jess to see if he's back. If he is, we'll go when you're dressed," he said.

"Why wait?" she asked, giving him a bewildered look.

"Because you've been wearing that same robe for the past two days. You can't go anywhere in that."

She glanced down as if surprised by the reminder. "I won't take long," she promised. "I know you need to get to work. Go ahead, if you want to. I can stop by on my own."

"Not a chance. I'm going with you," Mack said. He needed to see for himself if his wife intended something more than a kindhearted visit to an employee who'd just suffered a terrible loss.

Susie leveled a knowing gaze straight at him. "I'm not jumping off the deep end," she told him. "I know I can't go swooping in and take a little boy away from Sam, no matter how desperate I might be feeling."

Mack was relieved to hear her express his exact

concern. "I'm glad to hear that's not what you were thinking."

She touched his cheek. "I love you for caring so much and for worrying about me. I'm sad, but I'm not crazy."

He pulled her into his arms. "I never, for even a second, thought you were."

A faint smile tugged at her lips. "It crossed your mind, Mack Franklin. Don't you dare try to deny it. I honestly can't blame you. I have been sitting around here wallowing ever since Connor told us we weren't going to get our baby. I'll probably wallow some more before I'm done."

He rested his chin on the top of her head and held her close. "Take all the time you need. And if checking on Sam and his nephew will reassure you somehow, I'm all for it. I imagine he'll appreciate the gesture. He must be freaking out about now."

"I hope not," she said, her expression turning wistful. "I hope he's on his knees thanking God for the gift he's been given."

Mack tucked a finger under her chin. "Suze, if he's not there just yet, it doesn't mean he won't get there. Look how long it's taken me to believe I could be a decent parent. After growing up with poor examples in my life, I had more doubts than anyone could imagine, but you believed in me. So did your family. Sam needs our support, not somebody waiting in the wings to snatch that child away at the first sign of a misstep."

"I know that," she said, indignation in her voice, even as she was careful to avoid his gaze.

Mack wished she were half as convincing as she'd obviously intended to be. Instead, he feared what might happen if she seized on the situation to fill the empty space in her heart. The past few days of despair would seem like a picnic compared to the heartache in store if that happened.

<h1 style="text-align:center">❧ 4 ☙</h1>

With Susie still very much on her mind, Carrie walked the few blocks to the house that had been converted into Noah's medical offices on the ground floor. The upstairs had been turned into a cozy apartment for him, Cait and the baby. Once Cait was finished with her medical training and home for good, it would probably be much too small for a growing family, but for now Grandpa Mick had converted it into a warm, welcoming home. It was too bad, Carrie thought, that her twin was rarely here to enjoy it or her family.

Carrie used her key to the side entrance to the offices and found Noah's nurse, Wendy Kaine, already there, bustling around in the brightly painted examining rooms, getting ready for another busy day.

"You here to pick up the little man?" Wendy asked with a grin as a wail carried all the way from upstairs. "Good luck. He seems to be expressing himself quite clearly today. He is not a happy little boy."

Carrie winced at the sound. Noah, who prided himself on soothing even his most difficult young patients, must be at his wit's end about now. "I could hide out down here till his daddy gets him calmed down," she whispered to Wendy.

"Coward," the nurse accused. "March right on up there and show the two of them who's boss."

"Noah's probably trying to make him eat more of that boring baby cereal again," Carrie said. "Jackson really hates that stuff. I guess I should go up and save him."

"Him who? Jackson or Noah?" Wendy asked. "I'm sure the baby will appreciate it. Noah, too. I know I will."

Carrie hurried up the steps, tapped on the door to the living quarters—not that it could likely be heard over the baby's noisy sobs—and went inside.

Sure enough, Noah had a spoon in his hand, a frustrated expression on his face, and far more cereal on his shirt than could possibly be in the little boy who was waving his fists and had big, fat tears rolling down his chubby cheeks.

Jackson spotted Carrie and immediately held out his arms. A drooling smile lit up his face.

She grinned at Noah, then passed him and picked up the eight-month-old. "That's right, sweetie. Aunt Carrie is here to save you from having to eat that nasty old cereal."

Noah frowned at her. "You've been telling me he eats it for you."

She leaned closer, the baby clinging tightly to her. "Want to know my secret?"

"Please," he said, sounding a little desperate.

"I mix in a little applesauce. He loves apple-sauce."

Noah closed his eyes. "Of course. Why didn't I think of that?"

"Because you probably never tasted the cereal yourself and had no idea how awful it is. I believe peaches were the fruit of choice for Cait and me. And in the interest of full disclosure, I didn't dream this up on my own. Mom gave me the tip after I'd spent a week washing cereal out of my hair."

Noah laughed then. "I feel a whole lot better now." His expression sobered. "You say this worked for you and Cait?"

Carrie nodded.

"Hmm. She never suggested it, either. I'm thinking my wife deliberately omitted a few helpful tips when she left me in charge."

"Could be," Carrie agreed. "She does like to feel superior. Now, go. Change shirts and get to work. I have things under control here. As soon as I have Jackson fed and cleaned up, we'll head on over to my house so peace should reign here for you and your patients."

"Thank you," Noah said, his tone heartfelt. "I mean it, Carrie. I don't know what we'd do without you. The first couple of months, when Jackson was with Cait in Baltimore so she could breast-feed him, I had no idea of what she must be going through, even with help. I was so sure it would be easier for me here, with family all around. I'm a doctor. I deal with sick kids on a daily basis. They're not usually in the best mood, but they're mostly saints compared to my own son."

"Jackson is a sweet little angel," she corrected.

Noah smiled. "Well, it's a good thing you're smitten. Otherwise I'd be up a creek. Thanks again for pitching in." His expression turned serious. "I want you to let me know if it gets to be too much for you, if we're taking advantage."

"Not to worry. I love having Jackson with me," she assured her brother-in-law.

"But it doesn't leave much time for . . ." His voice trailed off.

"For what?" she asked, forcing a smile. "My busy schedule of watching the grass grow? My nonexistent social life? Pursuing my exciting career path?"

At her undisguised bitter tone, worry immediately spread across his face. "Carrie, are you okay? Seriously? Do you want to talk about any of this? I can make time."

"Absolutely not. I think one of the things I love most about watching the baby is that he doesn't ask questions I can't answer. I have Grandpa Mick doing enough of that. And Mom. Even Cait gets in a shot from time to time."

"I'm happy to listen, though," Noah said. "Being an outsider, I might be able to give you a different perspective."

"Noah, I love you for wanting to help, but we're talking about the O'Briens. I have so many perspectives about my life, my head is spinning. I'll figure it out, even if it's not on their timetable."

"Of course you will," he said with confidence. "I'll be by to get Jackson later."

"Or I can bring him back," she offered. "Whichever's easiest for you. Just let me know."

As soon as Noah had gone, she sat the baby back down, mixed some applesauce into his cereal and spooned it into his mouth at a steady clip. He gave her a toothless smile that always warmed her heart.

Today, thinking of Susie's longing to have a child and her own fantasy about a family, that smile made her heart ache. When would it be Susie's turn? Or hers?

First thing in the morning, with Bobby up and eager for the promised pancakes, Sam dug out some wrinkled but clean clothes for his nephew, then took him down to the inn's dining room. To his surprise he found Mack and Susie Franklin in the foyer. Susie's gaze immediately locked on Bobby and a smile spread across her face.

"You must be the young man I've been hearing so much about," she told Bobby.

Bobby regarded her shyly, then hid behind Sam. Sam knelt down and drew the boy up beside him. "Bobby, this is Mack Franklin. He's my boss at the newspaper. And this is his wife, Mrs. Franklin."

"Call me Susie, please," she said, her gaze never leaving Bobby.

"When I called this morning to see if you'd made it back, Jess told me you got in last night," Mack said. "Did the trip go okay?"

"It was smooth enough. I should have let you know we'd made it back to town," Sam apologized.

"Absolutely not. You had a lot to do to get settled, I'm sure," Mack said. "In fact, Susie insisted on coming over right away to see what she could do to help out." He gave Sam a reassuring look. "Things must feel pretty overwhelming about now, but you're not in this alone, okay? I want to make sure you know that. We all want to help."

"I appreciate that," Sam said, beginning to see what Carrie had been talking about. Even though he was new to town people were willing to pitch in. He hated that one of them happened to be his boss, a man he respected and wanted to impress. He couldn't help wondering what Mack thought of the chaos that had suddenly become his life.

"I'm not entirely sure where to start," Sam admitted candidly, then grinned at Bobby's impatient tug on his jeans. "Except to get some pancakes into my boy here."

"Yeah!" Bobby said.

"Well, I can definitely help with that," Susie said. "I'll go in the kitchen and speak to the chef myself."

Bobby regarded her hopefully. "Can I come, too? I want to see where they make the pancakes. When I get big, I want to make them myself."

"Absolutely," Susie agreed and held out her hand. She turned to Mack. "Why don't you grab a table by the window so we can see the water?"

As she and Bobby left, Mack watched them go with a surprisingly worried expression.

"Something wrong?" Sam asked him as they made their way to a table.

Mack shook off whatever was troubling him and forced a smile. "No, nothing for you to worry about. Do you need more time off? Like I told you when you called the other day, I can manage for another week. I might not have the creative-design expertise you have, and I definitely don't have your tech skills, but I can post stories and pictures." He regarded Sam with concern. "You must have a list a mile long of things you need to do to adjust to having custody of your nephew."

"You have no idea," Sam said. "Thank goodness my sister and brother-in-law had the foresight to have a will. Too many young couples think they're immortal, according to the lawyer. He says it's critical to plan ahead when there are children to consider. They even had a small life-insurance policy that will be set aside for Bobby's education."

He shook his head. "It's hard to imagine my sister being quite so organized. Neither one of us thought much beyond our next meal when we were kids."

"Maybe that's why," Mack suggested. "Kids who grew up in a chaotic household often feel the greatest need for a sense of stability. And, in case you're wondering, I know that from experience." He gave Sam a rueful look. "Of course, I had to go through a playboy stage and a career crisis before I figured out what I really needed and got my life on track."

Maybe Sam was more like Mack than he'd realized. He certainly hadn't changed dramatically from his early days of wanting to seize whatever adventure came along next. Now, though? He needed to figure out how to do the whole stable thing in a hurry for Bobby's sake.

"Maybe that explains it," he said, though he

was still skeptical. She might have bossed him around like a mature adult, but she'd had her own wild moments before she'd married. "I think it was probably Robert's doing. Laurel's husband was a real steady guy. Money in the bank every week for the future, oil changed in the car, tires rotated or replaced right on schedule. It was ironic, really, that it was a faulty tire blowing that caused their car to spin out of control on a busy highway."

"That just shows that we can't always plan for every curve life might throw at us," Mack said. "I'm so sorry, Sam."

Sam nodded, unexpected tears once more threatening. "Me, too," he said, his voice choked. He sighed heavily, then added, "All I know about the future is that I need to enroll Bobby in school this morning. After that, I don't have a real plan."

"School doesn't start for almost a month," Mack reminded him. "There's no rush. Why not wait at least till Monday? If you need to have any paperwork expedited, I'm sure someone in the family will be able to help. Susie's cousin Connor is a lawyer. And her uncle, Mick O'Brien, can get just about anything done around here with a phone call. Give Bobby a few days to get used to being here, let him get familiar with the town, meet a few kids. Give yourself time to get your feet back under you, too."

"I just thought maybe if he was enrolled in school and knew there was going to be a familiar routine, he'd feel more settled," Sam said. "I'm not sure he quite understands that this is his home now. He says all the right words about knowing Mommy and Daddy are in heaven, but I just have this sense he still expects them to find their way back to him."

"That must kill you," Mack said, then hesitated. "Look, I think a break before he has to think about anything except being a kid might be good, but run it by Susie. She's smarter about this sort of thing than I am. It just seems to me Bobby's already had to make a lot of big adjustments. A couple of extra days to hang out with you might make him feel more secure. You guys probably need some serious bonding time."

Sam nodded. "That does make sense. And, like you said, maybe it'll help me to wrap my head around everything that's happened, too."

"What about a place to live?" Mack asked. "I'm sure Jess will give you a break here, if you need to stay on for a while longer."

"She mentioned that when I got back last night," Sam responded. "But as convenient and wonderful as the inn is, it's not a long-term solution. The sooner I can find a permanent place for us, the better it will be."

"I can help with that," Susie said, returning just in time to overhear. "I know every property in town that's available for rent or for sale. Any preference?"

"I'd planned to rent a small apartment, if there is such a thing in Chesapeake Shores, but now . . ." His voice trailed off and he shrugged. "Bobby needs stability, so maybe a house."

"I agree," Susie said enthusiastically. "And I already know the perfect one. It's not too big and it's on Willow Brook Road, which is a wonderful street with lots of shade trees and nice yards. There are several children Bobby's age on the street, and a lot of the kids in our family are over there a lot, too. My cousin's daughter lives there and she watches them after school from time to time."

"Carrie?" Sam asked.

A startled look passed across Susie's face. "How on earth did you know that?"

"I ran into her last night when I was picking up dinner at O'Brien's. She mentioned she has children in and out all the time."

"It's not a formal day care or anything like that," Susie explained. "Carrie just happens to be really good with children, so all the O'Brien little ones gravitate to her. The adults take terrible advantage of that. I think we all know that sooner or later she'll decide on a new career and go back to the glamorous life she used to live, but in the meantime, she's a godsend."

The mention of Carrie's previously glamorous

life set off alarms for Sam. It only confirmed what he'd guessed the previous night just looking at her in an outfit even he could tell hadn't come off a rack at a discount store. Hadn't he already experienced one disastrous relationship that ended because he'd rather spend his money on adventures than clothes? Maybe Carrie Winters, despite her thoughtful offer, wasn't the best person to bring into Bobby's life . . . or his, especially if her future in Chesapeake Shores was as uncertain as Susie had just suggested. Bobby didn't need to form an attachment to another person who might disappear from his life at any moment.

He hesitated about even considering a house just down the street from Carrie. It seemed like a really bad idea. But looking into Susie's expectant face, he knew he couldn't afford to ignore a house with real potential, especially in a town where he already knew real estate came at a premium and was in short supply.

"Sure, let's take a look," he said. "I'll give you a call and we can set it up."

"You don't want to look this morning? I have time."

"Don't push," Mack said quietly. "Sam has a lot to do."

"Anything more important than this?" Susie asked, her voice tight.

With Mack's steady gaze holding hers, she

finally backed down. She reached in her purse and handed Sam a business card. "Call me whenever you're ready. But houses don't stay on the market long here," she cautioned.

Sam nodded, then turned to Bobby, noting that he was making slow but steady progress through a stack of pancakes more suited to Sam's appetite than a boy's. "You doing okay, buddy?"

Bobby nodded happily, his mouth full. When he'd swallowed, he took a big gulp of milk and said, "You were right, Sam. These are the best, even better than Mom's."

As if he'd suddenly realized what he said, his smile faded. "Is it okay that I like them?" he whispered. "It won't make Mom mad, will it?"

"No way," Sam said. "Your mom only wanted the very best for you always, whether it was pancakes or . . ." He searched his mind for something sufficiently yucky to appeal to Bobby's sense of the ridiculous. He grinned. "Or escargots."

Bobby wrinkled his nose. "What's that?" he asked suspiciously.

"Snails," Sam told him.

With Susie and Mack fighting smiles, Bobby made a gagging sound. "Mom would never make me eat snails." He gave Sam a wary look. "You're not gonna, either, are you?"

"They are considered a delicacy," Sam told him.

Bobby's jaw set stubbornly. "I don't care. I'm not eating them."

Sam laughed and ruffled his hair. "Okay. Good to know where you draw the line when it comes to food. No snails."

"No snails," Bobby repeated fervently. He bounced in his seat. "What are we gonna do today?"

Sam glanced at Mack, then back at his suddenly eager nephew. "I thought I'd play hooky and we could check out the shops on Main Street, maybe spend some time on the beach or swim in the pool. And I think I saw a playground on the town green. Would you like to check that out?"

"All right!" Bobby said with a fist pump that had everyone at the table smiling.

Sam breathed in a sigh of relief. Finally, after days of awkward, disapproving silences and difficult choices that had Bobby shifting from tantrums to outright rebellions, it seemed Sam had gotten something exactly right. Unfortunately, it was mostly thanks to Mack's instincts and not his own.

Even after giving Jackson a bath and dressing him in clean clothes after the cereal debacle, Carrie discovered it was still surprisingly pleasant for a morning in early August. Rather than pushing his stroller straight over to her house, she headed for Main Street and then Shore Road.

Her first stop was Grandma Megan's art gallery, which was currently showing an exhibition of Moira's local photographs, many of them taken of O'Brien children, as well as other Chesapeake Shores residents. Luke's wife had become a surprisingly successful photographer thanks to Megan's contacts in the New York art world. Out of loyalty to Megan, Moira always insisted on a show here in town in late summer. It had the added advantage of giving her a solid stretch of time at home with Luke.

When Grandma Megan spotted Carrie with the baby, she rushed over to hold open the door.

"There's my precious boy," she cooed, leaning down to scoop Jackson out of the stroller.

"I'm delighted to see you, too," Carrie said, amused by her grandmother's complete lack of interest in anything other than her first great-grandchild.

Megan glanced up at her. "I fussed over you from the day you were born. It's Jackson's turn now." She bounced the baby in her arms. "You're almost too big for me to hold."

"I'd suggest you not bounce him quite so energetically," Carrie cautioned. "He's just finished his breakfast."

"It wouldn't be the first time someone in this family spit up all over one of us," Megan said dismissively.

"Didn't you buy that scarf in Paris when

you and Grandpa Mick went there for your second honeymoon?" Carrie asked. "Isn't it your favorite?"

Her grandmother glanced down and shrugged. "I'll just make your grandfather take me back to buy another one."

"And he'd do it without batting an eye, wouldn't he?" Carrie said, envying them the devotion they'd found together the second time around.

Apparently something in her voice alerted Megan that Carrie was in an odd mood. She returned Jackson to his stroller with a little pat, then turned to Carrie, giving her the full attention she'd apparently concluded was required. "Would you care for some tea? It's Irish Breakfast tea, Nell's favorite."

"We should be going. You're probably busy."

"I'm never too busy for a visit with you. Sit. I'll get the tea."

When she came back, Carrie was pushing the stroller back and forth and watching Jackson fight sleep.

"Here's your tea," Megan said, handing her the delicate, old-fashioned chintz-patterned teacup. "Now tell me what's on your mind."

"I'm at loose ends," Carrie admitted.

"No news there," her grandmother agreed. "Any thoughts about what you intend to do about it?" She gave her a sly look. "Other than avoiding advice from your grandfather, that is?"

Carrie grinned. "How'd you guess?"

"The way you took off from the pub as if you didn't hear him calling after you last night," Megan said. "And the fact that you're in here right now, rather than in your own house where you could put the baby down for his nap."

"You know how Grandpa Mick is," Carrie said.

"I most certainly do," Megan replied. "That said, not all of his ideas should be dismissed so readily."

"But I need to find my own ideas," Carrie argued. "Isn't that the whole point of growing up, to figure out what we're meant to do? You didn't exactly have a handle on it, did you? You were how old and had five kids at home, when you decided it wasn't enough, divorced Grandpa Mick, moved to New York and discovered how much you loved art and working in a gallery?"

"Touché," her grandmother said. "But there was a little more to the divorce than my running off to find myself."

"I know that. It was because Grandpa Mick was a workaholic and you felt like he'd abandoned you to be a single mom, stuck at home with five kids."

Megan smiled at what even Carrie knew to be a simplistic version of a very difficult time in her grandparents' marriage.

"That does sum it up," Megan acknowledged. "Or at least the heart of what happened. Here's the difference between you and me. I didn't know just how unhappy I was for a very long time, and I hurt a lot of people when I took off, including your mother and your aunts and uncles. I've spent a lot of time making amends for that. You have the advantage of being on your own. Now's the perfect time for you to get serious about finding your dream. To make your mistakes when the only person likely to be hurt is you."

Carrie met her sympathetic gaze. "You're talking about Marc."

"Not exactly. I'm talking about what you did to yourself. You worked yourself into exhaustion to impress a man who didn't appreciate it," Megan corrected. "The good news is that you had sense enough to leave before you were trapped by a marriage that was doomed."

Carrie rolled her eyes. "Trust me, marriage was never on the table, except maybe in my fantasy. Marc had an entirely different agenda. He was a selfish, manipulative man who took advantage of the feelings he knew I had for him. I can see that now."

"Good for you! You won't make a similar mistake again, will you?"

"I sure hope not."

Her grandmother studied her worriedly. "You're not going to let that one mistake keep you from taking risks or opening your heart again, are you? Because that would be a real tragedy. You have so much potential, Carrie, so much love to give."

"But I need a purpose," Carrie told her. "Grandpa Mick has been harping on that ever since I left Europe."

"And he's right. Everyone needs a purpose, a passion that makes them want to get up in the morning."

"So you think I'm wasting time, too?"

"No, I think you're taking your time trying to avoid another mistake. That's not you. You're my impulsive, embrace-everything granddaughter, but suddenly you're scared. I think that's what I hate most about Marc Reynolds. He robbed you of that wonderful, spontaneous spirit that made you special. If I may offer one piece of advice, it's this. Start taking chances again, Carrie. If something feels right, try it. If *someone* feels right, open your heart."

"Maybe you're right," Carrie acknowledged. "Maybe I have been playing it safe."

She gave her grandmother a plaintive look. "Or maybe I simply have no idea where to go from here."

Her grandmother wrapped her in a tight embrace. "You'll know it when it comes along. In the meantime, I'll try to get your grandfather to give you some space."

Carrie laughed. "Thanks for the offer, but we both know that's a losing fight. I'll just tune him out."

She tried to imagine how well that would work and couldn't. "I'd better get Jackson home. He'll be awake again any minute and he tends to wake up cranky. We don't want him scaring off your customers."

"Wednesdays are usually slow. I'm not worried. I'm glad you came by, sweetheart."

"Me, too. Love you."

Surprisingly, though there had been no sudden bursts of inspiration during their conversation, Carrie felt at peace when she left. That lasted two whole blocks until she spotted Sam Winslow sitting on a bench by the playground, and his nephew heading straight for the top rungs of the jungle gym.

Carrie's breath caught in her throat as she pushed the stroller as fast as she could in their direction. She didn't dare call out for fear the boy would take a misstep and tumble straight to the ground.

With her eyes glued to the boy, she made it to the base of the jungle gym and stood there watching his every move, ready to catch him if he fell.

She sensed Sam's approach, but never looked away.

"What were you thinking?" she said in a quiet

voice. "Did you have any idea what he was doing?"

"Of course I did," Sam said defensively, his welcoming smile immediately fading. "I'm not completely incompetent. Bobby's been climbing jungle gyms since he was four. He's a little daredevil."

He leveled a look at her. "Don't believe me?" He whipped out his cell phone and showed her a picture of a triumphant little boy atop another jungle gym with a woman who was clearly his mom standing watch just below, a tremulous smile on her lips.

"Your sister?" Carrie asked.

Sam nodded.

"She looks terrified."

"But she let him do it," Sam pointed out.

"The difference is she was standing right below in case he fell."

"And I was sitting a few feet away. I may have looked distracted to you, but trust me, I saw his every move. And you saw firsthand how quickly I got over here when you turned up."

"I suppose."

"Carrie, I may be new at this, but I'm not going to let anything happen to Bobby. My sister trusted me to get it right, and I will."

She looked into his eyes then and heard the sincerity behind his words. "Then I should relax and leave you to it."

"Or you could go to the café with us. I promised

Bobby a milk shake and a grilled cheese sand-wich for lunch."

She was a little too tempted by the invitation. "I should probably get Jackson home."

Sam looked at the sleeping baby and smiled. "Is this your nephew?"

"The one and only Jackson McIlroy," she confirmed. "His dad's the doctor in town. With an adventurous kid in your life, you'll want to get to know him."

"Absolutely," Sam said. "Now, about lunch. How about it? You can grumble that nothing I'm feeding Bobby is healthy."

Carrie laughed and thought about what her grandmother had just advised, opening her heart to new experiences, even if she wasn't quite ready for a new man.

"Well, when you put it that way, it should be fun," she said. "Maybe I'll even let you hold the baby, if he wakes up crying. That could be even more entertaining."

"Hey, I'm barely holding my head above water as it is. One kid at a time, okay?"

"Okay," she relented. "I'll go save a table. It's going to be hopping in there soon."

Even as she walked away, she heard him trying to persuade Bobby to climb down. The boy promptly refused.

"Don't make me come up there after you," Sam warned.

As much as she wanted to turn around and watch the test of wills play out, she kept going to Sally's. Lunch promised to be one of those interesting adventures that had been in short supply recently.

❧ 5 ❧

"Twice in one day?" Sally commented when Carrie walked into the café. "To what do I owe the honor?"

"I'm meeting a friend. At least I am if he can get his nephew to leave the playground."

"Ah, you must be talking about Sam," Sally said, proving how efficient the Chesapeake Shores grapevine could be. "I heard about what happened, that out of the blue, he's got his nephew to raise." She shook her head. "Poor little thing. He must be feeling so lost without his mom and dad. And Sam must be feeling completely out of his depth. Your uncle Kevin would know what that was like."

Carrie immediately sat up a little straighter. "Why didn't I think of that? Uncle Kevin suddenly found himself a single dad when Georgia was killed. The whole family pitched in with Davey until Kevin got his feet back under him. I should arrange for Sam to meet him."

Sally gave her a long look. "How did this become your problem?"

"I told you. Sam's a friend."

"I thought he was new to town."

"Okay, we just met, but he obviously needs help. Kevin can give him some encouragement, tell him he won't feel as if he's floundering for long," Carrie said, warming to the idea. "Look at Kevin's life now. He's married to Shanna. They have Davey, and an adopted son, Henry, and two kids of their own."

"You planning to step in and be this man's Shanna?" Sally asked, a spark of devilment in her eyes.

Carrie's jaw dropped at the question. "No, of course not. I'm just being neighborly."

Sally looked doubtful. "Keep telling yourself that. You want your usual to drink—an iced tea?"

Carrie shook her head, determined not to be so predictable. Maybe it was silly, but she viewed it as a first step toward getting more spontaneity back into her life just as Grandma Megan had advised. She'd been right. Playing it safe wasn't Carrie's way.

"I think I'll go crazy and have another cup of coffee," she announced with a greater sense of triumph than the decision deserved.

Sally nodded and went to greet a group of tourists who'd just taken over two tables in the middle of the room, using half the chairs for all their packages. Clearly their visit had been good for the Chesapeake Shores economy.

Just then Sam came in the door, a firm hand on his nephew's shoulder. The boy wore a mutinous expression as Sam guided him to the booth where Carrie was waiting.

"Carrie, this is Bobby. Bobby, Carrie is the nice lady who helped me decide on that delicious Irish stew we had for dinner last night."

Ignoring both her and his uncle, Bobby crawled across the seat and settled in a corner of the booth, arms folded across his chest, his gaze downcast.

"Sorry," Sam mouthed.

Carrie debated her strategy, then opted to be direct, acting as if Bobby weren't so determined to punish Sam and pretend she didn't exist.

"I saw you climb that jungle gym on the playground just now," she said, her tone cheerful.

Bobby gave her a surprised look, but remained stubbornly silent.

Carrie was undaunted. "You were really high. You must be very brave. How old are you?"

She saw Sam start to answer for him, and shook her head. He sat back and waited.

"I think I was about your age when my twin sister and I climbed up on the railing on the porch at my grandfather's house and tried to walk it like a tightrope," she continued as if he'd responded. "It was pretty scary, but fun, too. At least till our mom caught us."

Bobby finally met her gaze, a faint interest sparking in his eyes. "Was it very high?"

"Not as high as the jungle gym, but pretty high."

"I like to climb stuff," he said. "And I never get scared."

"That's great, but it's important to understand that some things have risks. You don't want to do anything that might be dangerous. A broken arm or leg wouldn't be much fun."

Bobby shrugged. "My friend Pete had a cast on his arm. He said it itched. And there were lots of things he couldn't do for a long time."

"Something to remember," Carrie suggested. "I heard you might want a grilled cheese sandwich for lunch. That's my favorite, too. Sally's are the best."

Curiosity finally overcame his bad mood. "Is that the lady who owns this place?"

Carrie nodded. "And here's another tip. If you're nice to her, she sometimes has cookies still warm from the oven for her best-behaved customers."

Bobby's eyes widened. "Chocolate chip, like we had last night?"

"Even better," Carrie said, praying Nell would forgive her if she ever heard about that traitorous claim.

"I think you've said the magic words," Sam said. "Bobby and I are both suckers for warm chocolate-chip cookies."

"I can eat lots and lots of them," Bobby agreed.

"But only after lunch," Sam reminded him just as Sally arrived to take their orders for two grilled cheese sandwiches, a burger for Sam and an order of fries for the table.

Clearly more at ease now, Bobby glanced across the table and studied Jackson in his carrier. "Is that your baby?"

"No, Jackson is my nephew. He stays with me sometimes."

"Like I'm staying with Sam?"

"Not exactly," Carrie said. "He goes home to his dad at night. His dad's a doctor here in town and his mom is in school in Baltimore."

Bobby looked puzzled. "If she's a mom, isn't she too old for school?"

Carrie smiled. "This is a special school for people learning to be doctors."

"Is she gonna give shots?"

"I imagine so."

He gave an exaggerated shudder. "I don't like shots."

"Most people don't," Carrie agreed. "But I happen to know that Jackson's dad gives shots that you barely even notice."

"Did he give one to you?"

"More than one. I was going on a trip and needed several before I went."

Bobby shook his head. "I'd have stayed home."

"And missed out on a big adventure?" Carrie said. "I thought it was worth it."

"Where did you go?" Sam asked.

"Africa. My grandfather has taken on the task of designing and building medical facilities for several small villages, something that's increasingly critical with all of the outbreaks of Ebola that have been occurring in that part of the world. I went with him and my grandmother to talk to the people and see what they needed. While he did his thing, we worked with the women in the villages to help with their English and teach them some preventative care for their babies."

"That's impressive. Are you involved in his work on a regular basis?"

"Not really. Helping in underserved villages is my sister's passion. It's the reason she's studying to be a doctor. And the trip was my grandfather's way of trying to motivate me to get on with my life."

"What do you do now, aside from taking care of your nephew?" Sam asked.

"Not much," she said candidly. "And that's the problem." Relief washed over her when she saw Sally coming with their food. "Here's our lunch."

She stole a French fry from the plate the minute it was on the table, avoiding Sam's curious gaze.

She glanced his way again and realized she'd been wrong. It wasn't curiosity on his face. His expression had actually shut down as if he disapproved of her glib response.

Okay, maybe her life was a bit of a disorganized, unplanned mess at the moment, but who was he to judge? As she focused her attention on her meal, it dawned on her how annoying snap judgments could be. Perhaps that was exactly how Sam had felt earlier today and last night, when she'd been judging him.

Maybe she'd been a little premature in telling Sally they were friends. They were, at best, distrustful acquaintances. With surprising regret, she realized she didn't see that changing anytime soon.

Except for Carrie's ability to coax Bobby out of his stony silence, lunch had pretty much been a disaster, Sam decided as he headed back to the inn with his chattering nephew at his side. He couldn't exactly ponder what had gone wrong, though, with Bobby asking a million and one questions about the town, the bay and every bird they saw. Sam's answers were in short supply. Who knew a six-year-old could be so bright and inquisitive?

"Why don't we look for some books about all that the next time we're in town?" he suggested at last.

"We could go back now," Bobby said, gazing

up at him hopefully. "I saw a bookstore right next to where we ate."

"Are you sure you don't want to take a nap?"

"I don't take naps," Bobby scoffed. "I'm too big."

Sam sighed. "Okay, then. Let's go back."

This was Sam's first visit to the bookstore. He was surprised by how extensive the selection appeared to be. It even had a cozy little coffee area.

Bobby immediately gravitated toward the children's section, where books had been left scattered around and child-size furniture invited kids to sit and look at the books or play with the book-themed toys. Clearly the owner understood a lot about children. It was an atmosphere that invited curiosity and exploration, rather than one that said Hands Off!

A woman emerged from the back and beamed, first at Bobby, then at him. "Hi, I'm Shanna O'Brien," she said, holding out her hand to Sam. "And you're the new web designer working with Mack."

Sam blinked, astounded not only by her perceptiveness, but by her last name. "Excuse me for letting my jaw drop," he said. "But I'm beginning to think O'Briens are everywhere."

She laughed. "Pretty much, and with all the babies in the next generation, I don't see that changing."

"How did you know who I am?"

"I ran over to Sally's a half hour ago to pick up a sandwich. I spotted you with Carrie and this little guy. It didn't take long to put two and two together. We have very good math skills in this town, at least when it comes to that sort of thing."

"I'd better remember that," he said, not sure how he felt about so many people, no matter how well-intentioned, knowing his business.

Shanna had gone to kneel down next to Bobby. "So, what kind of books do you like?"

"All kinds," Bobby said. "My mom read to me every night before bed." He glanced up at Sam, his expression sad. "Will you do that? I packed some of my favorites, but I like new stories, too."

"Absolutely," Sam said readily, grateful to get a handle on something he was capable of doing to make Bobby's transition to this new life a tiny bit easier. "You pick out whatever books you want and we'll read them together."

Looking relieved, Bobby turned back to Shanna. "Do you have books about the bay and the birds around here?"

"I sure do," she said, pulling several off a shelf. "There are a lot more, but they're for grown-ups. If you want to know more when you've been through these, come back and we'll see if one of those appeals to you." She glanced at Sam. "I'm a big believer in encouraging children to read about whatever interests them, even if the books were meant for adults. They might stumble over some of the words, but it keeps them interested."

Bobby was already engrossed in a picture book about local shore birds, so she turned her attention back to Sam. "I'm trying to convince Thomas O'Brien to start a summer class for the younger kids in town. He already has an active group at the high school, but in my opinion children are never too young to develop a passion for the world right around them. Thomas runs the foundation to preserve the bay, and I've told him the best way to assure that the bay goes on being protected is to spark interest at an early age. Do you think Bobby would like to join?"

Sam glanced down at his nephew and smiled. "I think that's your answer. He's the one who insisted we come in today and find these books, and we just arrived back in town last night."

"Thomas and my husband will be thrilled about that enthusiasm. Kevin—and yes, he's an O'Brien, one of Mick's sons, in fact—works with Thomas. Between us we have three boys and a girl, ranging in age from a few months to seventeen. We'll have to have the two of you over for dinner, so Bobby can make some new friends."

"That would be great," Sam said, liking this open, generous woman at once.

"Should I invite Carrie, too?" she asked slyly.

He blinked at the obviousness of the question. "Up to you," he said. "It's your dinner."

She gave a nod of satisfaction. "I'll take that as a yes. Now let me ring up those books, unless you want to look around for some for yourself."

"I think I'm going to be spending all my spare time reading these with Bobby," he said. "I'll find some for myself the next time we come in."

"Any particular genre?"

"Adventure travel," he suggested. Books were probably the only way he was going to satisfy his wanderlust for the foreseeable future.

"You're in luck. I have a great selection. There are a few other people in town who have the time and money to travel, so I try to order the latest books for them."

"You must get to know your customers really well," Sam said, impressed.

"It's the only way for a small, independent bookstore to succeed these days," she said.

When their purchases were paid for and bagged in two separate bags so Bobby could carry a couple himself, she gave Sam another smile. "I'll be in touch about dinner. Probably one night next week. I know Tuesday is deadline night at the paper, so I'll aim for Wednesday or Thursday."

"Great," Sam said.

Outside Bobby was practically skipping across the street in excitement. "Can we read when we get back to the inn?"

"Would you rather do that than swim?" Sam asked, surprised.

"Uh-huh," Bobby said with a nod. "I always liked it when Mommy read to me."

"Then that's what we'll do," Sam said. He held out his hand. "Hold my hand when we cross the street, buddy."

Bobby tucked his hand trustingly into Sam's, then gave him a shy look. "I think maybe being here is going to be okay."

The softly spoken comment brought the sting of tears to Sam's eyes. He was glad for the sunglasses that kept those tears from his nephew. "I *know* it's going to be okay, Bobby," he said, his tone more reassuring than it might have been even twenty-four hours earlier. "We're going to be a team, you and me."

Bobby grinned. "I like being on a team. Do you think they have T-ball here?"

"I imagine they do."

"Can I play?"

"If you want to."

"Will you come to the games like Daddy did?"

"You bet."

Sam studied the satisfied expression on his nephew's face and realized turning into a dad wasn't going to be quite as terrifying as he'd imagined. Bobby was already showing him the way.

Jackson was down for his afternoon nap, though how he could sleep with Davey and Henry fighting over a video game in the living room was beyond Carrie.

"Hey, you two, a little quieter, please. The baby's sleeping."

"Oops," Henry said, his expression immediately turning serious.

"Shouldn't you have outgrown this competitive thing with your younger brother by now?" she teased. "You're only a year away from going to college."

He grinned. "I'm just warming up *for* college," he informed her. "I hear it gets pretty wild and competitive in the dorms and fraternity houses."

"Whatever happened to the sweet, serious little boy who first came to town to live with Shanna?" Carrie asked, remembering his arrival even though she'd been just a few years older.

"I got turned into an O'Brien," he said, then gave her a taunting look. "You want to play?"

Davey's eyes lit up. "Yeah, Carrie, take him down, okay?"

"I'm no good at this game," she protested innocently. "You both know that." Still, she sat down and took Davey's remote. "Don't be too hard on me, okay, Henry?"

Fifteen minutes later, she'd wiped the floor with the smug teenager, proving he and Davey weren't the only competitive people in the room. Davey hooted.

Henry's gaze narrowed suspiciously. "Have you been practicing behind our backs?"

"It is my game in my house," she told him. "What did you think, that I'd let you go on trouncing me?"

Henry laughed. "I was hoping. I need somebody around to keep my confidence high. Uncle Connor sure doesn't let me win and even Davey's getting to be more than I can handle. I guess I'll have to start playing with the babies if I want a surefire win."

"Are there any more of those cookies, Carrie?" Davey asked. "I'd like a couple for the road. We need to get home for dinner."

She gave him a stern look. "Which is exactly why I'm not giving you more cookies. I don't want your mom or dad over here yelling at me about spoiling your appetites."

Just then her phone rang and she spotted Shanna's name on the caller ID. "Speak of the devil."

"Is that Mom?" Davey asked.

Carrie nodded.

"Then we'd better move," Henry said, leaning down to give her a kiss on the cheek. "Bye, Carrie. See you."

"See you," Davey said, bounding out the door ahead of his big brother.

Carrie sighed and answered the phone. "Your boys are heading home right now."

"Good to know," Shanna said. "But that's not why I called."

"Oh? What's up?"

"Are you free for dinner next Wednesday or Thursday?"

"Sure, either one," Carrie said without bothering to check her calendar. "It's not as if I have a lot of commitments these days. Anything special going on?"

"Not really. We just haven't seen enough of you lately," Shanna said.

The comment was so completely untrue it was laughable. "I saw you this morning," Carrie reminded her. "And Henry and Davey just left my house. I see all of you at Sunday dinner at Grandpa Mick's. What's this really about? And don't fib. You're no good at it."

"I invited Sam Winslow and his nephew for dinner," Shanna admitted.

"Oh, boy," Carrie whispered. "If you're trying to do some matchmaking, quit it. Sam and I have some issues."

"Not that I could see at lunch today," Shanna argued. "It was quite the little family scene in Sally's."

"You saw us?"

"Of course I did. If it was supposed to be a secret rendezvous, it might have been better to have it someplace more secluded and minus the kids."

"You are so far off base," Carrie told her. "There is nothing at all between Sam and me. There's not likely to be, either. I'm not crazy about some of the decisions he's been making about Bobby and he doesn't seem all that crazy about me, period. Let this go, Shanna. I'm glad you invited him over. Earlier today I was thinking he and Kevin might have a lot in common, given how abruptly they both became single dads. Trust me, though. You'll have a much better time without me there."

"I already told him I was inviting you."

That gave Carrie pause. "And he didn't immediately come up with an excuse to avoid the whole thing?"

"Nope. He looked more like a man who was happy someone was stepping in to push the two of you together again."

"I seriously doubt that."

Shanna was surprisingly silent for about a minute. "You know, I take it back," she said.

Carrie was startled by the sudden turnaround. She didn't like the disappointment that immediately spread over her. "You're withdrawing the invitation? You're canceling dinner?"

"Nope," Shanna said decisively. "I'm moving it up. It's tomorrow night. I don't want you to have a whole week to talk yourself out of coming. Sam, either. Seven o'clock. I'll call him right now to confirm."

"But I never said yes."

"Oh, you'll be here," Shanna said confidently. "Don't you have enough issues with the family without adding coward to the list?"

"That's not fair," Carrie grumbled, knowing Shanna had set a very neat trap for her.

"Life is rarely fair," Shanna said brightly. "But O'Briens always cope. See you tomorrow, sweetie."

She hung up before Carrie could form another protest or think of a single way to wiggle out of the commitment. Maybe, if she were very, very lucky, Sam would do the wiggling. Sadly, with the way her luck was running lately, it wouldn't happen that way.

And somewhere, deep down inside, a traitorous spark of anticipation was doing a little jig about that.

6

Sam had been surprised to hear from Shanna so quickly about dinner. In fact, she'd caught him so completely off guard, he hadn't been able to come up with a single excuse to refuse, even though he wasn't crazy about her obvious attempt to throw him together with Carrie. He told himself he'd accepted for Bobby's sake. That was the only thing that gave him any comfort as he approached Shanna and Kevin's house on a quiet side street not far from downtown.

Though the house appeared small from the street, he discovered on entering that appearances had been deceiving. There had been additions onto the back, including a big sunroom where a baby in pink was bouncing in a child seat, a toddler was climbing all over a teenager as the boy tried to play a video game and yet another boy was laughing hysterically.

"Way to go," the laughing youngster told the toddler.

"Get him off of me," the older boy pleaded, still trying to concentrate.

"No way!" the other boy declared. "He's my secret weapon."

"I thought Carrie was your secret weapon. You loved it when she busted my chops yesterday."

Shanna stood in the doorway, shaking her head. "Welcome to my world," she told Sam. She raised her voice. "Boys! We have company."

"Henry, Davey and Johnny," she said as she pointed to each of them. "The baby's Kelly. Everyone, this is Sam. He's working with Mack at the paper. And this is his nephew, Bobby."

Bobby hung back shyly, but surprisingly it was the teenager who came over and held out a hand. "Hey, Bobby, do you like video games?"

Bobby nodded.

"Then you can be on my side. Davey's enlisted

the little monkey over there to try to distract me when it's my turn. You can do the same when it's Davey's turn."

"You want me to climb on him?" Bobby asked skeptically.

Henry laughed. "Whatever works," he said. "You'll think of something."

Bobby looked hesitantly up at Sam. "Is it okay?"

Before Sam could answer, Shanna stepped in. "Do whatever you need to do," she told Bobby. "Just no hitting or biting. Those are the house rules."

She turned to Sam. "We probably don't want to watch this. Come with me and I'll get you a glass of wine. Kevin should be here soon and Carrie's on her way. She's stopping to pick up dessert. Nell baked today. Honestly, I don't know how Nell does it. Once a week there's Kevin's favorite apple pie, a coconut cake for Connor and his family, chocolate cake for Abby and Trace, scones for anybody who wants them. She must have been a baker in her previous life. She'd do all the pastry for the inn, if Jess would let her. Now that she's in her eighties, we all think she should slow down, but she's having none of it. Have you met her yet?"

Sam shook his head. "But I have had a few of her chocolate chip-cookies," Sam said. "Carrie gave me some when I stopped by O'Briens the other night."

Shanna's eyes lit up. "Did you try the stew? That's Nell's recipe, too. In fact, most of the food in the pub is based on traditional recipes she learned when she stayed with her grandparents in Ireland years ago."

"So Luke inherited her skill in the kitchen?"

Shanna laughed. "Absolutely not. She despaired of teaching him a thing. He brought in a chef and Nell trained him. She still looks over his shoulder regularly to be sure he's not messing up. Nothing goes on the menu unless it has her stamp of approval. For a guy who learned to cook in a New York deli, he's adapted quite well to Nell's Irish favorites. Every now and then he sneaks a Reuben or a pastrami sandwich onto the menu as a special, and Nell pretends not to notice."

Just then Carrie's voice carried down the hallway to the big open kitchen. Sam felt an immediate and troubling spark of anticipation. Apparently he could tell himself a thousand times that getting involved with her was a bad idea, but his testosterone wasn't convinced.

"Anybody here?" she called out.

"In the kitchen," Shanna replied as she poured two glasses of wine. She handed one to Sam, then held out the other to Carrie as she set the pie on the counter.

"Gram says to heat this up before you serve it," Carrie instructed Shanna.

"As if she hasn't told me that every single week since the day I married Kevin," Shanna said.

Carrie laughed. "She doesn't like to leave anything to chance and I'm pretty sure she's convinced that not a one of us inherited a single bit of her culinary skill."

"Not true," Shanna said. "Kevin's actually quite adept in the kitchen. He's just never home to cook."

He walked in just in time to overhear the comment. "I'm here now," he said, giving her a thorough kiss. "And I always take care of the important things, right? Like this?"

Laughing, Shanna shoved him away when he clearly would have stolen another kiss. "Company, Kevin."

"It's just Carrie," he said.

"And Sam Winslow," Shanna said, giving him a gentle elbow in the ribs. "Sam, my husband, Kevin O'Brien."

Sam grinned at Kevin's suddenly chagrined expression. "I didn't realize we had *company* company," he apologized. "I thought it was just Carrie."

"Thanks," Carrie grumbled, feigning an insulted look. "Always a pleasure to see you, too." She glanced at Sam. "A minute ago I would have told you Kevin was my favorite uncle, but now he's on probation. I'm thinking Uncle Connor has the edge."

The teasing interaction was a revelation to

Sam, whose own family life, if it could even be called that, had always been filled with tension and long, awkward silences.

There was a sudden whoop of glee from the sunroom.

"Video game?" Kevin asked.

"Always," Shanna said with a sigh. "Sounds as if maybe Davey actually won this one."

Kevin glanced toward Sam. "You any good at those games?"

"I've played some," Sam said, though from what he'd observed tonight, he wasn't nearly as competitive as the males in this family.

"Want to go out there and take them on?" Kevin asked.

"Sure," Sam said at once, eager to get away from the kitchen and the unwanted attraction that seemed to be simmering between him and Carrie.

"Twenty minutes," Shanna reminded them sternly. "Once I get dinner on the table, I'm not calling you all twice. And make sure all the boys wash their hands. And don't forget the baby, the way you did last night."

Sam bit back a smile as he followed Kevin to the sunroom. "You forgot the baby?"

"Hey, she'd fallen asleep," Kevin explained in his own defense. "Since she's almost never quiet for more than a heartbeat, I think I should be forgiven for not realizing she was there."

"You have no idea how happy I am to hear you say that," Sam told him.

Kevin regarded him with a puzzled look. "Why's that?"

"Because I've only had responsibility for my nephew for a couple of weeks and I've spent most of that time terrified I was going to do something totally stupid. And as if I didn't have enough doubts myself, Carrie has caught me twice doing things she apparently considered unforgivable."

"What things?" Kevin asked.

"I left Bobby sleeping in the car while I ran into O'Briens to pick up takeout. Even though I kept my eye on him the whole time, that wasn't good enough for her. And the next day she thought I wasn't watching closely enough while he was climbing on the jungle gym at the playground."

"When it comes to kids, Carrie's a natural-born worrier," Kevin consoled him. "Just like her mom. And just like Abby, Carrie will be a great mom someday. We all trust her to keep an eye on our kids, but we also know she's overprotective. She'll get over it once she sees that not even she can be everywhere at once. Kids are adventurous. They do crazy things and sometimes they're too fast for us to catch 'em before they fall. All we can do is be alert and minimize the risks, then be ready to patch up any bumps and bruises, dry any tears."

"Voice of experience?" Sam asked.

"As a dad and as a former paramedic," Kevin confirmed. "There's a big difference between letting kids be kids and allowing them to take the occasional risk, and being a negligent parent. You'll figure it out, too."

Sam was doubtful. "I hope so. By the way, Bobby was asking if there's T-ball in town."

"Sure. Show up at the high school field on Saturday. We'll get him on a team."

In the sunroom, Kevin muscled Henry away from the controls for the video game, took the other remote from Davey and handed it to Sam. "Let us show you how it's done, boys."

"Oh, please," Henry taunted. "I've been beating you since I was a kid."

"Me, too," Davey gloated. "Dad, you're really bad."

Sam laughed. "Then maybe I have half a chance."

"Loser takes on Carrie," Henry said, his expression innocent. "You'll need a confidence boost."

Something told Sam he'd better win against Kevin. The last thing he wanted was to be humiliated for his ineptitude yet again by Carrie Winters.

"Are you convinced now?" Carrie asked Shanna as Kevin and Sam left the kitchen. "He barely even looked at me."

Shanna waved off the comment. "That meant nothing. If anything, it was more telling than it would have been if he'd fawned all over you."

"Seriously?" Carrie said, trying to follow her logic.

"Sure. Men act all indifferent when they're feeling exactly the opposite and don't want to give anything away."

"It was just plain awkward," Carrie corrected. "I should probably go so you all can have a pleasant evening."

"And let him think he chased you off?" Shanna asked. "I thought you were tougher than that."

"You're thinking of my twin. It's Cait who's tough. I'm all sweet and sensitive."

Shanna guffawed at that. "Since when? You didn't survive in the shark tank of fashion by being anybody's pushover."

"You're wrong," Carrie said, instantly somber. "I was Marc's pushover."

"Whole different story, sweetie," Shanna said. "It's time you put that behind you. Let Sam be your rebound guy. Practice being a whole new you on him."

"Now there's a charming approach," Carrie said. "I'm sure it'll make him feel all warm and fuzzy about being chosen to play such an important role in my life."

"You never know. He might like the idea of being a knight in shining armor for a little while."

Carrie gave her an impatient look. "Haven't you been married long enough to stop being such a romantic?"

"I hope I will always be a romantic," Shanna protested. "It's a good way to be. Look at your grandmother. Do you think she and Mick got back together without both of them being romantics at heart?"

"I certainly see the sparks," Carrie admitted, "but I try not to think about exactly how they got back together or what they do behind closed doors. In fact, I'd be content to go to my grave without having that particular image engraved on my brain."

"They're great examples," Shanna countered. "So are Nell and Dillon. Our family is crawling with wonderful role models who exemplify the importance of romance. Your mom and Trace are no slouches."

"Another image I prefer not to dwell on," Carrie said. "Though they are awfully cute together. And, just to be clear, I'm not denying the importance of romance. I'm just saying I've never encountered it, not in the way you're describing."

"And yet you tell us all the time that what you want most in life is to be a wife and mom. I'm telling you that requires romance and sappy, messy feelings and risks."

Carrie sighed. "I know you're right. But Sam? I

think that's a lost cause. He can't possibly have time for anything these days beyond discovering if he has what it takes to be a dad."

"He could probably use somebody to encourage him and show him the way," Shanna suggested. "Somebody who's a natural with kids."

"You're suggesting I coach him?"

"Something like that."

"He hasn't taken kindly to most of the advice I've offered so far," Carrie told her.

"Advice?" Shanna repeated, her brow lifted. "Or criticism?"

A guilty flush crept up Carrie's neck. "Criticism," she acknowledged. "Okay, I see your point—about that, anyway. As for Sam and me as a couple, I think you're way off base about that."

Shanna merely gave her a knowing smile. "I guess we'll see."

Despite the difference in their ages, Bobby seemed to flourish under all the attention of the older boys. He even held his own when it came to teasing them. Sam watched the interaction with amazement, then uttered a sigh of relief. Kevin apparently overheard him, because he gave him a puzzled look.

"What was that sigh about?" he asked Sam.

"I'm sure you've heard the story of how Bobby came to be my responsibility barely three weeks ago," Sam said, smiling when a belly laugh erupted from Bobby as Davey pinned him down and tickled him to get even for something.

Kevin glanced over. "Hey, watch it! Remember he's younger than you."

"He has it coming," Davey retorted. "He was supposed to be on my side for this game and he helped Henry just then."

"I didn't mean to," Bobby said, giggling and scrambling away. "Honest. I forgot. I was on his side before."

"Yeah, sure," Davey said, then tickled him some more.

Kevin turned to Sam. "You okay? Davey's just teasing, but if you think it's too much rough-housing, I can call a halt to it."

"Absolutely not," Sam said. "It's wonderful. This is the first time I've heard a real laugh from Bobby since, well, since he lost his mom and dad. I was afraid there'd been too many changes for him to handle. I was thinking about talking to Will, after Carrie mentioned he's a shrink. I thought he could help me figure out what to do to make this transition easier on him." He gestured toward the pile of laughing boys, which now included Henry and even the toddler. "Look at them."

Kevin shrugged. "Looks normal to me."

Sam couldn't seem to stop the smile spreading across his face. "I know."

Kevin gave him a slap on the back. "I'm no expert, but it looks to me as if you're doing just fine."

"Maybe you could mention that to your niece."

Kevin gave him a sly look. "Does her approval matter to you?"

Sam laughed. "Not the way you mean. I just don't want her reporting me to child protective services."

Just then he heard a shocked gasp behind him and turned to see Carrie, her complexion suddenly pale.

"I would never report you and risk having Bobby sent into foster care," she said. "Not unless you did something totally outrageous or dangerous. How could you say such a thing?"

"Well, it certainly doesn't seem as if you're very impressed with my parenting skills," Sam said, already regretting a comment he'd meant mostly in jest.

"Maybe you two should work this out on the patio," Kevin suggested, casting a pointed look toward the suddenly silent boys who'd turned to see why voices were raised. "I'll tell Shanna she'll have to hold dinner a few minutes."

"But it's ready now," Carrie protested. "She sent me to tell you. Besides, I have nothing to say to him."

Her uncle had the nerve to smile at her petulant

tone. He was a braver man than Sam. Sam could feel the anger radiating from her.

"I disagree, and this conversation takes precedence," Kevin insisted. "Go, settle this and get back in before dinner gets cold so my wife doesn't lose patience with all of us."

He turned to address the kids as he picked up the baby. "Hands washed and in the dining room. Davey, you show Bobby where to go. And make sure Johnny washes up, too."

Shoulders stiff, Carrie led the way past Sam, opened a pair of French doors and walked onto a flagstone patio. Keeping her back to him, she folded her arms across her chest.

Taking a deep breath, Sam walked up beside her. "Which one of us should go first? Kevin didn't mention that."

"You started it," she muttered.

She glanced his way and gave him a hurt look. To Sam's dismay there were tears in her eyes.

"What would make you think I'd turn you in to child protective services?" she asked.

"Isn't that what people are supposed to do when they think a parent's being negligent?" Sam responded. "You've made it pretty clear that you think I'm inept. I can't even argue with your perception. I'm floundering, no question about it."

She flushed, then sighed heavily. "And I should be cutting you a whole lot of slack under the circumstances. It's not as if I have tons of parental experience myself."

"But you're great with kids," Sam said. "Everyone I've run across says so. You have no idea how I envy that. I never expected to be a dad."

"You didn't want children?" she said, looking genuinely shocked.

"I never thought much about it. My parents weren't the best examples, so I figured I should avoid following in their footsteps. My sister always said she wasn't cut out for motherhood for the same reason, but then Laurel met Robert and he was solid and steady and completely unflappable—perfect dad material. He convinced her they could be great parents, and together, they really were. Bobby's a great kid, and I know it's because they knew what they were doing, unlike me."

"You can be a great dad, too," Carrie said with feeling. "I'm so sorry if the things I said made you feel inadequate, or should I say more inadequate than you were already feeling. I tend to open my mouth without thinking, especially when a child is involved."

"That's my point," Sam said. "You could tell right away that Bobby was in the hands of someone who didn't know what they were doing. And you cared enough to say something."

"But you did know more than I gave you credit for," she corrected. "When you left him in the car, instinct told you to keep an eye on him. I just jumped to conclusions. Same with the jungle gym. You knew it was something he loved and let him go for it, rather than hovering too close and making him scared to try something. I think really good parents have to find a balance between letting kids grow and being overly protective."

She met his gaze. "I'm sorry, Sam. I truly am. How about this? Next time I think you're handling something wrong, I'll mention it, but I won't get all judgmental and crazy on you."

He laughed. "Do you really think you can pull that off?"

She winced. "I can at least try."

"Well, don't try too hard. Despite not enjoying being the target of your indignation, I like that you were protective of a little boy you didn't even know. I admire you for caring that much. And just to reassure you about Bobby, I may be inexperienced and the situation may be totally unexpected, but I'm going to be the best stand-in for his dad that I can possibly be."

"I believe that," she said, then studied him. "So, we're good?"

He nodded. "We're good."

"Okay, then. I see Shanna at the kitchen window staring at us. I'm not sure if she's just curious to see if we're killing each other or ticked off about dinner getting ruined."

"Let's go inside, so she can check for injuries," Sam suggested. "And, to tell the truth, I've been looking forward to a home-cooked meal ever since she invited Bobby and me over. I'd hate for it to be spoiled."

Carrie fell into step beside him as they went back in. "Don't you cook?"

"I'm a single guy. I grill and I order pizza. I am also a master of cold cereal."

"Oh, dear," she said, regarding him with alarm.

"I know," he said, holding up a hand before she could say more. "As soon as Bobby and I have our own place, I will make sure he has healthy meals, even if I have to rely on somebody else to cook them. I'll get Shanna to recommend a foolproof cookbook."

She grinned. "An excellent plan. And knowing the single women in this town, I imagine you can count on casseroles and desserts turning up on a regular basis."

"Will you be one of those women?"

"You never know," she said lightly. "Of course, if I am, I'll make sure Nell does the cooking. Or maybe Luke's chef. My skill in the kitchen is only marginally better than you claim yours is." Her expression brightened. "Or how about this? We could both take lessons from Nell. She'd love it, and you and Bobby definitely wouldn't starve."

Sam was startled by the suggestion. "What do you get out of it?"

"I become one of the few O'Briens who actually knows her way around the kitchen. Nell's always been so good at cooking, we count on her for all the big family occasions. I wouldn't mind having bragging rights as a worthy successor someday down the road. Up till now Kevin's had them, but he doesn't exercise them enough to count anymore."

Sam laughed. "Ah, I finally see a chink in your armor of perfection. Sign me up, if Nell's willing."

Her face lit up. "Seriously? You'll do it?"

He shrugged. "Why not? Bobby and I have to eat."

And perhaps it would give him a chance to see Carrie in a setting in which she wasn't quite so sure of herself. He liked knowing she didn't excel at everything. And even with everything already on his plate and his determination to remain immune to the attraction, he had to admit that discovering more about Carrie Winters was an intriguing prospect.

7

She was crazy, Carrie thought as she walked to Nell's cottage the morning after dinner at Shanna and Kevin's. Why would she throw herself into the path of danger by spending even more time around Sam and Bobby? Just as Caitlyn had suggested during her last call, Carrie recognized that she was vulnerable right now and Sam—a floundering single dad—was exactly the sort of man she was likely to fall for when she was in such a vulnerable state. She could tell herself from now till doomsday that she was only interested in Bobby's well-being, but the little sizzle that ran through her when she was in close proximity to Sam said otherwise. Sizzles, as she knew all too well, could turn into dangerous fires.

When she tapped on her great-grandmother's front door, it was Dillon who answered.

"Well, if it isn't the prettiest great-granddaughter in the world," he said with that wonderful Irish lilt in his voice.

"You do know that Caitlyn and I look exactly alike," she responded.

Feigned surprise spread across his face. "Do you, now? There are two of you?"

Carrie laughed and kissed his cheek. "You

know there are. Where's Gram? She's not still asleep, is she?"

He looked appalled by the very thought. "This late in the day? Not a chance. She's on her knees in the garden, despite me telling her she has no business doing all the weeding herself. Since I can't make her see reason, see if you can't lure her inside for a cup of tea and a good long chat."

"It's such a lovely day, maybe I'll make the tea and take it outside, instead," Carrie suggested. "She's much more likely to take a break if she can enjoy her precious garden at the same time."

Dillon nodded approvingly. "And that's why you're the smartest great-granddaughter, as well as the prettiest."

Carrie laughed. "I'm so glad you brought that blarney with you from Dublin, right along with your love for Gram."

"No choice in the matter, my darling girl. No choice at all. There were far too many years when we were apart. I intend to spend whatever time we have left on this earth side by side, wherever that may be. Chesapeake Shores and her family are too much a part of my Nell to ask her to come to Ireland to be with me. And I'm blessed to have my own granddaughter Moira here now, too, with Luke."

"Funny how things work out, isn't it?" Carrie said, as she poured boiling water over the Irish

Breakfast tea leaves her grandmother preferred. Bringing a tea bag into this house would be considered practically sacrilegious. Tea was to be made the old-fashioned way, or not at all. "There are always surprising twists and turns."

"Life amazes me every day, to be sure," Dillon agreed. "That's how I know I'm living."

"Do you need help carrying that outside?" he asked as she put two of Nell's prettiest cups, the antique china teapot with its crackled finish, a matching sugar bowl and a few slices of lemon on a tray.

"I have it, but thanks," she said.

"Enjoy your visit." He reached for some wet wipes and a towel. "Take these along. Nell never wears gardening gloves the way she's promised to. She'll want to clean up before touching those precious cups of hers."

Carrie smiled as she left the kitchen of the cozy little cottage overlooking the bay. Dillon truly was a treasure, and his long-held love for Nell had been a wonderful discovery on the family's trip to Ireland several years ago. Reunited after years apart, they set an example for the whole family of how love could endure, despite nearly a lifetime with other people.

Carrie set the tea tray on a table beside two Adirondack chairs facing the bay, then crossed the lawn toward the gardens. She found her great-grandmother with her roses, humming an Irish tune that sounded familiar, though Carrie couldn't come up with the words.

"Does music make the roses bloom better?" she teased.

Nell looked up, startled, then laughed. "Not mine, I suspect. But it makes me happy. What brings you by on this lovely summer morning?"

"I was hoping for a cup of tea and a chat with my favorite person." She nodded in the direction of the chairs. "I've made it just the way you like it. Can you take a break?"

Nell frowned. "Did Dillon put you up to this? He's been pestering me all morning about the dampness making the arthritis in my knees worse."

"He worries about you."

"Oh, I know that, and I love him for it, but I've been gardening for enough years to know that the pleasure outweighs a few aches and pains. But a cup of tea and a chance to catch up with you would be welcome."

As she struggled to get to her feet, Carrie held out a hand, but as she'd expected, Nell ignored it and made it on her own. Carrie handed her the wipes and towel.

"I imagine these were Dillon's doing, too," she grumbled, though her blue eyes sparkled with affection.

"He says you forget to wear your gardening gloves."

"I don't forget a thing. Half the joy is getting a little dirty."

Carrie put an arm around Nell's waist. "Ornery old thing."

"I am that," Nell said with pride as they walked across the lawn. "How do you think I've lived so long?"

When they were seated and the tea had been poured, she turned a serious gaze on Carrie. "What's on your mind? You aren't letting Mick pressure you about what you're going to do next, are you?"

"He has a point," Carrie conceded. "I should make a decision of some kind."

"Well, my advice is to take your time. There's no rush. The right answer will come to you."

"I wish I believed that," Carrie said with a sigh, then shrugged off the way her indecision weighed on her. "That's not why I'm here, though. I was wondering if you'd have a little time to teach me to cook. Me, and a friend, that is."

Nell's eyes sparkled with delight. "I'd love that," she said enthusiastically. Her expression turned curious. "Tell me about this friend. It must be a man, since I can't imagine you wanting to spend time in the kitchen if it weren't."

"Maybe I just think it's time someone learns all your recipes," Carrie responded.

"Luke's chef knows a good many of them."

"He's not family."

"And your uncle Kevin has picked up a few."

"I want to know them all."

"And this friend, what's his motivation?"

Carrie explained about Sam and Bobby.

"Oh, the poor little thing," Nell said at once.

"He has a weakness for chocolate-chip cookies," Carrie reported. "I gave him a couple of yours at the pub the other night. I gather they were a hit."

"Well, he can't very well live on cookies and pizza and whatever Sam can take out of the freezer or pick up in town," Nell said briskly, her expression thoughtful. "If Sam is working for Mack and trying to manage a child for the first time, I imagine he doesn't have a lot of time. You find out when he has a couple of hours to spare, let me know and bring both of them by. Promise them there will be a good meal at the end of the lesson."

"Thanks, Gram."

"Now, tell me what this young man is like. Is he handsome?"

Carrie blushed. "I suppose."

Nell leveled a direct look at her that had her squirming. "Is it him you're drawn to or the boy?"

"Maybe both," she admitted.

"Oh, my darling girl, be careful."

"I will be, Gram. Nobody knows better than I do that I shouldn't even be thinking about a relationship right now. I have enough decisions to make."

"That's not at all what I'm saying. Love comes along on its own timetable. I just want you to be sure that you're spending time with this man for the right reasons. There's a little boy who's been through too much to be considered. When two adults try and fail, it's one thing, but you don't want to make a mistake that could hurt a child who's already suffered a terrible loss."

"It's not as if Sam and I are dating," Carrie protested. "We can barely call whatever's going on a friendship. I just want to help."

"And that's a lovely gesture. Just think carefully before it goes any further."

"Believe me, I will," Carrie promised. "Now let me take the tea things back inside. Are you coming?"

"I still have my roses to tend to," Nell said. "You can reassure Dillon that I'm not overdoing it and that if he's all that worried, he can get out here and pull a few weeds himself. I won't even tell him he's doing it all wrong."

Carrie laughed. "I'll pass that along." She hugged Nell. "I love you. I'll be in touch about the cooking."

"I'll be looking forward to the lessons and to meeting your young man."

"He's not my young man," Carrie reminded her, probably to no avail. No one in this family listened to such denials unless it suited their purposes. Romantics, the whole darn lot of them!

Determined not to dwell on Nell's speculation about her relationship with Sam, Carrie decided she'd wait before calling him. She didn't want to seem overly eager. And since she didn't have Jackson today, maybe she could go shopping for a few things that didn't practically scream *designer* when she put them on. She didn't want to think about why she felt that was necessary. Not scaring Sam off should not be a consideration.

She was on her way back from the nearest mall way out on the main north-south highway, when she spotted a day-care center on a large fenced-in patch of lawn with a colorful swing set in the backyard. With Luke's suggestion about a possible career still very much on her mind, she made a U-turn and went back, mostly out of curiosity. A look around wouldn't hurt anything, and maybe it would even inspire her.

Inside, she could hear shouts of gleeful laughter coming from the back. That sound made her smile.

The girl at the reception desk, who looked to be barely out of her teens, hung up the phone and grinned at Carrie. "It's snack time. It always gets noisier then. Can I help you?"

"I was wondering if I could speak to the owner

or manager for a few minutes," Carrie said.

"About? If you have a child you'd like to enroll, we're not taking any new clients right now."

"No, it's not that. Actually, it's a long story, but the short version is that I'm thinking of opening a day care over in Chesapeake Shores." She smiled reassuringly. "No competition for this one. I could use some advice and I'd like to look around if she or he doesn't mind."

"Hold on. Let me check," the girl said. "I'm Lucy, by the way. Lucy Morris."

"And I'm Carrie Winters. Do you work here full-time?"

"Pretty much, but I'm also studying early childhood education. My mom opened this day care when I was a baby, so I've pretty much grown up around the place. I've been working here ever since high school."

"You must love it since you chose early childhood education as a career."

"It's the best job ever," she said cheerfully, then made a face. "Except on the days it isn't."

"Which days are those?"

"When one kid is cranky and the mood seems to be contagious. Or when mom caves in and brings cookies for snack time. Twenty kids on a sugar high?" She shuddered. "Not pretty."

Carrie chuckled. "I know what you mean. I've had a houseful of kids at my house like that a time or two. The day after Halloween can be particularly dicey."

"Tell me about it." Lucy held up a finger to indicate her mother had finally picked up the phone. "Mom, there's a woman named Carrie Winters here who'd like to talk to you about running a day care. Can you take a minute? I'll come back and take over, if you want to come out here where it's quiet." She nodded. "Sure thing. I'll tell her."

When she'd hung up, she stood. "She told me to bring you back so you can get a firsthand look at the craziness. She'll spend a little time with you after that."

"Perfect. Thank you so much."

Lucy grinned at her. "I predict you'll either fall in love in the first five minutes or run for your life. Either way, you'll have some inkling if this is right for you."

"I sure hope so," Carrie said, following her through a set of double doors that led into a large play area.

A quick glance around had her smiling. The colors were bright and cheerful from a palette very similar to the one used in Noah's offices. Tiny tables and chairs were scattered around the room, along with boxes stuffed with toys. There was a chalkboard in an area where a few young children were apparently engrossed in lessons that would give them a head start for the upcoming school year. Some were reading, but others seemed to be getting tutoring from a boy who looked to be high school age. Everyone was finishing up a snack of cheese, crackers and carrot sticks, along with bottled water.

A woman who appeared to be in her early forties disentangled herself from three pre-schoolers who were begging for another story. "Sit quietly and Lucy will read to you," she promised. "Go pick out one book each."

The children scampered away and the woman came over. "I'm Julie Morris," she said. She nodded toward the younger children. "Lucy, you'll take over?"

"I'm on it," Lucy said. "Nice to meet you, Ms. Winters," she called over her shoulder as she rushed after the kids.

"I know it probably seems chaotic, but it's an organized chaos," Julie told her. "Lucy said you're interested in opening a day care."

"I'm exploring the possibility," Carrie said. "I had another career, but it turned out to be a bad fit. Someone suggested that Chesapeake Shores could use a good day-care center."

"So, out of the blue, you want to snap your fingers and do it?" Julie asked, her expression skeptical.

Carrie winced. It did sound crazy when her plan was described that way. "It's not quite as impulsive as it sounds. Ever since I got back to town, I've been caring for my nephew as a favor to his mom and dad. Other kids in my family are in and out of the house all the time. I love having them underfoot and everyone says I'm very good with them."

"Running a day care is a lot more difficult than babysitting," Julie cautioned.

"I know that. I did take a few early childhood education courses in college as electives, but I understand that's just the tip of the iceberg. That's one of the reasons I stopped by when I spotted your center as I was driving home just now. I realize there's a lot I need to learn and I don't want to do this by half measures if I'm going to do it. If you knew my family, you'd know we might make impulsive decisions, but we do our homework and we do things right. And to hear my grandfather tell it, failure's not an option."

Julie studied her intently, then seemed to reach a decision. "Look, I can sit down with you and go over regulations, your business plan and all the other things it takes to be successful in this business. I can even advise you on some courses if you want to fill in the educational blanks."

"That would be incredibly generous of you," Carrie said enthusiastically. "I'd be happy to pay you for your time."

Julie smiled. "Not a chance, because I'm not going to start advising you, at least not right away. You think you want to do this, then you sign up for those courses online, then come here a couple of days a week as a volunteer. You'll know soon enough if you're any good at it. When I see if you're serious, *then* I'll teach you everything you need to know. I've been running this center since Lucy was a baby and I've got an excellent reputation. If I'm going to be your mentor, then I'm going to be thorough."

Carrie was momentarily taken aback, but then she chuckled. "Done," she said, holding out her hand. "We'll do it your way. I have the baby a couple of days a week, but I can work here around that."

"Or you can bring the baby with you," Julie said. "I won't even charge you for it, since you're going to be pitching in as volunteer staff. I've worked that deal with a couple of moms who need child care while they hunt for work."

"Something tells me spotting this place was the luckiest thing to happen to me in a long time," Carrie said sincerely.

She liked that Julie wasn't going to hand over a bunch of facts and figures or dole out advice without being sure that Carrie was up to the job. She was obviously a woman who took her responsibility to the children in her care seriously and intended to do whatever she could for those who might be in Carrie's care down the road. For the first time Carrie was starting to view the whole day-care idea as a serious, viable option for her future.

"Monday morning," Julie told her. "I get here by five-thirty. A couple of parents work very early shifts and drop off their kids on the way to work. Six-thirty will be early enough for you."

"I'll be here," Carrie promised, managing to hide her startled reaction to the early hour. She'd grown used to late nights and laid-back mornings, a carryover from her lifestyle when she'd worked with Marc.

Julie nodded approvingly. "I expected you to react differently to the early hour."

"I'll admit that I've never been much of a morning person," Carrie conceded. "But I am a reliable one. I'll be here."

"Keep surprising me and we'll get along just fine. Now I'd better get over there and see how Lucy's holding up. The kids adore her, but they tend to try to take advantage of her. She's still working on being a disciplinarian when she needs to be."

She gave Carrie a distracted wave as she hurried off.

Carrie stood where she was for a moment longer, soaking up the high-pitched laughter, the sight of kids bouncing in their seats with excitement as their young tutor made whatever lesson they were having fun. The atmosphere in the room wrapped itself around her and warmed her heart in a way nothing had in a very long time.

Apparently Luke had been onto something when he'd pointed her in this direction. She supposed she'd find out for sure over the next few weeks or months or however long it took for Julie to decide if Carrie had passed her personal test.

Carrie already had a pretty good idea that this time she'd found a perfect fit.

When she finally got back to Chesapeake Shores, Carrie found her grandfather pacing up and down the front walk, a cell phone up to his ear. When he saw her, he disconnected and shoved the phone in his pocket.

"It's about time you got home. Why weren't you answering your phone?"

"The battery died," Carrie replied, thinking how convenient that was, given the expression on her grandfather's face. She kissed his cheek. "What's up?"

"That's what I want to know," he grumbled. "You've been avoiding me."

"I've been busy."

"Doing what?"

She held up her packages. "Shopping, for one thing."

"You couldn't possibly need more clothes. I helped haul all your things over here, in case you've forgotten."

"They were a little too fancy for every day in Chesapeake Shores," she said. "I bought a few more practical things."

His gaze narrowed. "So, you're not thinking of taking off again right away?"

"Nope," she said, setting all the bags down in a chair, then heading for the kitchen. "I could use some iced tea. How about you?"

"Tea's fine," he said. "Answers would be better."

"I haven't heard any questions yet." Her back to him, she pulled a pitcher of tea from the refrigerator, retrieved two glasses from a cabinet, added ice, then poured the tea, taking her time about it before facing him again.

He scowled at her. "Don't be smart with me, young lady."

She smiled. "Ask whatever you like, Grandpa Mick, but on the advice of counsel, I reserve the right not to answer."

The scowl deepened. "What counsel? What the devil are you talking about?"

Carrie laughed. "Grandma Megan told me I don't have to let you pry into my life unless I want to."

"My own wife told you that?" he demanded incredulously.

"She also said she was going to get you to stop bugging me." She sighed dramatically. "I guess that didn't work out so well."

He scrubbed a hand across his face and looked as if he were clinging to his last thread of patience. "I swear that woman is going to be the death of me."

Carrie gave him an impulsive hug. "But you love her like crazy."

"That I do." He looked into her eyes. "And I love you, too. I want you to be happy. That means getting on with your life. I don't see you doing that, though if you've made a decision to stay here, I suppose that's a start."

"I'm working on the rest," Carrie assured him. "Honest, Grandpa Mick. I'm seeing things more clearly than I have in a long time."

His expression brightened. "Tell me."

"Not just yet. I want to see how things go first."

"Not even a tiny hint so I don't worry?"

"Not even a tiny hint, but I promise you can stop worrying. The skies have cleared and the outlook around here is improving by the minute."

"Whatever that means," he grumbled again.

"It means you can go meet Grandma Megan at the gallery, take her out for a nice dinner and talk about something other than me and my problems for a change. I'm sure she'll appreciate that."

He shook his head, but smiled at last. "I'm sure she will. Okay, then. I'll stop pestering you." He gave her a meaningful look. "For now," he amended. "But if I don't like what I'm seeing, I reserve the right to speak up."

"I wouldn't have it any other way," she told him as she led the way to the door. "Love you."

"Love you, too, though how you turned out to be such a stubborn one is beyond me."

"Lots of examples," she reminded him. "And you're the best one of all."

As she closed the door behind him, she leaned against it for a moment, then realized she was smiling. For the first time in what felt like forever, she hadn't been fibbing to him. She headed for her computer to look for some of the classes Julie had suggested she could find online. Smiling as she signed up for two of them, she finally felt as if she was starting to have some control over her life again.

Sam had brought home pizza for the second night in a row, mostly because it was what Bobby had insisted he wanted and because Sam couldn't come up with a sensible alternative.

"We can't go on like this," he muttered mostly to himself.

"Why not?" Bobby asked, devouring his second slice.

At least it was a veggie pizza tonight, Sam thought, a concession to a healthier lifestyle.

"Because you need real food."

"Pizza is real food," Bobby said, looking confused. "This one even has yucky vegetables on it."

Sam noted the pile of said vegetables that Bobby had picked off and left on his plate. "They don't count unless you actually eat them."

"I don't like them," Bobby said reasonably. "If I ate them, I'd probably get sick."

"You wouldn't get sick, I promise." A thought struck him. "Did your mom ever let you have pizza every night of the week?"

Bobby hesitated, clearly debating between the truth and an answer that would keep the pizza coming. "No," he conceded finally. "It was for Saturday night." His expression brightened. "And tomorrow's Saturday, so we can have it again!"

Sam shook his head. "I don't think so, pal."

He grabbed his cell phone, checked for Carrie's phone number, which he'd programmed in, and called before he could think about the wisdom of it.

"Well, hi," she said. "Everything okay?"

"You said something about cooking lessons," he reminded her. "I'm on our second night in a row of pizza with a third one in store unless you can save us."

She laughed. "I spoke to Gram this morning and she's eager to start whenever we're ready. I was going to call you to check your schedule, but I had a busy day today."

"Would tomorrow be too soon? I need to break this pizza habit as quickly as possible."

"Are you good with anytime tomorrow?"

"I'm taking Bobby to check into T-ball first thing in the morning, but we should be free by eleven. Any time after that if it works for Nell," he told her. "And you."

"Let me check and I'll get right back to you."

"You have my number?"

"On caller ID," she responded. "I'll call you in a couple of minutes."

"Thanks."

"Was that Carrie?" Bobby asked when Sam set his phone within reach on the table.

"It was. She's going to set up some cooking classes for us with her great-grandmother."

Bobby immediately looked worried.

"Something wrong?" Sam asked.

"Do I get to come, too?"

Over the past few days, Sam had noticed that Bobby rarely let him out of his sight. It was understandable, but it probably needed to change or the first day of school was going to be a problem. Still, he couldn't very well break the habit until he had good alternatives. He considered calling Shanna or even Kevin to see if they'd take Bobby to T-ball in the morning, but one look at the fear in Bobby's eyes told him he couldn't do it.

"Sure you can come."

When Carrie called back, he walked out onto the balcony of their room at the inn and finalized the plans.

"Is it okay if Bobby comes along?" he asked, explaining Bobby's reaction to the prospect of being separated from Sam even for a little while.

"Gram's counting on it," Carrie assured him. "And, by the way, good job picking up on his fear."

"Picking up on it is one thing," Sam said. "But not every situation will be resolved as easily as this one. I have to go back to work next week. School starts not long after that."

"You'll figure it out," Carrie assured him.

When Sam remained silent, she said, "Did you hear me?"

"I did. I just couldn't quite believe what I was hearing."

"I learned my lesson," she told him. "Positive reinforcement from here on out. Does it help?"

"Surprisingly, it does," Sam said. "See you tomorrow."

"Looking forward to it. Want me to pick you up, so I can show you the way to the cottage?"

"Sure," Sam said, though he already had a pretty good idea where it was. Anything to spend a little more time around the positive energy she was suddenly exuding. It was pitiful how badly he needed that right now.

8

When Mack couldn't find Susie at home, he drove into town and headed for the real estate office. Susie rarely stayed late, but for the past couple of days she'd been there until eight or later. When he'd asked, she'd told him that paperwork had piled up because of the days she'd stayed home. He hadn't bought her excuse, and when he'd run into her dad earlier, Jeff had confirmed that there was no backlog of paperwork.

"Any idea what's going on?" Jeff had asked him. "I know having the adoption fall through was a blow, but she's bounced back a lot more quickly than I'd anticipated. And since she came back to the office, she's been working harder than ever."

"I noticed the same thing," Mack had said, not even trying to hide his concern.

"Want me to have Jo talk to her?" Jeff had asked.

Susie and her mom were close, but Mack wanted to get to the bottom of this himself. "I'll handle it, but thanks. If I think Jo needs to get involved, I'll ask."

Jeff had slapped him on the back. "I know you love my girl, Mack, but so do we. If you need help, all you have to do is ask. Unlike my brother

Mick, I don't meddle. Neither does Jo, but we're only a phone call away if you think something's not right. Just because Susie's a grown woman and married, doesn't mean she's not still our child."

"Trust me, I know exactly how strong the bond is," Mack said, meaning it and grateful for it, too. "You two were every bit as important to her cancer recovery as I was. She needed us all. She may again."

In Mack's opinion, something definitely wasn't right. After two days of staring at the bay and showing no interest in anything, Susie had demonstrated a sudden surge of energy right after meeting Sam's nephew, Bobby, on Wednesday. There was little doubt in Mack's mind that the two things were connected.

After parking on a side street when he couldn't find a spot along Main or on Shore Road, he headed for the real estate office. As he'd expected, the lights were burning brightly despite the lateness of the hour. He could see Susie at her desk staring at the phone. Taking a deep breath and praying for guidance, he went inside, a smile plastered on his face.

"Here you are," he said cheerfully, dropping a kiss on her forehead. "I thought you'd be home by now. Friday night's always been our date night."

She flushed guiltily. "I forgot all about it

144

being Friday. I got caught up in something here," she said.

"What?" he inquired mildly.

She frowned at the question. "Why the doubt in your voice? You know I work late sometimes."

"Of course you do. I was just curious about what had kept you tonight. Is there a big deal pending?"

"Something like that," she said, not meeting his gaze.

Mack concluded that dancing around the subject wasn't going to get answers. He sat in the chair beside her desk. "Suze, what's going on?"

"I told you I'm working."

"It looked to me as if you might be waiting for the phone to ring." Suddenly the answer came to him, though he didn't like it. "Are you waiting for Sam to call about taking a look at that house?"

"He said he would," she replied defensively. "Getting Bobby settled is important, so why hasn't he done it?" She regarded him with alarm. "Nothing's happened to Bobby, has it?"

"Bobby's just fine as far as I know. They had dinner with Kevin and Shanna and the kids last night. When I spoke to Sam earlier this evening, he mentioned that he's signing Bobby up for T-ball in the morning, then Nell's giving him a cooking lesson."

For the first time since he'd arrived, there was a

spark of interest in Susie's eyes. "How'd that happen?"

"I gather Sam threw himself on Carrie's mercy and she set it up. She's taking lessons from Nell, too."

"Of course she is," Susie said, a surprising edge to her voice.

Mack knew there'd once been a family rivalry between Susie and Jess, but this was something new. "Hey, why the attitude?"

"He's single. He has a kid. Of course Carrie would latch on to him, the same way she made herself available to Noah when he first got to town."

Mack regarded her with shock. In all the years he'd known her and through some very tough times, he'd never heard her be so mean-spirited, except perhaps when he'd stupidly invited an ex-girlfriend to work at the paper. Even then, his wife had struggled hard to hide her distaste for the woman and how much the situation upset her.

"You know perfectly well that Carrie and Abby pitched in to help Noah get settled because Caitlyn was starting her internship at the hospital in Baltimore," he said quietly. "There was nothing more to it, certainly not anything like what you're implying."

"You're so naive," Susie said.

Mack found the whole conversation

increasingly puzzling. If Susie was going down the path he feared she might be, her jealousy of Carrie was a worrisome sign.

"Since when do you have such a jaded attitude toward Carrie?" he asked, keeping his tone as level as he could. Sparking a fight would get him nowhere.

She winced at the question, but didn't respond. That left him no choice but to be direct.

"Is it because she's spending time helping Sam with Bobby and you wanted to be the one to do that? If so, Suze, that's a problem."

He tried to hold her gaze, but eventually she sighed and looked away, though not before he saw tears forming in her eyes. She buried her face in her hands.

"I'm turning into such a witch, aren't I? How can I be jealous of someone who's just trying to be nice?"

When the tears began to fall in earnest, Mack gathered her close. "You're the furthest thing from a witch. You're just hurting right now. I know you, babe. You'd never say things like this if you weren't."

"I can't seem to stop myself. These awful thoughts keep coming to me and I get so angry. Thank goodness it's you and not someone else in the family. They'd probably want me to go into therapy."

When Mack didn't reply right away, she

regarded him with dismay. "That's what you want, too, isn't it?"

Rather than answering directly, he asked, "Do you think therapy might help? You've been through a lot. Not many people could have handled it as well as you have."

"You have. You were a rock through all of my cancer treatments. You handled every curve that was thrown at us. Even when we found out we weren't getting the baby, you were so blasted strong. I wanted to be like that, but this adoption fiasco was the final straw. I don't have any hope or strength left in me."

"Of course you do. Give it time, Susie. You can't expect to go through something like this without it taking a toll. I was probably pushing too hard for us to try again, because I thought that would help. I was wrong. You need time to mourn."

"That's exactly it," she said, seizing on his comment. "I'm mourning this child that was almost ours. When I lash out at Carrie the way I did just now, I can hear the words as if someone else is saying them and I'm horrified at the spitefulness, but I can't seem to stop." She sighed. "Maybe I *should* see Will."

"That's your decision, but it might help to have another perspective. I may be too close to this to give you the sort of unbiased support you need."

"I'll think about it," she promised. "And now, if you're not totally turned off by my mood swings, how would you feel about taking me to dinner? It's not too late for our date night, is it?"

"It's never too late for me to spend an evening with you, anyplace you want to go," Mack said readily, relieved for now.

"Brady's, I think. I'd like some wine and some excellent rockfish and maybe even a decadent dessert."

Mack smiled. "Now you're talking my language. Great food and a date with the woman I love more than anything in this world. Let's do it."

Though she cast one last look at the still-silent phone, she grabbed her purse and locked up. Just outside she looked up at him. "Have I mentioned how much I love you and how lucky I am that you're hanging in here with me?"

"No chance of me doing anything else," he assured her. "You're my world, Suze. And whether we ever have kids or we don't, you will always be more than enough. Please try to remember that."

When Carrie arrived at the inn in the morning to pick up Sam and Bobby, there was no sign of them. Her aunt Jess found her pacing in the lobby.

"There you are," Jess said. "It's crazy around here this weekend. We're packed, so I've been helping in the kitchen and dining room, but I've been trying to watch for you. Sam wanted me to ask if you could pick them up at the ball field.

Kevin came by earlier and drove Sam and Bobby to T-ball. Kevin thought it would be easier for Bobby if Davey and Johnny arrived at the field with him. Sometimes my big brother demonstrates amazing sensitivity." She grinned. "Of course it was probably Shanna's idea."

Carrie laughed. "More than likely. Thanks for passing along the message. I'd better get over there."

"Not before you have a cup of coffee with me," Jess said. "Call Gram and tell her you're running late. She won't mind. I spoke to her a few minutes ago and said you might be."

Carrie regarded her suspiciously. "You told Gram I'd be late?"

"I said it was a possibility, because of having to go by the ball field," her aunt said blithely.

Carrie tried to protest any further delay, but Jess had a firm grip on her elbow as she guided her into the busy dining room. "There's a table over by the window. I'll get the coffee and join you in a minute."

"Jess, I really don't have time," Carrie argued, then glimpsed her mother at the table Jess had pointed out. "Ah, I see. An ambush."

Jess laughed. "You can choose to see it that way if you want, but I tend to do my big sister's bidding, especially after she's handed me a nice, fat dividend check from the investments she's made for me."

As Carrie crossed the room, she noticed her mom was distractedly stirring her own coffee. Since she took neither cream nor sugar in it, it was clearly a nervous gesture just to pass the time.

"Hi, Mom. You're out bright and early on a Saturday morning," Carrie said, giving her a hug. "How'd you manage that?"

"Trace took Patrick to the ball field. He wants to play T-ball, even though he can barely hold the bat."

"So, rather than taking advantage of a little time to yourself, you just happened to come by here?"

"I had a check for Jess, but then I heard you were stopping by to pick up Sam Winslow and I was hoping to catch a glimpse of both of you. Apparently I missed Sam, but here you are."

"Sorry you're not getting a twofer," Carrie teased. "And why would you want to meet Sam, anyway?"

"The O'Brien rumor mill has been buzzing. I wanted to see if there was any truth to what I was hearing." She gave Carrie a chiding look. "You might have mentioned yourself that you'd met a nice young man."

"Everybody is making way too much of this," Carrie said. "Sam's single and he's attractive. However, he just started a new job and he just assumed custody of his nephew after a terrible tragedy. I'm sure he's not looking for a relationship any more than I am. We both are way too busy trying to get our lives on track."

"And yet you're taking time this morning to have Nell teach you how to cook," Abby said. She grinned. "Clever move, by the way."

"It wasn't some sort of ploy," Carrie claimed. "Sam can't cook. He has a six-year-old who needs to eat."

"Very logical," Abby said, her eyes sparkling. "And you? Where did your sudden desire to learn your way around a kitchen come from? Up till now you've been perfectly content to take your meals with family or at the pub or Sally's. And I know you'd have a ton of frequent diner points at Panini Bistro or the pizza place if they offered them."

"And who set that example for me?" Carrie retorted, drawing a startled laugh from her mom.

"Touché. I am a master of takeout. Thankfully that hasn't driven Trace away yet. He knew what he was getting when he married me, and it wasn't gourmet cooking."

Since she'd managed to one-up her mom and doubted she'd pull it off again, Carrie stood up. "Mom, I'd love to stay and chat, but I really do need to pick up Sam and Bobby and get over to Gram's."

"Fine. Go, but I expect to meet them very soon. If you don't bring them around, I'll go looking for them. At least I know where to find the lot of you on Saturday mornings. You'll be in Nell's kitchen." She grinned. "How convenient!"

"Weren't you banned from Nell's kitchen a long time ago?"

"Only if I try to get near the stove," Abby retorted, laughing. "Now go. Have fun."

"Love you," Carrie said, kissing her cheek.

"Hey," Abby called when she was just a few feet away.

Carrie turned back.

"I hear you've decided to stay in town. I'm so glad about that. We all are."

"Boy, it didn't take Grandpa Mick long to spread that word."

"I suspect he was texting before he left your house," Abby replied. "He said it was the best news he'd had in weeks."

"I'm glad I could make his day."

It remained to be seen if the decision was going to work out half as well for her, but she was definitely hopeful.

Kevin's offer to pick them up for T-ball had been a stroke of genius, Sam thought as he watched Bobby shadowing the older, very friendly Davey on the field. Soon Bobby was talking to other boys his own age, taking his turn at bat and listening closely to whatever the coaches had to say.

Of course, Sam also noticed that Bobby never went more than a couple of minutes without glancing his way. With some kids, he suspected that would be no more than a quick check for parental approval, but in Bobby's case, Sam had a feeling it was another example of the boy's need to reassure himself that Sam was close by.

It was Bobby's team's last at-bat when he felt Carrie's presence nearby. He turned and grinned at her. "We're almost done."

"How's he doing?"

"The kid has pretty good eye-hand coordination. He's had more hits than the other kids on the team. That's made him an instant hero."

She glanced around the field and spotted Bobby waiting for his turn at bat. He was laughing with another little boy. For the first time since she'd set eyes on him, he looked like every other child his age having a great time at the ball field.

"Whose idea was it for him to play T-ball?" she asked.

"His. He asked if there were teams. I checked with Kevin and here we are."

"He's obviously played before."

"Apparently," Sam said. "Not that I knew much about his life before I got custody. Thankfully he's starting to speak up about the things he likes to do."

Carrie gave him a curious look. "You knew about his fondness for the jungle gym."

"My sister sent pictures from time to time. It was one of her ways of keeping the lines of communication open. When we spoke, we tended to butt heads, so we didn't do it often."

"That surprises me," Carrie said. "Especially since she trusted you to take custody of Bobby."

"It surprised me, too," Sam confessed. "I think maybe she thought it would never come to that." He sighed. "I guess now I'll never know what she was thinking."

"I'm sorry."

"Yeah, me, too."

The batter before Bobby was called out at first base, and the game ended before he could go to bat. He dropped the bat and ran to Sam, his face flushed with excitement.

"Did you see me? I got two hits!"

"I saw," Sam said. "You're pretty good."

"Not just pretty good," Bobby corrected. "I'm great!"

"Well, definitely no lack of confidence when it comes to T-ball," Sam said dryly. "I haven't heard you say hi to Carrie, yet."

"Hi," Bobby said, instantly shy.

"I only saw the last couple of minutes of the game, but I heard very good things about how well you played," Carrie said.

"Maybe you could come next week," Bobby suggested.

"I'd love that. Maybe I will." She ruffled his hair. "Are you ready to learn to cook?"

Bobby looked doubtful, so Sam stepped in. "I

certainly am, especially since you told me we get to eat what we cook."

Bobby's expression brightened at once. "We do? Then I hope we're learning to make cookies."

Kevin approached just then with Davey and Johnny in tow. "We're going to Sally's for milk shakes, Bobby. You want to come along?" He glanced at Sam. "I can bring him by Gram's after that."

Sam watched Bobby closely. At first the idea of a postgame treat seemed to interest him, but then he gazed up at Sam.

"You wouldn't be there?"

"I can't go, buddy. I'm going with Carrie for that cooking lesson, but you can go if you want to."

Bobby took his hand and held on tight. "No. I want to go with you."

Kevin gave him an understanding look. "No problem. Maybe next time." He gave Carrie a quick kiss on the cheek. "Don't wear Gram out."

"It's more likely to be the other way around," Carrie said.

When Kevin and his boys had gone, Sam realized Bobby was regarding Carrie with curiosity.

"How come Kevin kissed you? Is he your boyfriend? I thought Shanna was his wife."

Carrie laughed. "She absolutely is. He's my uncle. He and my mom are brother and sister."

"Did you ever live with him?"

"Just for a little while at my grandpa's house when we first moved back to Chesapeake Shores. Then my mom got married again and we moved to another house."

"Oh," Bobby said, his expression thoughtful as if he was trying to fit together a puzzle.

"You guys ready?" Carrie asked.

"We can't wait, right, Bobby?"

"I guess," he said, sounding doubtful.

Carrie leaned down and whispered something in his ear that made him smile.

"What did you tell him?" Sam asked as they walked to the car.

"That no matter what we cooked, there are bound to be cookies. And if I know Gram, she'll have a whole plate fresh from the oven when we get there."

"Isn't that great?" Bobby asked excitedly.

"Best news ever," Sam agreed.

He wasn't holding out a lot of hope that whatever he and Carrie learned to make would be received quite so enthusiastically.

Sam glanced across the small butcher-block island in Nell's kitchen and smiled at the frown of concentration on Carrie's face as she diced vegetables into perfectly matched pieces.

"Need a ruler?" he inquired.

She scowled at him. "Gram said they should

be the same size so they cook through evenly."

"I'm not sure she meant you had to be quite that precise," he said, grinning as he gestured to his own haphazardly diced veggies.

"I guess we'll see when she and Bobby get back from checking out the garden and picking the fresh herbs we need," Carrie said, finally putting down her knife and regarding her neat piles of vegetables with obvious satisfaction.

Sam glanced out the window and saw Nell leaning down to listen to Bobby as they walked toward the house. To his surprise and relief, Bobby had been chattering nonstop ever since he'd met Nell. Either it was her natural warmth or the chocolate-chip cookies just out of the oven, but she'd won Bobby over at once.

Carrie followed the direction of his gaze and smiled. "They make quite a pair, don't they?"

"Is she this way with all kids, sort of a natural Pied Piper?"

"Pretty much. When my grandmother left my grandfather while my mom was a teenager and her siblings were still pretty young, Gram moved in and took over. There were five of them and it could have worn her out, especially with Grandpa Mick on the road with work so much. Instead, she always said that being around them and the great-grandchildren who've come since has kept her young. She has this free spirit that all of us appreciate. And watching her fall in love with

Dillon all over again when they reconnected in Dublin was an inspiration."

"It's nice to know that things do work out, even if it's not on the timetable we anticipated."

"That's what she says, that love has its own timetable, and we need to pay attention to it. Not everyone gets that second chance."

Sam studied her and noticed a sadness he hadn't seen since that first night when he'd spotted her at the bar at O'Brien's.

"How do you feel about second chances?"

"Given how often we manage to mess up our own lives, I'm all for them," she said. "You?"

"Same thing. Have you messed up your life? It seems to me you have it all—a big, wonderful family, a whole town that's practically a family business in some crazy way. You're beautiful."

"I'll accept the compliment, but those are blessings that I really had nothing to do with. My looks can be attributed to great genes. This town is Grandpa Mick's baby. The family, well, that's Nell's doing. Even when there have been tensions, she's made certain that we all stick together. It's nice knowing that kind of support is always there when we need it."

"Is that why you came back here? I heard you were living in Europe."

"In a way," she said. "This is home, and I do love it here."

"Are you planning to stay or is there another

glamorous job on the horizon. I've heard from a couple of people you were involved in the fashion industry."

"All behind me," she said. "It turned out it wasn't right for me."

He grinned. "You wore the clothes well." He glanced at the bright blue T-shirt and capris she was wearing today, along with a pair of flip-flops with a big white daisy between her toes. No more sexy heels. No designer wardrobe. "Is this a new look?"

"You have a good eye," she said. "I decided I needed some more practical clothes for the life I'm living now. I loved some of the things I was able to buy at a discount because of my connection to a designer, but I would have had heart failure if I'd splattered grease on them." She gestured toward the apron Nell had given her, which was covered already with various stains. "Look at me. I sure wouldn't have made one of those perfect housewives portrayed in those old TV sitcoms." She glanced his way and caught a puzzled look. "You know, the ones who could cook entire meals in a dress and heels without getting a thing on them."

"Ah, yes," he said with dawning understanding. "Well, just so you know, you look like a million bucks in these clothes, too."

She blushed. "Sam Winslow, are you flirting with me?"

"Just calling it like I see it," he said, then winked. "I've also heard that a little flirting is good for your health. If that blush on your cheeks is any indication, it definitely has an impact on blood flow."

She laughed. "I never thought of it quite that way. I'll have to brush up on my flirting skills."

A sudden image of her flirting with any man who crossed her path gave Sam pause. And the fact that it did scared him in a way that little else in his life had. The only thing scarier was knowing that as tricky as the past three weeks of adjusting to being a dad had been, he still had years in that role to figure it out.

That thought had him moving quickly to the door to hold it open for Nell and Bobby, relieved to have a distraction. He could feel Carrie's puzzled gaze for the rest of the morning as he focused his attention on mastering Nell's instructions and answering her questions.

When they finally sat down at the big kitchen table to sample what they'd cooked, he smiled when Bobby took his first taste of the Irish stew and looked up, his face alight with surprise.

"This is really good," he said, already spooning up more. "It's like the stew we had when we got to town."

"It is," Carrie agreed, looking triumphant. She met his gaze. "How about that? We didn't mess it up."

"You both get an A plus," Nell said approvingly.

"Never had better, not even back in Dublin," Dillon added.

Sam studied their expressions, still harboring doubts about their success. Eventually he took a tentative taste. As the flavors of the beef, fresh herbs and vegetables burst on his tongue, he regarded the stew with amazement.

"Who knew I could cook?" he said, an unmistakable hint of wonder in his voice.

Nell chuckled. "Boy, you're just scratching the surface. You can't live on Irish stew alone, even as good as it is. Next week we'll move on to my chicken and dumplings. Now those dumplings are the test that separates the men from the boys."

Carrie murmured something under her breath that drew a sharp look from Nell.

"What's that, girl? Speak up."

"I said Uncle Kevin's dumplings are pretty light and fluffy."

Nell gave her a chiding look. "You mean compared to mine?"

Carrie shrugged. "He does seem to have a magical touch."

"And where'd he get that from, I ask you?" Nell inquired with a touch of indignation.

"I'm guessing he learned it from you," Sam said quickly.

Nell gave a nod of satisfaction. "Of course he

did," she said, then frowned. "But do you know the ungrateful brat won't tell me what he's done to improve on my recipe."

"So you're admitting his are better?" Carrie pressed.

"Maybe a smidgen," Nell conceded, "but if you tell him I said that, I'll call you a liar."

Sam noticed that Bobby was thoroughly engrossed in his meal, thank goodness. Because while the rest of them might be wise enough to keep Nell's admission to themselves, if Bobby heard it, he'd blurt it out without a second thought.

"Hey, Bobby," Sam said, just to see if he was as distracted as he'd hoped.

Bobby glanced up from his food. "Chicken and dumplings next week. I know."

Sam winced. "And?"

"Kevin's are better but we're not telling."

Dillon's boom of laughter filled the kitchen. He reached over and squeezed Nell's hand. "That'll teach you to say things you don't want repeated, my darlin' Nell."

A twinkle in her eyes, she focused on Bobby. "How many cookies would it take to make sure you forget what I said?"

Bobby's face lit up. "I can have all I want?"

Carrie intervened. "No bribery, Gram."

Nell sat back with a sigh. "I suppose I'll just have to hope that Bobby has a very short memory or that he and Kevin don't cross paths."

"Something tells me you're doomed on both scores," Carrie said. "Kids always remember the things you don't want them to and Kevin's likely to be at Bobby's T-ball practice every Saturday."

As he had at Kevin and Shanna's, Sam listened with growing amazement to the banter at the table. This was what it would be like to have a real family, connected not just by the chance of DNA, but by genuine caring. For the first time in his life, he wanted that, not just because it was what Bobby had lost and deserved to have again, but for himself. Also, for the first time, he could appreciate just how much effort Laurel had put into trying to give him some semblance of normalcy amid the chaos their parents' dysfunction had created.

9

On Monday morning Carrie dragged herself out of bed at the ungodly hour of 5:00 a.m. to shower, dress and make the drive to the Happily-Ever-After Day-Care Center. At least the sun was still coming up fairly early, so she wasn't driving the winding road in the pitch-dark of winter.

At the center she found the lights on and Julie and two other women busy making sandwiches for lunch. Julie gave her an approving look, made quick introductions, then nodded toward a shelf where a box of disposable gloves had been left open.

"Get busy," Julie said. "We need to have these made before the next round of kids starts to arrive. Lucy has the early arrivals entertained for now, but she'll need help as soon as it starts getting crazy in here."

Studying the turkey, tomato and lettuce sandwiches being assembled, Carrie pitched in and went to work, then dared to ask, "Wouldn't peanut butter and jelly be a lot easier and more popular?"

"Peanut allergy," Julie explained. "We know we have one boy who has it. Once we open that jar, who knows who might get their hands on it. Why take chances? And we try to stick to healthy options, not popular ones."

"We shake things up with grilled cheese and tuna on pita bread," Lucy said, joining them and reporting that the three early arrivals were occupied within view with picture books. "It's never boring and the younger kids will pretty much try anything once. For a couple of them, the meal they get here will be the healthiest one they get all day. Add in some fruit and added veggies at snack time and they get decent nutrition from us. It makes the older ones more alert, too, so we can actually get in a few lessons during the day when the littlest ones are down for their naps."

"What ages do you have?" Carrie asked. "I noticed some older kids here with a tutor the other day."

"We have six up to the age of eight who come here after school. During the summer they're often here all day. They've been with us since they were toddlers. I won't take babies," Julie said. "I just don't have the staff, but we'll take them as early as two as long as they're reasonably potty trained."

Just then a loud *No!* carried from the lobby.

Julie shook her head, her expression resigned. "Lucy?"

"I'm on it," her daughter said.

"Problem child?" Carrie guessed.

"She just started here a week ago and has big-time separation anxiety, at least until we can get her so interested in something, she doesn't realize her mom has left. Once the other kids are here, she's pretty good."

Thinking of Bobby, Carrie asked, "How do you deal with the separation thing? I have a friend who just assumed full custody of his nephew after the parents died in an accident. So he's in a new town with an uncle he barely knows. I noticed the other day that he's not letting his uncle out of his sight. That's going to be a problem when school starts."

"Totally understandable," Julie said. "How old is he? Does he have friends?"

"He's six and he's started making some friends."

"The same age?"

"A couple are older, but he started playing T-ball on Saturday and that looks promising. He seemed to fit in pretty quickly, though that's when I noticed he was keeping a close eye on his uncle the whole time."

"If he's socializing that well already, I'll bet he'll be fine," one of the other women making sandwiches piped up, then gave a shrug, her expression wry. "Lots of psychology classes before I had to quit college. I know just enough to be dangerous."

"Alicia, right?" Carrie said, determined to keep as many names as possible straight from the beginning. She'd been a master at it during her career in fashion. Remembering names was the first step in great PR.

Alicia nodded.

"Listen to her," Julie said. "I may have been at this a long time, but Alicia does have the advantage of all those classes. One of these days we're going to convince her to finish her degree and hang out her shingle in child psychology. Or I'll put her on staff right here and brag about her."

Carrie noticed that the women had an easy rapport and a demeanor that would be warm and welcoming with the children. When Lucy returned with a little girl whose face was tear-stained, Alicia rushed over to give her a hug.

"We're so glad you're here," she told the child. "Want to come with me and draw a picture?"

"No!"

"Finger paints?" Alicia suggested, even as Julie winced.

"Okay," the girl said with a spark of interest.

"Be sure she wears a smock over that pretty dress," Julie called after them, then sighed. "The person who invented finger painting should be made to clean up a day care at the end of the day for a year. I swear I'd ban it from the premises if I could."

"No, you wouldn't," Lucy said, giving her a hug. "You are in charge here, so you could easily toss all the paints in the garbage and never mention the activity again."

Julie's expression brightened. "I could, couldn't I?"

"And let all those smocks you bought go to waste? Come on, Mom, you know the kids love all those bright colors and getting messy. Nothing on earth makes you happier than a room filled with smiling faces."

Three more children arrived in rapid succession. The adults made quick work of getting them settled with toys or other age-appropriate activities before the next wave arrived. By seven-thirty the room was filled with noisy, but definitely cheerful, chaos.

By nine Carrie's clothes were streaked with

finger paint, and her hair, which she'd pinned atop her head, had tumbled to her shoulders. But she was as happy as those children Lucy had described. She'd read at least a dozen stories, helped clumsy fingers play with blocks and doled out praise for unidentifiable art projects.

After lunch, with the littlest children down for naps, and others looking at picture books during their own quiet time, she finally had a minute to draw in a deep breath.

"How are you doing?" Julie asked. "Is the indoctrination by fire helping or destroying this crazy impulse of yours?"

"I love it," Carrie responded without hesitation.

Julie smiled. "Then there may be hope for you. You'll be back tomorrow? Or Wednesday? We didn't settle on a schedule."

"Tomorrow," Carrie said at once, eager to learn all she could as fast as she could.

For the first time in months, she was actually excited about getting up in the morning, even if it was at 5:00 a.m. when no sensible person should be expected to be awake.

Since she didn't want to reveal her plans to the whole family just yet and it had been Luke's idea in the first place, as soon as she'd showered and changed, Carrie headed to the pub. It was still early enough to be deserted and she found Luke, as expected, behind the bar.

He studied her curiously. "Something's different."

"I've had a very good day," she said.

"Have you, now? Well, it's definitely agreed with you. Your face is glowing and your eyes are bright. And there's a lovely streak of something that looks like blue paint in your hair. What was so special about today?"

Carrie reached for her hair, regretting that she'd simply twisted it into a loose knot again, rather than washing it as she probably should have. "Where?" she asked Luke.

"It's the strand that's pulled loose and curled along your neck. If I didn't know you better, I'd think you were making some sort of rebellious fashion statement, the kind meant to drive your grandfather to distraction."

"Hardly," she said, then shrugged. "Oh, well, it'll wash out."

Luke stared at her with feigned shock. "Who are you and what's happened to my perfectly groomed, fashion-forward cousin? You're not rushing home to deal with it right now?"

"Nope," she said, grinning. "This is the new me, relaxed and taking life as it comes."

"Now that's a fine attitude, if you ask me," he said. "What brought it on?"

She extracted his promise that on pain of death he'd never reveal a word of their conversation.

"Bartender's confidentiality," he intoned seriously. "You've got it."

"I took your advice."

"What advice is that? I hand out so much of it and I'm not used to anyone taking it seriously."

"Maybe the rest of it is suspect, but this was right on target. I'm volunteering at a day-care center to see if I like it and to learn everything I can about possibly running my own. I even signed up for two online classes the owner recommended I take."

"Now, there's a bit of news worth celebrating," he said at once, tapping his glass of soda with her glass of wine. "Judging by the way you look, I'm guessing you're finding that it's a good fit."

"It's the best," she told him enthusiastically. "The work is hard. There is a huge amount of responsibility, but I've never been happier. I actually can't wait to get back there tomorrow."

"No difficult children to ruin it for you?"

"Sure, there are problem kids or, I should say, kids who have problems from time to time, but nothing I can't handle." She hesitated, then amended, "At least so far."

"Tell me everything."

She described how she'd discovered the day care, stopped in and met Julie and Lucy and asked for advice. "I got a whole lot more than I'd ever imagined," she said. "Julie's incredible. It's not just that she has a wealth of information to share, but she cares almost as much as I do about making sure I'm not making a mistake. Not for my sake, of course, since she doesn't even know me, but for any kids who might be placed in my care. In just one day, I've already learned so much. I'm also beginning to see how much I don't know."

"And the blue paint?"

She smiled. "Some of the kids are a little aggressive with the finger paints," she said, then shrugged. "It'll wash out."

Luke tapped her glass again. "And that sort of acceptance is what will make you very good at this, if it turns out to be the right career for you."

"I already know it is," Carrie said eagerly. "But I'm not rushing into anything. For one thing, Julie won't teach me the nuts and bolts till she's satisfied that I'm not going to mess up. For another, this experience is invaluable."

"When will you tell the rest of the family?"

She sighed heavily at the question. "No idea. Not yet, that's for sure. Grandpa Mick will think I'm grasping at straws. For someone who's always been a huge supporter of the schools and education, he'll view this as glorified babysitting and a waste of my talents. I can hear him now."

To her regret, Luke nodded. "I can hear him doing just that. Nothing less than lofty ambitions for his family. My side was much the same. Can you tune him out?"

"Today? Probably not," she conceded with

regret. "Once I'm 100 percent certain I'm on the right path, I won't let him intimidate me."

"Good for you." He glanced toward the door. "You might want to brace yourself. I see him outside chatting with someone right now."

"I don't suppose you'd let me sneak out through the kitchen?" she asked wistfully.

"Of course I would, but you'd hate yourself for running away."

"Surprisingly, not that much," she replied, but she did stay where she was. "Not a word, remember? You promised."

"He won't hear this from me," Luke agreed. "But don't wait too long to fill him in, Carrie. It'll only annoy him when he does find out."

No question about it, she thought to herself, then managed a bright and hopefully innocent smile as her grandparents came through the door. She stood up and gave them both hugs.

"Sorry to bolt, but I have things to do," she said, thinking of the reading she needed to do for her online classes. She'd ordered the books from the university bookstore and they'd been on her doorstep earlier. She could hardly wait to check them out and do her first assignment. Her enthusiasm was a far cry from the days when she'd hated wasting time on studying in college.

Her grandfather regarded her with suspicion. "You've barely touched your wine."

"No time," she said. "Love you."

"Enjoy your evening," her grandmother called after her. "I hope it's a hot date that has you rushing off."

"Hot date?" Grandpa Mick echoed indignantly. "What's wrong with you, woman? You don't say something like that to our granddaughter."

"*You* don't," she corrected. "I'm the realist. If we want her to be truly happy, she needs someone in her life."

Carrie didn't linger to hear what her grandfather had to say to that, but she had a hunch her grandmother was about to get an earful. Better Grandma Megan than her!

Sam looked down into Bobby's tearstained face and felt the urge to shed a few tears of his own. They'd just finished dinner at Sally's—another burger and fries for Bobby—when Sam had tried to explain that he needed to get Bobby enrolled in school first thing in the morning and then he had to go back to work.

"I don't want to go to school here," Bobby had shouted, drawing stares from the other customers. "I want to go at home with my friends."

"You have friends here," Sam reminded him, unable to keep a note of desperation out of his voice.

"They're not my real friends. I miss my old friends. I miss Mommy and Daddy. I want to go home."

Sam knew that deep down Bobby understood that simply wasn't possible. He even knew that Bobby had started to like Chesapeake Shores. He'd just bumped up against the reality of the huge change in his life. Sam seemed to do the same thing about a million times a day. The shock of it still hadn't worn off, and he hadn't come close to dealing with his own feelings about the loss of his sister.

Focused on Bobby now, Sam urged him out of their booth and headed outside, hoping to finish this delicate negotiation with some degree of privacy. He took Bobby's hand and crossed the street to the playground on the town green. He chose a secluded bench under a majestic old oak tree and sat down, then patted the seat beside him.

For a minute, it looked as if Bobby might stubbornly resist, his little jaw set and more of those heartbreaking tears rolling down his cheeks, but eventually he heaved a sigh and climbed onto the bench. He did, however, keep some distance between himself and Sam.

Flying by the seat of his pants, Sam said quietly, "You know you live here now with me. I know how confusing it's been and what a huge change it is, but we're in this together."

"But you're going to work," Bobby said, looking lost and scared. "What will I do?"

"In another couple of weeks, you'll start school,

you'll meet lots and lots of new friends, and you'll be so busy you won't even have time to think about me."

"What about tomorrow?"

Sam made an impulsive decision, one he prayed that Mack wouldn't object to. "You can come to the newspaper office with me tomorrow, if you want to. You can bring your books and your games."

Bobby's silence suggested he was considering the idea. "I guess that would be okay," he said eventually, though he didn't sound very happy about it.

"Would you rather spend the day with Davey and Johnny?" Sam asked. "I can check with Shanna and Kevin to see who's taking care of them and maybe work that out."

Bobby fell silent, then heaved a sigh. "That might be okay."

But when Sam called Shanna and learned that Henry was caring for his younger siblings, he couldn't bring himself to ask that Bobby be added to the mix. While Davey might not be a problem, Johnny and the baby would be enough of a handful for the teenager.

"Are you looking for something for Bobby to do tomorrow, so you can work?" Shanna asked perceptively.

"How'd you guess?"

"It was bound to come up," she said. "Call

Carrie. She'll be more than willing to pitch in, I'm sure."

"She did offer when we first met," Sam conceded, though he didn't like the idea of taking advantage of her.

"Well, there you go. She's wonderful with kids and Bobby already knows her."

Sam glanced up and spotted Carrie crossing the green. "Thanks for the suggestion," he told Shanna. "I'll check into it."

Just then it seemed Bobby saw her, too, and called out. "Hi, Carrie!" he yelled, scrambling down and running across the green to meet her. "I just had a hamburger for dinner. That's my favorite."

She laughed. "I thought pizza was your favorite."

Bobby nodded. "They're *both* the best food ever!"

Sam winced at her reproachful expression as she approached. "Don't look at me like that. I'm weak. What can I say? Hamburgers and pizza are my favorites, too."

"Mine, too, when it comes right down to it," she admitted, sitting next to him. "What happened to your resolve to have healthy meals?"

"Guilt," he said at once. "I had to break some news and this was meant to pave the way."

She immediately frowned. "What news?"

"Sam's gotta work tomorrow," Bobby announced sorrowfully.

"Ah, I see," she said. "And school hasn't started yet."

"Exactly." Sam hesitated. "I just spoke to Shanna, but Henry is watching her whole gang. I didn't want to add one more. She suggested you might have an idea."

"I'm sure she suggested I'd be happy to have him at my house, and normally I would, but I'm not going to be around tomorrow."

"That's okay, no problem," Sam said at once. "I'll figure something out. Worst case, he'll come to work with me."

Her expression turned thoughtful. "I do have an alternative. Can I make a quick call?"

"If you think it might lead to a solution, go right ahead," he said at once. "You know, though, this is not your problem to solve."

"I know, but this could work out." She held up a finger as her call connected, then stepped away so the conversation couldn't be overheard.

"Done," she said, smiling when she rejoined them.

"Please tell me you didn't change your plans on my account," Sam said.

"Not at all. I just checked to make sure it would be okay if Bobby came along."

"Where?" Bobby asked suspiciously.

"First you have to tell me if you're any good at keeping secrets," she said.

"I never told Kevin about the dumplings, just like I promised," he said solemnly.

"Excellent."

Sam regarded her curiously. "What on earth are you up to and why is it a secret?"

"Because I'm not sure how my family will react," she said, then shook her head. "No, actually I know exactly how they'll react and I'm not quite ready to take them on."

"This is getting more intriguing by the minute. Do I really want Bobby drawn into this scheme of yours?"

"I'm volunteering at a day-care place over on the highway," she said. "You have to admit taking Bobby along is an ideal solution." She turned to Bobby. "Today was my first day and we had lots and lots of fun. We did finger painting and played games outside. You'll be one of the older kids, so you even get to help with the little ones, like a big brother. There were snacks and a really good lunch. I think you'll like it. Do you want to come with me?"

Bobby looked skeptical, his worried gaze going from her to Sam and back again. "You'll be there the whole time? You promise?"

"Absolutely."

"I guess it would be more fun than going to the paper with Sam."

"It'll be tons more fun," Carrie agreed. She met Sam's gaze. "How does it sound to you?"

"If you're sure it's not a problem and Bobby's willing, it's okay with me. They don't mind that you're bringing him?"

"Not for the next couple of weeks. School will start then, so it won't be an issue any longer, right?"

"Right," Sam confirmed. "I'd be happy to pay their fee."

"Hey, they're getting me free. That's an extra pair of hands. The owner had already offered to let me bring Jackson, my nephew, on the days I have him. And, as I said, Bobby will be a big help with the littler kids."

Sam studied Bobby's face. "You're okay with this? Carrie will have my phone number, so you can call me anytime."

"It could be fun to be like a big brother," Bobby said. "Davey says it's really cool having Johnny around."

"Then I guess it's decided," Sam said, not even trying to hide his relief. "Thanks, Carrie. You're a lifesaver."

"Can I go climb on the jungle gym?" Bobby asked, his mood improved.

"Sure," Sam said, standing up to follow along behind, as did Carrie.

"So, tell me," he began. "Why wouldn't you want your family to know you're doing volunteer work at a day care?"

"Because the whole purpose of it is to get

enough experience to see if I really want to open my own," she said.

"Ah," Sam said. "And you don't think they'd approve?"

"Some will. Some won't. I'm not sure which side will be in the majority."

"And their approval is that important to you?"

"Sure. They're my family," she replied simply. "Life is a whole lot easier when they're on your side."

"I've heard enough about Mick to imagine he must be a force to be reckoned with," Sam conceded.

"*Stubborn* and *opinionated* are a couple of words that usually come to mind." She met his gaze. "Which reminds me, I was probably remiss in not swearing you to secrecy, too."

Sam laughed. "A little late now, don't you think? I think maybe I like having something to hold over your head."

"You'd blackmail me?"

"I'm beginning to think I'd be foolish not to," he said. "This incredible opportunity just fell into my lap."

She shook her head at his teasing. "Okay, what's it going to be? You already have my great-grandmother teaching you to cook, thanks to me, and now I'm providing day care for Bobby. That's a pretty good deal, if you ask me."

"It's an excellent deal, but I'm thinking there

could be one more thing," he said, not sure why he was heading in this direction despite all of his reservations about timing, and even about Carrie herself. He just knew he felt better when he was around her, happier and more in control of things. "Have dinner with me."

Her eyes widened with shock. "You're black-mailing me into going on a date with you?"

"I'm *asking* you to go on a date," he corrected. "Keeping your secret is just a tiny incentive for you to consider saying yes."

She laughed. "And if I say no?"

He shrugged. "I guess we'll see what sort of a risk taker you are."

Even as he uttered the taunt, Sam wasn't sure which answer he really wanted. He'd always been drawn to daring, adventurous women. Everything he knew about Carrie told him she fit that description. But was that the sort of woman he needed in his life now? He and Bobby needed stability more than just about anything. He had a feeling it would be impossible to find both in one woman.

Then, again, he was already discovering that Carrie was pretty remarkable.

✈ 10 ✈

Mick took his wife's offhand comment about Carrie needing someone in her life to heart. He'd been so focused on getting her grounded and working at something that would fulfill her, he'd forgotten about the importance of a strong relationship with someone suitable.

As he and Megan strolled home from the pub, he sensed Megan studying him with concern.

"What?" he asked, to get whatever was on her mind out in the open.

"You've been awfully quiet," she said. "That usually means you're up to something."

"I'm right here with you," he reminded her. "What could I possibly be up to?"

"I don't know and that worries me," she replied.

"Okay, the truth is that I've been thinking about what you said earlier," he admitted. "About Carrie needing someone in her life."

Alarm immediately filled her eyes. "I was not suggesting that you go out and find that someone, Mick O'Brien! Carrie can do that all on her own. She's a very resourceful young woman."

"Isn't she the one who found that Marc person, who overworked her and broke her heart? Are you suggesting her judgment's better than mine?"

She chuckled. "I'll give you that one. I certainly can't defend Marc Reynolds, but Carrie learned from the experience. She'll be more discerning next time."

"Meggie, I love you for having faith in our granddaughter, but I wasn't blind to the fact that she dated every man who crossed her path all through college."

"And had sense enough not to choose one who was wrong for her," Megan reminded him. "An old expression comes to mind, something about having to kiss a lot of frogs before finding a prince."

"I don't want our girl kissing any blasted frogs," Mick grumbled.

"Darling, it's a metaphor."

"Whatever. This will go better if I give things a little push. Now, who do we know who's available?"

As they approached the town green, he noticed that Megan was no longer listening to him. He followed the direction of her gaze and spotted Carrie with a young man and, apparently, a boy who'd climbed to the top of the jungle gym. She and the man were laughing and applauding the boy's achievement.

"Who's that?" Mick demanded, studying the scene intently and trying to assess any potential there. Was the man a married acquaintance or an available single dad?

"I'm not 100 percent sure," Megan equivocated.

Mick frowned at her. "Who do you *think* it is?" he asked with considerable patience. Sometimes it required ingenuity and a trained prosecutor's skills to get his wife to reveal anything she wanted to keep to herself. This appeared to be one of those times.

"I've heard that the young man Mack hired as a web designer at the paper just took custody of his nephew. I'm guessing that's him. Sam Winslow, I believe."

Relieved to know that the man was employed by a family member and likely both single and responsible enough to be given custody of a child, Mick eagerly turned to head in that direction. "Let's go over there and say hello," he suggested, only to have his wife take a firm grip on his arm.

"Not on your life. They're obviously enjoying themselves, and that's the goal you had in mind, right? Leave them alone. Let nature take its course."

"Sometimes nature takes too darn long," Mick said, but he did allow himself to be persuaded to take the long way around the green en route home in order to keep the peace with his wife.

Tomorrow, he vowed, he'd do a little investigating and determine if this young man was the right sort for his precious granddaughter. After all, not just anyone would do.

• • •

Carrie felt as if she'd been frozen in place for a solid ten minutes. First there'd been Sam's unexpected dare that she go on a real date with him. While she was still absorbing that and deciding how to answer, she saw her grandfather and fully expected him to charge right on over and start interrogating Sam about his intentions. Grandpa Mick was not known for his discretion, his subtlety or his timing.

The one man she'd risked bringing home from college had been reduced to stuttering once Mick got started. Despite an impeccable background, a path to a law partnership in his father's very respectable New York law firm, poor Nathan hadn't been able to withstand Mick's cross-examination. Carrie had concluded that didn't bode well for his career in a courtroom or for their relationship. Any man who couldn't hold his own with Grandpa Mick was doomed. Surprisingly, she wasn't quite ready to put Sam through that test.

"Carrie?"

Sam's questioning tone snapped her attention right back to him. "Sorry. I just saw my grandparents."

He grinned. "And what? It required all your concentration to will them not to come over here?"

She laughed. "You're amazingly perceptive.

See how well it worked? They've already moved on."

"Which raises the question of why you didn't want them to meet me," he said. "Or am I misinterpreting?"

"Oh, no, you got it exactly right. Well, not about them meeting *you*. The other way around." She sighed. "It's complicated. It's not that I don't want you to meet them *ever*, just not yet."

"Because?"

"Let's just say that once Grandpa Mick gets an idea in his head, he tends to run with it, and that includes running roughshod over anyone in his path. Neither of us needs that sort of pressure."

"So he's a meddler," Sam concluded.

"And a master manipulator," she confirmed. "Much to my dismay, I'm his current project. I don't think you need to get tangled up in whatever plans he decides to pursue for me."

Amusement danced in Sam's eyes, but he said very solemnly, "Okay, then. I'll watch my step if we happen to cross paths."

"Oh, you'll cross paths," she said with regret. "I predict he'll have figured out who you are within the hour if he doesn't know already, and you'll find him waiting on the doorstep at the paper first thing tomorrow morning."

Sam laughed. "Then it's a good thing I don't go in till ten. Mack can deal with him." He held her gaze. "Now, you and I have some business to conclude. Where do we stand on dinner?"

"The three of us, you, me and Bobby?" she hedged, trying a little manipulation of her own.

"Nope. A real date, the way it was meant to be, just two people getting to know each other. Friday night. I'll make arrangements for Bobby."

As tempted as she was, Carrie thought it was too soon for Sam to be abandoning Bobby to some anonymous sitter. It was the perfect excuse, so she seized on it. "Sam, you've seen the way Bobby keeps you in sight no matter what he's doing. Maybe after he's started school and really settled in here, he'll be ready for you to go out and leave him with a sitter. But now?" She shook her head. "I think it's a bad idea."

He nodded slowly. "So, just to be clear, you're saying no because of Bobby, not because you're not interested or because you've concluded I'm an irresponsible jerk?"

She drew in a deep breath and examined her motives, then nodded. "It's just about Bobby. And, again, I really am sorry about jumping to conclusions about you. You've given me reason to revise my first impression."

"Okay, then, if we're past that particular hurdle, how about this? On Friday night the three of us will go out for pizza and two weeks after that, when school's started and Bobby's ready to spend some time with a friend, you and I can go on a real date, just the two of us."

"You're only giving him two weeks to adjust?" she said, unable to keep a note of panic out of her voice. She realized that panic had nothing to do with Bobby and everything to do with her.

Sam apparently saw that, too. "Do *you* need longer to adjust to the idea of a date with me?" he taunted.

"Could be," she conceded honestly. "But I really am thinking about all the changes in Bobby's life. His adjustment may not happen on some precise timetable. Why don't we just agree to play it by ear?"

"Only if you agree that we'll see each other in the interim doing things Bobby can do, too."

Carrie found his determination flattering, but she wasn't quite ready to give in. In days gone by, playing hard to get would have been part of some strategy, but with Sam? It was panic, no question about it.

"I've already said I'd come to a T-ball game," she reminded him. "And we're all going to Gram's on Saturdays, too. I'll see you tomorrow when I bring Bobby home."

Sam frowned. "Speaking of that, I usually wind up at the office till at least nine or ten at night getting the latest edition up online. You'll have to bring him to the office."

"Where he'll be bored to tears, hungry and pestering you the whole time?" she objected. "That will be fun for both of you. No. I'll take him to the inn, see that he gets dinner and hang out till you get there. If he goes to sleep, Jess can keep me company."

"That's too much," Sam protested. "I don't expect you to make a career of babysitting him."

"But that's exactly the career I'm thinking of pursuing," she reminded him. "Consider this part of my professional training."

"Then you should get paid."

"Not a chance. This is just a friendly gesture. If I do open a day care and Bobby needs a place to come after school at some point, then we can talk about fees and such."

Sam didn't look all that happy about the arrangement. "Are you sure? I don't want to take advantage of you."

"You're not," she assured him. "I offered." For just an instant she had a flashback to all the times she'd said much the same thing to Marc, jumping in to take care of things that weren't her responsibility and doing it to please him. The difference now, she told herself, was that this pleased *her*. If it bailed Sam out of a jam, so much the better.

After studying her as if to assess her sincerity, Sam nodded. "Then I owe you a whole lot more than pizza."

"You can give me a lovely quote that I can use in my advertising when the time comes," she teased. "Or you can design my website and online advertising. If you're good enough that Mack trusts you with his precious paper, that'll be great for me. Now I'd better get moving. I have to be up at five."

Sam's gaze narrowed. "What time do you need Bobby to be ready?"

"Five-thirty," she said brightly. "Didn't I mention that? You'll be able to get a nice, early start on your day, too. In fact, you just might get to the paper in time to cross paths with Grandpa Mick, after all. Isn't that something fun to look forward to?"

He groaned. "And just when I was starting to have all these warm and fuzzy thoughts about you, I discover that you have a slightly twisted streak."

"That's only when it comes to the adults in my life. Bobby's perfectly safe."

Sam gave her a long look, his lips curving slightly. "Never doubted that for a minute."

After sending a still-sleepy Bobby off with Carrie just before dawn, Sam went down to the inn's kitchen to beg the biggest take-out cup of coffee to be had, then headed to the newspaper office.

The walk through the quiet streets of Chesapeake Shores with the sun just beginning to streak the sky in the east over the bay with brilliant splashes of pink and orange was surprisingly invigorating. Sam thought it might even be worth getting up at this hour more often, though he doubted he'd do it. He'd been a night person most of his life and it was probably a little late to adjust his body's clock now.

As early as it was, he found Mack at the office before him. Mack looked up from his computer screen with shock.

"I wasn't expecting you for a few hours."

"I was up. I had to get Bobby ready to spend the day with Carrie," he said, censoring himself quickly to keep from spilling the beans about the day-care volunteer work she was doing.

"Carrie got Bobby at the crack of dawn? That has to be a first. She's a night owl."

Sam shrugged. "They have plans."

Mack regarded him with suspicion. "Carrie and Bobby have plans?"

"What can I say? It worked out for me, so I didn't ask a lot of questions."

"They're not getting too attached, are they?" Mack asked.

Sam frowned. "No idea what you mean." He held up his coffee cup. "I need a lot more of this before I start delving into motivations. Why don't you fill me in on the log of stories for this week's edition? I have some ideas for a home page redesign I want to run by you, something that will make it even more user-friendly."

Mack looked as if he wanted to protest, but instead he let the subject drop. "Before I get into that, there is one thing I should probably ask you."

"As long as it doesn't involve deep thought, shoot."

"Susie's been wondering why you haven't called about looking at houses."

"Because I took your advice and decided to spend a lot of time with Bobby helping him to get acclimated. I know we need to get out of the inn and into our own place. I'll have more time to look once he's started school."

Mack nodded. "She was just worried maybe you'd decided to stay at the inn or maybe even use another Realtor."

"No other Realtor. I wouldn't do that to her," Sam assured him. "Tell her I'll be in touch as soon as school starts. I really am anxious to see what she's come up with."

"Will do," Mack said, looking satisfied. He handed over a printout. "These are the news stories for this week. You can see the lead right there on top. There are three features, too. A couple of important meetings are coming up in town after our print deadline, but I want you to get the coverage of those up online as soon as the stories are written. I'll do those myself."

"Photos?"

Mack turned the computer screen in his direction, made a few clicks on his keypad, and a dozen pictures came up. "I sorted through a lot more and narrowed it down to these. I'll use some in the print edition, but the joy of the online edition is that you can use all of them, especially the shots that showcase a lot of locals. They eat that up."

"Got it," Sam said. "Everyone ID'd okay? I may not recognize faces just yet."

"I think so, but anyone you're not certain about, ask."

"Okay, then. I'm on it."

He was about to take his coffee across the room to his own desk when the door opened and Mick O'Brien walked in. *So,* he thought, *Carrie had nailed it.* Sam had to turn away to hide a smile.

Mack made the introductions, then looked at Mick expectantly. "What brings you by at this hour? I hope you're here to take out a big full-page ad."

Mick laughed. "For what? Haven't you heard? I'm retired."

"That's not what I hear from the guys who work for your company," Mack responded.

"Has my nephew been grumbling again about being overworked?" Mick asked without rancor. "Matthew doesn't know how easy I've been on him, on all of them, now that I've mellowed out."

"So, if you're not here to advertise something, what does bring you by?" Mack asked.

"I was hoping to catch Sam if he has a couple of minutes," Mick said.

Clearly surprised, Mack looked from Mick to Sam, then chuckled. "Sure thing."

Sam headed for his desk, then gestured toward the chair beside it. "Have a seat. I don't have a lot of time. We're on deadline today."

"This won't take long," Mick said, sitting down and taking his time studying Sam. "You know my granddaughter Carrie?"

"I do," he said solemnly.

"Wonderful girl," Mick said.

"I don't know her well, but I'm sure she is."

"I saw the two of you together last night. The boy with you, that's your nephew?"

"Bobby, yes. I just gained full custody of him after his parents died."

Seemingly genuine dismay registered on Mick's face. "Terrible thing to lose both parents like that. He's lucky to have you."

"I guess we'll see about that," Sam said. "But I'm going to try my best."

"Can't ask more than that."

"Sir, if there's nothing else on your mind, I really do need to get to work. Bobby's with Carrie right now, and I need to get my job done, so I can take over again." So what if the time-line for that wasn't as tight as he was implying.

Mick nodded. "I understand all about work taking priority, but a piece of advice from a man who got his own priorities all out of whack. Family's what counts."

"I'll take that to heart," Sam promised.

Mick held his gaze for a long time, then gave a little nod that Sam couldn't interpret. He hadn't known Mick long enough to conclude if the interview had gone well or if he'd failed miserably. He supposed time would tell. Time would also tell if Mick O'Brien's approval was necessary if Sam was to have any hope of getting any closer to Carrie. Right now that might not matter, but he had a hunch things were heading in that direction a little faster than he'd originally anticipated.

At the day-care center Bobby had shadowed Carrie's every move until Lucy finally interceded and managed to get him to play a game with several other children. Alicia drew Carrie aside.

"That's the boy you were so concerned about last week?" she asked with a nod in Bobby's direction.

"Yes," Carrie confirmed.

"And now he's attached himself to you?"

"I'm the only person he knows here. Sam was in a bind today and Julie said I could bring Bobby with me when I'm here, at least until he starts school." She frowned at the look of concern on Alicia's face. "Is there something wrong?"

"You said he'd lost both parents. Obviously Sam is filling in for his dad these days, but what about you? Are you ready to take the place of his mom?"

"No, of course not. I'm a friend. Barely even that."

"Bobby doesn't seem to feel that way. He's looking for replacements, Carrie. Unless you're ready to step into that role, be careful how you handle things. We both know I'm not an expert, but I can see how attached he is already."

"He's a wonderful little boy," Carrie said. "I'm just trying to help out in a tough situation."

"Best intentions in the world," Alicia agreed. "But a six-year-old . . ." She hesitated. "Is that right? He's six?"

Carrie nodded.

"He's going to gravitate toward the first person who can fill that huge void that's been left in his life."

"I don't know how to handle this any other way," Carrie replied, frustrated. "He needs to know there are people who care about him."

"Then make sure there are lots of them," Alicia advised. "Not just you."

Carrie could see her point, which meant that the sooner there were more loving adults surrounding Bobby and her role in his life was minimized, the better. It also meant those plans she'd made the night before with Sam should probably be put on hold for now. Creating an ongoing threesome might suggest something completely unintended to a little boy looking desperately for a family.

She tried telling herself the disappointment that

washed over her was all about not spending more time around a bright, inquisitive little boy, but it was the image of his grown-up uncle that she couldn't seem to get out of her head.

Sam had left word with Jess that she could let Carrie into his suite when she arrived with Bobby. Not that Carrie couldn't have persuaded her aunt to let her in, but why should she be bothered with the hassle?

He'd hoped to be able to join them in time for dinner, given the early start he'd gotten in the morning, but one crisis after another with their internet server had made that impossible. At eight, he called Carrie's cell phone.

"I'm so sorry. I thought I'd be there by now to have dessert with you or at least to take over, but we seem to be in a holding pattern here."

"Not a problem," Carrie assured him. "Bobby's had dinner, taken his bath and is watching a video. What's his bedtime?"

"I aim for nine, but we sometimes get distracted," Sam said, thinking of how often that had actually happened. Nine had been a pretty unrealistic goal apparently.

She laughed. "I'll make sure we're not distracted. He should be in that routine by the time school starts, anyway."

"You're right," Sam said. "Tell him I'll try to be there in time to read him a story."

"He's already picked out tonight's book—or five based on the pile he showed me. I'll fill in, if need be, though I bet you do better voices than I can."

"He's not an especially tough critic," Sam said. "But I will try to make it. See you in an hour."

He actually came close to making it, too. It was 9:45 when he walked into the suite carrying a pizza and a bottle of wine. He regarded Carrie apologetically.

"He's already asleep?"

"Out like a light. He had a big day at the day-care center. He was yawning by the time I got off the phone with you and asleep two pages into his first story."

"I don't know how to thank you. This was way above and beyond."

"No thanks necessary. We had fun," she replied simply. "He really is a great kid."

"Well, I won't start depending on you to fill in," he promised.

"Sam, it's not a big deal. If I have Jackson, he can hang out with us. On the days I'm at the center, I already have Julie's permission to bring him along. He was great with the other kids today. Everybody loved him."

"Okay, then. When I'm in a bind, I'll check with you," Sam said. "Now, then, are you hungry? Can you stay for a while and share the pizza and wine?"

She hesitated for a surprisingly long time.

"Carrie? What's going on? It's pizza and wine, not a lifetime commitment."

"It's something someone at the center said today," she told him. "They thought Bobby might be getting too attached to me. We already know you're his lifeline. I can't be one, too. You and I . . . well, we hardly even know each other. Bobby's emotions are pretty precarious right now. We don't want him to get any ideas about how I'm going to fit into his new world."

Sam set down the pizza and wine and crossed the room. He rested his hands on her shoulders and looked into her troubled eyes. "The fact that you care so darned much is proof of how special you are. It's the reason I'd like to get to know you better."

"How am I supposed to trust that?" she asked. "You're in a difficult situation. I'm able and willing to help out. Don't you see how tangled up that could get? Add in the possibility that Bobby could get hurt and it's too big a risk."

Sam's heart sank. "So, you're not only saying no to pizza and wine tonight, but next week and beyond, is that right?"

She nodded. "I think that's for the best. I'll still come to his T-ball game on Saturday and I'll be at Gram's for our cooking lesson, but you should probably make sure he gets to know lots of other people right now, so he doesn't get overly attached to me or anyone else."

"You've really thought about this, haven't you?"

"Ever since it was brought to my attention that the situation might not be healthy."

"For Bobby?" he said, wondering yet again if his nephew was the only one she didn't want to risk getting hurt.

"Of course."

Sam didn't consider himself to be all that intuitive when it came to women, but this situation was plain as day even to him. "Somebody did a real number on you, didn't they?"

She immediately looked so flustered, Sam knew he'd gotten it exactly right. "What happened, Carrie?"

"It doesn't matter."

"I think it does. It's not that I don't believe you're concerned for Bobby. I know you are. But you've been taken advantage of by someone and this situation is bringing up bad memories."

"Maybe," she finally admitted. "In a way. But the situations are nothing alike, honestly. And believe me, you are nothing like Marc Reynolds."

Sam regarded her with shock. He didn't know a lot about fashion, but he knew that name. The man had a rich tabloid history with several of his top models. "He was your last relationship?"

She shrugged. "If you could call it that. Look,

it's messy and it's not one of my finer moments. Can we leave it at that?"

Discussing it obviously brought back painful memories. Sam quickly realized this might not be the time to probe for details. "Sure," he said. "I'm sorry, Carrie. I may not know what happened, but I'd be willing to lay odds you didn't deserve it."

She smiled at his vehemence. "Thanks for that. I'd better go."

"You're here now," he protested. "Bobby's asleep. I hate eating alone. Stick around for one glass of wine and keep me company. Can you do that?"

For a moment she looked torn, but then her gaze was drawn to the pizza box. "What kind?"

"Veggie," he said.

A smile broke across her face. "You win!" she said, throwing open the box and taking a slice, then curling into a corner of the sofa.

Sam grinned. "Make yourself at home, why don't you?"

"What can I say? I made Bobby eat a healthy dinner downstairs, but it was pretty darn boring. This, however, is the food of the gods. Pizza like this may or may not be truly Italian, but I'm giving them credit for making the food world a better place."

Sam laughed, sat beside her and poured the wine, then took his own slice. "Amen to that! Ask any unattached male over eighteen who lives on his own and it's probably pizza that keeps us alive."

Carrie held out her wineglass and tapped it to his. Sam met her gaze and held it. A wicked current of electricity sparked between them. No matter what she'd said earlier, no matter how wise her decision, this thing between them wasn't over. It was just temporarily on hold.

❧ 11 ❧

Carrie was shaken by how intense things had gotten with Sam the night before. That one long, sizzling look even after she'd declared what a bad idea it was for them to spend time together had told her that she was crazy if she thought a bunch of words and good intentions were going to keep them apart. She had to try, though. For Bobby's sake and, as Sam had guessed, her own. She'd made one truly terrible judgment about a man and it had torn her emotional life apart. She wasn't quite ready to trust herself again.

And it wasn't as if Sam hadn't given her cause for concern. Look how badly he'd bungled things with Bobby when they'd first met. Sure, there were extenuating circumstances and he seemed to have learned from those mistakes, but one of the things she wanted most desperately was a man who'd be a great dad.

Hers sure hadn't fit the bill. Wes Winters had been controlling and had demonstrated the morals of an alley cat when he'd gotten involved with one of her mom's coworkers. Since the divorce and their move to Chesapeake Shores, he'd been mostly an absentee father, rarely putting in an appearance even on big occasions such as Cait's wedding. He'd sent an extravagant gift and a lame excuse for his absence.

Her stepfather, though, was something else. Trace had been a loving, warm, thoughtful presence in her life and Cait's from the minute he'd started trying to win back her mom. He'd been tough, but fair, a lot like Grandpa Mick, but without the meddling gene.

On Wednesday morning with all those thoughts still tumbling around in her head, Carrie was at Sally's for coffee in time to catch up with Shanna, Bree and Heather. She'd arranged to do the day-care center again on Thursday, but had kept today and Friday open to babysit Jackson as usual. Even though the offer to bring him along had been made by Julie, Carrie thought the early hour would be too hard on the baby and on Noah, who had precious little time with his son as it was. Their early-morning ritual, even when it included gobs of smeared cereal, mattered.

"Where have you been the past couple of mornings?" Bree asked.

"I was busy," Carrie said evasively.

"Not just sleeping in after late nights with you-know-who?" Shanna taunted.

Bree's eyes lit up. "If that were the case, then this morning wouldn't have been an exception," she said, clearly delighted that Shanna had broken the ice and opened up this particular topic. "I have it on good authority, she was at the inn till all hours last night."

Carrie barely contained a groan. "Not that I'm surprised, since Aunt Jess has never been one to keep a tidbit of gossip to herself, but did she also happen to mention I was there babysitting Bobby while Sam was on deadline at the paper?"

"Till after midnight?" her aunt Bree retorted with undisguised skepticism. "Jake was picking up a pizza for a late snack after he finished a big landscaping job and he happened to run into Sam at the pizza place. So, I know Sam got back to the inn before ten. Your car was in the lot till much, much later." This final revelation was made with a certain degree of triumph in her voice.

Carrie sighed. "I really need to reevaluate whether I can stand to live in Chesapeake Shores."

Though the comment had come out impulsively, she couldn't have chosen her threat more carefully. All three women immediately looked alarmed.

"We'll cut it out—I promise," Shanna said at once.

"Absolutely," Bree chimed in. "I don't want my sister on my case for chasing off her daughter. Abby's upset enough that Caitlyn's still living in Baltimore, even though Noah and their baby are here."

"Then let that be a lesson to you," Carrie scolded, to take advantage of their momentary chagrin. "My roots here are not firmly planted in the ground quite yet."

"You bought a house," Heather said tentatively. "You want to stay. You know you do."

"A house doesn't make a life," Carrie reminded them. "All O'Briens eventually want to have a home here to come back to, even for short visits. It was a smart investment."

"And an indication of how you're leaning. All the other pieces will fall into place," Bree said with certainty. "I didn't know I wanted to stay when I first moved back from Chicago after that disastrous experience I had at the regional theater. But then I opened Flowers on Main, Jake and I got back together and I opened the theater. This is what my life was meant to be."

"It worked a lot like that for all of us. Living in Chesapeake Shores was the first step into our futures," Shanna said, then added with confidence, "That's what it is for you, too, Carrie."

"And now we're officially dropping the subject," Bree said.

The other two nodded, though Heather gave

Carrie a hopeful look. "Unless there's something you wanted to tell us about you and Sam."

"Incorrigible!" Carrie decreed, laughing. "All of you."

"Only because we love you and want you to be happy," Shanna insisted. "We're not just nosy, honestly."

"And now you sound like Grandpa Mick," Carrie said with an exaggerated shudder.

The three women exchanged looks, then shuddered themselves.

"That's it. Message received," Bree declared. "Let's move on to Susie. Have any of you seen her?"

"Not since the adoption fiasco," Heather said. "I know she's working again, but she's obviously avoiding us."

"I've called," Shanna said. "I even poked my head in the office on Monday, but she picked up the phone and waved me off."

"Not unusual," Bree said. "She's pretty focused when it comes to work."

"Ah, but that's the thing," Shanna said. "The phone hadn't rung."

"Oh, dear," Carrie said. "She's shutting every-one out. That can't be good."

"I have one thought," Shanna said. "We're due for a book-club meeting and it's her turn to host it. I can remind her of that and see how she feels about it. Maybe if I approach her and the conversation's not about her and how she's feeling, she'll relax and let us back in."

"It's worth a shot," Bree said. "Somebody needs to do something. Gram was beside herself when Susie and Mack skipped Sunday dinner again this week. I don't like seeing her upset."

"Me, either," Shanna said. "Though I've never known Nell to sit on the sidelines for long. She'll be on Susie's doorstep any day now, if she hasn't been already."

"No doubt about it," Carrie said. "I'll try to get Gram to hold off another week, if you'll see if you can get this book-club meeting organized."

"Done," the others agreed, practically in unison.

"Okay, then, if we're all in agreement, I'd better head to the flower shop," Bree said. "Jake's bringing my order in early." She grinned wickedly. "If I'm lucky, we can make out in the back room for a couple of minutes."

Heather laughed. "We may be the luckiest women in the world."

"How so?" Carrie asked, curious because it did seem to her that they were. She couldn't help wondering what their secret was.

"We're all married to men we still think are hot," Heather replied. "Better yet, they can't keep their hands off us, either."

Carrie slapped her hands over her ears. "Too much information!" she protested even though she was the one who'd asked for the insight.

"Not so," Bree said. "We're setting a good example for you. When you find the guy who makes you feel like that you'll know he's the right one."

An image of Sam and that sizzling moment they'd shared the night before immediately came to mind. She could say it was a bad idea from now till doomsday, but she was having more and more trouble believing it.

Mack stopped by the real estate management office to try to lure Susie to lunch and found her with Shanna.

"Come on, Susie. Tomorrow's book-club night and it's your turn. Please don't back out. We've been missing you like crazy at Sally's in the morning. We want to catch up."

Susie opened her mouth, about to decline again if Mack knew anything at all about his wife, but Shanna kept right on talking over her. "You won't have to do a thing," she promised. "We'll bring the food, the drinks, all of it. We'll even clean up."

"Sounds like a great deal," Mack said, watching his wife closely.

Susie barely spared him a glance before shaking her head. "I'm not ready for a girls' night. And I haven't even read the book."

Shanna grinned. "When has that ever mattered to anyone except me? Half the time I'm the only one who's read it. You know this is just an excuse for all the O'Brien women to get together."

Mack kept silent, praying that Susie would break down and say yes. She needed her friends, whether she wanted to admit it or not.

"Okay," she said at last. "But not one word about what happened to Mack and me, okay? I can't talk about not getting the baby."

"Promise," Shanna said. "I'd better get back to the store. I'm training a new salesclerk and she panics if we have more than one customer at a time. See you tomorrow at seven. Don't lift a finger. We'll do everything."

Susie nodded, though she still didn't look especially happy about agreeing to it.

When Shanna had gone, Mack took her place beside his wife's desk. "That should be fun. You need to spend some time with the girls."

She gave him a wry look. "So you're free to play hoops with the guys? Don't think I haven't noticed how closely you've been sticking to home."

"It's not as if spending time with my wife is a huge sacrifice," he responded. "In fact, I came by now to see if you have time for lunch."

"At Sally's?" she asked, a frown in place.

"Unless you'd prefer someplace else."

"Anyplace else," she said fervently.

"Panini Bistro, the pizza place, Brady's? Your choice."

"Home," she said at once. "I can make salads there."

"Are you sure you wouldn't rather go out?"

"Very sure."

"Because you don't want to run into anyone who might ask about the adoption?" he guessed.

She nodded. "I'd told everybody it was happening, Mack. I was so excited. Now I just don't know what to say. It hurts seeing the pity in their eyes."

He reached for her hand. "I'm so sorry, babe."

"It'll get better eventually," she said with more hope than confidence in her voice. "People will hear what happened, if they haven't already, and will avoid the topic."

"They will, you know. If they don't drop it, if they do ask, it's only because everyone in this town adores you."

"I suppose."

"Before I forget, Sam told me last night that he'll be in touch about looking at houses as soon as school starts and he has more time. He's been spending most of his spare time with Bobby."

Her expression brightened marginally. "They're doing okay?"

"It sounds like it. I know Carrie's been helping out," he said, then could have kicked himself when dismay once again washed over Susie's face. "Let's go have lunch. I think it's cool enough to sit on the porch."

She nodded, but it was clear some of the life had gone out of her again. When she stood up, Mack drew her into his arms and pressed a kiss to her forehead.

"I love you more than anything," he told her. "And I hate that you're hurting."

"I'm trying to get past what happened, Mack. I really am."

Mack believed her, but they both knew that pain that deep simply didn't vanish overnight.

With the morning off after working late the night before, Sam bought Bobby a fishing pole at Ethel's Emporium, then took him to the town pier to see what they could catch. Bobby eyed the worms with distaste.

"They're yucky!" he declared.

Sam laughed. "I'll grant you that, but the fish love them."

He glanced up with relief when he heard Henry, Davey and Johnny approaching. Shanna had called that morning and offered to send them along to help with a fishing lesson.

"Every boy in this town needs to learn to fish," she'd declared. "It's a rite of passage. I taught Henry myself. Of course, Kevin came along and improved on my lessons. He didn't think a woman, especially one who moved here from a big city, could possibly know anything about doing it right."

"How'd you feel about that?" Sam asked, curious.

"Oh, he was right, no question about it," Shanna admitted. "But the important thing was Henry gave it a try and came to love it."

Henry took over with the younger boys and Sam settled onto a bench to enjoy the morning. Not only did Henry know what he was doing, it seemed he had endless patience with the kids. Davey, of course, needed no coaching. He caught his first fish before the others even had the bait on their lines.

"Now we throw him back," Davey said.

"But why?" Bobby asked, clearly fascinated with the fish in Davey's hand.

"Because he's too little to eat," Davey told him solemnly. "He should have a chance to grow up."

While catch and release was obviously a lesson ingrained by Kevin, it didn't seem to resonate well with Bobby. Tears filled his eyes and he came running for Sam.

"What's wrong?" Sam asked, at a loss to understand the obviously heartfelt emotion.

"What if he can't find his mommy and daddy again?" he whispered to Sam.

"I'll bet they're close by waiting for him," Sam said.

"That's what moms and dads do," Davey said in his own attempt to be reassuring.

That only made Bobby cry harder. "Not mine," he said between sobs.

All Sam could do was hold him close while the tears flowed.

"I'm sorry," Davey said, looking shaken. "I forgot about his mom and dad."

"It's okay," Sam assured him. "Sometimes it just hits him. Maybe we should all go for some ice cream and forget about fishing this morning."

"Sounds good to me," Henry said at once, taking his cue from Sam. "These guys are always up for ice cream, right, Davey?"

"Right," Davey said at once.

"Bobby? Johnny? Does that sound okay to you?" Sam prodded.

Johnny kept his solemn gaze trained on Bobby, as if he understood that Bobby was the key to whether ice cream was an option.

"I guess," Bobby said with a loud sniff. "Can I have chocolate?"

"You can have any flavor you want," Sam said, relieved.

"Maybe Carrie could come?" Bobby suggested.

Sam thought of her declaration that they do nothing that would feed into Bobby's growing attachment to her. "I think she's out of town today, pal. Remember?"

Bobby looked puzzled, but then his expression brightened. "Oh, yeah, the day-care place."

Even as the innocent words left Bobby's mouth, Sam winced.

"Day-care place?" Henry echoed, looking confused. "What's that?"

Even Bobby realized his mistake. He stared sheepishly at Sam. "Uh-oh," he whispered. "Is she gonna be mad at me?"

"No way," Sam soothed, though he knew no such thing. For now, though, he had to do damage control. He offered a bright smile for Henry. "Just a project she's been working on. She doesn't want anyone to know about it yet."

Henry studied him with that solemn, knowing expression that suggested he was wise beyond his years. "Got it," he said readily. "No one will hear about it from me." He scowled fiercely at Davey. "Got that?"

"My lips are zipped," Davey confirmed.

Henry gave a nod of satisfaction. "We're good, then."

"Okay. Let's get that ice cream," Sam said eagerly.

As soon as the kids were settled on a bench facing the bay with their cones, he stepped aside, pulled out his cell and called Carrie. Since she was working, he'd anticipated voice mail, but she picked up at once.

"I hope I'm not disturbing you at work," he said.

"Actually I'm at home. I have Jackson today. I won't be going to the day care again until tomorrow. What's up?"

215

"Just something I thought you needed to know."

"Is it about Bobby? Is he okay?"

"He had a little meltdown earlier," he said, explaining what had happened. "He wanted me to call you. I reminded him you were working today—or at least I thought you were—and he kind of blurted out something about the day-care center."

"And Henry and Davey caught it?"

"Oh, yeah, though they have promised to keep what they heard to themselves. I just thought you should know that your secret's not so secret anymore."

She sighed heavily. "I should have known it wouldn't last. I guess I'll have to come clean about this sooner, rather than later. It's not as if I don't know already that this is something I want to pursue. I think I'm ready to do battle with anyone in the family who tells me I'm crazy or not thinking rationally or whatever."

"I can't say if this is the right career path for you or not, but I do know how great you are with kids," Sam said. "If this is something that you believe will fulfill you, then I say go for it."

"Could you put that in writing? Maybe if I have a few testimonials, my grandfather and my parents won't go berserk."

"Happy to do that," Sam said. "Want to have a strategy session later?"

"Sam," she protested.

"After Bobby's in bed," he persisted. "The suite's big. We didn't wake him up the other night. I'm very good at making pro-con lists."

She laughed. "You haven't met my twin. She is the grand master of the pro-con list."

"I'll bet I could give her a run for her money." He thought of how frequently Laurel had forced him to sit down and evaluate decisions rationally, when he'd wanted to jump into something impulsively. He'd hated her for it at the time, but the skill had stayed with him.

She hesitated for so long, he thought he'd lost, but eventually she said, "Okay. Honestly, I could use the help to weed out the emotional arguments from the sound, rational ones."

"Then I'll make sure Bobby's in bed by nine and asleep. I'll ask Jess to send up some brain food for snacks."

She laughed. "What on earth would that be?"

"You know . . . healthy stuff. Almonds. Carrot sticks. Whatever."

"Maybe I should bring the snacks," Carrie replied. "And the less Jess knows about this little get-together the better. The whole blasted family apparently knew about me being over there last night."

"You could swear her to secrecy," Sam suggested.

"It's divulging secrets to the wrong people that

got me into this," she retorted. "I'm not telling my aunt a thing."

He laughed. "I see your point."

"Sam, thanks."

"For what? Letting my nephew blab your secret?"

"For scrambling to make it right," she corrected. "And for offering to help me sort this out."

"Not a problem. See you tonight."

He hung up and glanced over at Bobby, who was now covered with chocolate ice cream and giggling happily again. He was starting to see that the difficult moments in parenting were somehow balanced out quite nicely with moments just like this. He hadn't felt this optimistic in weeks.

Even though a part of Carrie very much regretted being pushed to reveal her plans much sooner than she'd hoped to, she couldn't help feeling a faint sense of relief that soon everyone would know and she could start moving on with her life.

She arrived at Sam's with a grocery bag filled with her idea of appropriate snack food—chips, guacamole and a pint of Ben & Jerry's ice cream. The combination was pretty sickening when she really thought about it, but it's what had appealed to her when she shopped.

"Bobby asleep?" she asked, her voice low when Sam answered the door to his suite.

"In bed by eight-thirty and asleep a few sentences into his second book," Sam assured her, then peeked into the bag. One brow shot up when he got a good look at the contents. "Seriously? Spicy guacamole and Chunky Monkey?"

"It seemed like a good idea at the time," she told him blithely.

"Well, one thing's for sure, it ought to keep us wide-awake all night."

"Maybe we should divide it up," she suggested, rethinking the whole thing. "Dibs on the ice cream."

"The chips work for me," Sam said agreeably.

Carrie pulled her tablet out of her purse and curled into the same corner of the sofa where she'd sat on her previous visit. She'd have to compliment Jess on her furniture choices one of these days. This was much more comfortable than her sofa at home.

"Okay, Mr. Organization, where do we start?"

"Pros," he said at once. "Let's be positive."

"Okay, then," she said and typed that she loved spending time with kids at the top of the list. "And I'm good with them, too," she added.

"Put that down, too. What else?"

"I've been getting practical experience," she said. "Maybe it's only a few days so far, but it's been the best thing I've done in a long time. I'm truly happy at the end of the day. Julie already agrees I have a knack for working with kids, and she's been at it for years."

"How are you when things don't go so smoothly?"

"I don't get flustered or impatient, if that's what you're asking. I'm calm in a crisis."

"Another plus," he said.

"And I'm great with all ages. I love being with Jackson, but I think I'm pretty good with the older kids, too."

Sam nodded. "All valid reasons why this would be a good fit for you. Any business reasons it's a good choice?"

"That's easy. The town needs a good day care. There's some help available at one of the churches, but it's run by volunteers and they can't handle all the children who need a place to go. Jackson's there a couple of days a week, but that's all they could accommodate. That's one reason I've been pitching in. Noah's actually lucky they would take him at all. A lot of places don't take babies."

Sam was smiling. "You are so into this. How could your family doubt for a second that it's exactly right for you?"

"Experience?" she suggested with a shrug. "The whole fashion thing was something I was passionate about for about a minute. Before that I worked with a sports team, also for about a minute." She made a face. "And the big draw with both of those jobs? I was attracted to a man."

He laughed. "Well, that's obviously not the case with this. And it will be your business, not someone else's."

"They might have bought that a couple of weeks ago," she said.

"Why wouldn't they buy it now?"

"You," she said candidly. "You need help with Bobby and they know what a sucker I can be for a man who needs me."

Sudden understanding dawned on Sam's face. "That's why you were comparing our situation to your relationship with the fashion jerk, isn't it?"

"Afraid so."

"But didn't you tell me that Luke had proposed this idea to you even before me met?"

"About fifteen minutes before, to be exact. So you see why people might be skeptical. The timing is suspicious."

"Do *you* think this has anything to do with me?" he asked.

She hesitated, then shook her head. "Running into you that night might have stirred up all my maternal feelings, but the day care? After working with Julie this week, I know it's about doing something that will make me happy, something I'll be good at. The classes I started online are only reinforcing that. Best of all, it's something I can do right here in Chesapeake

Shores. I don't have to go chasing all over the world to find fulfillment."

"There you go," he said with satisfaction. "You can clearly defend yourself against any arguments they might try."

She ate the last bite of ice cream in the container, then put it aside. "We're close, but we're not there quite yet."

"No?"

"We need that con list. That's where things could get tricky. Let's start with the fact that two days of volunteer work don't exactly make me experienced. Add in that I've never run any kind of business before. There are rules and regulations to contend with, finding a location, advertising, hiring help." She covered her face. "I don't even *know* what I don't know."

"So, there's a learning curve," Sam said, dismissing her concern. "It won't take forever to get up to speed. And didn't you tell me that Julie had promised to be your mentor? You have a cousin who can help you find a location, an uncle who can help with legal work. Sounds to me as if you're covered."

He studied her intently, then added, "Unless you're looking for excuses not to take a chance and possibly fail."

Her chin shot up. "Failing's not an option."

And just like that, her confidence that she was making the right decision was restored. She moved quickly to give Sam a fierce hug. "Thank you!"

"I didn't do much."

"Yes, you did. You helped me sort through this until I could see it clearly. You made me believe I might not be making a mistake."

"So what if you are?" he asked. "Mistakes often provide the cornerstone for getting the next phase of your life exactly right."

"O'Briens aren't supposed to make a lot of mistakes," she told him.

He grinned. "Then you can be the first."

"Not a road I particularly want to go down, but thanks for making it sound less than awful."

"I have faith in you," he said simply.

Surprisingly, that was just the boost her confidence needed as she made plans to face her family and the likely ruckus that was going to ensue.

❧ 12 ❧

Thursday morning at the day-care center was an eye-opener. After all the positive notes she'd made the night before, Carrie found herself questioning whether she was truly cut out for this. Every child at the center seemed to be having a very bad day. Even the unflappable Julie and Lucy seemed to be at their wit's end. And even at their worst, the children who passed through Carrie's house on a regular basis had never been this out of control. Or maybe it was just that here, there were so many more of them, all needing attention and discipline at once.

As Lucy tried to calm two sobbing children and Alicia took charge of three more who'd been throwing food at each other just seconds before, Julie and Carrie took the instigators of the trouble to Julie's office for a supervised time-out.

"I am so disappointed in you," Julie said, looking into each little face as they sat across from her at her tiny desk with its overflowing piles of folders. Jaws wobbled and eyes filled with tears.

Carrie knew they deserved Julie's harsh words, but she felt so bad for the three of them. It was hard to believe that just minutes ago they'd been hurling fruit and taunts at children even younger than they were.

Though she knew she ought to let Julie handle it, she couldn't seem to stop herself from asking, "Reed, you started it. Can you tell us why?"

Big blue eyes met hers. "Bailey was being mean to Javier. He said bad things about his mom. Bailey said Javier's mom didn't even know who his dad is. And that they weren't real Americans."

Carrie heard Julie's sharp intake of breath and barely managed not to visibly react herself.

"Javier, is that true? Is that what Bailey said?" Julie asked gently.

Julie had filled Carrie in on the story. Javier's mother had come here legally from El Salvador years earlier with Javier's two older siblings to join his father. After Javier's father had brought them here and before Javier was even born, the man abandoned them. His mother worked two jobs to keep food on the table and a roof over their heads. She pitched in at the center whenever she had the time to help pay Javier's fees. And, though legally documented to remain, she was studying hard and working through the process to become a citizen.

With Julie holding his gaze, Javier finally nodded, his expression sad.

"It is not true, what he said. I know who my father is and I am American," he said with a touch of proud defiance.

Julie came around the desk and put a gentle hand on his shoulder. "I know, sweetie. I'll deal with this." She turned to Reed. "I appreciate your wanting to stand up for your friend, but next time, just tell me and let me handle it, okay? You saw how quickly things got out of control. Someone could have gotten hurt."

"I promise," Reed said solemnly.

"You've been coming here a long time," Julie continued. "I count on you to look out for the littler kids, but not like this."

"Okay," Reed said. "I just knew it was wrong and I didn't like it. Bailey shouldn't have said something like that."

"No, he shouldn't have," Julie agreed. "I'll deal with Bailey. Carrie, you want to take these troublemakers out onto the playground and shoot some baskets with them while I have a word with Bailey?"

"Absolutely," Carrie said.

"I can watch everybody," Reed protested.

"You probably can," Julie agreed. "But rules are rules. Nobody's on the playground without an adult present."

With the chaos now under control and its cause determined, Carrie felt better. Being outside in the fresh air and working off some of their aggression in a more positive way was just what they needed. She couldn't help wondering, though, if she'd have been as quick as Julie to recognize that. Or if she would have been so incensed by the racial profiling by a child too young to even know what that meant, she would have been on the phone telling off the parents.

"What if I'm no good at this, after all," she murmured to herself as she followed the three boys outside.

"Hey, Carrie, do you want to play, too?" Reed called out with a grin that reminded her of Davey.

She recognized a challenge when she heard one. "You're on," she said at once, then stole the basketball from his grasp and made a quick shot.

The three boys stared at her in amazement.

"Still want me to play?" she asked.

"You bet," Javier said, his tone heartfelt. "You can be on my team."

"How come?" Reed demanded. "I'm the one who asked her."

"Yes, but I'm the shortest," Javier replied reasonably. "I need the help."

Carrie laughed. "It's so nice to be wanted," she told them. "Javier, I'll play with you first, then we'll switch. How about that?"

"Works for me," Reed said.

Carrie looked into their happy, expectant faces and concluded maybe she wasn't quite as bad at handling controversy as she'd feared.

Sam discovered a whole new side to Bobby when he took him over to the school to get registered and take a look around. Since his dad had been pretty mellow and easygoing, the kid's stubborn streak had to have come from the Winslow genes, but he couldn't recall Laurel or him ever digging in their heels and throwing a royal tantrum.

"I'm not going," Bobby declared mutinously, arms crossed tightly, his jaw set. His eyes welled with tears.

"The school looks really nice," Sam said. "And did you see the playground? It has lots more equipment than the one on the town green."

"I don't care. I want to go to my old school."

Sam clung to his patience by a thread. He understood what was going on, but coping with it was something else entirely. He was way, way out of his depth. He was sure Carrie could have coaxed Bobby out of the car and into the school by now, but short of dragging him, he didn't have a plan for accomplishing that. Reason didn't appear to be working.

"You already know lots of kids here from playing T-ball," he reminded Bobby. "I'll bet some of them will be in your class."

"I like my old friends."

Sam seized on a bribe. "And maybe we can take a trip some weekend to see them, but you live here now and this is going to be your school."

"NO!"

The emphatic shout echoed in the car.

Sam took a deep breath and tried to imagine what it must be like for his nephew. He'd lost his mom and dad. He'd moved to a new town with an uncle he barely knew. It probably shouldn't have come as a surprise that sooner or later Bobby was going to dig in his heels. Sam tried another tact.

"It wasn't that long ago that I was new here, too," he reminded Bobby. "I didn't know anybody in town except my boss. Starting a new job is a lot like starting at a new school. It can be pretty scary."

"I'm not scared," Bobby declared, though he

couldn't quite bring himself to meet Sam's gaze.

"Of course not. You're the bravest kid I know," Sam agreed readily. "You've been handling stuff that would be hard for anybody. This is just one more thing you have to face, but I know you can do it, Bobby. And a couple of weeks from now, I'll probably have trouble getting you to come home, because you'll be having so much fun with all your new friends. It's just this first step that's hard."

"What if my teacher's mean?" he asked, his voice small and filled with the fear he'd been trying so valiantly to hide.

"I can't imagine any teacher in this town being mean," Sam said. "We haven't met one single mean person yet, have we?"

"I guess not," Bobby conceded grudgingly.

Inspiration struck. "I have an idea," Sam said. "Davey went to this school. I'll bet his mom knows all the teachers. Want to go by the book-store and Shanna can tell you all about her?"

Bobby nodded eagerly. Anything to delay the inevitable, apparently.

"Okay, we'll do that first."

"And then lunch at Sally's?" Bobby wheedled. "I'd probably feel better after a grilled cheese sandwich."

Sam nodded. "But after lunch we come straight back here and get you registered. Deal?"

Bobby clearly realized it was the best deal he

was likely to get. "I guess," he said eventually.

Sam started the car and drove into town. Five minutes later, he'd explained the situation to Shanna. "So, do you happen to know the first-grade teacher?"

Shanna's expression brightened. "You bet I do. Her name is Amy Pennington."

"Is she mean?" Bobby asked, trepidation in his voice.

"No way. She's very nice. She's been here for a very long time." She sat down on one of the low chairs in the children's section right next to Bobby, then leaned in to confide, "You know who she reminds me of?"

"Who?" Bobby asked.

"Mrs. Claus."

Bobby's eyes went wide. "Santa's wife?"

Shanna nodded, a smile tugging at her lips. "Don't ever tell her I said that, though. Here, I'll show you." She pulled a Christmas picture book from a nearby shelf and flipped through the pages, then pointed. "There you go. You wait till you meet Mrs. Pennington and then tell me if I'm right."

Bobby giggled, and Sam's heart filled with a mix of emotions he couldn't quite identify. Happiness at the sound, to be sure, and relief, but it was more than that. He felt a tiny bit like a dad who'd faced a monumental hurdle and somehow gotten over it just right.

"Thanks, Shanna," he said as Bobby scampered off to choose a new book for his collection.

"Not a problem. I'm so glad you thought to bring him here." She gave him a reassuring look. "You might want to remember that you won't always have all the answers when it comes to your kids, but knowing when to ask for help and where to go to get it is sometimes just as important."

"How about bribing him with the promise of lunch at Sally's? Is that as smart?"

She laughed. "Sometimes you have to wing it and do whatever it takes to get the job done. Just don't back down once you're back at the school. Remind him he made a deal with you and hold him to it."

Sam sighed. "Does it ever get any easier?"

"You've been at this for what, a month maybe? I've been at this parenting thing for a whole lot of years now. I'll let you know when I finally start to see easy." Her expression sobered. "Of course, it helps that I have Kevin right there to pick up the slack. You could always ask Carrie for backup."

"I'm already relying on her a lot, maybe even too much," he said. "I don't want to take advantage of her. I gather she's still recovering from the last jerk in her life who did just that."

Shanna looked surprised. "She told you about Marc?"

"Enough that I understand why she's gun-shy about getting involved with anyone else she perceives could be using her."

"Recognizing that just proves you're a thousand times more sensitive than he was. You have my stamp of approval, for whatever that's worth." She gave him a long look. "Just don't ever force me to admit that I was wrong about you. I hate being wrong."

He laughed. "Most people do. And I'll do my best not to hurt Carrie. That's a promise."

She nodded. "Good enough for me."

Sam looked around for Bobby and found him absorbed in a book he'd chosen. "Come on, kiddo. Let's pay for that and grab some lunch."

Bobby jumped up and headed for the register. Sam paid Shanna for the book. "I owe you a lot more than this for the advice."

"Nope. That was on the house." She grinned at Bobby. "Remember what I said about Mrs. Pennington. That's just between us."

Sam thought of Carrie's secret that Bobby had inadvertently blurted out all too recently. "You might not want to count on that," he warned Shanna.

She shrugged. "I'll recommend her to Bree for this year's Christmas production. Amy will be so flattered she'll thank me for making the comparison."

"Do you have a positive spin for everything?"

"I do these days," she replied cheerfully. "That's what a happy marriage will do for you. You might keep that in mind."

"So Mick's not the only meddler in the family," he said wryly.

"He's just the tip of the iceberg," she confirmed.

For some reason that didn't bother Sam half as much as it probably should.

"Dinner with Trace and me tonight!" Abby declared in a brief, but pointed voice mail.

Carrie listened to her mom's message and recognized a command when she heard it.

Sighing, she returned the call. "Are you cooking?" she asked when Abby picked up.

Her mom chuckled. "What do you think? I know my food's never going to lure you over here. Jess is sending over a roasted chicken, red bliss mashed potatoes, veggies and the inn's chocolate decadence cake."

"Wow! Is this a big occasion?"

"It is if one of my daughters is coming for dinner after a long absence," Abby said.

"I just saw you at the inn," Carrie protested.

"Two weeks ago. And you haven't seen Trace for even longer, to say nothing of your little brother. We miss you, sweetheart."

Since she knew she'd been deliberately avoiding them, Carrie could hardly deny that her absence had gone on too long. "What time?"

"Dinner will be at seven, but come whenever you're ready." There was a slight pause before her mother added, "Anyone you'd like to bring along?"

There it was, Carrie thought triumphantly. The ulterior motive. "So this isn't really about catching up with me. It's about Sam. You want to check him out."

"I thought it might be nice for his nephew to get to know Patrick," her mother contradicted.

"I'm sure it would be, but I am not bringing Sam within ten miles of anyone in this family just yet. O'Briens tend to get ideas and then try to ram them down the throats of innocent people."

"Have you ever known me to do such a thing?" Abby asked, an almost believable note of hurt in her voice.

"Only because I've never dated anyone seriously in Chesapeake Shores," Carrie replied. "And because you don't want me to accuse you of taking after your father."

Abby laughed then. "Well, that's true. Okay, come on your own. We'll try to make do with just your company."

"I'm so flattered. Love you, Mom."

"Back at you. See you tonight."

As soon as she'd disconnected the call, Carrie regretted not agreeing to bring Sam and Bobby along. At least they would have provided a very nice distraction from the night's likely remaining mission: getting a fix on her plans for the future. She couldn't help wondering how surprised they were going to be when she arrived with a written list of answers all prepared for them.

Carrie walked into the house that had been her home for most of her life just as her stepfather came down the stairs looking as if he'd just been for a swim fully clothed. She couldn't seem to stop the grin spreading across her face.

"Did Patrick win the bath war?" she teased.

"Of course he did," Trace said. "I'm not sure why your mother insists he take a bath when he's spent the entire day swimming. Nor do I understand why a kid who's a little fish from morning till night balks at getting into a bathtub."

Carrie kissed his cheek. "Just to give you a rough time."

"You and your sister were never this impossible," Trace said.

"Because we were your little angels," Carrie replied sweetly. "And we wanted you and Mom to get back together, so we were always on our very best behavior."

Her mother walked into the foyer just in time to overhear her. "I don't recall any of that," she said. "I recall bath times with protests at decibel levels that could have registered down the block. I recall two girls who ran away from home and scared the daylights out of me. I recall—"

Carrie laughed and cut her off. "Mom, you don't need to recount all of our bad behavior. Let Trace have his illusions."

Abby slipped an arm affectionately around Trace's waist, then jerked away. "You're soaking wet!"

"Thus the comparison of Patrick's bath-time behavior to Cait's and mine," Carrie said. She glanced at Trace, then shook her head at his besotted expression as he stared at his wife. It had always been that way. Unlike her memories of her dad and the nonstop arguments, her memories of her mom and Trace were all colored by the absolute conviction that they loved each other and her and Caitlyn like crazy.

"Maybe I should go upstairs and check on my little brother," she murmured and moved toward the stairs. "Is he supposed to be in bed or is he coming down here to have dinner with us?"

"He'll join us," Abby responded distractedly. "Trace, you need to get out of these wet clothes."

"Anything you say," he said, a wicked twinkle in his eyes as he reached for the buttons on his shirt.

"Not here," Abby protested, but she was laughing. "Impossible man!"

Carrie laughed and left them to their flirting. That, she thought as she climbed the stairs, was what she wanted, a marriage in which the romance stayed alive. It was exactly as Bree, Shanna and Heather had suggested earlier.

She found her little brother, still damp and wearing nothing more than his favorite Spider-Man underpants, sitting on the floor playing with his LEGOs. Her grandfather, who'd given Patrick the most expensive set he could find, claimed he was already seeing signs that Patrick would follow in his footsteps as an architect. Given the wobbling structure he was working on now, Carrie wasn't so sure.

"Hey, bro," she said, earning a glance and a grin.

"Did you bring me something?" he asked. Patrick was well aware that his big sisters were put on this earth to spoil him.

"Broccoli and spinach," she replied, keeping her expression serious.

"Yuck!"

"That is no way to show your appreciation for a gift," she admonished.

"Broccoli and spinach aren't presents," he replied reasonably.

"Oh, okay," she grumbled. She reached into her purse and tossed him the bag of penny candy she'd brought.

His eyes lit up and he tore into the bag.

"Hold it! After dinner," she said firmly. "Or Mom will kill us both."

He giggled. "She told Grandpa Mick never, ever to bring candy into this house again."

"Has he paid any attention to her?"

Patrick nodded. "He hides it outside, and then I go out and find it."

A typically sneaky Grandpa Mick maneuver, Carrie concluded. She reached for the bag. "Then maybe, if you already have candy hidden away, you shouldn't have this."

"Yes, I should," he said, tightening his grip. "It's my present. You can't take it back."

"What have you got for me, then?"

He scrambled up and hugged her. "Thank you."

She ruffled his strawberry blond hair, creating a halo of the curls he hated. "You're welcome, peanut. Now put on your pj's and come downstairs. We'll be eating dinner soon. I hear there's cake for dessert."

That earned a fist pump. He searched through a drawer, tossing things on the floor, till he found a pair of pajamas he liked, then pulled them on. The top was inside out, but Carrie refrained from pointing that out. Even as a toddler her little brother had had a well-developed independent streak. It was only strengthening as he prepared to go off to preschool this year.

As they reached the top of the stairs, he gave her an impish grin. "Wanna race?"

Before she could reply, he'd perched on the banister and was flying down the railing. Carrie watched, heart in her throat, till he reached the bottom. She recognized for the first time how much her mom must have aged watching her and Cait test their limits.

As she followed her little brother downstairs using the actual steps, she spotted her mother waiting at the bottom.

"You know," Abby said a little too casually, "if you're going to open a day care, you're going to have to keep a much closer eye on the kids."

Carrie regarded her with shock. "Who said . . . ? How did you . . . ?"

"Word travels," she said. "You should know that by now."

"But I haven't discussed this with anyone except Luke. He took a vow to keep it to himself."

"And I didn't hear about it from Luke."

"Who then?"

"Does it matter? Is it true? Are you considering opening a day care?"

Carrie ignored the question, still trying to figure out where the leak had been. Then it hit her. Davey, of course. Sam had told her himself that Bobby had let it slip around the boys. Henry would never reveal a word, but Davey was a loose cannon.

"Have you spent any time with Kevin lately?" she inquired innocently.

A faint blush tinted her mother's cheeks. "I've spoken to your uncle. Why?"

"Did he happen to pass along any tidbits of family gossip?"

Her mom frowned. "Okay, yes, but what I want to know is why my brother knew about this before I did?"

"He didn't hear it from me, if that makes you feel any better," Carrie said, and explained the likely scenario that led from Bobby to Davey to Kevin.

Abby laughed. "Oh, sweet heaven, if the next generation is starting this early spreading family gossip, we'll never be able to keep another secret."

She linked her arm through Carrie's and led the way into the kitchen. "You can fill us in over dinner."

Trace looked up. "Fill us in about what?"

"Carrie has decided what she wants to do with her life."

Her stepfather's gaze narrowed. "Does it involve going anywhere near that fashion designer?"

"Definitely not," Carrie assured him.

"Okay, then. Whatever it is, I'm all for it."

Carrie heard the unconditional support in his voice and felt her heart lift. She knew he meant every word. From the moment Trace had come into their lives, he'd been not only a devoted husband to her mom, but a steadying influence for her and Cait. He thought they were capable of anything. And, in part, because of that unwavering faith in them, they believed it, too.

❧ 13 ❧

"You have to understand that I'm just at the beginning stages of thinking this through," Carrie told her mom and Trace after a bored Patrick had gone back to his room after dinner. "I don't have all the details worked out. Or any of them, for that matter. I just have lists, a whole lot of very long lists."

"You've always been a natural with kids," Abby said, her expression thoughtful. "You know, there was a time when I thought you might want to go to medical school just like your sister and become a pediatrician."

"Not me," Carrie said at once. "The process takes way too long. You know how impatient I am. I couldn't wait to get on with my life, even though I obviously didn't know quite what I wanted that life to be. As for the whole medical thing, that's Caitlyn's passion."

"And you think opening a day-care center could be yours?" Trace asked, studying her closely. "You honestly think you'll be happy staying here and looking after kids? Kids, who aren't your own, that is. I think your mother and I figured you'd be settled down with a whole brood by now."

Carrie shrugged. "So did I, but it hasn't

happened. I'm trying to find an alternative that will be a good fit, something I can be as excited about as Cait is about medicine."

"It's a big decision," he reminded her, as if she weren't already very well aware of that.

Carrie knew he was making his point only to be sure she wasn't diving into something this demanding on a whim. Taking care of other people's children was a huge responsibility. She'd seen that firsthand since she'd been working with Julie. And once she'd committed to it, it wasn't something she could walk away from on yet another whim. People would be counting on her.

"I know it must seem as if this whole idea has come to me out of the blue and I can't deny that a few months ago, it had never once crossed my mind," she conceded.

"What happened?" Trace asked.

"You mean besides realizing that I was in a dead-end relationship and quitting my job with no prospects for another one?" she said dryly.

"Leaving Marc and that job were the smartest things you'd done in a while, if you ask me," Trace told her, not even trying to hide the disdain he'd managed to mask while the relationship had been new and, she'd claimed, everything she'd ever wanted. "You were too good for him and that job wore you out. It didn't make you happy."

"I loved my job," she protested. And at first Marc had been as attentive as she could possibly have wanted. It was only later that she'd realized that all that attention she'd basked in was nothing more than a jaded attempt to make sure she continued to do his bidding.

Trace regarded her skeptically. "Which part of the job made you want to jump out of bed in the morning? And before you answer, remember my history. I was dragged into banking by my father —a nice, stable career path I was supposedly destined to follow. It would have meant good money and stability for sure, but I hated every minute of it. It wasn't until I convinced Dad that my sister was more suited to that career and I was free to continue with my design business that I was truly happy." He gave her a long look. "So I know a little bit about how important it is to choose what you were truly meant to do and not let anyone or anything stand in your way."

Carrie heard what he was saying. "Okay, it wasn't the PR job I loved so much. It was Marc. You're right about that. I wanted to impress him." She shrugged. "And I happened to be good at public relations. There's a lot to be said just for being good at what you do. Especially in that world, praise is seductive. And I wanted to do something that would make the family take notice and be proud of me."

"Darling, we've always been proud of you," her mother said, looking shocked.

"Sure, in sort of a you're-our-daughter-and-we'll-love-you-no-matter-what way. Mom, you and everyone else in our family set the bar pretty darn high."

Abby sighed. "I suppose we did, and your grandfather's certainly not above reminding everyone about his lofty standards. Still, we all know how that job worked out. It's over and done with now," her mother said briskly. "Tell us why you think opening a day care is what you were meant to do? How did you reach that conclusion?"

"I was talking to Luke about my options. We just started batting around ideas and he pointed out that half the kids in our family are in and out of my house on a regular basis. I'm good with them. I love being with them."

"But that's all pretty casual," her mom said worriedly. "This will be a full-time commitment, Carrie. It's not something to take lightly."

"I know that," she said impatiently. She reached in her pocket and pulled out the pro-con list she'd printed. She handed it over to her mom. "And that's why I'm taking it very seriously. Look those over and you'll see just how carefully I've been analyzing this."

"Pros and cons?" Abby said with a smile. "This is something your sister would do."

"Since I've been watching her analyze things to death practically since birth, I decided to give it a try," Carrie said wryly. "And I've been volunteering, just for a few days so far, at a day care outside of town. The owner's been in the business for years. She's promised to be my mentor and guide me through everything I need to do, but only if I prove to her that I can handle the job. There's no telling how long I'll have to pay my dues before she's convinced, so I definitely won't be taking the next step impulsively. I'm even taking a couple of classes she recommended online."

"Ah, so the day care's where you've been going at the crack of dawn," her mom concluded. "Now it makes sense. I couldn't believe it when someone said my little night owl was up and out before daybreak."

Carrie didn't even bother asking who'd filed that report. It hardly mattered. She looked expectantly from Trace to her mom, trying to gauge their reactions.

"So, what do you think?" she prodded when she couldn't stand the silence another minute.

"Now that we've talked, I can see how it would be exactly right for you," her mother said. "I'm a little surprised no one suggested it sooner."

Carrie rolled her eyes. "Who? Grandpa Mick? You know he's going to have plenty to say about me wasting my potential by babysitting."

"And I think you're selling him short," Abby contradicted. "He wants you close by. This will keep you here. He wants to see you happy. If this achieves that, he'll have no complaints."

"And it shouldn't matter what Mick or anyone else thinks," Trace emphasized. "If this is what you want, that's all that counts. Have you spoken to my dad or Laila at the bank about getting a small-business loan for your start-up?"

Carrie held up her hands. "Slow down. I'm not that far along yet. And I still have trust-fund money to underwrite the first-year costs when I am ready."

Trace shook his head. "Speak to Dad or my sister. Don't put your trust fund at risk. Part of opening any business is establishing good credit. Let them help with that. It will make Dad's day. You know he's always had a soft spot for you and your sister. And anytime an O'Brien succeeds, it's good for the bank and good for the town. He's well aware of that."

"I suppose it wouldn't hurt to talk to him when the time is right," Carrie agreed, though she wasn't enthusiastic about laying out her plans for a man as hardheaded about business as Trace's dad. He'd spot every single flaw and make no concessions because she was family.

"Seems to me that the end of summer and the start of the school year would be a good time to get things rolling," Abby suggested casually.

"No way," Carrie said, horrified. "School starts in a couple of weeks. This isn't something I can rush into. Even if I wanted to open quickly and on a very small scale, there are too many regulations and licenses to deal with. Plus I have to find a location, do renovations. There are a million things that need to be done before I could even consider opening."

"Stop by and see Susie about suitable property," Abby suggested. "She knows every house or retail space around here that's zoned for something like this."

Carrie studied her mom. Something was going on here. "Why are you suddenly in such a rush for me to make this happen? It's not just so I'll stay close by, is it? I've already told you I intend to stay in Chesapeake Shores. That decision definitely isn't a whim. I want this town to continue to be home."

Abby glanced across the table at Trace, who nodded. "The thing is," she began, color blooming in her cheeks, "we're expecting another baby."

Carrie stared at her in shock. "A baby? But, Mom, you can't be. You're . . ."

"Old. Go ahead and say it," Abby said, her expression wry. "Believe me, no one is more shocked than the two of us. I thought I was a lot closer to menopause than I was to becoming a mother again."

"Who knows? Have you told anyone else?" Carrie asked.

"No. So far, it's just us," Trace said, then

cautioned, "And we want it to stay that way for another couple of months. But you can see why the idea of a day care right here in town and run by someone we trust could be a lifesaver for us. Trying to keep an eye on Patrick while working at home almost drove me over the brink. With this baby, I want him or her out of the house and in the hands of a professional. Your mom and I are agreed on that. I'm not expecting her to put her career on the back burner, either, so reliable day care is a must."

Carrie bounced out of her chair and hugged her mom, then Trace. "I am so, so happy for you. Does Caitlyn know?"

"Not yet," Abby replied. "We wanted to wait a little longer. We'll fill her in next time she comes home for a weekend."

"Then I don't suppose Patrick knows he's going to be a big brother," Carrie said.

"Absolutely not," Trace said. "The pint-size O'Briens are not even remotely trustworthy with secrets of any kind. The leaking of your news is proof enough of that."

"Point taken," Carrie agreed. "Remind me to beat the tar out of Davey next time I play a video game with him just to get even."

"Hey, it's not all bad, having us in on your plans, is it?" her mom asked.

"Actually, no. Your enthusiasm has been reassuring, even if I have discovered it's due to an ulterior motive." She studied her mother worriedly. "Are you feeling okay? Is the pregnancy going okay so far?"

"I'm a little tired, but the doctor says everything's right on track. We'll do an amniocentesis down the road just like we did when Patrick was on the way."

"We're not going to take any chances with your mother's health or the baby's," Trace assured her.

"Well, if you need anything, anything at all, I'm just a phone call away," Carrie told both of them. "I am so happy for you. And Gram's going to be over the moon."

Abby smiled. "She will be, won't she? There's nothing Nell loves more than a new O'Brien to fuss over."

Thinking of all the babies in the family, Carrie figured her great-grandmother would be in seventh heaven for a long time to come.

For a full week after dinner with her mom and Trace, Carrie tried to absorb their big news, while continuing to babysit Jackson and volunteer at the day-care center. She didn't hear much from Sam beyond a quick call to let her know that he'd successfully enrolled Bobby in school.

"Now I just have to get him in the door on the first day," he'd said, sounding unconvinced that he could do it.

"He's going to be fine," Carrie had assured him.

"It would help if you'd tell me that in person," he suggested slyly.

She'd laughed. "Remind me next time we're at Gram's."

"No sooner than that?"

"Sorry. I'm swamped."

And it was true. As her confidence in her plan had started to grow, impatience had set in. She downloaded forms and studied the requirements for licensing. Then, when she'd been at the center for three weeks, she sat down with Julie.

"How am I doing?" she asked directly.

Julie smiled. "I wondered how long it was going to take before you started getting antsy to get started."

"To be honest I've been hoping for some sign from you that you feel I'm qualified."

"Qualified? In less than a month?"

"Okay, maybe not qualified, but capable of getting there."

"Truthfully, I've been impressed," Julie admitted. "So much so, in fact, that I wish I could talk you into staying right here and continuing to work with me." She studied Carrie, then shook her head. "But you want to open your own place, don't you?"

Carrie nodded. "I really do. Working with you has just solidified my resolve. This may have started on a whim, but I'm committed to it now, but only if you believe I'm going to be able to do this the way it should be done. And I'm not going to bail on the training I've been getting here or on my classes. I will keep coming here at least a couple of days a week until all the pieces of my plan come together. I owe you that and I can use every second of practical experience I can get."

Julie nodded. "Okay, then, you have my blessing to get started with your own plans." She gestured toward the tablet Carrie had brought to the meeting. "Get ready to take some notes. We'll start your crash course right now."

For the next two hours, she filled Carrie in on everything from the costs of doing business, the licensing process, liability insurance, what to charge and the best quality toys and supplies available and where to get them.

"And that's just the tip of the iceberg," Julie concluded. "But it's enough for today. You get started on all of that and when you're here next time, we'll go over some more."

She smiled at Carrie's apparently glazed expression. "Don't worry. It will all fall into place and start to make sense once you start chipping away at that list. And when you find a place you like, invite me down and I'll walk through it with you and help you figure out what changes will be required to meet code. It's been years since I've been to Chesapeake Shores despite how close by it is. I've heard wonderful things about the Inn at Eagle Point. Maybe Lucy and I will spend a mother-daughter weekend there."

"You're a godsend," Carrie said fervently. "And my aunt Jess owns the inn. I'll talk her into comping your room."

Julie smiled. "Well, how about that? I won't say no. As for whatever I've done to help you, it's in my own interests as much as yours. I can't very well let someone I've trained go off and make a mess of things, can I?"

"I'll get started on all this tonight," Carrie said. "By the time I see you day after tomorrow, I'll have a full report on what I've accomplished."

Julie gave a little nod of satisfaction. "Of course you will."

As Carrie was leaving her office, Julie called her back. "I'm proud of you. You've caught on quickly. You've never once blinked no matter what I've asked of you. And you're great with the kids."

Touched by the praise from a woman she'd come to respect, Carrie blinked back tears. "Thank you."

"Don't thank me yet. There are going to be days in the months and years to come when you'll probably hate me for encouraging you to take this on."

Carrie couldn't imagine such a day, but she nodded. Julie hadn't been wrong about anything else. She was probably right about this, too. But it didn't really matter. She'd never been more excited about anything she'd ever tackled before. And O'Briens were made of tough stuff. Difficulties didn't deter them one little bit.

Sam was on his way to the pizza shop with Bobby for a celebration of the first day of school when he spotted Carrie heading toward O'Brien's. He changed direction and intercepted her. A smile spread across her face when she saw them.

"A first day of school celebration?" she guessed right away.

Bobby nodded enthusiastically. "We're having pizza!"

"Not exactly a rare treat," she commented, her gaze on Sam.

He caught the glimmer of amusement in her eyes. "I'm reformed, but not obsessed about it," he told her. "Besides, this is Bobby's celebration, so it's his choice. Want to join us?"

"Yes!" Bobby said eagerly. "Please, Carrie."

"Well, I can hardly turn down the chance to have dinner with two handsome guys. It will have to be a quick one, though. I have a ton of work to do tonight."

Sam cast a cautious glance toward Bobby, who was already running ahead to the pizza shop. "Day-care plans?"

She nodded, a brilliant smile lighting up her

face. "I'm moving forward with Julie's stamp of approval," she confirmed. "Only my mom and stepfather know, though, so please keep it to yourself a little longer. I'm going to see Susie tomorrow about locating a property, so I suspect everyone in the family will know after that."

Sam winced at the mention of Susie.

"What?" Carrie asked, obviously catching his guilty expression.

"I've been meaning to call her ever since I got to town about looking at houses. Time keeps getting away from me. Mack's even mentioned to me twice now that Susie's wondering if I'm just going to go on living at the inn."

"It is a pretty comfortable place," Carrie said.

"But it's not a home. And it's above my budget long-term, even with the deep discount Jess has been giving me." He waved off the topic. "I'll get to Susie sometime this week. Right now I want to hear all about your plans."

"Hurry up!" Bobby's urgent command interrupted them.

Sam sighed. "But I suppose now's not the time."

"Probably not."

"I don't suppose you've changed your mind about dating?" he asked hopefully. "We could have a quiet, adults-only dinner this weekend."

"Didn't you tell me that Bobby's still uneasy about being at a new school?"

"Yes, but today seemed to go okay."

"That's one day, Sam. Give it a week and then we'll talk about it. I need some space to pull all this paperwork together, anyway. And you need to spend your spare time house-hunting."

Sam conceded defeat reluctantly. "I'm calling you first thing on Monday and asking you out," he informed her. "And make no mistake, I'm not taking no for an answer."

"Then I'll practice saying yes," she told him with a grin. "Who knows? I might be very good at it."

The next morning, determined to turn her dream into reality, she was in the real estate office five minutes after it opened, sitting across from Susie.

"I need a house," she told her second cousin.

Susie regarded her blankly. "You have a house."

"But it's not zoned for what I have in mind."

"And that would be?"

"I'm planning to get licensed and open a small day-care center."

Rather than applauding her decision, as Carrie had expected, Susie frowned.

"I know you love having the kids over for visits every day, but an actual day care, Carrie? Have you really thought this through?"

Carrie discovered that having each new person she told question her decision was annoying. "Of course I have," she said impatiently. "Since everybody in the family has been regarding me like a slacker for months now, I thought this would come as good news. Carrie's finally figured out what to do with her life. Yippee!"

Susie's smile was only halfhearted. "Nobody thinks you're a slacker."

"Seriously? I get a lecture from Grandpa Mick on an almost-daily basis. I could see the worry every time Mom looked at me, at least until I filled her in about this. I'm pretty sure Gram has been lighting extra candles at church."

Susie finally chuckled. "Being an O'Brien does come with a fair share of pressure," she conceded. "But day care? I thought you were destined to return to Paris or Milan. Why settle for Chesapeake Shores, when you've led such a glamorous life? We all envied you getting to work in such amazing locations."

Carrie shrugged. "I'm hardly settling. The reality is, I'm an O'Brien and this is home. Despite all the worried looks I've endured since coming back, I know this is where I belong. Opening a day care just seems like a natural. I've done my homework on the number of children with working parents and the options available. The only facility open right now is at the church and it's filled to capacity. The town needs a day-care center."

"So it's not enough for you that most of the kids in our family are already in and out of your house on a daily basis?"

Carrie thought she heard a surprisingly bitter note in Susie's voice. She also thought she understood it. Thanks to that adoption falling through at the last minute, Susie was bound to be touchy about anything having to do with kids these days.

Regarding her cousin with sympathy, she said, "I'm sorry the adoption didn't work out this time, Susie, but there will be other chances. You and Mack will have children."

"I'm done," Susie said flatly. "And I don't want to talk about it."

"Is Mack ready to give up?"

Susie just stared at her, her expression completely shut down. Carrie got the message and dropped the subject.

"I'm sorry if I upset you," Carrie apologized.

Susie sighed. "And I'm sorry for taking my lousy mood out on you."

"Please. I'm family, and I know how badly you want children. I do, too, but I know it's not the same."

"Right. You could get pregnant anytime. I can't." Susie winced at her tone. "Sorry. *Again.* It's ironic how all of the O'Briens seem to procreate at the drop of the hat, and then there's me. Look at your sister. Caitlyn didn't want to get married or have a baby, but here she is with a great husband and a darling little boy, and I'm not sure she appreciates either one."

"Of course she does," Carrie said, immediately jumping to the defense of her twin. "It was just a big adjustment. She had her whole life mapped out."

"I guess what they say about best-laid plans is true," Susie said. "They do tend to go awry. I thought if I could eventually convince Mack to look at me twice, we'd live happily ever after."

"You and Mack are solid," Carrie reminded her.

Susie's eyes turned misty. "I know, and I thank God for that every single day. Mack stood by me—he even married me not knowing how long I might live. Most men would have bailed."

"And you'll get that baby, just maybe not on the timetable you'd hoped for," Carrie said confidently.

Susie managed a faint smile. "From your lips to God's ear," she whispered.

Carrie squeezed her hand. "It'll happen. O'Briens always make things happen."

Susie drew in a deep breath, then squared her shoulders and faced the computer. "Let's see about finding a spot for that day care. Who knows? Maybe I'll come and work for you and get my fix of babies that way."

"Suze," Carrie said quietly, then waited for her cousin to face her. "There will always be a spot for you, even if you just want to spend your lunch hour hanging out, okay?"

"Thanks."

But they both knew that caring for other people's children, no matter how rewarding, would never quite fill the empty place in either of their hearts.

A few days later Carrie had just pulled a hot cookie sheet from the oven when her grandfather barged into her kitchen without bothering to knock.

"What's this I hear about you opening a day-care center?" Mick asked, his voice booming through the small space.

"You've been talking to Susie," she concluded.

"Actually I was talking to my brother. Jeff told me Susie has been showing you properties and that you've already applied for a license. What sort of nonsense is going on in that head of yours? Why didn't you discuss this cockamamy plan with me before you dived in?"

Carrie dropped the cookie sheet onto the table with a clatter she hoped would be a hint of just how annoyed she was. Naturally her grandfather was oblivious. She'd expected this reaction from him, but that didn't keep it from hurting.

"You're an O'Brien," he declared. "You're meant to be doing great things, not babysitting other people's children."

"Even if some of those children are O'Briens?"

He scowled at her. "There are plenty of people in this family to look out for our own. Not a one of them needs to be in some impersonal day care."

"So now I'm providing impersonal care?" she challenged.

"You know what I mean," he said.

"Actually I do. You mean that I'm letting you down yet again. You didn't approve of it when I was in Europe working in fashion. Then you were disappointed in me for quitting that job and coming back here. You were thoroughly frustrated when I didn't jump on the bandwagon and take up Caitlyn's favorite cause in Africa. Sorry, Grandpa Mick, I guess I'm just destined to be a huge failure in your eyes."

As her heated words and the tears stinging her eyes registered with him, he looked stunned. "I never said any such thing."

"Didn't you? Worse, you just referred to something I'm truly excited about as a cockamamy idea."

"Carrie, sweetheart, all I want is for you to be happy."

"And I think this will make me happy," she told him, swiping angrily at her tears. "I really do. I love kids. Right now I don't see any children of my own in my immediate future, so this works for me. I'm good with kids. Ask anyone."

"Well, of course you are. I've seen you at the house reading stories and playing games with all your little cousins. You've a gift, no question about it," he said, clearly backpedaling as fast as he could.

His expression turned thoughtful. "Seems to me, though, what you really need is a man and a houseful of kids of your own."

Carrie gave him a horrified look. "Do not get any ideas about matchmaking, Grandpa Mick. I mean it. Right now I need to focus on this new business. I want to do it right. When it's up and running and such a huge success that even you will be impressed, then I'll think about my social life. And when that day comes, I want you to remember that I'm perfectly capable of finding the right man without any help from you."

Her grandfather didn't appear impressed by her declaration. "Are you, now? Is there one lurking about I've not seen? That Sam Winslow fellow, perhaps?"

"Leave Sam out of this. There are lots of men lurking about, as you put it," she said, silently begging forgiveness for the blatant lie. "Everywhere I turn, in fact."

"Then you'll be bringing one to Sunday dinner, I imagine," he said.

Check and checkmate, she thought with a resigned sigh. "Sure," she said, wondering who she might draft for the assignment. It needed to be somebody tough enough to withstand Mick's scrutiny and willing to play the game for a few hours on a Sunday afternoon.

Because his name had just come up and because an image of Sam popped into her head all too regularly, she considered him as a possibility. *Bad idea,* she told herself. Then again, at least he would come away with a decent meal and some new friends for his little boy.

She wouldn't go looking for him, but if they crossed paths between now and Sunday, what was the harm in asking?

She glanced up to find her grandfather munching on a warm chocolate-chip cookie and regarding her suspiciously.

"You aren't thinking of trying to put one over on me, are you?" he asked.

She mustered her most innocent expression. Given the number of times she'd been called upon to use it with this very man, she had it down pat. "Absolutely not," she told him.

He gave a little nod of satisfaction. "Then I'll see you on Sunday."

He picked up another couple of cookies and left through the kitchen door. Carrie sighed heavily. That gave her exactly three days to find the man of her dreams . . . or at least someone willing to play the role.

❧ 14 ❧

On Saturday Sam stood just inside the front door of the little house on Willow Brook Road as Bobby raced through the rooms, the sound of his footsteps on the shiny hardwood floors echoing in the empty space.

He'd just bought himself a house, he thought, amazement and panic washing over him. Here he was, a man who'd never planned to put down roots, and he was suddenly the owner of a house with a mortgage and the parent of a grief-stricken little boy. Somewhere God must be having a really good laugh at his expense, because the carefree life he'd envisioned for himself had definitely gone up in smoke.

He was a little astonished at how quickly and smoothly the purchase had happened. When he'd finally called after his dinner with Carrie, Susie had leaped into action. She'd clearly been highly motivated and apparently in Chesapeake Shores when O'Briens were in your corner, credit reports and paperwork could be handled with lightning speed.

Susie hadn't wasted time dragging him all over town. She'd brought him straight to this house and let the cozy little cottage speak for itself. Sam might have hesitated for days, weighed the merits of buying a house at all, rather than renting, but Bobby's initial enthusiasm had been contagious. Listening to his exuberant shouts echo through the empty rooms and watching his eyes widen with delight when he spotted both a swing and a tree house in the backyard had clinched the deal for Sam. Everything after that had been all about the paperwork.

"Not to worry," Susie had assured him. "I've already spoken to the seller and you can move in as soon as you want to. Mack spoke to the bank and reassured them your job is solid. All you need to do is sign an endless number of papers, pack up, get some furniture in here and you're all set. My cousin Connor will handle all the legalities."

Sam had been astonished. "Just like that? Do things always go this smoothly? I've heard horror stories about buying a house."

She'd simply shrugged. "In this town, connections help."

They certainly did, Sam concluded. He'd even been able to arrange for the beds he'd bought just yesterday—a king for him, the bunk beds Bobby had insisted on—to be delivered first thing this morning. Susie or someone she'd designated had made a call and the store had been more than happy to cooperate. He'd had to call Carrie and Nell to cancel this week's cooking lesson, but this delivery had taken precedence. The truck had been waiting in the driveway by eight o'clock and the hastily purchased furniture was already in place.

Susie had made a few more calls and O'Briens had offered additional furniture from attics and extra sets of dishes they swore weren't being used, but that would happen during this next week. In the meantime, he and Bobby could put their clothes in the freshly painted closets and sleep in their own beds. Bobby was elated by the new Spider-Man sheets on his lower bunk and the matching night-light that had already been plugged in.

The only thing missing, Sam concluded with a sigh, was a refrigerator stocked with cold beer. He could really use one about now as he faced his new reality.

"Knock, knock."

The hesitant, musical voice cut into his thoughts. Or maybe it was the aroma of freshly baked cookies that caught his attention first. He turned, and there was Carrie, her cheeks naturally rosy from baking, her auburn hair curling about her face. She was wearing shorts and a Chesapeake Shores T-shirt and looked a little too approachable. He could suddenly envision coming home to her every night and finding her in his kitchen looking just like this, the aroma of one of Nell's specialties they were mastering wafting from the kitchen.

"Hi," he said, then gestured around the empty

space. "I'd invite you in, but, as you can see, chairs are in short supply."

"That's okay. I'm just dropping off cookies to welcome you to the neighborhood. I'm a little stunned by how quickly you pulled this off."

"Me, too," he admitted. "I hadn't even thought about this move making us neighbors. You okay with that?"

Carrie frowned. "Why wouldn't I be?"

"We sort of agreed to keep our distance, right? For Bobby's sake?"

"We'll just have to work a little harder to make sure he doesn't get the wrong idea," she said.

Sam wondered what she'd think of the ideas *he* was getting right now. Was it possible that chocolate-chip cookies were an aphrodisiac? She looked far more tempting than that plate of cookies.

He suddenly realized she was studying him with a puzzled look.

"If you're really worried, you should know that I don't intend to make a habit of this. I just wanted to welcome you. It's a great neighborhood. I didn't even realize this house was on the market or I'd have mentioned it to you myself. The location couldn't be more convenient to town and the house is absolutely charming."

Sam didn't know what qualified a house as charming, but this one did feel exactly right somehow. It even had a working fireplace in the living room, built-in bookshelves and one of

266

those white picket fences he'd always thought to be the worst sort of cliché for the kind of quaint, suburban life he didn't intend to live. How often had he expressed his disdain for such a life to his sister. She must be having a good laugh at the way she'd turned his life upside down.

He realized Carrie was again studying him intently. "Sorry," he apologized. "I guess I'm a little distracted."

"I know you're just settling in and must have a million things to do, so I won't bother you, but if there's anything I can do to help, let me know, okay?" She glanced around at the empty room again. "How are you going to manage without furniture?"

He smiled. "We have beds. That'll do for a couple of nights."

"What about dishes? Pots and pans?"

"All in due time," he said. "I gather from Susie that she's been raiding various O'Brien attics and will be bringing in castoffs on Monday. After that, I'll be shopping for whatever else we need."

"Well, then, I guess I'll take off," she said and started down the steps. As she reached the sidewalk, she turned back. "I don't suppose the two of you would like to go to my grandfather's for dinner tomorrow, would you? It'll be the usual Sunday madhouse, but Nell's cooking, so I can promise you a delicious meal, and it'll give Bobby a chance to make some more friends."

Sam hesitated. Given what she'd told him about her grandfather's matchmaking tendencies and what he'd seen for himself when Mick had come by the newspaper office, maybe this wasn't such a hot idea. Carrie was skittish enough and neither of them needed extra pressure these days. He was overwhelmed by all the sudden changes in his lifestyle and she was sorting through a million details to decide whether to open that day care. All very valid considerations, he concluded.

In the end, though, he had to think about Bobby. It would be a whole lot easier for him to adjust to Chesapeake Shores if he was surrounded by even more kids his age. Sam wanted him to feel as if he belonged here, rather than constantly hearing that he wanted to go back home to see his real friends.

"Are you sure it'll be okay if you bring a couple of last-minute guests?"

She laughed at that. "You'll see. In the mob scene at Grandpa Mick's, they'll barely notice two more. And you already know Susie and Mack, plus me and Luke, so you won't feel that out of place. And you've met my grandfather and survived, so it should be all good. Nell will, no doubt, seize the chance to give us both another cooking lesson. She's complained about us missing the past couple of Saturdays."

Sam nodded. "Okay, then. Thanks for the invitation."

"Would you like to ride over with me?" she asked. "There's no reason to take two cars, since we're neighbors."

"Why don't I drive?" he suggested instead. "My car has Bobby's booster seat."

"Sure. I'll walk over here just before five." She gave him a wave and took off.

Sam stood in the doorway and watched her go, enjoying the sway of her hips in those shorts probably a little more than he should. Bobby slipped up beside him and tucked a hand in his.

"Was that Carrie?" he asked.

"It was."

"Why was she here and why didn't I get to see her?"

"She came to invite us to Sunday dinner with her family tomorrow." He ruffled Bobby's hair and waved the plate of cookies under his nose. "And she brought a housewarming present."

"Cookies!" Bobby guessed at once. "Can I have some?"

"Just one," Sam said. "Then we need to go to the grocery store to buy milk and some other supplies."

"Peanut butter and jelly for school lunches?"

"If that's what you want."

"And cheese and bread to make grilled cheese sandwiches for here?"

"Sure."

"And pancakes?"

When Sam hesitated, Bobby said, "They make frozen ones. Do we have a toaster?"

"Not yet, but we will," Sam said, moving that to the top of his mental list of necessities. "If we drive to the big Walmart on the main highway, we can get food and a toaster."

"All right!" Bobby enthused, shoving the last of his cookie into his mouth. "Let's go."

Sam couldn't help chuckling. Apparently when properly motivated, Bobby forgot all about how much he missed home and was ready to embrace Chesapeake Shores. All it took was the promise of a few familiar treats . . . and warm cookies from a neighbor who was sneaking past Sam's defenses, too.

On Sunday, Carrie introduced Sam and Bobby to her relatives, taking great care to stress that he was a neighbor and new to town, then adding his connection to Susie and Mack. At least that's what she did until they reached her grandfather.

"Grandpa Mick, you already know Sam Winslow," she said. "I understand you met him at the newspaper office."

If there was a tiny flicker of guilt in her grandfather's eyes, it was hastily replaced by a satisfied gleam. She hoped Sam was oblivious to it.

"And who would this be?" Mick asked, reaching out a hand to Bobby.

"This is my nephew, Bobby," Sam said. "I

believe I mentioned to you that he's just come to live with me. Bobby, shake Mr. O'Brien's hand."

Bobby hesitantly reached out for Mick's hand, then looked surprised when he came away with a wrapped piece of penny candy. Carrie chuckled.

"Bobby, you're going to find that my grandfather has a never-ending supply of candy from Ethel's Emporium."

Bobby grinned shyly. "Cool." He looked up at Sam. "Can I have it now?"

"I don't think one piece will spoil your appetite," Sam said, then gave him a look of mock severity. "But just one, understood?"

"You may be telling that to the wrong person," Carrie told him, nodding toward her grandfather.

"Oh, stop your fussing," Mick grumbled. "You enjoyed your share of treats from me when you were his age. Now why don't you introduce Bobby to some of the other kids, while Sam and I have a chat."

Carrie regarded her grandfather with alarm, but knew better than to argue. "Come on, Bobby. I think there's a whole slew of kids playing in the yard. Shall we look for them?"

Bobby looked hesitant, but Sam gave his shoulder a reassuring squeeze. "I'll be right here," he promised.

Carrie held out her hand and Bobby immediately took it, then followed her outside where a half a dozen O'Brien grandchildren were racing across the lawn in an improvised game of hide-and-seek. The instant they spotted Carrie, they stopped and ran over.

"Carrie, are you going to play with us?" Sean asked, his blue eyes regarding her hopefully. Sean was the surprise blessing who'd come into her uncle Thomas's life after he and the younger Connie had married.

"Not right now, but I've brought along someone who would love to join you," Carrie told him. "This is Bobby." She knelt down and put her arm around Bobby's waist, then pointed out each of the children. "This is Sean, and that's Emily Rose. You already know Davey and Johnny. And this little guy here is my brother, Patrick. He doesn't run as fast as the others yet, so maybe you can look out for him."

Bobby's chest swelled just a little at being asked to be the younger boy's protector. "I can do that."

"Come on, then," Sean encouraged. "Henry's it and we're supposed to be hiding from him. I can show you the best spots."

Bobby glanced up at her. "Is it okay?"

"Of course. I'll be waiting for you right here on the porch." She lowered herself to the top step and watched as Bobby joined in, hesitantly at first, and then with the exuberance of a typical six-year-old.

"He's having fun."

She heard the surprise in Sam's voice and glanced up. "Sometimes the chance to just be a kid can help with all the grown-up emotions a little boy doesn't know how to handle."

Sam dropped down beside her. "I've tried so hard not to let him see how sad and scared I am."

"I'm sure you're doing fine."

"I wish I could believe that." He glanced sideways at her, his eyes shadowed. "It's pretty overwhelming sometimes. I can't believe Laurel and Robert are gone or that they left Bobby in my care. What were they thinking?"

"That you'd do a great job with him," Carrie said. "You are, you know. Despite all the adjustments you're having to make, you're managing."

He looked startled. "That's high praise coming from you."

"You've earned it." She nodded in the direction of the house. "How'd it go in there?"

Sam turned to face her and grinned. "I had the oddest sensation that once again I was being interrogated as potential husband material. You wouldn't know anything about that, would you?"

Carrie could feel a blush staining her cheeks. "Grandpa Mick is an inveterate matchmaker. I warned you about that. Pay no attention to him."

He nudged her with an elbow. "Tell the truth, Carrie. Did you invite me here today to give him the idea that we're dating?"

She sighed. "Maybe, just a little. He stopped by

the house the other day and got on my case about finding a man. I told him I had lots of prospects, when the truth is there are none. Since I didn't want him to decide to fill that particular void in my life, I decided to invite you here today. All the stuff about Bobby making new friends was true, too. It seemed like a win-win." She gave him an imploring look. "Can you play along, just for the afternoon?"

To her relief, Sam looked more amused than distressed, "Gee, pretend to be interested in a beautiful woman for a couple of hours? Especially when I've had no luck up till now getting her to go out with me? Hmm, I don't know." He held her gaze. "That's asking a lot."

She nudged him back. "Are you up to the task?"

"Just how serious does your grandfather get about his matchmaking? Will he be booking the church for a wedding next week? Should I avoid signing the final papers for the house just in case I need to make a hasty getaway?"

Carrie laughed. "I think I can hold him off on that. We've all had a lot of experience at keeping Grandpa Mick from getting ahead of himself. It's just that it's easier to play along and let him think there's someone special in our lives. I'm catching enough grief over my career choice these days. I don't need him bugging me about men, too."

"How is the day-care location hunt coming along? We haven't had much of a chance to talk about it since you started looking at property."

Carrie beamed at him. "Not quite as crazy fast as your house hunt, but I think I've found the perfect spot for it just off of Main Street. The kids would be able to play on the town green in good weather. It has a big yard, too. Julie and her daughter are going to come over next weekend to take a look. If they think it's as perfect as I do, I'll put in an offer. They've promised to walk me through any necessary renovations. I have a hunch once I can get my grandfather involved in that project, he'll back off on his search for the perfect man for me. The truth is he revels in being involved in our lives and a project like that will be totally absorbing, even if it's a thousand times smaller than what he used to do when he designed and supervised the building of whole towns the way he did with Chesapeake Shores."

"How long are those renovations likely to take?" Sam inquired.

"Probably not long enough to keep us safe from his meddling for more than a month. Brace yourself."

She realized Sam was studying her curiously. "What?" she asked.

"I'm surprised, that's all. Not that long ago you were making a pro-con list and now you're obviously all in."

She laughed. "I am, and you're not the first to

comment on my sudden enthusiasm. My whole family seems torn between relief that I've found a new direction and shock that it's something like day care." She shrugged. "What can I say? Working at Julie's place has reinforced what I already knew about myself."

"Which is?"

"I love being around kids, especially little ones. They're endlessly curious and sweetly innocent."

"And you're sure this is what you want to do with your life? No lingering longing to run off to Europe or New York?"

"I'm more sure of this than I have been about anything in a long time," she said with confidence, then smiled as Patrick wandered over and snuggled against her. "My little brother," she told Sam. "Mom got a late start on a second family. We're a family that's just full of surprises."

"I can see that," Sam said, his warm gaze filled with appreciation.

"What about your family?"

"There's just Bobby and me now," he said, grief once again darkening his eyes. "My folks died a couple of years ago, just months apart. And you already know about the accident that took my sister."

"No other siblings?"

He shook his head.

"I can't imagine growing up without a huge

family," she said. "I was so lucky to be part of this one."

Sam gazed around at the children, who'd now been joined by several of the adults in an increasingly rambunctious game of tag. His expression turned wistful. "I can understand that."

Something in his voice, though, suggested otherwise. "Even so, you find it a little overwhelming, don't you?"

He shrugged. "To be honest, yes. I've always been a bit of a loner. Now that there's Bobby to consider, I'm going to have to change my ways. No more all-nighters for work. No more forgetting to eat or even to buy groceries. Bobby and I hit the store to stock up yesterday and the amount of food in my grocery cart was probably more than I bought in six months in the past. I might even have to figure out how to use the washing machine and, heaven forbid, an iron." He shuddered dramatically.

"Kids do need food," she said. "And attention, and sleep, and a routine. It probably doesn't matter so much if their clothes aren't ironed."

"All stuff I'm not very good at," Sam said.

"You'll learn," she said confidently. "And you already have the one thing Bobby needs the most right now."

"What's that?"

"You love him."

She could see it in his eyes as he watched his nephew. Sam might be terrified at being thrust into this new role of being responsible for another person, but he loved that little boy. Seeing that made her fall just a little bit in love with both of them. And that definitely wasn't meant to be part of today's hastily devised scheme to get her grandfather off her back.

Sam was surprisingly content sitting on the porch step next to Carrie as kids raced around the yard, shouting exuberantly. While it was a far cry from the quiet, carefree existence he'd lived up till now, there was something alluring about the friendly competitiveness and the laughter that echoed through the air.

"I thought I'd heard that the two of you were out here," a voice said from above them.

Sam looked around to see Nell on the porch, hands on her hips. Despite the scolding note in her voice, there was a twinkle in her eyes.

"Hi, Gram," Carrie said, flushing. "Did you need something?"

"I need a little help from two people who missed their cooking lesson again yesterday with a bunch of flimsy excuses. I imagine you could both use some experience with getting pot roast for this crowd onto the table."

Sam readily jumped to his feet. "What can we do to help?"

"Come with me," Nell commanded. When Carrie stayed put, she frowned. "You, too."

"Somebody needs to keep an eye on Bobby," Carrie protested.

"There are at least ten responsible adults in the yard," Nell countered. "Including Kevin. Tell your uncle to keep an eye on Bobby along with his own kids."

"Yes, ma'am," Carrie said dutifully.

In the meantime Sam followed Nell into the kitchen. She already had the bulk of the meal well under way, but she assigned him the task of making gravy.

"But I've never made gravy in my life," Sam protested.

Nell chuckled. "Exactly why I'm here to teach you, young man."

"Oh, gravy!" Carrie said when she joined them. "Gram's gravy is the best."

"It might be wise to avoid it today," Sam said, a grim expression on his face as he stirred what looked to him like a glutinous mess.

Nell glanced over his shoulder. "Did you measure the cornstarch or just dump in half the box?"

"It didn't look as if it was thickening at first," Sam admitted. "So I added a little more."

"Cooking is like a lot of things in life. It can't be rushed," Nell admonished. "It requires patience."

"Something in short supply in this family," Carrie commented.

"Unfortunately true," Gram replied. "Let's see if you're any better at this than he was."

She gestured toward another pan of drippings from the roast, then coached her through the steps and ingredients needed to make her smooth, rich gravy.

"Better," she said approvingly. "You get a little red star."

"Not gold?" Carrie asked.

"Is it perfect?" Nell asked.

"No," Carrie admitted with a chagrined expression.

"Then you don't get gold, do you?"

"How about Sam?" Carrie asked, proving that competitiveness existed everywhere with O'Briens.

"He gets to do it again at my house next Saturday till he gets it right. I'd make him try again right now, but we need to get this food on the table. Start dishing it up, Carrie. Sam, you can put it on the dining-room table."

"Is she always this bossy?" he asked in an undertone that he meant to be overheard.

Carrie laughed. "Even Grandpa Mick and his brothers cower when she speaks," she said.

"Now that I'd like to see," Sam said.

"Stick around," Nell told him, smiling. "My sons usually give me some reason or another to take them to task before the day is out."

Somehow Sam found the thought of this wonderful, diminutive woman being able to handle the all-powerful Mick O'Brien very reassuring. Maybe he could follow her example and learn to hold his own with Mick—and even Carrie—when he had to.

"Have you watched her?" Susie was saying to Jess just as Carrie was about to walk onto the porch after lunch. Her cousin's voice carried inside and something made Carrie come to a stop long enough to listen.

"The way she's latched on to Sam is so obvious. All this talk about opening a day care doesn't mean a thing," Susie continued. "What she's really interested in is finding a man and a ready-made family."

Carrie knew there was little question that Susie was talking about her. She waited for her aunt Jess's response.

"I'm not seeing that," Jess responded quietly. "Sure, Carrie's been pitching in to help out, but anyone in this family would do the same. You've certainly done your share to get Sam and Bobby into a new house with a minimum of fuss. And you've been scouring attics for furniture they could use. Does that mean you're after Sam?"

"Of course not," Susie said. "That's entirely different."

"How?"

"I'm just helping. Carrie obviously has an ulterior motive."

Carrie froze in place at the horrible accusation. Before she could work up a full head of steam and confront Susie herself, Jess did it for her.

"That's a pretty terrible thing to accuse your cousin of doing," Jess said. "Since I know you're not interested in Sam yourself because you're happily married to Mack, something tells me this is really about Bobby. Am I right? Did you want to be the one who helped that little boy adapt to being in a new town?"

Silence fell, and for a moment, Carrie thought Susie might not answer.

"Maybe," she finally admitted in a small voice. She regarded Jess miserably. "It's so obvious that Sam's not qualified to be anyone's father. Even Carrie saw that for herself. He left that child in a car all alone, for one thing. Who knows how many mistakes he's going to make and what could happen to Bobby because Sam's so careless? And Carrie, of all people, is going to jump in and save the day? One minute she's living it up in Europe. The next she's opening a day care. Come on. What does that tell you about her stability?"

Carrie felt as if she'd been slapped. Rather than going outside to defend herself, she whirled around to go through the house and leave for home.

"Don't you dare run away," her mother said gently, standing in her path. She'd obviously overheard most of Susie's remarks, as well. "You know she's wrong. Susie is just upset with her own situation. She's lashing out at anyone and everyone right now. The situation with Sam and Bobby has stirred up all those unrequited maternal instincts she has and she's made you the enemy."

"I get that," Carrie conceded. "But no one in this family has ever said such spiteful things about me or anyone else before." She regarded her mom with real dismay twisting in her gut. "You don't think I'm that frivolous, do you? And you don't think I'm trying to latch on to Sam, just so I can have a family? I would never do that. If anything, I've been ignoring the spark of attraction between us because I don't think it would be smart to start something up with Sam when there's a scared little boy in the mix who could get hurt."

"Try reserving some of that compassion for Susie," her mother said. "She's hurting right now. She doesn't know what she's saying. Try to remember how much pain she must be in to feel the need to attack you. Don't think I'm suggesting for a minute that she doesn't owe you an apology, but consider the circumstances and try to cut her a little slack. Once she has her feet back under her, she'll see how wrong she's been."

"Well, it's pretty unlikely that's going to happen today. I should leave before we get into it and ruin the day for everyone."

"Didn't you ride over with Sam?"

"Yes, but you can tell him something came up and I had to leave. I can walk home." She gave her mom a pleading look. "Please."

Abby looked as if she didn't agree, but eventually she nodded. "I'll tell him." She gave Carrie a fierce hug. "Try to put this whole incident out of your head and please don't let it spoil all of your excitement about opening a day-care center."

"I'll try," she promised.

But Susie's cruel comments, no matter the pain that was underlying them, weren't something she was likely to be able to get out of her head anytime soon.

❧ 15 ❧

"I'm worried about Susie," Mack confided to Jake and Will, his two best friends. It was after Sunday dinner at Mick's and the three lifelong friends—all of them married to O'Briens—had retreated to the Adirondack chairs overlooking the bay, where they had some privacy amid the raucous games being played by the younger generation.

"Why is that?" Will asked. A psychologist, he

had insights they all relied on from time to time. As the husband of Mick's youngest daughter, Jess, the owner of the Inn at Eagle Point, Will understood the family dynamics as well as any of them.

"The whole adoption process is taking a lot longer than either of us imagined," Mack said, his own frustration evident. Around Susie, he did his best to be upbeat and encouraging, but the situation was getting to him, too. "Having this private adoption fall through at the last minute was devastating for her. Susie insists she's through trying, but I can see the longing in her eyes every time we're around the other kids in the family. She almost balked at coming today. When I asked why, she came up with some lame excuse, but I know it's because she wants her own baby so badly. I got her here by warning her that Nell would start asking questions if she missed another Sunday dinner."

"Still, I can understand her desire to avoid these family meals," Will said. "Everywhere she turns, there's either a new baby or one on the way. That's bound to hurt."

"Exactly," Mack said. "It's killing her. It's turning her into someone I hardly recognize anymore."

"Bree's worried about her, too," Jake admitted. "Susie was coming around the house pretty regularly to spend time with Emily Rose, but she suddenly stopped. Bree can't decide whether to talk to her about it or to let it go. And she mentioned that Susie's been avoiding the women in the family who gather at the café in the mornings, too. Sounds as if she's withdrawing from everyone."

"Not everyone," Abby said, pulling up another chair and joining them. "Sorry for eavesdropping, but Mack, I was looking for you."

"Any particular reason?" Mack asked.

"Did you need to speak to him alone?" Will asked, obviously sensing Abby's mood. Even Mack, who could be pretty oblivious to such things, could tell she wasn't happy.

"Actually, you should probably all hear this. Will, you might have some ideas about how to handle the situation," Abby said.

Mack regarded her warily. "This is about Susie?" he concluded.

She nodded. "I was coming out of the house just now and overheard her talking to Jess about Sam, Bobby and Carrie."

Mack could guess from Abby's protective expression what the gist of the conversation had been. He knew because he'd heard the same or similar comments. "She thinks Carrie's making a move on Sam because of Bobby and that Sam's completely lacking in parenting skills."

Abby gave him a startled look. "Pretty much. She's said the same to you?"

Mack nodded. "She knows she's wrong, but she can't seem to help herself. It's this whole adoption fiasco. She's not thinking straight. For some reason she's seized on Bobby like some sort of lifeline, a child who might need her."

"Well, I don't know how often she's been talking like this or to whom," Abby said, "but this time not only did I overhear her, so did Carrie."

"Blast it!" Mack said heatedly. "I am so sorry, Abby. Did they get into it?"

"No, Carrie walked away. I don't know if Susie even realized she was there. I'm afraid my daughter might not be quite so forgiving next time. She was hurt and angry, but she was trying very hard to put herself into Susie's position." She leveled a look at Mack. "The last thing we want is an open feud between those two with everyone in the family taking sides."

"Of course not," Mack agreed, then turned to Will. "How am I supposed to fix this?"

"Talk to her," Will said. "Get her to open up to you."

"Do you think it's that freaking easy?" Mack retorted. "She won't talk about it. If I bring up the adoption, she snaps my head off. I get it. I really do, but it's taking a toll. I swear there are days when I think dealing with the cancer was easier than this. At least we knew what we had to do then. And we stuck together. Neither of us knows how to fix this and it's evident to me that she thinks she's facing it all alone."

Will regarded him thoughtfully. "I noticed something today that fits what both of you are saying. When Susie was watching Carrie with Sam and Bobby, she looked almost angry, as if Carrie had stolen something from her."

Mack sighed heavily. "I know. It's just as I feared when I took her over to the inn to meet Bobby. I think she got this crazy idea of jumping in to save this poor motherless little boy. Except now Carrie's obviously beat her to it."

"If she won't open up to you, do you think she'd talk to someone else?" Abby asked gently.

Mack frowned. "You mean a professional?"

Abby nodded, then gave his hand a sympathetic squeeze. "Look, I'm going to let you handle this. Me butting in beyond alerting you to the problem won't help. I may be open-minded and rational about a lot of things, but when it comes to my kids, I'm going to stand up for them, no matter who gets hurt in the process. I know Susie doesn't need me coming down on her. If there's anything I can do, though, let me know. I know how hard this is and I feel for Susie. I really do. I'll leave you all to figure out your next step."

After she went, Mack sighed.

"This really does suck," Jake said. "It doesn't sound like there are any easy answers."

"Certainly none Susie's going to be happy

288

about," Mack agreed. "She doesn't like asking for help, even when she recognizes how desperately she might need it. On top of that, she's pretty private. I can't see her talking to a stranger."

"What about me?" Will asked. "We've always been close. She used to open up to me about her feelings for you, Mack. At least she did back in the day. I'd be happy to spend some time with her, though somebody completely impartial with no connection to the O'Briens at all might be better."

It was the obvious next step, but Mack thought he knew how his wife would react. She'd think he was siding with the enemy in some way. "I can suggest it," he said, resigned to a messy confrontation. "Something tells me, though, that it won't go over well. I'm afraid it's going to drive another wedge between us."

"Try," Will encouraged him. "It's important, especially if you think her feelings could cause a real rift between her and Carrie. Abby's right. That would have everybody in the family taking sides. O'Briens are used to sticking together. I'm not sure how well they'd handle something that's bound to divide them, especially when it comes to something like this. And we sure don't want to see Sam and that innocent nephew of his caught up in some messy family dispute."

"Believe me, I get it," Mack said. "None of us wants that. Keep in mind that Sam works for me.

He's a decent guy who's doing the best he can in an already tough situation." He shook his head wearily. "At the same time, I want my wife to be happy and to have everything she needs."

Will regarded him with compassion. "If what she needs is a child right here and now, you might have to accept this one is beyond your control."

"Could you, if Jess were this upset?"

Will leveled a look at him, then smiled ruefully. "Of course not. I'm just saying that none of us mere mortals, not even the all-powerful Mick, can make dreams come true on command every single time."

"But Mick certainly has been the role model for trying," Mack said.

The other two nodded.

"Oh, yeah," Jake said.

The truth was that Mick O'Brien had set the bar impossibly high for all of them. And the women in their lives were used to success, not failure.

While Abby had offered a totally plausible explanation for Carrie's abrupt departure from her grandfather's—that she had paperwork for the day care due in the morning—Sam couldn't shake the feeling that there was a lot more to it. Even though he barely knew Carrie's mother, he thought he'd detected a real hint of worry in her eyes.

As he made the turn onto Willow Brook Road,

he drove slowly by the house he'd determined was Carrie's. He saw no signs of life, not a light on inside, no movement.

Of course she could be taking a nap or maybe she wasn't even home, but he was struck once again by the sense that something wasn't right.

He parked in his own driveway, hesitated just long enough to draw a puzzled look from Bobby, then said, "How about taking a walk before we go inside?"

"How come?" Bobby asked.

"I thought we might stop by to see Carrie."

Bobby's eyes brightened at once. "Okay. Maybe she'll have more cookies."

Sam laughed. "Didn't you get enough to eat today?"

"Sure, but cookies are always good. Or they could go into my backpack for school tomorrow."

"An interesting line of thought," Sam agreed. "But you don't ask for cookies. You can accept them if she offers you some, okay?"

Bobby shrugged. "Whatever."

Carrie's house still seemed uncommonly quiet to Sam as he and Bobby approached, then rang the bell. He heard no sounds coming from inside, so he rang the bell again. Then he decided to walk around back.

That's where he found Carrie at the far edge of the property, her feet dangling into Willow Brook, tears on her cheeks. She swiped at them impatiently when she realized she had company.

Bobby instantly took note of the tears and sat down close to her. "Are you sad?"

"A little," she admitted as he snuggled closer.

"I'm sorry."

"Having you here makes me feel a whole lot better," she told him, draping an arm over his shoulders.

"Are you sure?" Sam asked, studying her intently. "We don't have to stick around if you'd rather be alone. I was just worried that something had happened at your grandfather's."

"Nothing I can't figure out," she said, though she didn't sound convincing.

"Want to talk about it?" he asked, despite his lack of experience in solving the sort of problems that brought on tears. He could handle computer crashes or internet provider glitches right at the newspaper's deadline without batting an eye, but this sensitivity business was new territory.

"If I do, it will only convince you that you've gotten tangled up in a very messy family dynamic that it would take Solomon to sort out. Since you're just settling into Chesapeake Shores, it might be better to let you keep your illusions about my family a little longer."

He gave her a long look. "I haven't signed the final papers on the house. I'm not stuck here yet."

She tried for a smile, but it wobbled and failed. "That's the problem, isn't it? If I start blabbing and blubbering, you could take off faster than one of those rockets they fire from Wallops Island to get supplies to the International Space Station."

"I'd like to think I'm a little tougher than that." He sat on her other side and stretched out his legs, then reached over and brushed away the dampness that lingered on her cheek. "Seriously— you've stood by me in some tough spots the past few weeks. I'd like to return the favor if I can."

"Maybe a cookie and some milk would help," Bobby suggested hopefully. "That always makes me feel better."

Over the top of his head, Sam caught Carrie's gaze and held it. "Or we can take off."

She tried another smile and this one held. "I think cookies and milk sound like the best idea ever," she said, getting to her feet and leading the way inside.

She flipped on the kitchen lights to reveal a small space, but one that would have been a gourmet chef's dream with its granite counter-tops, stainless steel appliances and a door that opened into a walk-in pantry stocked with every conceivable snack, healthy and otherwise. Bobby stood in the doorway, clearly mesmerized.

"It's better than the grocery store," he said, awe in his voice.

Carrie laughed. "I like to be prepared when the kids come over," she told Sam, her expression chagrined. "I told you I like being the go-to aunt."

"Well, I can see I'm going to have difficulty getting Bobby back to our house ever again," Sam said. "In fact, I might want you to adopt me, too."

The color washed out of her cheeks at his words and she quickly turned away. Sam walked around to face her. "What did I say?"

"Nothing. Honestly," she claimed, though she wouldn't look him in the eye. "If you could get three glasses from the cabinet above the sink, I'll get the milk and the cookie jar."

Behind them, Bobby was doing an inventory of the pantry. "There are those fruity things I love, and chips, and Oreo cookies, and peanut-butter crackers and pretzels and apples and bananas and lots and lots of cereal and—"

"Enough," Sam said, chuckling. "I'm sure Carrie is well aware of what's in there. Stop being nosy."

"But the door was open," Bobby protested.

Once the milk was poured and the cookies placed on a plate, Carrie focused her attention on Bobby. "Did you have fun today?"

He nodded, his mouth already full of crumbling chocolate-chip cookie.

She finally turned to Sam. "And you?"

"It was a revelation."

"It seemed as if you'd lost that glazed-over, overwhelmed expression by the end of dinner," she observed.

"Pretty much. It was fascinating watching the ebb and flow as people moved from one conversation and one group to another."

"Sort of like witnessing a social experiment in person," she suggested.

"Not at all. It's evident that O'Briens love and respect each other. I found that pretty impressive."

"Oh, believe me, we have our share of squabbles," she said, an odd note in her voice. "In some ways they're worse when they happen, because the expectation is that we'll all get along all the time."

"Personal experience?"

Rather than answering directly, she told the story of the warfare among her grandfather and his brothers when the town was being built. "Uncle Thomas took Grandpa Mick to court because he didn't think he was working hard enough to protect the bay. Uncle Jeff sided with Thomas and war was declared. It was Gram who brokered peace, mostly by insisting that the Sunday-dinner tradition would not be broken and that they had to get over themselves."

"And just like that, they did?"

Carrie laughed. "Hardly. It took years. According to Mom, Sunday dinners were sometimes very tense if anyone ventured onto a dangerous topic. Of course by the time Caitlyn and I came along, Chesapeake Shores had been built and peace once again reigned, at least most of the time."

"Well, I certainly didn't notice any strain today," Sam said.

Again, though, he had the sense that Carrie wanted to dispute that, but she remained discreetly silent.

"We should go," he said eventually. "Thanks for asking us to join you today."

"I'm sorry I bailed on you. I hope Mom explained."

"She did," Sam said, though with no mountain of paperwork in sight, he was well aware he still didn't have the whole picture. Given Carrie's reticence just now, he wondered if he ever would.

Or why he had a gut feeling that it mattered.

"Book club is on again for tomorrow night at Susie's," Shanna announced happily on Monday morning.

"I thought she'd agreed the other day when you first spoke to her about it, then canceled an hour later." Heather said, looking surprised. "What makes you think she won't cancel again?"

"I pinned her down yesterday at Mick's and badgered her till she couldn't say no," Shanna said, clearly pleased with herself. "You'll all be there, right? And you'll bring something. I promised her she wouldn't have to lift a finger."

Heather and Bree immediately offered to shop

for sandwich wraps and salads from Panini Bistro.

"And I'll bake brownies," Shanna said. "And I'll ask Jess to bring another dessert from the inn. What about you, Carrie?"

"I can't make it," Carrie said stiffly. "I'm swamped with paperwork for the day-care center."

Bree studied her with a narrowed gaze. "And that's more important than being there for Susie?"

"Actually it is," Carrie said defensively. "I have to get the ball rolling, and Connor needs this paperwork to file all the applications."

"Surely one night won't make that big a difference," Shanna said.

"Sorry. Not this time," Carrie repeated.

Bree gave her a penetrating look, then sighed. "So it's true."

The other women stared at her curiously, even as Carrie wanted to jump up and leave before her aunt opened this can of worms.

"What's true?" Heather asked.

"There's some sort of rift between Carrie and Susie," Bree said, her gaze on Carrie. "Am I right?"

"No idea what you're talking about," Carrie said. "And I have to run. I need to pick up Jackson."

"Sit still. You don't have Jackson on Monday," Bree said.

"Change of plans," Carrie said, trying to keep a note of desperation out of her voice. "Noah asked me to fill in. That's why I'm not volunteering at Julie's day-care center today." She gave Bree a challenging look. "Would you like to call him to check?"

Bree relented. "That won't be necessary," she said eventually. "But sweetie, if there is something going on between you and Susie, you need to mend fences. That makes it even more important for you to be there for book club."

"It's up to me? Why?" Carrie snapped before she could stop herself. She fought to bring her annoyance under control. "You have no idea what you're talking about and I really think you should stay out of it."

She stood up and this time no one made any effort to stop her. She was halfway out the door before she heard the murmur of voices start again and knew that heated speculation was under way.

This whole thing was destined to turn into a huge disaster before all was said and done and she couldn't think of any way to stop it. How was she supposed to defend herself against Susie's irrational suspicions and cruel comments without making matters even worse? Talking to her cousin in Susie's present frame of mind would only escalate the situation.

Of course, walking out of Sally's just now probably hadn't helped, either. Whatever her aunt

Bree knew or thought she knew was going to be common knowledge before noon. And then what? Battle lines would be drawn? Not only did Carrie not want that, but in Susie's fragile state these days, it was the last thing she needed, as well.

Sam had gotten Bobby off to school and was having a second cup of coffee to brace himself for a busy day at the newspaper, when he heard a car pull up outside. He glanced out the living room window and saw instead a pickup loaded with furniture. Susie was just getting out of the cab of the truck.

Sam opened the front door. "Where on earth did you find all of that stuff?"

She laughed. "I made the rounds after dinner yesterday and raided attics."

As Sam approached the truck he spotted what looked to be some decent antiques and a like-new sofa. "*That's* what O'Briens store in their attics?"

"The women in the family like to redecorate on a regular basis," Susie said with a shrug. "It's a curse. Heaven forbid a perfectly good sofa clashes with the new paint color."

"Yes, heaven forbid!" Sam replied, astonished. "Look, I really appreciate this more than I can say, but I don't think you and I can get it into the house on our own. And I need to get to the office for an early meeting with your husband."

"Don't fret. He's on his way, along with other

reinforcements. All you need to do is decide where you want things and point them in the right direction."

Sure enough, several cars pulled into spaces along the street and men he'd met just yesterday, plus Mack and Kevin and even Mick, piled out of them. For the next twenty minutes or so, all he did was direct traffic to various rooms.

"I don't know what to say," he told them when the furniture and boxes of pots and pans and dishes had been unloaded. "This is way above and beyond."

"All things that should be put to good use," Mick said. "Now all you need is a woman's touch and you'll have yourself a very nice home."

"Which is exactly why I'm going to stick around and put things in their proper places," Susie said brightly. "Plus I have a few more little things in the truck that will brighten things up."

"Susie, you've already done more than enough," Sam said. "Rounding all of this up and getting the paperwork in order so quickly—you've been a real godsend."

"Absolutely," Mick said. "You just leave the rest of this to Carrie. She has a good eye for details."

Sam couldn't read the expression that washed over Susie's face, but Mack was at her side in an instant. "Sam's right, sweetheart. What you've done here is amazing, but let him figure out the rest. I'm sure Bobby will want to have a say, too."

"You can bet on that," Sam said.

"I picked up a few toys for him," Susie said stiffly. "Can I at least leave those?"

"Of course," Mack said quickly. "Are they in the cab of the truck? I'll get them."

As the other men waved good-bye and headed out, Susie stood beside Sam, her shoulders hunched, her face downcast. Sam could tell she was upset, but figuring out exactly why was beyond him.

"I really do appreciate everything you've done," he told her again. "This situation could have been so much harder and you've made it painless."

"I just wanted to help any way I could," she said, lifting her chin until their gazes caught.

Something in her tone left Sam puzzled. "I know that." Had someone suggested otherwise? Before he could ask, Mack was back with bags of toys for Bobby. Sam could only stare.

"Wow! Did you buy out the store?"

She gave him a sheepish grin. "I might have gotten a little carried away. Once I got started, I was having so much fun, I couldn't seem to stop. Please don't ask me to take them back."

Sam had been about to do just that, but at a subtle shake of Mack's head, he said only, "I was going to suggest that I put them into a closet and that you come back later and give them to Bobby yourself. You deserve the reward of seeing his face light up when he sees everything."

At that Susie's expression finally brightened. "You wouldn't mind?"

"Not at all. I'm planning to get back from work in time to be here when Bobby gets home from school. Do you want to stop by around four? Mack, you, too?"

"Sure," Mack said awfully quickly. "We wouldn't miss it, would we, Suze?"

"We'll see you at four," Susie promised.

"Well, I'll see you at the office a lot sooner than that," Mack said.

"On my way," Sam promised and watched the two of them leave.

He still had the sense that despite the generosity behind everything that had happened here this morning, there was an undertone of something he was missing. And whatever it was, it seemed to have left a lot of people on edge.

❧ 16 ❧

Carrie was taking Jackson for a walk in his stroller Monday afternoon when she spotted Mack and Susie pulling into Sam's driveway. She was about to make a U-turn and go back home, when Bobby spotted her and came running across the lawn, shouting her name. Susie's head snapped around, Mack winced and Carrie wished the ground would open up and swallow her.

"Stop it!" she muttered under her breath. After all, this was her neighborhood. She had a perfect right to take a walk on this street. Plastering a smile on her face, she called out a greeting to Bobby.

"There's a surprise for me at the house," Bobby told her excitedly when he reached her. "Sam won't tell, but I'm gonna find out in a minute. You wanna see? Maybe Jackson would like it, too."

She glanced in Sam's direction for guidance and he nodded. "Absolutely," she told Bobby. "Let's see what this amazing surprise might be."

On her way to the house, she managed a civilized greeting for her cousin and Mack, but she could tell by the look in Susie's eyes that she was unhappy with the addition to the celebration, whatever it was. On any other day, maybe Carrie would have been more sensitive and made herself scarce, but after overhearing Susie's accusations yesterday, she wasn't about to do that. O'Briens didn't hide. Of course, what they eventually did was speak their minds, and she wasn't quite ready to do that, either, especially not in front of an audience.

At the front door, Carrie paused in amazement. "You have furniture!" The living room had been transformed from an empty shell practically overnight into a charming, cozy room with the addition of a sofa, chair and tables she'd last seen in Susie's apartment before she and Mack had built their home on Beach Lane.

"Yes, but that's not the surprise," Bobby told her. "Sam says it's something else, something just for me."

Carrie glanced at her cousin. "I heard you were gathering up things for Sam's house. You did a great job. This looks wonderful."

"Thanks," Susie said tightly.

"She also picked up a few things she thought Bobby might like," Sam said. He pointed toward a closet. "Check in there, pal."

Bobby raced across the living room and threw open the door. His eyes widened even as he gave a whoop of delight. "For me? All of it?"

"That's what I hear," Sam said. "This is all Susie's doing, so be sure you thank her."

As Bobby started bringing out bags and investigating the contents, there were more whoops and gasps. Even Carrie was a little in awe of the magnitude of Susie's generosity.

Bobby paused midway through checking out his unexpected haul and threw his arms around Susie. "Thank you, thank you!"

"You really did go above and beyond, yet again," Sam said, clearly taken aback.

Susie's face flushed. "I just wanted him to feel at home here. I was pretty sure you'd left a lot of things behind in storage and I thought new might be nice, anyway. Sort of a fresh start."

"That was really thoughtful," Mack told her, giving her hand a squeeze.

"It was," Carrie agreed, though she suspected she and Mack both understood there was a lot more behind the magnanimous gesture. Susie, with all the best intentions in the world, was trying to buy Bobby's affections and fill the void in her heart.

Carrie could understand all that. She could sympathize, knowing how Susie had been counting on the adoption that had fallen through at the very last minute. What she was having a hard time with was Susie trying to cast her as the bad guy because she was forming a bond with Bobby and Sam, too.

"How about something to drink?" Sam suggested, getting to his feet. "I have sodas, beer, water."

"I should probably go," Carrie said. "I need to get Jackson over to Noah's."

She saw the undisguised relief in Susie's eyes as she spoke. Sam didn't argue, but he did walk her to the door. Outside he studied her, his expression puzzled.

"What happened just now?"

She looked into his eyes. "No idea what you mean."

"The tension in there was so thick I could have

cut it with a knife. Are you and Susie fighting about something?"

"No," she said. And that much was true. They hadn't exchanged a single harsh word with each other. But those blasted battle lines had been drawn just the same. She wondered if things between her and her cousin would ever be the same. The irony was that they both knew Susie was madly in love with her husband, so it wasn't as if they were fighting over the same man. No, the battle was for the heart of a little boy, who needed all the love he could get from both of them and anyone else in this new world to which he was adapting.

After delivering Jackson to Noah, Carrie couldn't bring herself to go back to her empty house. If she discovered that Susie and Mack were still hanging out at Sam's, her sour mood would sink even lower. Instead, she headed to O'Brien's, though she wondered if that was a good choice. This was hardly a problem she could dump in Luke's lap. Susie was his sister.

Fortunately the pub was already busy and there were no seats at the bar, so she found a table in a corner near the front window and settled in with a glass of wine. With the view of the bay across the street, it was surprisingly soothing. There was time to listen to her own thoughts . . . about the day care, about her cousin and, of course, about

Sam. Individually she could have coped with any one thing, but combined? Was she destined to make a bad decision about any one of them, just because she was too busy to think things through? All were too important for missteps.

She'd been there less than half an hour with no resolution to any of her dilemmas and was debating ordering dinner, when she looked up and found Sam by her table.

"Interested in company?" he asked.

"Sure," she said, then glanced around. "Where's Bobby?"

"Susie and Mack are at the house with him. He didn't want to leave his haul of toys, so they offered to hang out."

"Are you sure that's a good idea?" she asked, then winced. "Sorry. Not my business."

Sam reached across the table and took her hand. "Carrie, what's going on? That's the second time I've picked up on some sort of tension between you and Susie. You carefully avoided giving me a straight answer earlier. How about now?"

She debated brushing off his observation for a second time, but couldn't quite bring herself to do it. This was a man she might want to have a future of some kind with. Lying or even hedging was no way to move forward.

"Okay, maybe there is an issue," she conceded, then added earnestly, "but it's not my doing."

She hesitated, still not convinced she wanted to air this particular bit of family laundry.

Sam didn't press. He ordered an ale, then watched her and waited. When Carrie realized he apparently had an endless supply of patience to go along with his keen powers of observation, she continued.

"Did you know that Mack and Susie were in the process of adopting?"

He nodded. "Mack mentioned how excited they were."

"Well, the baby, a girl, was born a few weeks ago, but the mom backed out of the adoption."

Sam looked shocked. "Can she do that?"

"Apparently."

"That must have been heartbreaking," he said. "But what does it have to do with you?"

"It shouldn't have a thing in the world to do with me," she said. "But you brought Bobby to town around the same time. Susie's apparently focusing all that love she was so desperate to give a new baby on Bobby now."

Sam looked momentarily stunned, then nodded slowly as understanding dawned. "A lot of things suddenly make sense to me. The very first day Mack brought her by to see Bobby, he was clearly worried. He thought she was going to get a little carried away, didn't he?"

"More than likely."

"And those toys she picked out. That's part of

her attempt to be a part of Bobby's life," he concluded.

"I'd say so."

"Is it more than that? Is she waiting for me to screw up, so she can take legal action or something?"

Carrie was stunned by that possibility. "Of course not," she said, then hesitated. "Honestly, I don't know what she's likely to do. She's not thinking clearly right now. I'm trying to make allowances for that myself."

"Because you're somehow caught up in whatever's going on with her," he concluded. "But how? I still don't see the connection."

She smiled. Typical male, oblivious to any nuances when it came to women. "Don't you see? She thinks I'm in her way, because you and I have gotten to be friends. You've turned to me a couple of times when you needed help with Bobby."

"But that's crazy," Sam said at once. "She's married to my boss, happily as near as I can tell."

"Sam, it's not about you. It's about my relationship with Bobby or the access that my friendship with you has given me to him."

"Oh, boy," Sam murmured.

"See what I mean about how complicated things have suddenly become?" She noticed the worry building in his eyes and knew she had to offset any panic she might inadvertently have caused. "Susie's really a good person. She's just

309

going through a truly terrible time. You don't have to worry about Bobby or anything like that. He's in perfectly good hands, especially with Mack there. And it can't hurt, having so many people caring about him, right?"

"I suppose not," he agreed, though he still looked concerned.

"You're thinking you should rush right home, aren't you?"

"Should I? Is the fact that I left to see you going to go on some list she's keeping of my questionable parenting?"

"You have to trust your instincts, but mine are telling me that all Susie wants is to spend time with Bobby and to have a relationship with him. You'll have to watch that the attachment doesn't get too intense or that she doesn't go overboard with the presents again, but beyond that, the Susie I've known my whole life would never do anything to hurt anyone. And I can't imagine her trying to take him from you, any more than I would have."

Sam gave her a wry look. "That remark I made at Shanna and Kevin's house is going to come back to haunt me, isn't it?"

"It could come up from time to time," she said, "when you need to be reminded about leaping to conclusions. Of course, I was guilty of the same thing where you were concerned. We're okay now that we know each other better."

"You think this thing with Susie will eventually work itself out?"

Carrie thought about that. She honestly couldn't say. If Susie focused all her attention on Bobby and continued to refuse to consider another adoption, how healthy would that be? That was a question for someone a whole lot wiser than she was.

"Eventually," she said, though with more hope than conviction.

"Maybe I'll just touch base with Mack, see how things are going at the house," Sam said. "It's the first time I've left Bobby with anyone other than you. I'll tell him that, so he doesn't jump to the conclusion that I don't trust him or Susie. Or figure out that you've filled me in."

"Good idea."

Sam made the call, looking more and more relieved as he listened to Mack's responses. "If you're sure things are under control. I might stick around the pub and have dinner with Carrie. Do you mind?" He listened intently, then smiled. "Sure, order a pizza. That's Bobby's favorite, so that would be great. Thanks."

He disconnected the call, put the phone back in his pocket, then focused on her. "Looks as if we can finally have that date. Maybe I should be thanking Susie, instead of worrying about her."

"I let you join me," Carrie reminded him. "Nothing was said about dinner or a date."

A sparkle lit Sam's eyes. "Carrie, would you like to have dinner with me? Then I can walk you home after, maybe even steal a kiss at your front door. That seems like a reasonable first date."

"Mighty big plans," she commented.

"A first step," he corrected. "The big plans are for much later."

"And what if I don't kiss on the first date?"

"I'll see if I can change your mind. I can be pretty persuasive when I put my mind to it."

"An interesting challenge. So, what's the time-table for these big plans of yours?"

"I was thinking down the road a day or two at least," he said, chuckling. "But I'm a guy. I'm happy to speed the process along."

Carrie laughed, but she had a little trouble catching her breath. She liked where this seemed to be heading. The old wisdom seemed to be true; the right man sometimes did come along just when a person stopped looking.

Sam's expression sobered. "So, what's the decision? Will you join me for dinner and what-ever comes after?"

"Let's start with dinner and see how it goes."

He reached for her hand and held it. "I think it's going to go very well."

Carrie couldn't seem to stop herself from nod-ding in agreement. For an evening that had started out fraught with tension, it was definitely turning around into something very intriguing.

Sam listened to Carrie going on and on about her plans for the day-care center. Her enthusiasm was contagious. He could envision exactly what it was going to look like when renovations were completed and what the children in her care would be doing every minute of the day.

She stopped for breath. "I'm boring you to tears, aren't I?"

"Absolutely not. It's wonderful to see you so caught up in your plans. You've obviously found your passion. From what you told me when we met, it's something you were struggling with."

"I truly think I have," she said. She glanced at the untouched food on her plate. "Of course, because I've been talking so much, my food's gone cold. How about you? Tell me about your passion, while I eat. Was web design it for you from the very beginning, the thing you knew you were meant to do?"

"Not entirely," Sam admitted. "It was a career I knew I could take anywhere I wanted to live. Whether I have one client like the newspaper or fifty clients all over the world, I can do the work wherever I go."

"So it's more a convenience than a passion?"

"That probably makes it sound a little more calculating than I meant to. I love the work. I always enjoyed art and design and the tech stuff came easily to me. The web side of design just seemed to be a natural fit for my passion and for my desire to be footloose and travel. And these days there's a huge demand for what I do. Newspapers are in transition. Eventually they'll be mostly online. Everybody wants an online presence for their business."

"There are two parts of that we should talk about," Carrie said. "You'll have to get to know my stepfather better. His first love was graphic design. His father tried to steer him into running the community bank here in town, but Trace balked and focused on his design career. He gets to work from home, so he was there for Caitlyn and me when Mom couldn't be. The same with Patrick, though Trace and Mom claim my brother is not the little angel my twin and I were."

Sam laughed "They say that or you do?"

"Okay, that's my interpretation."

"And the other thing we need to discuss?"

"Your desire to wander. What's that about?"

"I've never analyzed it, but I suppose it's because my mom had always wanted to see the world. She must have had a hundred travel memoirs in the house and read them to us instead of storybooks. I was fascinated by those books."

"Did she ever get to see all of those exotic places?"

Sam shook his head, surprised by the depth of sorrow that washed over him. "She had gotten pregnant with Laurel, married my father and spent her life stuck in a tiny three-bedroom house in the suburbs of Cleveland. The longest trip she ever took was down to Columbus, and that was only because my dad wanted to go tailgating with his buddies and their wives at an Ohio State football game."

"No girlfriends she could travel with?" Carrie asked.

"No friends of her own," Sam corrected. "In hindsight, I think my dad abused her psychologically by isolating her and controlling her. She didn't have the strength to walk away, though there were some pretty intense fights from time to time. Laurel tried to protect me from all that, but I heard way too much."

"Kids usually do," Carrie said.

"In some crazy way I wanted to shape my life to do the things my mother hadn't been able to do. I always intended to take her along to the places she'd dreamed about, but by the time I could have done that, she was too sick to travel. At the end, I sat beside her bed and told her stories and showed her pictures from my travels."

"Oh, Sam," Carrie whispered, her eyes damp with tears.

He tried to shrug off the memories. "Anyway, there will be no more trips for me for the foreseeable future now that I have Bobby in my life."

"Are you afraid you'll resent him because of

that?" Carrie asked with surprising insight. "Do you somehow see this as a repeat of what happened to your mom?"

"I was worried about that when all of this first hit me, but you know what? I'm starting to realize being a parent is its own kind of adventure. And I'm very glad that if it had to happen, it happened after I'd moved to Chesapeake Shores. I wasn't thinking about it when I took the job, but now I truly appreciate what a great place this will be to raise a child."

He leveled a look into her eyes. "And then there's you. I certainly can't regret anything that has brought me closer to you. If you hadn't jumped all over me for leaving Bobby in the car the night we got back to town, who knows how long it might have been before we crossed paths."

She smiled. "You think that was fate?"

"I'm not sure how I feel about fate or destiny or whatever you want to call it. What about you? Any thoughts about whether there's one right person for all of us?"

"I've grown up in a family of romantics," Carrie told him. "How could I not believe that? I just spent a long time looking for my soul mate in all the wrong places."

"Any regrets about that?"

Her expression turned thoughtful. "You know what? Not really. I think I learned something from all of my mistakes, even miserable Marc. I figured out what I don't need in my life." She met his gaze. "And lately I've started discovering what I do need."

"A shift in priorities?"

"No, just a sudden awareness that there's more than one way to approach those priorities. Family will always be first for me, with a fulfilling career a close second. If you study my family, you'll discover that most of them have achieved a balance between those two things, even if it took a few of them a little longer than it did others."

"I never gave much thought to having a family," Sam said, drawing a shocked look. "I know that must be strange to an O'Brien, but my family was very different from yours. Laurel and I were fairly close as kids, but we've had our differences as adults."

"But your sister left you custody of her son. That must mean she trusted you."

"There was no one else," he replied simply. "I was the default guy. I know she believed I'd do right by Bobby. So did Robert. But if they'd had any other viable option, they probably would have taken it. Robert's parents are around, but they're older and a little too set in their ways for the chaos a kid Bobby's age would bring into their lives. They did talk to a lawyer about fighting me for custody, but I think they were relieved when he advised them they were unlikely to win."

"Will they continue to be a part of his life?"

"Of course, if they want to be. I'll take him to visit or invite them here. I can see the value of Bobby knowing I'm not the only family he has."

"Now that you've had some time, how do you feel about becoming a dad overnight?"

"It's an adjustment," he admitted. "I was a pretty carefree guy. Now I have no choice but to think of someone other than myself. Fortunately Bobby's a terrific kid. I think we're going to do okay. It may be rocky from time to time while I find my way, but there's nothing like a kid to keep a guy honest."

He smiled at her. "You've been doing that, too. I don't want to let either of you down. That's a scary prospect, because I know sooner or later I will. Until this happened, I'd led a pretty selfish existence, doing whatever appealed to me, taking off at a moment's notice if something that sounded exciting came up. Those days are done."

He was surprised to realize that he no longer regretted that the way he had when he'd first grasped all the changes he was going to have to make to life as he'd known it.

"As long as you're doing the best you can, you won't let either of us down," Carrie assured him.

Her confidence, especially given their rocky first meeting, meant a lot. "I've already made mistakes, as you can attest."

"Find me one human being who hasn't," she countered. "Or one parent who hasn't made a boatload of them. My grandparents, the ultimate role models for a family matriarch and patriarch now, made some doozies. I'll fill you in sometime. Mistakes are part of life. It's what you do to fix things that really matters."

"I'm going to remind you of that next time you're scolding me for the error of my ways."

"I vowed to give you gentle advice, not scoldings, remember?"

Sam touched her hand to make sure he had her full attention. "I think I might miss the fire in your eyes when you're telling me I've gotten it all wrong."

She glanced up at his words and he met her gaze.

"There's something about a redhead with a full head of steam that gets to me," he said. "Makes me want to discover what else she might be so passionate about."

"I guess we'll see, won't we?" she said, a telling hitch in her voice.

For the first time since they'd begun this dance, Sam was starting to believe they might get the steps just right.

"This house is amazing," Lucy enthused as she walked from room to room in the property Carrie was hoping to turn into her day-care center.

"Lucy's right," Julie added. "The open concept is very workable for keeping an eye on the kids from anyplace you happen to be, yet it's easily divided into activity areas."

"Then you think it will work?" Carrie said, excited by their enthusiasm. She'd been holding her breath awaiting their reaction. If they approved, she was ready to move forward first thing Monday morning. Connor was on standby to close the deal. She knew even then she'd be weeks, if not months, away from opening, but owning the right property would make the dream feel real. She'd have something concrete to show for all the steps she'd taken in this new direction.

"Not a doubt in my mind," Julie said. She handed over a few pages from a notebook she'd been writing in since she'd arrived. "Notes on things you'll need to address to bring it up to code for a day-care center. An inspector might have more, but this should cover most of it. When are you thinking of opening?"

"As soon as I can take care of this list and get all the licenses and approvals I need."

"That could take a while," Julie cautioned. "Bureaucracy doesn't move quickly."

"I know. My cousin's a lawyer. He's warned me not to get ahead of myself."

"And I imagine you'll have your grandfather's help with the renovations?" Julie said.

Carrie chuckled. "Yes, but not just because he's an outstanding architect and has years of construction experience."

"Then why?" Lucy asked, regarding her curiously.

"It will keep him focused on this, instead of my social life," Carrie said candidly.

Lucy's expression brightened. "Tell us more!"

"Stop being nosy," Julie chided her daughter, then grinned. "Unless of course you'd like to share, Carrie. It's been so long since I've been on a date I can barely remember what it was like. I yearn to live vicariously, and Lucy is pretty tight-lipped about sharing any details about the men in her life. She hasn't brought one to the house to meet me in years."

"Because you interrogate them," Lucy grumbled, though her eyes were twinkling.

"Been there, done that," Carrie said.

"So, is the father of that little boy who came to the center with you part of the social-life equation?" Julie asked.

"Now who's being nosy?" Lucy teased.

Carrie laughed. "Let me take you on a tour of the town, then I'll fill you in over lunch. There's not much to tell, though."

Though after dinner the other night, there were a few additional details. Those she thought she probably ought to keep to herself for now. To her surprise and delight, it turned out that Sam had the whole kissing thing down pat. It had taken every ounce of her willpower not to drag him inside to find out what else he'd mastered!

She caught Lucy nudging her mom.

"Carrie's blushing. Did you notice?"

Julie laughed. "I noticed. Maybe we should skip the tour and go straight to lunch."

"Not a chance," Carrie said, chuckling. "I want to show off Chesapeake Shores."

An hour later they'd had a condensed tour of the town and were seated at a waterfront table on the outside deck at Brady's.

"This is a fantastic little town," Julie said as she drank her iced tea. "I can see why you love it. I can't imagine why I haven't driven over this way in so long."

"Well, this may be the first time, but it definitely won't be the last," Lucy said. "Mom, I think we should look for a house. The commute to the center wouldn't be that awful and I've seen some very attractive men in town."

"I'm too old to be looking for a man," Julie said. "But you are right about the town. I can almost imagine how relaxing it would be to come home to a place like this after a tough day. I could see myself sitting out here with a glass of wine and unwinding."

"My cousin Luke has a pub that's great for unwinding and spending time hanging out with locals. Sally's Café has its own crowd in the mornings and on weekends, especially when it's not tourist season," Carrie said. "You really should consider it, Julie. I love it because it's been home for most of my life, but I've lived in a lot of other places and, believe me, nothing compares."

"We'll see," Julie said.

"Mom, what's holding you back?" Lucy prodded. "You hate our house. You hate the traffic and how crowded everything's gotten."

"But it is a much longer commute from here," Julie protested, though not very convincingly.

"Mostly on a country road that's not that busy," Carrie said, adding her encouragement to Lucy's. "And you'd get to keep an eye on me, make sure your protégé isn't messing up."

Julie shook her head. "I'm not worried about that. You're going to do just fine."

"Maybe we should back off," Carrie suggested to Lucy. "Give her some time to draw her own conclusions."

"Now there's an intriguing concept," Julie said wryly. "I raised a little bulldozer. When Lucy wants something, she tends to roll right over anyone or anything that gets in her way."

Carrie laughed. "Welcome to my world! I have a whole slew of people in my life exactly like that. If you figure out how to stay out of the way, let me know."

Julie nodded. "I'll add it to those lists I'm passing along to you." She turned her attention to the plate the waiter had just placed in front of her and sighed. "Now I am going to focus on these scallops and savor every single bite. This is so far beyond my usual salad diet I may never leave."

Lucy and Carrie gave each other high fives.

"Mission accomplished," Lucy said triumphantly.

Julie just gave her daughter a long, hard look and kept right on eating.

Carrie envied them the bond they'd formed both as mother and daughter and as coworkers. She was close to her own mom, so she knew how rare it was to view a parent as a person and not just an authority figure. She hoped Bobby and Sam found that sort of relationship one day. Ironically, she couldn't help thinking in some way it might be easier because of how they'd come to be together. The hard part for both of them might be the adjustment to thinking of Sam as the authority person in Bobby's life, rather than the fun uncle who breezed into his life and out again.

One of these days she needed to think about Sam's wandering ways and whether they truly were behind him. Even though he seemed to have accepted his responsibility for Bobby didn't mean the two of them couldn't relocate at the drop of a hat. And where would that leave her? Every time she started to think she was ready to take another risk with her heart, her head jumped in with something just like this to renew her caution.

❧ 17 ❧

Sam didn't have a chance to talk to Mack privately until late on Tuesday after they'd gotten the web edition of the paper online and the print edition to the company that printed it and delivered the bundles of papers to town on Wednesday morning.

Unsure of exactly how to begin, Sam fumbled through a few attempts, then finally settled for saying again how generous Susie had been.

Mack gave him a long look, then sighed heavily. "I know it was too much," he said eventually. "And I appreciate you not calling her on it. Susie's struggling right now."

"I heard about the adoption," Sam said. "I'm sorry, but—"

"But Bobby can't be the substitute for the baby we didn't get," Mack said, completing the thought. "I know that, Sam. But I can't tell you how worried I've been about her. Being around Bobby makes her happy. Don't take that lifeline away from her."

"I wasn't going to," Sam said. "But maybe we should have some boundaries."

"That makes sense," Mack agreed readily. "Do you have something in mind?"

Sam shook his head. "I have no idea what they

ought to be. Maybe that she needs to check with me first before showering him with gifts or making arrangements to spend a little time with him. Do you think she can do those two things without feeling as if she's being cut off from contact with him or that I'm retaliating in some way? Parenting is still brand-new to me, and this particular situation with Susie definitely wasn't one I anticipated."

"Seems to me you're managing just fine," Mack said. "Then again, I didn't exactly have an ideal background to compare it to. I wasn't at all sure I was prepared to be a father." He sighed. "Maybe no one with any sense ever is. You just do the best you can."

"I sure hope that's what it takes," Sam said, "because I wake up every day feeling as if I'm about to fail abysmally."

"And yet you didn't take the easy way out."

"What way was that?"

"You didn't turn Bobby over to his grand-parents. You've said they wanted to fight you for custody. You could have walked away with a clear conscience."

Sam shrugged. "Laurel and Robert chose me. They must have had their reasons. I couldn't let them—or Bobby—down without at least trying. There have been a couple of moments here and there when I've actually thought things will work out okay. Bobby's a great kid."

"He really is," Mack agreed. "You should have heard him with Susie." The words were no sooner out of his mouth, than he heaved a sigh. "About those boundaries, I think what you suggested is perfectly logical. That said, I don't know how much logic enters into anything with my wife these days. I'll do my best to make her see that the boundaries are in Bobby's best interests."

"I'd really appreciate that," Sam told him.

"Under normal conditions, Susie is great with all the kids, but she seems to have created some sort of special attachment to Bobby. Just this morning, she mentioned casually that she wondered who'd be looking after him tonight while you're here. I told her I was sure you'd made arrangements. It took all of my persuasive powers to keep her from calling you with an offer to babysit."

Mack frowned even as he told the story, then asked, "Or would you have welcomed the offer? I feel as if I'm walking a tightrope here."

"I had already made plans for Bobby. He's over at Kevin's." Sam recalled that conversation, then gave Mack a curious look. "I thought Shanna was supposed to be at your house for some family book-club thing that Susie's hosting."

"Susie was ready to cancel that if you needed her," Mack admitted with a grimace. "See what I mean? She's made Bobby a top priority." He studied Sam for a minute, then said a little too casually, "I figured Bobby would be with Carrie."

Sam recognized that there was more to the question—that Mack, like everyone else in the family, was trying to figure out their relationship.

"Carrie's not my designated babysitter," he said, keeping his tone neutral. He might be annoyed by the probing, but it was second nature to O'Briens and anyone connected to them. "She's a good friend. Right now she's trying to get her day care ready to open. She has plenty on her plate with that. She's offered to pitch in when I need her, but I'm not going to take advantage of her."

"Susie seems to think you two are an item." As soon as Mack spoke, he winced. "Listen to me. I'm turning into as bad a gossip as the rest of the town, trying to wheedle information out of you."

At least Mack obviously felt guilty, which allowed Sam to chuckle at his discomfort. "Very little information to wheedle," he said with complete candor. "We're exploring the possibilities and that is the last I intend to say about that." He leveled a look that was intended to make Mack squirm. "Unless your role as my boss extends to my life outside the office."

"Nope. The topic is closed," Mack said. "I should be getting home. Susie wasn't looking forward to this whole book-club gathering. She was convinced the women planned to stage some sort of intervention."

"Are they qualified to do that?" Sam asked, startled.

"Hardly, but it doesn't matter to an O'Brien. When they perceive that one of their own is struggling with anything, they jump on the case. It's a blessing and a curse. Right now, my wife considers it to be a curse. She wants to wallow a bit and, if you ask me, she has a right to. It's not the wallowing that worries me half as much as the manic stuff that involves your nephew. Thanks for trying to overlook that or at least keep it in perspective. I'll do my best to see that it doesn't get out of hand."

Sam nodded. "Fair enough. I am sorry as hell about the whole adoption thing. Here the two of you are so anxious to be parents and I wind up with custody of my nephew. Life sure takes some unexpected twists."

"It does that," Mack agreed. "I've given up on trying to figure out the plan and tried to learn just to go with the flow. Susie's cancer taught me that life's precarious and a smart person makes the most of whatever's he's given."

"Not a bad philosophy," Sam said. It might be one he'd do well to follow himself, instead of questioning every unanticipated twist and turn.

Carrie had papers spread all over her dining-room table and a checklist which seemed to be growing, rather than getting shorter. When her cell phone rang, she answered it with an unmistakable touch of impatience.

Her tone was met by an equally testy question. "Why aren't you at my house?"

Carrie stared at the phone in shock before answering. "Susie?"

"Of course it's me. It's book-club night and everyone else is here and they're all wondering what I've done to offend you. Of course no one has actually said a word, but I can tell by the way they're looking at me. Is that what you wanted, to get the whole family on your side? It's not enough that this great little kid just fell into your life?"

Carrie sighed. "Susie, this is a conversation we probably need to have face-to-face, but certainly not tonight in front of half the family."

"Then you agree there's a problem?"

"I think maybe you've seen one that doesn't exist, at least not from my perspective."

"So now you're saying I'm, what, crazy? Imagining that you're moving in on Sam and Bobby?"

Carrie clung to her patience by a thread. "I'm not discussing this with you, not like this."

Silence greeted her remark. Then she heard what sounded like a sob.

"Susie?" When there was no reply, just more choked sobs, Carrie tried again. "Susie, say something. Are you okay?"

"Of course I'm not okay," Susie said, a note of near hysteria in her voice. "If I were, I wouldn't be acting like this. Carrie, I'm sorry. I truly am. I've gotten into this awful, dark place and I can't seem to drag myself out."

Every bit of anger drained away as Carrie heard the sincerity and fear behind her cousin's words. "I'm coming over," she said quietly.

"No, you were right. This isn't the time to have some sort of confrontation."

"How about just a conversation," Carrie suggested. "Every single person over there tonight loves you and wants to help. *I* want to help, but none of us know what you really need."

"I need a baby of my own, a child I can hold," Susie whispered, a hitch in her voice. "And none of you can give me that."

"Connor desperately wants to help you find that baby," Carrie told her. "You just need to tell him you're ready to try again. Everybody in this family wants you and Mack to find the perfect child."

"I'll take any child. He or she doesn't have to be perfect. Goodness knows, Mack and I have our flaws. Irrational jealousy comes to mind."

"It was irrational," Carrie agreed. "But understandable. Now I'm heading over there. How's the supply of Ben & Jerry's?"

"There were at least six pints by my count," Susie said. "Everyone must have thought I was teetering on the brink."

Carrie laughed. "I'll bring a few more. One pint apiece seems about right on a night like this."

"Thank you."

"It's ice cream. No big deal."

"No, for forgiving my craziness. You have forgiven me, right?"

"Forgiven and forgotten," Carrie promised. That's what she hoped anyone in the family would do for her if she ever went off the deep end.

Sam found Carrie at the café first thing on Wednesday morning, sitting with the usual group of O'Brien women. To his surprise Susie was among them, looking more relaxed than he'd seen her since they'd first met. Maybe that intervention thing they'd supposedly staged had helped, after all.

"Mind if I borrow Carrie?" he inquired, though he honestly didn't expect any objections.

"You don't want to join us?" Bree asked hopefully.

"Yes, do join us," Heather said. "We wouldn't mind observing the dynamics between you two so we could draw our own conclusions. Carrie won't tell us a thing."

Sam laughed. "Good for Carrie." He met her gaze. "Do you mind coming with me?"

"To get away from these meddlers? I'm all yours," she said eagerly.

"Of course you are," Bree commented with satisfaction.

Outside, he studied Carrie's face, smiling at the scattering of freckles across her nose and imagining how those probably irritated her. He couldn't help wondering exactly when the sight of her had started to fill him with such an intense burst of happiness. He'd never thought of himself as lonely or incomplete, but that was before he'd met this woman who made him feel as if he were whole. Add in Bobby, and his life was full in ways he'd never anticipated. It was a little scary, but not so terrifying that he didn't want to stick around to see what came next.

"Okay, you've gotten me away from my family, for which I am profoundly grateful," Carrie said eventually as they headed toward Shore Road. "What's on your mind?"

He regarded her blankly. "Nothing in particular. Why?"

"You realize that makes no sense. You interrupted a get-together, dragged me away, and for what? You have no idea?"

He grinned. "I spotted you inside at Sally's and suddenly felt this need to have you all to myself."

"Really?" she said, sounding surprised, even as a smile seemed to be spreading across her face.

"I can't get enough of you, I guess. Do you mind?"

333

"Since they were about ten seconds away from interrogating me yet again about our relationship, your timing couldn't have been better from my perspective, though I imagine my disappearance just now will only fuel their already overactive imaginations."

"Sorry."

She shrugged it off. "It's what they do."

"How about a cappuccino?" he asked as they turned the corner. "I can get them to go at Panini Bistro and we can sit on one of the benches across the street. Do you have time?"

Carrie nodded. "Sure. Jackson is at the church day care today and I'm not volunteering at Julie's. I have a million and one things to do at my new building, but Grandpa Mick is overseeing that and the less time I spend underfoot, the better. His help comes with too many intrusive questions."

"So I've saved you on several fronts this morning?"

"At least two," she agreed. "Yay, you!"

Yay, indeed, Sam thought. "I'll get the coffees. Why don't you snag a bench before the tourists grab them all?"

When Sam rejoined her, she was staring at her cell phone with a frown on her face.

"Problem?" he asked as he handed over her coffee, then sat next to her.

She looked startled by his return. She quickly

jammed the phone in her purse, the gesture oddly angry. "No," she said tersely.

Sam regarded her in silence and waited.

"Okay, it was a text from Marc," she said.

"The designer jerk," Sam said, drawing a faint smile.

"Couldn't have described him better myself," she said.

"What did he want?"

"He wanted me to return his calls or one of the previous ten texts he's sent overnight."

Sam felt his heartbeat accelerate in something that felt like panic. "Seems to be important."

She drew in a deep breath, then forced a bright smile that didn't fool either one of them. "Not to me." She glanced toward the bay. "It's an absolutely beautiful morning, isn't it?"

The bay, sparkling with morning sunlight, was spread before them. The blue sky was dotted with the merest wisps of white clouds. Ospreys swooped overhead, then headed for impressive nests atop poles that had been erected specifically for that purpose. The town had installed them in an attempt to keep the osprey from choosing these waterfront benches for their nests, as they had one year, forcing the humans to remain at a distance. Bobby had told him about that. Apparently a delighted Davey had filled him in, while explaining that the osprey were protected.

"Beautiful," Sam agreed, though his gaze was on Carrie.

"We're moving into fall. I wonder how many more glorious days we'll have like this," Carrie said, her face turned up to the sun. "When it's like this, I wish I could sit right here all day long."

"Courting sunburn?" Sam teased, touching a fingertip to her nose.

"Enough SPF30 and I can sit here indefinitely," she countered.

"These freckles suggest you've forgotten it a time or two."

"Yes, well, Mom and Gram couldn't always catch me before I got outside," she said with a laugh, then suddenly pulled her cell phone from her purse.

Sam regarded her curiously. "Are you going to respond to that text, after all?"

"Not a chance. You just reminded me to add suntan lotion to my list of supplies for the day care," she said, typing a quick note to herself.

Sam plucked the phone from her grasp and tucked it into his own pocket. "Obviously my mere presence isn't enough to distract you," he murmured.

Her eyes widened. "What did you have in mind?"

"The same thing I've had in mind ever since the first time I did it," he said, moving closer until he could claim her lips.

The kiss was as intoxicating as he'd remembered, maybe even a little more potent. Champagne intoxicating, rather than beer, perhaps. Whatever it was, he couldn't recall a single time in his life when a simple kiss had made him long to leap into something more than bed, something lasting.

When he pulled away, he kept a hand against her cheek in a caress. "Just the way I remembered it from the other night," he said. "Better even."

Carrie smiled. "Is my technique improving?"

"No, you just get more infatuating every time I see you."

"Who knew you had such a way with words? Does Mack know about that? He'll have you writing articles as well as designing the paper, if you're not careful."

Sam chuckled. "Trust me, Mack does not inspire me to wax poetic." He held her gaze. "I really want to kiss you again," he murmured.

"Why don't you?"

"Because I am suddenly very much aware that we are sitting in public in broad daylight just across the street from shops owned by your grandmother and Heather, as well as Luke's pub."

"Good point," she said, though her sigh suggested she was as disappointed by that as he was.

"Maybe we could continue this later, someplace a little more private. I can't abandon Bobby again tonight, but you could come over for dinner.

Maybe hang out till after he's asleep. Any interest?"

"What's for dinner?"

"I think I can manage burgers on the grill and a salad."

"Why don't I bring dessert? I'm thinking vanilla ice cream and some peaches. I found some at the farm stand yesterday, last of the season more than likely."

"Bobby will love that."

She regarded him with surprise. "Not you?"

Sam winked at her. "I have a much more grown-up dessert in mind."

Carrie laughed. "Then you're in for a big disappointment. Not with Bobby in the house."

He realized she was dead serious and sighed. "You're right. We don't want him to catch us in the act and start getting ideas."

"Exactly," she said. "You're starting to think like a parent."

"But I still want some of the perks of being a bachelor," he told her, leaning in to steal one more quick kiss meant to hold him.

"Patience," she said. "I'm not going anywhere."

She'd told Sam that before, but he certainly didn't mind the reassurance. Because despite her enthusiasm for her day-care project and her avowed love for Chesapeake Shores, he couldn't help wondering if someday down the road the allure of Paris or Italy would suddenly become too strong to resist. And with Marc Reynolds

338

seemingly trying to get back into the picture, it was a concern he couldn't seem to shake. Was Carrie as immune to the man as she seemed to be? Or did he have the power to hurt her yet again?

Carrie had been surprised by how much red tape was involved with getting herself licensed to open a day-care facility. She probably shouldn't have been, given all the instructions Julie had given her. Maybe it was the fact that in so many ways being an O'Brien made life easy. Her grandfather was usually able to make hurdles disappear. Not this time. She was dealing with a new, by-the-books bureaucracy, and she relished the challenge.

Between the paperwork, doing the renovations she felt were necessary to create a bright comfortable space for the kids, interviewing for help and doing background checks on her top candidates, keeping up with her online classes and still volunteering at Julie's, she had precious little time for babysitting her nephew or the other O'Brien children who'd been coming around for the past few months. The few stolen moments she'd shared with Sam on the waterfront this morning had been a rare break from sending off forms, answering endless questions, establishing an account at the bank and going through catalogs for supplies. Everything seemed to take a lot longer than she'd anticipated.

She was in the small office she'd carved out for herself in what had once been a walk-in coat closet and had just hung up the telephone after dealing with yet another request for information she thought she'd already supplied—in triplicate, in fact—when Connor wandered in to check on the progress. Since his law office was just up the street, his visits were pretty much daily. So were those of almost everyone else in the family, especially since her grandfather had assigned one of his crews to do the renovations she wanted.

Today, though, she suddenly realized something was different. Connor had an envelope in his hand and a cat-that-swallowed-the-canary spark in his eyes.

"Is that it?" she asked excitedly. "Am I legal?"

"Mostly," he told her, handing over the paperwork. "There will be a final inspection once all the work in here is finished, but you've passed all the screenings. The state of Maryland has deemed you fit to be trusted with children."

She grinned at him. "You sound surprised. I told you I was never in any legal trouble. I might have gotten into a lot of mischief over the years, but I never crossed a line. And unlike some people we could probably name, Grandpa Mick never had to step in and clean up any of my messes."

Connor scowled at her. "Hey, I had one speeding ticket when I was just a teenager. That's it."

Her grin spread. "But it was in Grandpa Mick's prized classic Mustang, which you did not have permission to drive, as I recall."

Her uncle's scowl deepened. "My mother obviously has a big mouth. She was supposed to take that secret to her grave."

Carrie laughed. "Afraid not. We all heard the story. Grandma Megan seems to enjoy sharing it, especially when she knows it will get Grandpa Mick all riled up."

"Let's stay focused on business, not my misdeeds, okay?" Connor grumbled in a way that reminded her of just how much he'd matured from those rebellious teen years.

"Fine with me," Carrie said, fighting for a more serious expression.

"When were you hoping to open?"

"Grandpa Mick says his crews will be out of here by the end of September. All the furniture and supplies are scheduled for the following week. I'd say we should be ready for that final inspection by mid-October, or November 1 at the latest. I've already had inquiries from a few people about whether I'll be open in time to accept kids for the fall school holiday periods that parents can't always get off from work. And I have a half dozen names of families looking for a permanent place for their toddlers that's closer to home."

"You haven't guaranteed anything, have you?"

"Of course not. I've told them I'll call the

minute I have all the necessary approvals. I want to be careful not to take on too many children at once. With me being new to this and a new staff, I can't risk us being overwhelmed and making mistakes. To be honest, I'd be happy enough to get open by the end of the year once I've finished my classes and gotten in a few more weeks of working with Julie."

Connor nodded approvingly. "Smart thinking."

Carrie couldn't seem to stop a smile from spreading across her face. "Connor, this is really going to happen, isn't it?"

"Looks that way." His expression suddenly turned worried. "You aren't going to panic and change your mind, are you?"

This was about the tenth member of the family to ask her the same question this week alone. She was out of patience with it. "How flighty do you all think I am? How many times were you asked if you were sure about going to law school? I doubt anybody questioned my mom about going to work on Wall Street."

Connor gave her an incredulous look. "Are you kidding me? Even after I'd graduated from law school and gone to work in Baltimore, the family was all over me for choosing divorce law. Nobody was very happy with me until I'd moved my practice down here. And your mom chose to work in New York initially. That caused its own sort of ruckus. Let's not forget Kevin deciding to go to work for Uncle Thomas, which set my dad's teeth on edge. Or Bree going off to Chicago to be a playwright, which is not exactly a stable profession. This family is incredibly supportive, but they don't hesitate to nudge and maneuver and speak their minds until we're living according to some grand plan Dad has in mind for us."

Carrie winced. "I see your point. This just seems really personal."

He laughed. "Well, of course it does. It's focused on you. Just remember that in your case, they're not just asking because they think you made the wrong choice. They're asking to give you an opening to change your mind. O'Briens may push and prod to get any of us to go in a particular direction, but the bottom line is all they really care about is whether we're happy. It took me a while to grasp that myself, especially since living in Chesapeake Shores once Mom came back was not part of my life plan."

She studied him. "No regrets now, though, right?"

"Not a one. And all of my issues with Mom leaving years ago are in the past. I may never totally understand her choices, but I've stopped reacting like an immature kid. She's actually a pretty great person and she's really pulled through for Heather and me more than once."

Carrie knew how hard her grandmother had worked to make amends for leaving Grandpa

Mick and moving to New York, leaving her children to be raised by him and Nell. Everyone in the family had finally made peace with that difficult time.

"I'm glad you've moved on," she told her uncle.

He shrugged. "It was past time. How about you? Any regrets about not going back to Europe or New York?"

She shook her head without a moment's hesitation. "I *know* this is right. I *know* it's going to make me happy," Carrie said with certainty. She was convinced enough to go right on ignoring all of Marc's texts and voice mails.

"Then give the family six months, show them how deliriously content you are, and they'll all be claiming it was their idea," Connor said.

Carrie laughed. He was right. Taking credit, even for decisions they'd discouraged that turned out okay, was definitely the O'Brien way.

❧ 18 ❧

Though he'd had no experience dealing with them, Sam had heard plenty about the terrible twos when Bobby had been that age. Laurel had called from time to time in tears, because her stubborn son seemed to know only one word, *no,* said emphatically in response to anything she asked of him.

Tonight it seemed Bobby had reverted to those days or something very close to it. When Sam asked him to pick up his new toys that had been left scattered all over the living room floor, Bobby scowled at him, turned his back and ran from the room. Since it was the first time he'd been openly defiant in quite this way, Sam was shocked.

"Young man, come back here," he commanded in what he thought sounded like a sufficiently parental tone.

Bobby kept right on running, his footsteps echoing on the hardwood floors. When he evidently reached his room, he slammed that door behind him.

Sam stared after him in dismay. Working to keep a rein on his own temper, he took a deep breath, walked down the hall and opened the door. He knew he needed to get an explanation before tackling the boy's intolerable behavior. This was the first time he'd felt the need to establish some basic ground rules. It was a reminder that Bobby, for all of his good traits, was still a little boy in need of the kind of guidance Sam wasn't sure he was qualified to give.

Bobby was sitting on the floor with his new Transformers, listlessly moving them around. He didn't give Sam so much as a glance. Sam wanted to scream at the kid and remind him who was the boss around here, but something in the dejected set of Bobby's shoulders kept him from doing that. Instead, he sat on the floor next to him.

After several minutes of continued silence, which gave both of them time to calm down and think, he asked, "Okay, pal, talk to me. What's up?"

Bobby continued to pretend Sam wasn't even there. When Sam touched his shoulder, Bobby jerked away. Even though Sam reminded himself that the kid was in some sort of turmoil, he was surprised by just how much the rejection hurt.

"How was school today?" Sam asked, searching for some logical explanation for Bobby's mood. A bad day at school was the first thing that came to mind. He could recall a few of those in his own past.

He drew a shrug in response, which was better than being ignored, but not exactly illuminating.

"Did you have a test?" Sam persisted. Failing a spelling test or getting a math problem wrong in front of the class might seem devastating to a kid Bobby's age. Or did they even have those sort of tests in first grade? It had been a very long time since Sam had started school.

Sam got nothing in response.

"At least recess must have been fun. Or did you fall down? Skin your knee?"

Again, nothing. Sam bit back a sigh.

"Did your teacher read to you today? I know you like that."

Bobby's scowl deepened and tears leaked out and trickled down his cheeks. "It's not about school, okay?" he blurted finally. "Leave me alone."

Sam inched closer, but didn't reach out. "Sorry, buddy. I can't do that. I know you're upset about something. Remember what we decided when you first came to town?"

Bobby sniffed, but kept his gaze downcast. "What?"

"That we're a team," Sam reminded him. "That means I'm your backup, so if something or somebody makes you feel bad, I'm here to help."

"You can't fix this," Bobby said wearily, clearly resigned to suffering alone.

His attitude made Sam want to cry. No six-year-old should be feeling this defeated. "Fix what? Maybe I can't, but you have to tell me so I can at least try."

Bobby gave him a what's-the-point look, but when Sam continued to wait for a reply, he finally said, "Grandma called."

"That's nice," Sam said carefully. Usually calls from his grandparents perked up Bobby's spirits, but clearly there had been something different about this one. "What did she have to say?"

The forlorn expression that washed over Bobby's face once more made Sam want to cry.

"She said it was Daddy's birthday and asked me what I was doing to celebrate." He turned to

Sam, tears streaming now. "But I wasn't doing any-thing, because I forgot."

This time when Sam reached out to gather Bobby close, the boy practically threw himself into Sam's arms, his shoulders shaking as he sobbed. Sam felt like joining in, letting go of the emotions that he'd kept mostly buried ever since the accident. Instead, he focused on Bobby, who was clinging to him as if he was afraid to let go.

"It's okay," he soothed, even though he knew nothing would ever be totally okay again.

Sam wished Robert's mother were here so he could give her a piece of his mind, but rationally he knew she'd only reached out to her grandson as a way to feel connected to her son on a day she could no longer celebrate with Robert. She hadn't meant to make Bobby feel bad for forgetting. Heck, even she probably knew that Bobby could barely remember where he'd kicked off his shoes the night before, much less important dates.

"I didn't mean to forget," Bobby whispered brokenly. "It doesn't mean I've forgotten my dad."

"I know, pal. And, believe me, your grand-mother's not mad at you. She's probably just feeling a little sad today. You know, the way you feel sometimes when you think about your dad or your mom and realize you can't see them."

His cheeks still damp, Bobby gave Sam a hopeful look. "Could we do something for Dad's birthday? It's not too late, is it?"

"It is definitely not too late," Sam said, making a spontaneous decision to make this right. This, thank goodness, was the sort of problem he could handle. "Carrie's coming over in a little while. She's bringing peaches and ice cream for dessert. Why don't I ask if she can pick up some cupcakes and some birthday candles?"

The spark returned to Bobby's eyes. "Sometimes people have balloons and let them float into the air, so people can see them from heaven. Could we do that, too?"

"I'll check to see if anyplace is still open that sells balloons with helium in them," Sam promised. "How does that sound? And we'll take pictures with the cell phone and send them to your grandmother. I think it will make her smile to see how we've celebrated your dad's birthday."

"All right!" Bobby enthused with the fist pump Sam had concluded always accompanied his solid approval for any plan.

"Now, while I call Carrie and get the ball rolling for this birthday celebration, why don't you pick up those toys so she doesn't trip on them and fall on her face when she walks in the door?"

"Okay," Bobby said agreeably and raced off.

Sam stayed where he was and drew in a deep breath. He'd averted one crisis, but how many hundreds more would there be like it? Was he really up to providing the support that Bobby needed?

"No choice," he reminded himself firmly. "We're a team."

That was the promise he'd made and he had every intention of doing whatever was required to keep it. As crazy as it seemed, it appeared he and his nephew would be growing up together.

When Sam told Carrie what had happened, she added a few extra things to her shopping list. Fortunately Ethel's Emporium was always well stocked with birthday supplies. She found balloons, a banner that spelled out Happy Birthday in colorful letters along with birthday paper plates, matching bowls for ice cream and napkins. She even found a silly pair of sunglasses for Bobby that had birthday candles and wishes on the frame.

"Did I miss a birthday?" Ethel asked. "I usually know when one's coming up because half your family is in here buying up most of my stock."

"Long story," Carrie said. "But it's not for an O'Brien this time."

"I imagine there are going to be quite a few birthday parties in your future," Ethel said, backing off from her natural tendency to ask too many questions. "Seems to me a day care will probably be having parties on a regular basis."

Carrie regarded Ethel with surprise as she recognized the validity of her statement, then immediately dug in her purse for her cell phone.

She added another note to her long to-do list, then met Ethel's curious gaze. "Adding a reminder," she explained. "Do I need to find a supplier or could we work something out?"

Ethel beamed at her. "I wasn't angling to make a sale, but I'm happy to help out. I'll get you anything you need and give you a proper discount, too. Your family practically keeps me in business. I can do this to return the favor."

"I know we shop in here a lot, but it's the tourists who keep this town afloat economically," Carrie said. "I've seen for myself how many bags they carry out of here on any given day."

"On any given *summer* day," Ethel corrected, then paused, her expression thoughtful as she apparently considered her business trends. "Okay, and maybe in the spring and fall, but it's the locals who see to it I make it through the winter. I'm not likely to forget that. It helps that your granddaddy is in here most every day buying a big sack of penny candy for all the kids he spoils."

Carrie laughed. "Cait and I were the first beneficiaries of that. Between him and Trace, it's a wonder our teeth didn't rot."

"Well, you and your twin still have those pretty smiles, so it didn't do either of you any harm. I imagine the other grandchildren and great-grandchildren will do just fine with all that sugar, too." She put Carrie's purchases into a bag, then tied a half dozen ribbons around her wrist to keep the balloons from sailing away.

"Have a good time tonight," Ethel called after her.

Ethel's words lingered as Carrie left the store. She thought of what Sam had in mind for dessert. Maybe they wouldn't quite get to that, given their pint-size chaperone, but the appetizer leading up to it promised to be superb.

Tears forgotten, Bobby was bouncing with excitement by the time Carrie arrived on their doorstep laden down with bags. To Bobby's unmistakable delight, she had a bunch of colorful balloons on long, matching ribbons.

"You'd better tie these to the back of a chair or something," she advised Sam when she handed them over. "Otherwise, they'll be on the ceiling when it comes time to release them." She grinned at Bobby. "Is that what you had in mind—letting them go, so they'd float into the sky where your dad can see them?"

Bobby nodded. "Won't that be cool?"

"It will be amazing." She brushed his hair back from his forehead, the tender gesture reminding Sam that Bobby was in need of a haircut, something else he'd forgotten about. "And you're so sweet to have thought of it."

Sam bit back a chuckle as Bobby made an exaggerated gagging sound.

"Not sweet?" Carrie asked innocently. "How about awesome? Incredible? Stupendous?"

Bobby's expression faltered at the last suggestion. "I don't know what that one means."

"It means amazing."

His smile came back. "Cool."

"Let's see what else we have here for the party," Sam said as he started poking through the bags. "Cupcakes with chocolate frosting."

"The very best kind," Bobby said. "Daddy loved chocolate. That's what he always wanted for his birthday."

Carrie studied him. "Is chocolate okay for you, too?"

"I *love* chocolate," he confirmed.

She nodded with evident satisfaction. "I had a feeling about that."

"Candles, plates, and what's this?" Sam drew a pair of brightly colored birthday sunglasses from the bag. "Who's wearing these? Not me, I hope," he said, even as he put them on.

Bobby doubled over with giggles. "You look silly."

Carrie smiled. "I think they make you look very handsome. Not every guy is man enough to carry off that style."

Sam felt his heart flip over just a little at the teasing. "And you, Ms. Fashion Expert, think I am?" he asked, holding her gaze.

"Definitely."

Something warm and almost tangible shimmered in the air between them until Bobby cut in impatiently.

"I think I should get to wear the glasses," he said.

Sam feigned reluctance as he removed them. "I suppose since this party is for your dad, you probably should get to wear the glasses, but it's going to be really hard for me to part with them."

Bobby looked as if he weren't quite sure if Sam was serious. Eventually he seemed to conclude he might be. "You can have them back when the party's over."

"Thanks, pal," Sam said. "Now let's get this party started before it gets dark out. Bobby, help Carrie put the ice cream in the freezer, so we don't wind up eating vanilla soup."

"Yuck!" Bobby said, grabbing her hand and pulling her toward the kitchen.

As they passed close by, Sam leaned toward her and whispered, "I am really, really looking forward to dessert."

She gave him a bland look, even though her eyes were twinkling. "I intend to savor every bite of the main course."

Bobby gave the two of them an odd look. "I want everything," he declared.

"Then get that ice cream put away and let's get the grill fired up for the burgers. The buttered corn is ready to go on, too. The guy at the farm stand says it's about the last of the Silver Queen variety for this year. Bring the salad with you when you come out. Bottles of dressing are in the door of the fridge."

Twenty minutes later Sam and Carrie were eating cheeseburgers with thick slices of tomato, while Bobby ate a hot dog, a last-minute substitution in the menu. Sam had cut the grilled cobs of corn into manageable, sweetly delicious bite-size sections.

"Best burger I've had all summer," Carrie declared.

"I thought your family had big barbecues all the time," Sam said. "Or is that just wishful thinking on my part?"

"Oh, no. Grandpa Mick considers himself king of the grill. He's in his glory at our annual Fourth of July celebration, the biggest family event of the year aside from Christmas and Thanksgiving. Unfortunately, he's easily distracted, so we sometimes get very, very well-done hamburgers, and that's being kind." She took another bite of her cheeseburger, closed her eyes and sighed. "These, however, are perfect."

"Amazing, considering how easily you can distract me," Sam said.

"That's why I stayed busy inside for so long," Carrie claimed, grinning. "If you think about it, I did not appear until you'd put these burgers onto their buns."

"So we owe the success of my cooking to your forethought and consideration?" he asked, laughing.

She nodded solemnly. "I think so."

"When are we gonna have cupcakes and ice cream?" Bobby asked, his mouth full of hot dog.

"When you finish eating," Sam told him. "Swallow, please, before you speak."

"Oh, yeah," Bobby said, then made a show of chewing. He put the rest of the hot dog on his plate. "I'm done."

Carrie stood up. "Okay, then. Ice cream and cupcakes coming up."

"I'll help you get them," Sam said, standing to follow her.

Inside, he moved close, turned her around and tilted her chin, then claimed her lips. "I've been wanting to do that since you got here," he said, even as he reluctantly took a step back. "But that's probably going to have to hold me. Given Bobby's impatience, he could walk in here any second."

"Good thinking," Carrie said. "But just so you know, it's been on my mind, too."

"That's encouraging." When she turned and would have reached out to open the freezer door, he put his hand over hers. "Carrie, are we crazy?"

"What do you mean?"

"You're in the middle of this life-altering career change. I'm an overnight single dad. Are either of us in any position to make our lives more complicated?"

"I don't know," she said softly. "But I know what my grandmother would say."

"What's that?"

"That love doesn't always come along when it's convenient." No sooner had the words left her lips than she blushed. "Not that we're talking about love, of course. This is lust, right? That's all it is."

She sounded so desperate, Sam barely resisted laughing. "Are you asking me or telling me?"

"I honestly don't know. How about you? What do you think is going on?"

Before Sam could answer, Bobby burst into the kitchen. "What's taking so long?"

Sam drew in a deep breath. "We'll be there in a minute. Why don't you get the balloons from the dining room. Hang on tight, though, and I'll tie them to something outside as soon as I get there."

"Hurry up!" Bobby commanded excitedly. "It's gonna be too dark to see 'em float away pretty soon."

As he ran off, Sam once again turned Carrie to face him. "To be continued," he assured her, then touched her cheek with a quick caress. "That's a promise."

"Agreed."

Bobby chose that moment to race back through, the balloons clutched tightly in his hand. Sam and

Carrie followed with bowls, plates, ice cream, cupcakes and candles. Sam pulled out his cell phone, ready to record the impromptu party.

As Bobby had reminded them, the sun was sinking toward the horizon in a final burst of color. Carrie quickly lit the candles on the cupcakes and they all made wishes and blew them out, then Bobby solemnly released the balloons into the air.

"Happy birthday, Dad!" he said, his head tilted up to follow the path of the balloons as they drifted away, bright spots of red, blue, green and purple dotting the last streaks of orange-tinted sky.

Carrie started singing "Happy Birthday" and Bobby and Sam chimed in. Nearly overwhelmed by the sweet poignance of the moment, Sam recorded it all with his cell phone, then shut it off as the final notes of the song and the last balloon drifted away on the evening breeze.

"That was the best birthday party ever!" Carrie said, giving Bobby's shoulder a squeeze. "I know your dad is so happy you thought of it."

"I miss him," Bobby whispered, then reached out for Sam's hand. "But now I have you."

"That's right," Sam said, his voice oddly choked. "Now you have me."

For better or worse. And every single day, he intended to pray like crazy that it would be for the best for this little boy who'd lost so much.

• • •

The call from the school the morning after the birthday celebration caught Sam completely off guard. He was up to his eyeballs with trying to correct a serious glitch on the paper's website when the counselor called to tell him Bobby had been in a fight on the playground. He'd gotten a split lip, which the school nurse thought might need stitches.

"What's wrong?" Mack asked when he hung up the phone, obviously shaken.

Sam filled him in. "I can't imagine Bobby in a fight. I have to go. He needs to see a doctor."

"Go," Mack said at once.

"Or I could get him," Susie offered. She had brought in lunch for them since correcting the tech problem had both Mack and Sam tearing their hair out. Sam had discovered that Susie was convinced that Mack forgot to eat far too often. "Just call the school back and tell them I have permission to pick him up, then call Noah's office and tell them it's okay to treat him. I'll bring him by here after that, so you can see for yourself how he's doing."

Sam was sorely tempted to let her go. "I don't know . . ." He hesitated, thinking of the boundaries that had barely been put into place. Relying on Susie, even in an emergency like this one, seemed risky. Still, this web problem needed to be resolved.

Susie gave him a look that was almost pleading. "Please, let me do this, Sam. Bobby probably needs a mom's touch right now."

Alarmed by her choice of words, Sam glanced at Mack, who gave a subtle shake of his head. That was enough to convince him his instinct to do this himself was right.

"I've got it," he said, standing up. "Thanks for the offer, Susie, but he's bound to be scared. Besides, I need to get to the bottom of what the fight was about in the first place."

Susie looked as if she was about to protest, but Mack reached for her hand and gave her a pointed look.

"Go," Mack told him.

"I'll be back as soon as I can," Sam promised. "Here are a couple of things you might try while I'm gone. I think we were getting close to fixing the problem."

"Don't worry about it. Focus on what Bobby needs," Mack said.

Sam had a hunch this was yet another of those tests of parenthood, and for just a minute there, he'd almost failed it.

Mack steeled himself for a fight with his wife as Sam left the newspaper office.

"Why did you do that?" Susie immediately demanded. "I could have taken Bobby to the doctor."

"Of course you could have," Mack agreed reasonably. "But it wasn't your place."

"A friend can't step in to help?"

Mack sighed. "Sweetheart, if I thought it was nothing more than a friendly gesture, I'd have gone along with it, but it was more than that and we both know it. So does Sam."

Susie scowled at him. "Such as?"

"You said it yourself. You thought Bobby needed a mother's touch. You're not his mother."

"I *know* that."

Mack held her gaze and this time he knew he could no longer dance around the issue in an attempt to protect his wife's feelings. "Do you really? I've seen how you are with Bobby. I've seen the longing in your eyes. I have to wonder sometimes if you're not hoping Sam will decide being a dad is too much trouble, so we can step in."

"That's a terrible thing to say!" she said, but she was trembling and the sad look in her eyes told the real story.

"Can you deny it?" Mack asked gently.

He saw how much she wanted to, but Susie never had been very good at lying, even to herself.

"Okay, no, I can't deny it," she conceded wearily. "On some awful, selfish level, I think that child deserves two parents who would love and nourish him the way we could."

"Sam's doing his best. And today is a chance

for him to take one more step along the difficult learning curve of being a parent. You might have been able to handle the situation, but in the end, Sam has to fill the role of Bobby's dad and we need to give him that chance."

Tears spilled down Susie's cheeks. "You're right. I know you are."

Mack stood up and closed the door to his office, then pulled his wife onto his lap. "Suze, I know how badly you want a child," he said, holding her tight and brushing the tears from her cheeks. "I want that for you, for us. And it will happen when the time is right. If I could make it happen today, I would."

"I know," she whispered, resting her head on his shoulder. "I'm sorry I get so crazy. And I'm sorry I keep doing things that necessitate my apologizing to you, to Carrie, to practically everyone in my family. Sometimes I think this is the only thing in my entire life that matters, even though when I'm rational I recognize that I have so much to be thankful for." She gazed into Sam's eyes with regret. "I'm sorry if I make you feel as if you don't matter enough."

"Come on, sweetheart," Mack chided. "It's not about me. I know that."

She sighed heavily. "I hope so, because I do love you more than anything."

"And we are going to get through this," he said, praying it was a promise he could keep.

❧ 19 ❧

Sam found Bobby in the nurse's office, holding a bandage to his lip, a bruise already forming under his eye.

"Hey, buddy," Sam said, sitting down next to him. "You've got quite a shiner coming on. How'd that happen?"

The six-year-old regarded him with stoic silence. The nurse gave him a shrug suggesting that she knew no more than he did about whatever had caused the fight.

"Let's get over to the doctor's office and let him take a look at your lip," Sam suggested. "That's a pretty bad cut."

Fear sparked in Bobby's eyes. "Will he have to use a needle?"

"He might," Sam told him honestly.

Bobby crossed his arms over his chest. "No!"

"Buddy, we have to let the doctor decide and do whatever he thinks is best."

"No!" Bobby repeated.

Sam cast a helpless look at the nurse. She sat down on Bobby's other side.

"You know he'll give you something so it won't hurt," she told him gently. "And the rumor is that he has lollipops for his bravest patients."

"Gram'pa Mick has candy, too," Bobby said, as if the doctor's offering weren't all that special.

"But Grandpa Mick can't fix up your cut," Sam reminded him.

Bobby seemed to be considering the truth of that. "I'll go if Carrie comes, too," he said finally, startling Sam.

"I think this is something you and I can handle," Sam told him, determined to hold his ground. He wasn't sure why he was so insistent, but it seemed important to prove, if only to himself, that he could care for Bobby on his own.

Bobby's expression turned even darker. "No! I want Carrie."

As badly as he wanted to stay firm, Sam concluded this wasn't the time or place for an argument. "I'll call Carrie when we get in the car and ask her to meet us there," he conceded. "If she's free and close by, she'll be there when we get there. How's that?"

"I guess that's okay," Bobby relented.

A few minutes later Carrie met them at the doctor's office, which was in the same block as her new business. She gave Bobby a reassuring hug, then glanced curiously at Sam as Bobby drifted off toward a selection of toys in the waiting room.

"When you called, it almost sounded as if you weren't sure I'd come," she said quietly.

"You have a lot going on right now. I wasn't

even sure if you'd be in town. I didn't want to drag you all the way back from Julie's."

"Nothing I have to do is more important than this," she said, regarding him curiously. After glancing down to make sure that Bobby's attention was focused on some LEGOs in the waiting-room play area, she said, "Didn't you want me here? If that's it, why did you bother calling?"

Sam sighed. "It's just that I rely on you a lot, most recently last night, to bail me out of yet another tight spot."

"The impromptu birthday party?" she said incredulously. "That was fun. It wasn't an imposition. Sam, I know you and I have a whole lot of things we need to figure out."

"One of the things we agreed to was that we didn't want to confuse Bobby while we were figuring out the rest," he reminded her.

"True, but I thought we were friends. Friends step up in a bind, no matter what else might be going on."

Sam suddenly felt ridiculous for making too much out of this. Had he wanted to use this incident to prove he was up to the task of fatherhood? Now wasn't the time for his pride to kick in. Since he didn't want to admit to that, he said, "But Bobby isn't your responsibility."

Carrie held his gaze for a very long time, disappointment in her eyes. "One of these days we need to talk about the difference between responsibility and caring enough to be around for the people we love," she said. "If you don't get that, then maybe we shouldn't even consider anything more."

Before Sam could say a word in his own defense—assuming he even had one—Noah McIlroy came out of the back to get Bobby and the moment ended, leaving Sam more shaken than he'd been in a long time. Not even the call from the school had gotten to him the same way that Carrie's quietly spoken rebuke had.

Bobby isn't your responsibility.

The entire time Carrie was in the examining room, Bobby clutching her hand tightly as Noah put two stitches into his lip, she was fighting the hurt that had spread through her at Sam's comment. How could they possibly have been so close last night, only to have him utter such careless words today? She'd thought they'd been making real progress toward something meaningful, and in a split second, he'd destroyed that illusion and put her in her place.

She was aware of Noah studying her curiously, but knew he would never ask the questions that were so clearly on his mind, such as why she was here with Bobby or why she and Sam couldn't even look each other in the eye.

"Good job!" Noah told Bobby when he was finished. "You were very brave."

"The nurse at school said you might have lollipops," Bobby said hopefully.

Noah chuckled. "I do, indeed." He pulled a carton with an assortment of flavors from one of the drawers. "Now here's the deal. It might be best if you don't eat this right now. Your lip's going to be numb for a little bit longer and you don't want to dribble all over yourself. Can you save this till tomorrow?"

"Tomorrow?" Bobby repeated as if it were an eternity until then.

"But by tonight, I think perhaps you could have a Popsicle," Noah offered as a consolation. "Maybe even two. The ice would feel real good on your lip."

Bobby turned to Sam. "Can we get some?"

"I'll stop at the store," Sam promised.

"I could take him home, while you do that," Carrie offered, then couldn't seem to stop herself from adding, "Unless I'd be overstepping."

Sam winced at her words. Noah looked even more intrigued. Carrie simply stood there and waited to see what Sam would say.

"If you have the time, that would be great," he said.

"I'll give Bobby a small dose of children's Tylenol before you leave," Noah said. "He'll probably sleep for a while this afternoon. You can give him more later if he's in pain, but as brave as he is, he should be just fine. Bring him back next week and I'll remove the stitches. Call or stop by if you have any questions or if anything doesn't seem right."

"Thanks," Sam said, shaking his hand. "I appreciate your seeing us on short notice."

"Hey, playground war wounds always get priority around here," Noah told him.

Carrie added her own thanks.

"How's the day-care center coming?" Noah asked her.

"All I need are the final inspection approvals and we'll be ready to open. A few more weeks should do it," she said, hoping her optimism wasn't misplaced.

"Great. I'll have Jackson there on day one. Maybe you can give Cait and me a tour when she's home this weekend."

"Absolutely," Carrie promised, though she had a hunch that they were going to be far more interested in her relationship with Sam than they were in the selection of toys and the color scheme at her new enterprise.

Outside, Sam handed her a house key. "Thanks for taking Bobby home. I'll be there as quickly as possible, so you can get back to work."

"Sure," she said, barely resisting the desire to start a fight with him about his attitude toward her involvement. He'd called her, blast it all. And she wasn't Susie, likely to misconstrue what his request meant. "We'll see you at the house."

In the backseat of her car with his seat belt on, Bobby's eyelids were already drooping from the day's excitement. When she pulled to a stop in front of the house, though, his eyes blinked open.

"We're home," she said, walking quickly around to help him get out. "You feeling steady on your feet?"

"Uh-huh," he said, then wobbled a little.

Still he looked indignant when she offered to carry him. "I can walk," he said, then headed unsteadily for the front door.

Carrie opened it, then took him straight to his room. She removed his shoes and helped him onto the bed. His eyes were closed by the time his head hit the pillow. She sat next to him, her heart aching as she brushed his hair from his forehead. Long lashes that girls would one day envy brushed his cheeks. His sweet little mouth was swollen and red and there was already a bruise under one eye.

"What on earth were you fighting about?" she murmured to herself as she watched the rise and fall of his chest. She wondered if Sam had any idea.

She was still sitting there when Sam got home. She tensed at the sound of the front door closing, then made herself get up and go into the kitchen where he was putting away the Popsicles.

He turned slowly when she came into the room. "How is he?"

"Down for the count," she said, noting the raw anguish in his eyes. "Are you okay?"

He shook his head. "When I got my first look at him in the nurse's office, I think my heart stopped."

"Get used to it," she advised, wishing she had the right to put her arms around him and offer comfort. Less than a day ago, she would have. Now she felt entirely too uncertain of her status around here. "Little boys are prone to cuts and scrapes."

"And fights? At his age?"

"That's probably not quite as typical," she conceded, though she'd mediated several at Julie's day-care center involving boys not much older. "Any idea what on earth he was fighting about?"

"None. The nurse had no idea either and Bobby wasn't talking. I should probably give the teacher a call now that the immediate crisis is over and see what she has to say." He paused and muttered a curse under his breath. "I need to call Mack, too."

"He knows about what's going on already, right?"

"Yes, but I took off in the middle of a website crash. I was supposed to come back to deal with it."

"Then go," she said at once. "I can stay here till you get home." She saw another of those annoying looks that suggested he didn't want to

370

inconvenience her. "Or I'll stay till you can get somebody else, if you don't want me here."

Guilt darkened his eyes. He scrubbed his hand over his face. "Carrie, I am so sorry if I've made you feel as if you have no place here. I'm not even sure why I let myself get so crazy today. Maybe it was because Susie was trying to take over and I got defensive about that. Then Bobby wanted you with him, not me, and I hate relying on you, on anyone, right now. I need to know I can handle this stuff on my own, but the truth is that I can't. When I arrived at the nurse's office at school and saw that black eye and split lip, I felt completely helpless. I wanted to burst into tears myself and curse Laurel for putting me into this position."

Carrie felt the start of her tension easing. "Welcome to parenthood! Do you think there's a parent on earth who hasn't felt that way the first time his or her baby gets a cut or bruise that they couldn't prevent? The only adult I know who seems to handle that with complete aplomb is Gram. Nell has seen more than her share of injuries and come to accept that the vast majority are messy, but not life-threatening. She's really the one you want around in a crisis. The rest of us just do the best we can."

The corners of Sam's mouth lifted. "Are you suggesting you were as scared as I was?"

"Not so much scared as wanting to cry because Bobby was in pain."

"But you didn't."

"Neither did you," she reminded him. "You did everything just right, Sam. You even called me when Bobby asked for me, rather than making him tough it out."

She risked taking a step closer and this time she did put her hand on his cheek. "You did just fine, Sam."

"I have to wonder if every day is going to bring some new challenge that's going to make me feel completely inept."

"More than likely," she said candidly. "But think about last night. When Bobby was sad and lost, you pulled together exactly the right sort of celebration of his dad. You made everything okay again."

Sam sighed. "His mom and dad are gone. Nothing will ever be okay again."

"It won't be the same again," she corrected. "But it will be okay, because he has you." She hesitated, then added, "And me, if you want me around."

He reached for her then and pulled her into his arms. Carrie accepted the embrace and the apology that was in his actions, if not exactly in his words.

"I want you around," he said. "More than I probably should. You're going to get sick of being my go-to person."

Carrie touched a finger to his lips. "Kiss me."

Sam looked startled, but then he bent his head and claimed her lips. Like a drowning man, he clung to her and kissed her until they were both breathing hard.

When he finally pulled away, Carrie caught her breath, then smiled. "There are some definite perks that go with being the go-to person in your life."

"It's not nearly enough compared to what I owe you."

"Let me be the judge of that. Now go back to work. I'll be here when you come home. If we're lucky, Bobby will be sleeping soundly."

A grin tugged at his lips. "What on earth will we do, then?"

"I have a few ideas. We'll discuss them when you get home." She shrugged. "Or not. Maybe I'll just show you."

She laughed as Sam pulled out his cell phone and hit speed dial. "What are you doing?" she asked.

"Calling Mack. If there's a God in heaven, he will have solved that website problem without me."

"But you won't be really happy until you see for yourself that it's been handled properly. Go."

He hesitated, then asked, "We're okay, even after my slight lapse into idiocy?"

"We're okay," she assured him.

He claimed her lips one more time, then headed for the door.

"Hurry home," she called after him.

"I like how that sounds," he said, then closed the door behind him.

Carrie liked it, too, probably a little too much, given how prone Sam was to panicking over where things were headed between them.

Unfortunately the tech issue at the paper hadn't been resolved. It took Sam and Mack hours of frustrating work and way too many calls to their service provider to get everything back online and functioning properly.

"Do you think Kristin Lewis deliberately left some sort of bug in there just to yank your chain?" Sam asked, referring to the woman who'd initially designed the website and gotten it up and running. He knew she and Mack had a romantic history she'd hoped to recapture when she'd come to town. It had been a messy situation, complicated when a subsequent relationship with Luke O'Brien had fallen apart, as well.

Mack looked startled by the suggestion. "I can't imagine that. I thought Kristin and I were on decent terms by the time she left."

"She was still the woman scorned," Sam reminded him.

"Well, it doesn't matter," Mack said. "Kristin got a better job clear across the country, and we've solved the problem once and for all." He slapped Sam's hand in a celebratory high five.

"We *think* we've solved the problem," Sam corrected. "I thought I had it fixed last week, remember? If it crops up again, I'm serious about looking into sabotage. If Kristin is the web genius everyone says she was, she could be hacking in from anywhere."

"I am not going there," Mack said. "In fact, the only thing I'm going to do right now is go home and spend what's left of the evening with my wife. I honestly think we may have turned a corner earlier today." He gave Sam a weary look. "Of course I've thought that before."

"Did she understand why I had to pick Bobby up myself?"

"Eventually," Mack said. "But I don't think I'll mention that Carrie got involved. It might set her off again. Every time I think those two have mended fences, another incident crops up."

"Carrie is going to be involved with Bobby and me," Sam said flatly. "Susie needs to accept that."

"Then it's gotten serious?" Mack asked.

"It's definitely moving in that direction," Sam said. "I'm scared to death about that. Things in my life are changing way too fast for me. Not that long ago I was the guy who was always ready to move on or go on some dangerous adventure at the drop of a hat. Now, here I am, a dad and putting down roots and thinking about adding a woman to the mix for the long haul. A few months ago, I wouldn't have bet fifty cents on any of that ever happening."

Mack laughed. "Was that panic that just washed across your face?"

Sam nodded. "More than likely." He paused, thought about it, then added, "You know what, though? It's not quite as terrifying as I expected it to be, because it's Bobby and it's Carrie. Do you know what I mean?"

"Believe me—I know exactly what you mean. I was the ultimate player," Mack admitted, his expression nostalgic. "I had no intention of ever allowing a relationship to get serious. Susie wisely vowed she'd never even go out with a guy who tossed women away the way I did."

Mack laughed. "And then lightning struck and I realized Susie was the one. For the first time in my life I knew exactly what I wanted and who I wanted to be with." He laughed. "To my ever-lasting regret, it took a lot longer to convince her to take a chance that I'd mended my ways."

"No regrets?"

"Not for me," Mack said without hesitation. "Not a one, even now when things are rocky. I know we belong together and I believe we will have a child. Susie and I are in this together for the rest of our lives."

Listening to the deeply held conviction behind Mack's words, Sam nodded. He wanted to believe that strongly in what he had with Carrie.

He was more than halfway there. He thought she might be, too. He wasn't sure what it would take to get the rest of the way or if either of them were up to the challenge, but, if determination to take that final leap counted for anything, they'd get there.

Bobby had grape Popsicle dribbling down his chin and all over his hands and shirt. Carrie had given up trying to keep up with the drips and figured this shirt, like the one he'd worn earlier, would either come clean in the wash or make an excellent dust cloth.

They were sitting on the back deck to save the kitchen floor from the inevitable stickiness, when Sam found them.

"Hey, buddy! How are you feeling?"

"Better," Bobby reported. "I'm having Popsicles for dinner."

"Excellent." His gaze sought out Carrie's and held. "Everything okay around here?"

"We're doing fine, if you don't count the fact that this is the second shirt we've probably lost to Popsicle stains."

Sam shrugged. "They're T-shirts. They're expendable."

"My sentiment exactly."

Sam's expression sobered. He lifted Bobby up and sat him on his lap. In a tone he obviously meant to be casual, he said, "So, pal, maybe you should fill us in on what actually happened at school today."

"I was in a fight," Bobby said, as if it were of no consequence.

"I know that much," Sam said, his tone still light. "You have the black eye and split lip to prove it. But since fighting isn't on the approved list of school activities and you're aware of that, maybe you could tell me who hit you and why? Did someone else start it?"

Bobby's expression shut down and he dropped the remainder of his icy treat on the ground. "I don't want to talk about it." He struggled to break free. "I want to go to bed."

"Not an option," Sam said. "What happened?"

When Bobby tried once more to squirm off his lap, Sam held him in place.

"Bobby, it's okay to tell us," Carrie said gently. "It's not tattling."

"I don't care about tattling," Bobby said angrily. "What Patsy said was a lie, so I shoved her."

Shock spread across Sam's face. "You shoved a girl?"

"Don't feel sorry for her," Bobby said mutinously. "Because then she hit me in the eye and busted my lip." His cheeks colored pink with obvious embarrassment.

"The fight was with a girl?" Sam repeated, as if he couldn't quite grasp the reality of that.

"She's mean," Bobby declared. "And she told a big old lie."

"What was the lie?" Carrie asked, understanding that was at the heart of the fight.

"She said my mom and dad went away and left me on purpose because I was a dumb, stupid boy."

Carrie gasped at the cruelty of that. More than likely a six-year-old hadn't understood the depth of pain such a comment would cause, but it was shocking just the same. No wonder Bobby had reacted the way he had.

"You know your mom and dad didn't want to leave you," Sam said, clearly shaken. "They loved you more than anything."

"I know," Bobby said impatiently. "That's why it was a lie."

Sam cast a what-now look in Carrie's direction.

"Bobby, you still don't shove someone just because they say mean things that hurt you," Carrie said, even though she wouldn't mind giving the girl's mother a good hard shove. Clearly little Patsy had heard some comment at home that encouraged such talk.

"I had to do something," Bobby said in frustration.

Carrie recognized the childish sense of impotence behind the rage he must have felt. "I know, sweetheart. You should have walked away and told the teacher. Wouldn't that have been better than shoving Patsy and having her punch you? If you'd done that, you wouldn't have needed stitches."

"It was worth it," Bobby said stubbornly. "Because I got stitches, you're here and I got Popsicles for dinner."

Carrie saw that Sam was struggling to fight a smile. Eventually he was able to face Bobby with a sober expression.

"And because you were fighting when you knew better, you now get to go to your room and think about how wrong it is to hit someone else or to shove them," he said sternly. "It's not the way we solve problems." He pointed toward the house. "Go."

Bobby climbed down and headed inside, though he didn't look the least bit repentant. Just inside the door, he turned back. "If you'd been there, I'll bet you'd have shoved her, too."

When he was out of earshot, Sam met Carrie's gaze. "I sure would have wanted to," he admitted.

"You're not alone there," Carrie told him. "You probably should have a conversation with little Miss Patsy's mother or father."

Sam looked as if he'd rather eat dirt. "Do I have to?"

Carrie laughed. "Scared she's going to split your lip, too?"

"Nope."

"Oh?"

"I'm not 100 percent sure I won't throw the first punch."

"I have faith in you," Carrie assured him. "Not only does fighting not resolve anything, which you perfectly well know, but hitting a girl is never acceptable, something you also know."

He gave her a long look. "That child told Bobby that his mom and dad left him on purpose. Am I supposed to forget about that?"

Carrie felt her own anger stir again at his reminder of the hurtful exchange that had started all this. "Maybe I should come along," she suggested. "Not to keep you in check, but so that I can throw a punch. There's not a soul in this town who wouldn't back me up."

Sam moved to sit beside her and draped an arm over her shoulders. "And that is why I know you and I belong together. We're of one mind." He gave her a sideways glance. "And maybe we're meant to keep each other's tempers in check."

"Too bad. I do have red hair and those Irish genes, you know, and I haven't been in a good brawl in years," she said, then rested her head on his shoulder.

Sitting just like that, with the memory of the previous night's glorious sunset and poignant birthday celebration still very much on her mind, she felt contentment steal over her. She glanced at Sam and saw that the tension in his jaw had eased, as well.

This, she thought, was what real couples did. They faced problems together, worked through them, and their families were stronger because of it. The only issues she and Marc ever resolved together were work related. Anytime she'd tried to bring up his neglect or anything else personal, he'd tuned her out. She should have recognized they were missing out on a key aspect of any good relationship.

She had her own crazy family with all of its ups and downs to look to as prime examples of the way it should be done. Not every day was sunshine and roses. Those hurdles, faced together, were the strength behind every O'Brien family.

❧ 20 ❧

Sam requested a meeting with Bobby's teacher, Amy Pennington, and Patsy's mother, Allison Rogers. The three of them met in the first-grade classroom after school the day after the fight that had sent Bobby to Noah's office.

Allison Rogers appeared to be a nice enough woman, a little harried and a bit indignant about being dragged away from work in the middle of the afternoon, but otherwise reasonably pleasant. She seemed genuinely mystified about why she was there.

Bobby's teacher, who did, indeed, look a little

like Mrs. Claus with her white hair and frameless glasses, took charge of the meeting.

"Allison, I'm not sure if you're aware that we had a problem on the playground yesterday. I did leave you a message, but since you didn't call back, I can't be sure if you got it," Mrs. Pennington said.

"Last night was insane. I never checked for messages," Mrs. Rogers admitted. "Was it anything serious? If so, the office has my cell number."

"I tried that, as well." The teacher waved off the issue. "It doesn't matter now, since you obviously received the request to be here this afternoon."

"The principal called me this morning at work and made it seem like a matter of life or death," she said. "I certainly hope it's at least that important. My boss hates it when I leave early and I need this job."

"Then let's address this quickly," Mrs. Pennington suggested briskly. "Yesterday Patsy was involved in a fight with Sam's nephew, Bobby. She said something quite cruel and he, naturally, took offense. He gave her a shove, and then she split his lip and gave him a black eye."

"That's what he gets for shoving her," Allison said defensively, frowning at Sam. "Surely he knows better."

Sam had left the entire conversation up to the teacher until now, but he couldn't let that pass. "How would you react if you were a scared six-year-old living with an uncle you barely know in a new town, attending a new school and someone told you that your recently deceased parents had deliberately left you because you were a no-good, stupid boy?"

To her credit, Mrs. Rogers looked shocked. "That's what Patsy said?"

"I'm afraid so," the teacher confirmed. "I overheard her myself, but before I could intervene, Bobby had lashed out and Patsy had hit him hard enough that he required stitches."

Patsy's mom regarded Sam with what appeared to be genuine regret. "I am so sorry. I hate to admit it, but I think I have some idea where this is coming from. Patsy's father recently left us. One of his parting shots was that he was going because I was a failure at discipline and the kids —I have a son, too—are out-of-control brats. Naturally that was shouted at the top of his lungs from the front lawn. Patsy and her brother heard every word."

Of course with that piece of information added in, the whole incident made perfect sense to Sam. In Patsy's head, if a parent went away, it had to be on purpose and it had to be because the children were no good. She'd been taking her own pain out on Bobby.

"I'm sorry," Sam said.

"Hey, he wasn't a very nice man and we were a terrible couple," she said bitterly. "I think we'd forgotten why we'd fallen in love by the time the ceremony was over, but we hung in there until Patsy turned five. Her brother's four. My delightful husband figured by then Teddy would be old enough for preschool and Patsy would be going into first grade, so I could go back to work to support them."

"I'm sorry," Sam said again, realizing it was possible for children to suffer losses almost as emotionally devastating as losing two parents in an accident.

"I think we can see very clearly that there are two sides to every story," the teacher said. "That doesn't excuse the behavior, but at least it gives us some context. Mr. Winslow, do you agree?"

"Absolutely," Sam said.

"I'll talk to Patsy," Mrs. Rogers promised. "I'll make sure she apologizes to Bobby. I'll bring her to school myself in the morning and stand there to see that she does it."

"Ditto with Bobby for his part in the fight," Sam said. "I'll be here before school, as well."

The teacher beamed at them. "I knew we could work this out. I'll see each of you before class starts tomorrow morning."

Sam walked Patsy's mother back to the parking lot. "I really am sorry you're going through such a tough time."

She shrugged. "No more than I deserve for not listening to a single soul who tried to tell me my husband-to-be was a jerk." She managed a smile, though it seemed a bit forced. "I'm getting better every day. I've almost concluded that I'm not the terrible person he said I was, either." She regarded Sam with a chagrined expression. "God help her, is it any wonder Patsy can't get past his parting shot? I certainly haven't and I'm supposed to be the mature grown-up."

"But you will," Sam said with confidence. "I saw your fighting spirit returning back in that classroom."

She seemed surprised by his assessment. "You know, it is. Thanks for noticing. I'll see you in the morning. And I truly regret that Patsy said something that cruel to Bobby, to say nothing of the split lip. I'd be happy to cover the medical bill." The last was obviously added on impulse, one she clearly regretted the moment she'd spoken.

Recognizing that financial difficulties were weighing on her, Sam let her off the hook. "Not necessary. My insurance has it covered."

"If you ever have time for a cup of coffee," she began hesitantly.

Sam cut her off before she could complete the invitation. "Thanks, but I'm seeing someone."

She flushed. "You're single and good-looking. Of course you are. I was just thinking that our situations might give us a lot in common. Sometimes I'm afraid I'll go crazy if I don't have another adult around who gets it."

Before he could think of what to say to smooth over the uncomfortable moment, she hurried away, clearly embarrassed.

"Well, that was something new," he murmured as he headed for his car. He realized he'd recently joined the apparently desirable group of available single dads. Sure, he'd been hit on by plenty of women, but this was the first time the attraction had been based on the shared complexities of single parenthood.

Carrie agreed to meet her twin, Noah and Jackson for a tour of her new day-care center on Sunday morning before they all headed to Grandpa Mick's for dinner. As proud as she was of the facility and as eager as she was to show it off, she was anticipating a lively cross-examination from Caitlyn as the main agenda for the get-together.

Sure enough, as soon as Noah wheeled Jackson's stroller into the main activity room, Cait pulled Carrie into the kitchen, where they had a little privacy.

"What do you think of the place?" Carrie asked cheerfully, hoping to forestall the interrogation.

"It's lovely. You'll be a huge success. *Yada-yada*. I'm sure you've heard all that from every member of our family. Now tell me what's going on with you and Sam. I thought I warned you to stay away from him."

"It's not the first time I've ignored your advice," Carrie reminded her.

"Yes, I believe the last time was when I told you not to get involved with your boss," Caitlyn reminded her. "Given how things worked out with Marc Reynolds, I'd think my credibility would be pretty good right now."

"This is nothing like that," Carrie insisted.

"At least Sam seems to be more substance than flash—I'll give you that," her sister said. "Everyone I've spoken to really likes him."

"So the O'Brien hotline is working well," Carrie commented dryly. "Good to know. What's the method of choice? Still texting?"

"Mostly," Cait admitted. "At least from Grandpa Mick. Our aunts prefer to talk on the phone. And, of course, Noah and I are on Skype almost daily so I can see how Jackson is growing."

"How's the long-distance thing working for you?" Carrie asked, seizing on a particularly delicate debate between husband and wife and the rest of the family. Cait and Noah usually claimed it was working just fine. No one else could quite believe it.

Cait sighed heavily. "I hate being separated from them, okay? I admit it. But this is the way it has to be. I'm just in Baltimore until I finish my internship and residency. Then Noah and I will be together. I can be here in a couple of hours, tops, if anything comes up. Noah comes up whenever

I'm off on a weekend or I come down here. It's stressful at times, but we're making it work."

"Then why are you wasting even one second of that time in here lecturing me, when you could be alone with your husband?" Carrie demanded. "I'll even keep Jackson for the next couple of hours and bring him with me to Grandpa Mick's."

"A tempting offer, to be sure," Cait said, her regret plain. "But I'm on a mission to figure out whether or not you're about to ruin your life. Noah said things were awfully tense between you and Sam when he brought Bobby in the other day. He got the feeling Sam didn't really want you there."

Carrie gave up trying to avoid the whole discussion. "He had his reasons. We've worked it out. Like you said, that's what adults in a committed relationship do, right? They work through things. Not every day is a festival of love and laughter."

Cait laughed. "I wish. Okay, so things are fine with Sam. How fine? Any talk of a future?"

"Not beyond whether he and Bobby will be at Grandpa Mick's today. I'm thinking I should warn him to stay home."

"Don't you dare. I want to see him for myself and see you with him."

"We're not that interesting."

Cait put an arm around her shoulders. "Hey, you're my baby sister—"

"By two minutes," Carrie reminded her.

"It still counts. I have to look out for your best interests."

"Don't you think I get enough of that from the O'Briens right here on the scene?" Carrie asked wearily. "Mom, Trace and Grandpa Mick have made me their pet project lately."

"But I have special insight," Cait claimed, then linked an arm through Carrie's. "Now show me around in here. I still can't believe you're opening a day-care center."

"Believe it. If there are no more last-minute glitches, the doors open after Thanksgiving. The inspectors found a half dozen nits to pick on their last visit." She sighed. "Oh, well, it was to be expected they tell me. My only real regret is that I still haven't found the perfect assistant manager. I've hired a couple of great people with experience with kids and good educational requirements, but I'd really like someone with a solid background at a day-care center."

"Are you excited?"

"Excited, terrified, all of that," Carrie admitted. "What if the kids are miserable and the parents yank them out? Maybe I should have stuck to babysitting O'Brien babies on Willow Brook Road."

"Stop that! The children will be safe and blissfully happy. You're not going to fail," Cait said with total confidence. "And not just because

O'Briens don't fail, but because you're you and even I can see that this is the perfect fit for you. Mom was right. We all should have seen it much sooner."

"And saved me the disaster that was my life in Paris?"

"Something like that," Cait said.

In an example of perfect timing, or more precisely, perfectly *terrible* timing, Carrie's cell phone chirped out its alert for an incoming text. She ignored it.

"You're not going to check that?" Cait asked, her expression curious.

"I'm busy with you. Whatever it is can wait."

"And you know that how?" Cait asked suspiciously. "Do you know who's texting, Carrie?"

"I have some idea."

Before she could react to prevent it, her twin grabbed the cell. Her eyes widened in dismay. "Marc? You're in touch with Marc?"

"I am not in touch with Marc," Carrie replied defensively. "He's been texting." She hesitated, then added, "And calling. I've been ignoring him. Usually I just shut off my phone, so I don't have to be bothered looking at the texts. I've deleted the voice mails without listening to them."

"Good for you," Cait said. She studied Carrie a little too intently. "You're not even a little curious about what he wants?"

"Not enough to open that door again," Carrie

said firmly. "My life is falling into place just the way I want it, too. Marc is not a part of it."

"Okay, then. I won't freak out over him trying to contact you. Now, show me just how fabulous this place is going to be."

For the next half hour, Carrie showed her sister every nook and cranny of the center, watching her face closely. That, rather than her words, would tell the real story about what she thought of Carrie's seemingly impulsive career choice.

"Noah, isn't it fantastic?" Cait said at last, whirling around in a pool of sunlight in the middle of the main room. "It's such a happy place."

Noah chuckled. "I imagine you can hear the laughter already."

"Well, I can," Cait said. "Jackson's going to love it here. And, Carrie, you're going to be a huge success!"

"I agree," Noah said. "I checked out all of your first-aid supplies and can't think of a thing you missed."

"Thanks for doing that," Carrie said. "Though it's a big comfort knowing your office is right up the street."

"I wish I could stay an extra couple of days to throw a big open-house party for you to spread the word," Cait said.

"I appreciate the thought, but I don't need a party. I just want to get the doors open and get to work," Carrie said.

"But the entire region needs to know about this place," Cait argued. "You were in marketing and PR. You know that."

"I already have a waiting list for places," Carrie told her. "It's killing me to turn people down. The last thing I need is even more people wanting to get on that list."

"I suppose you have a point," Cait conceded. "There's no reason to create a demand you already know you can't meet. What about a family party?"

Carrie laughed. "Are you kidding me? You said it yourself just a minute ago. I don't think there's a single person in our family who hasn't wandered in and out of here on an almost-daily basis. Everybody wants to be the first to see how it's coming along. Grandpa Mick is basking in the glory of being both construction foreman and tour guide. He may not entirely agree with my plans, but he takes great pride in his workmanship."

"Of course he does," Cait said. "Then just let me add my stamp of approval."

Carrie gave her sister a fierce hug. "That means a lot. You know that, don't you?"

"The same way it means the world to me that when my son isn't with Noah or me, he's in your hands," Cait said. "Love you."

"Right back at you."

Something deep inside Carrie eased after the

exchange. Though she would never have admitted it aloud, her sister's approval—the whole family's for that matter—meant everything to her.

Over the course of the afternoon at Mick's, Sam found himself fascinated by watching Carrie with her twin sister. It seemed to him that the two women couldn't have been more different. Oh, not in appearance. There was no mistaking that they were identical twins. But Caitlyn looked as if she'd dressed in a hurry and perhaps in the dark. At the same time Carrie, even in her new day-to-day wardrobe, looked as if she'd stepped out of a fashion magazine. Apparently once she'd learned the skill of dressing, she could achieve a stylish look with a simple twist of a scarf or a well-chosen piece of costume jewelry, though something told him that was 18-karat gold she was wearing and that the stones were real gems, not fakes.

He was pondering the differences in style and personality, when Noah came over and asked about Bobby.

"I got a quick look at his stitches as he raced past a minute ago," Noah said. "No sign of infection. Bring him in this week and we'll get them out. Any afternoon's okay. Just drop in."

"Thanks," Sam said.

"How did things go at school? Problem resolved?"

"For now," Sam said. "I suppose there are always going to be kids who say hateful things. I just want to be sure Bobby doesn't become one of them."

"A goal every parent should have," Noah agreed. "Even though it's tough to monitor them every second of the day." He studied Sam more intently. "You doing okay? You were thrust into parenthood pretty unexpectedly."

"I'd like to think I'm getting better every day at figuring out how not to mess things up," Sam said. "Carrie's been a huge help on that front."

"If you don't mind me saying so, you didn't seem all that thrilled to have her help the other day."

"You saw that?" Sam said, chagrined. "My insecurities were in full swing. I thought I should be the adult dealing with the crisis. Bobby wanted Carrie. I hate to admit it, but on some level I was jealous."

To his surprise, Noah laughed. "I've been there a time or two myself. Carrie has a way with kids, including my son. You have no idea how my heart twists when he's sobbing and throwing his food at me. Then she walks in and it's as if the sun's come out. He's suddenly all smiles. Worse, he cooperates with whatever she wants from him. Maybe it's because she reminds him of his mom or maybe she has a magic touch with kids. Either way I feel like a failure, and then I feel like a jerk.

I should want my child to be happy, right? It's not about who assures that."

"So you're telling me the whole wounded-pride thing is probably a bit of macho craziness?" Sam suggested.

Noah shrugged. "Pretty much. There are plenty of times when Jackson's falling asleep on my chest or when I try to coax him to say Da-Da and he almost gets it right, that I realize he and I are making our own memories. When he's bigger, I'm the one who'll teach him to put a worm on a hook and clean a fish. Trust me, Cait may not be squeamish when it comes to people, but she isn't touching worms or the innards of a fish. Carrie's not fond of that, either."

"So I can create the guy memories with Bobby," Sam concluded.

"You're also his connection to his parents," Noah said quietly. "Nobody else can fill that role."

"He does have grandparents on his dad's side. I'm encouraging them to be a part of his life."

"But you grew up with his mom. Who else is there to tell him stories about what she was like as a little girl?"

"She was a pest," Sam said emphatically, but fondly.

"Tell him that. I bet he'll love hearing all about it."

Just then Carrie joined them. "You two look

awfully serious," she said, then frowned at her brother-in-law. "You're not interrogating him, are you?"

"Not at all," Noah said at once. "I'll leave that to my wife and Mick."

Carrie rolled her eyes. "Exactly why I came over here," she told Sam, "to lure you away before Cait or my grandfather find the time to question you about your intentions. I think a well-timed retreat is in order."

Noah laughed. "Good luck with that," he said, wandering off in search of his wife and son.

"You really want to go?" Sam asked Carrie.

"Don't you? I'd think you'd be tired of being in the midst of this crowd after a few hours of speculative looks and probably way too many intrusive questions."

"I'm up to it. I thought you'd probably want to spend more time with your sister. Isn't she heading back to Baltimore this evening?"

"I've endured about as many of her pointed questions as I can handle for one day. I'll be glad to see the last of her."

Sam regarded her with shock. "You don't mean that."

Carrie chuckled. "Of course not. We'll be on the phone at least twice tomorrow, but when we're on the phone, I can always hang up if she gets too nosy. In person, I can't get away."

"Somebody ought to do a study of the dynamics

of this family. It would probably make a great PhD dissertation."

"I'll mention that to Will," she said, taking him seriously. "He's still in touch with some of his psychology professors." She took his hand. "Now let's scoot while we can."

Sam looked into her eyes. "Did you have something in mind for the rest of the day?"

"A quiet walk along Shore Road, then some ice cream," she said, much to his disappointment.

"Sounds good," he said, trying to muster up some enthusiasm when his mind had already wandered to much more enjoyable pursuits.

Carrie tucked an arm through his and gave him a knowing look. "I'm thinking all this activity here, plus the sugar from an ice-cream cone will have Bobby down for the count in an hour."

"Ah," Sam said, understanding at last. "And then?"

"I bet if we use our imaginations, we'll be able to think of something."

"Already on it," Sam said. In fact, he was several wicked steps ahead.

Carrie obviously knew kids pretty darn well, Sam concluded as he tucked Bobby into bed five minutes after they returned home after eating ice cream. Bobby barely mustered up a mild protest at the early hour.

"Told you," Carrie said, smiling up at him

when he joined her on the deck out back.

She'd opened a bottle of red wine and poured two glasses. When he picked his up, she tapped hers to it. "Cheers!"

Sam held her gaze. "It was a good day, wasn't it?"

She nodded. "It felt right somehow, you and Bobby being there with me."

Sam drew in a deep breath, then admitted, "It felt that way to me, too. The last time I was there it was a little intimidating."

"O'Briens, cumulatively anyway, can be a scary bunch. They've been known to terrify me from time to time. One-on-one, though, they're just family." She gave him a long look. "I think they're all wondering how long it's going to be before you're a part of the family." When Sam opened his mouth to speak, she held up a hand. "Let them wonder, Sam. That's on them. You and I have agreed we're taking one step at a time."

To his surprise, she didn't seem to be bothered by the slow, steady pace toward an uncertain ending. He smiled at her deliberate nonchalance.

"Any thoughts on how we'll know when we get to the last step?" he asked, taking her hand and weaving their fingers together as they sat side by side with darkness falling.

"Since I've never gotten there with anyone before, I'm not sure, but based on evidence I've seen around me, I think we'll recognize it when it happens."

"Are you okay with waiting?"

She turned to him then, her expression earnest. "Do we have a choice? Sam, I like you. No, more than that, I think I may be falling in love with you, but it's not a one-sided decision. I can wait till you get there, and then we can decide what happens next."

"Some people think sex comes into play at some point," he said, fighting a smile and a rush of hormones stirred just by the suggestion.

"Don't think for one second that the thought hasn't crossed my mind," she said. "You?"

"It's front and center right now, as a matter of fact."

He saw her lips curve at that. Then she sighed. "Good to know."

"But it's not going to happen, is it?" he said with regret.

"Not tonight with the possibility that Bobby could wake up and wander in on us," she said.

"Run away with me," he pleaded with some urgency.

Carrie laughed. "Much as I might want to, I can wait. Anticipation is half the fun."

"It's not the half I'd like to get to right now," Sam grumbled. He lifted her hand to his lips and kissed her knuckles, then took each finger into his mouth. He heard her breath hitch, even as his blood hummed. "You wouldn't want to come over and share this lounge chair with me, would you?"

"Sounds dangerous," she said.

"Exactly what I was thinking."

A second later, she was stretched out beside him, her head on his shoulder, her body fit snugly against his. It was a form of sweet torture to be sure, but it definitely clarified the direction in which they were heading.

❧ 21 ❧

Carrie was going through the stack of résumés on her desk once again, hoping to spot the perfect candidate for assistant manager. Unfortunately, she kept getting distracted by memories of her evening with Sam.

The more time they spent together, the closer they were getting. And, she thought wryly, the more frustrated they were becoming. Despite their reaffirmation just last night that they wouldn't sleep together with Bobby in the house, that rule was getting more and more difficult to abide by.

Nor were they in any position to suddenly take off for a day or two on their own, even though Kevin and Shanna had offered more than once to let Bobby have a sleepover at their house. They both had too much work right now to take advantage of the offer.

Plus, if she were being totally honest, Carrie wasn't sure she was ready to deal with all the questions that were bound to follow if the family discovered they'd gone on a trip together. With O'Briens that was tantamount to an admission that a wedding was right around the corner. Inquiries along that line would add way too much pressure.

And then there was Marc. As diligent as she'd been about ignoring his texts and calls, his insistent attempts to contact her kept that part of her life very much alive. She didn't want any part of that old life, but she couldn't quite forget it—or him—completely. What did that say about her feelings for Sam?

Since wrestling with all of this was getting her nowhere, she sighed and forced her attention back to the résumés. She reached the bottom of the pile and concluded that there was nothing she'd missed the first time around. There simply were no good candidates.

Just then, a tap on the front door of the center startled her. Most people just walked in, even with the CLOSED sign on the door. She hurried across the room, wondering if there was some inspection she hadn't known about or possibly a parent desperate to find child care and hoping not to be turned away if they came in person.

Instead, she discovered Lucy on the porch.

"Hi," Lucy said, shifting nervously from foot to foot, a tentative smile on her face. "I know you must be swamped with details, but do you have some time to talk to me?"

"For you, absolutely," Carrie said with delight. "What brings you here? Come on in. I have some bottled water if you're thirsty, but not much else."

"That's okay. I'm good. Well, mostly good. Actually I'm a little rattled, because I don't know how you're going to react to this, but Mom told me I had to try."

Carrie led the way to her cramped office, then regarded her nervous guest with confusion. "Lucy, you're always welcome here. After everything you and your mom have done for me, are *still* doing for me, I consider you to be much more than mentors. You're friends. Now have a seat and tell me what's on your mind. Is your mom in town with you? She didn't mention you were planning a visit."

Lucy shook her head. "No, she's been at the day-care center since dawn as usual, but we did come down yesterday. It was a last-minute thing. I talked her into it. She didn't want to admit it when we were here the last time, but she fell in love with Chesapeake Shores the same way I did."

Carrie laughed. "Everybody does. Did you go back to Brady's?"

"Actually we just grabbed a sandwich at Sally's Café, and then spent some time with a real estate agent, a woman named Susie Franklin. She said she's your cousin."

Ah, so that explained Susie's absence from yesterday's dinner. Carrie had feared she was avoiding Sam and Bobby. Maybe her, as well.

"Susie's great, and she certainly knows every single piece of property in the town. Are you all seriously thinking of relocating? That would be fantastic!" She frowned as a thought crossed her mind. "Your mom's not worried that I'll think she's watching over my shoulder, is she?"

"Not at all. I actually think I've just about convinced her that it's time to retire, or will be when her current clients are too old to need her anymore. That'll take another two or three years, but for that long she could commute, just like you told her."

"She'd close her center?" Carrie asked, startled.

"She's done really well with it, but to be honest, she's had no life. I'll be graduating from college this year, so that financial burden will be behind her."

"How were you able to persuade your mom to consider this move?" Carrie asked.

"I told her she's not getting any younger."

Carrie winced, but said nothing.

"I told her it's way past time for her to do something for herself," Lucy continued earnestly.

"I think this town is the place for her to reinvent herself. She's starting to agree."

Her expression brightened with the bubbly enthusiasm that made her so great with kids. "We actually made an offer on a house yesterday," she revealed. "Your cousin called last night and the offer was accepted. My mom turned pale, but I really think she's as excited as I am, just a little scared about taking such a huge step."

"Oh, my gosh, that's incredible!" Carrie said. "I'm so happy you're going to be close by." She studied Lucy and saw that she was still a bundle of nerves. "But you didn't come by just to share that news with me, did you?"

"No," she admitted, then drew in a deep breath. "I came to ask if you'd consider hiring me, part-time till I graduate in the spring, and then maybe full-time."

Carrie's jaw dropped. "You're serious? You'd want to work with me here?"

"I like you. I can already tell I'll love this town. This facility is beautiful. You've created a wonderful environment for kids. For me it's exactly where I'd want to wind up after graduation. I don't like where we're located now, even if it would mean taking over an established day care." She shrugged. "I might as well seize the opportunity now, if there is one."

"And your mom doesn't care that you're abandoning her?"

"Like I said, she's already cutting back. Pretty soon she won't have a place for me, anyway. She was the one who suggested this, as a matter of fact. Do you still need any help? Please tell me I'm not too late."

Carrie stood up and threw her arms around the girl. "You, my friend, are the answer to my prayers. I've hired a couple of promising employees, but I'd despaired of ever finding a good candidate for assistant manager. You have the experience and qualifications for that, if you're interested. I know it wouldn't be full-time at first, but I think we could get through this year okay till you're finished with school. I know how good you are, Lucy. Not just with the kids, but with the business side of things. When your mom was hitting me with too much information that sounded like a foreign language, you turned it into plain English. Please, please say you'll do it."

A smile spread across Lucy's face. "I came in here scared to death to ask you for a favor, and now it almost seems as if I'm doing one for you."

"You would be. Bringing you on board would free up a little of my time."

A knowing expression passed over Lucy's face. "So there is a guy? I knew it. I told Mom you were too fantastic not to have a special man hidden away."

An image of Sam came to mind, of the way his

kisses continued to knock her socks off, of how much more she thought there could be between them. "Yeah, there is a man," she conceded. "Not that making a success of this business isn't my top priority right now."

"Of course it is, but I've been telling Mom for years that her life shouldn't be all about me and business. I think when Dad left it took something out of her. I'm hoping living here will give her back that part of herself."

"Chesapeake Shores does have a way of creating that kind of magic," Carrie said. "So, except for talking salary and schedule, do we have a deal?"

Lucy nodded eagerly. "We have a deal."

For the very first time since she'd set her career plan into motion, Carrie was truly filled with confidence that she would succeed. And, in time, with Lucy's energy, exuberance and experience on board, she'd be able to get the sort of balance into her life that her mom and every other woman in the O'Brien clan worked so hard to achieve.

When Sam walked into Sally's to grab an iced tea and a sandwich to go, the black Cadillac Escalade with its uniformed driver and handsome, semi-famous occupant was the talk of the café. Sam overheard just enough to make his blood run cold.

He nodded toward the gossiping trio of female

tourists in the closest booth, then asked Sally, "What's that about?"

"That designer, the one Carrie used to work for, was in here a few minutes ago looking for her. Obviously those women don't know the kind of man he is or they wouldn't be acting like fools over him."

"Any idea what he wanted, aside from Carrie, that is?" Sam asked, his heart in his throat. Was this it? Had she finally responded to those texts and messages she'd claimed to be ignoring? Was this Carrie's chance to go back to the life that so obviously suited her? He'd never understood how any sane man could let her go. Had Reynolds finally seen the light and come to claim her? He'd charmed her once. Could he do it again?

"I'm afraid he didn't fill me in on his plans," Sally said dryly. "I am, after all, just the owner of a small-town café in the middle of nowhere."

Sam smiled at her attitude. "A bit of a snob, was he?"

"More like an oily snake charmer," she corrected. "I recognize the type. Smooth as silk if they think it will get 'em what they want."

"And did he get what he wanted?" Sam asked.

"You mean did I tell him where to find Carrie?" She shrugged. "If I hadn't, someone else would have. Of course, I did direct him up to Mick's place, not to the day care. Let him do a little explaining to Carrie's grandfather, if he wants to get to her."

Impulsively, Sam planted a kiss on Sally's cheek. "You truly are a treasure."

"No question about it," she said, laughing. "Now take your lunch and go. If you don't mind a piece of advice, I suggest you eat it with Carrie at the day care, instead of going back to your own office and stewing all afternoon."

"You suggesting I should stake my claim?"

"It wouldn't hurt. I put an extra sandwich in there, just in case you have more sense than pride."

Sam nodded. "I'll definitely take that under advisement."

"See that you do."

Sam left the café, then drew in a deep breath, filling his lungs with the clean salty air. This fresh, invigorating air was something Carrie wouldn't get if she jetted off across the globe again. Who was he, though, to try to stand in her way? What could he offer that this Marc Reynolds couldn't offer a hundred times over?

Reason told him to look around. Chesapeake Shores was what she claimed to want. She seemed to have deep feelings for him, too. And she certainly had feelings for Bobby. Family, she claimed was her top priority, and her new day-care center promised a deep sense of professional fulfillment.

Was that enough? It would be for the woman he thought he'd come to know.

Just in case you have more sense than pride. Sally's words rang in his head, taunting him. He wanted to believe he did, but he also had a healthy respect for being realistic. This might be Carrie's chance to grab everything she'd lost. And if that's what she needed, what she wanted, he wasn't going to be the one to try to stop her, even though in his opinion Marc Reynolds had already shown himself to be unworthy of a woman with Carrie's kindness and generosity. If he had the chance, he'd tell her that, too.

He took yet another deep, cleansing breath and turned toward the newspaper office. If they were going to make it, he had to trust Carrie to make the right choice. He had to have faith that she would choose him—and family and home—over flash and glamour.

But as strong as his faith in her might be, it was going to be a very long afternoon.

Mick had gone outside with his father's pipe and was enjoying the fall afternoon, when the big black SUV drove up. His gaze narrowed as he recognized the perfectly groomed man who climbed out of the back, every hair in place, his clothes impeccable. Mick's blood promptly came to a boil, but he could hear Megan's voice in his head telling him to wait and see what the designer wanted before kicking him off his land and out of town.

"Mr. O'Brien?"

"That's me," Mick confirmed. "What can I do for you, Mr. Reynolds?"

The man's expression didn't register so much as a hint of surprise. Clearly he expected to be recognized wherever he went. Another black mark, in Mick's opinion.

"I'm looking for Carrie."

"Oh? A little late for that, isn't it?"

The direct remark hit its target. Reynolds looked taken aback.

"Letting her leave was a foolish decision on my part," he conceded. "I'm afraid I underestimated her value to my business."

"But not to you?"

The man looked completely befuddled by the question, which told Mick all he needed to know. Marc Reynolds hadn't shown up here because he'd discovered some deep, abiding love for Carrie. He was here because of what she could do for him. Well, not if Mick had anything to say about it. No man was going to get a second chance to break his girl's heart.

"I doubt she's interested in anything you're offering," Mick told him.

"Shouldn't you let her decide that for herself?"

"More than likely," Mick said, taking a long draw on his pipe and releasing the fragrant smoke

411

into the air. "But I'm comfortable with telling you to get out of my town and out of my girl's life."

"Mick O'Brien!"

Mick winced. Unfortunately he hadn't taken into account that Ma was inside. Apparently she'd overheard enough to guess the identity of their unwanted guest and to figure out what Mick was up to.

Marc Reynolds's gaze immediately went to Nell, who emerged from the house and was regarding both of them with displeasure.

"You must be Carrie's great-grandmother. Nell, isn't that right?"

"I am."

"I've heard a lot about you, about all of you. Family means the world to Carrie."

"Now that's the first thing we've agreed on," Mick said. "Which is why she belongs right here in Chesapeake Shores."

Ma put a hand on his shoulder. "She knows that, Mick. But she needs to be the one to explain it to Mr. Reynolds. I'd say the two of them have some unfinished business."

Mick frowned at that. "If the man were here because he wanted to tell her he was in love with her, I might agree, but that's not it, is it, Mr. Reynolds? He wants her to come back and be his workhorse again, the way she was before."

"I imagine Carrie will be smart enough to

understand the distinction," Nell said. "And if it's a job she wants to go back to, we'll have to live with that."

"Ma!"

Nell ignored him. "Mr. Reynolds, I think if you truly want our Carrie back working for you, you'll need to improve your presentation. She's not as gullible as she once was. I suggest you spend the night at the Inn at Eagle Point and put your best proposal on paper. We'll let Carrie know you're in town and, if she's interested, she'll meet you in the dining room there first thing tomorrow morning."

"I don't have time for this," the designer snapped impatiently. "I've come all the way from New York as it is. I'm scheduled to fly to Milan tomorrow."

"I'm sure you have an assistant who can change your travel arrangements," Nell said mildly.

"I don't," he grumbled. "That's the sort of thing that Carrie handled. The last two people in that position quit."

"It's so difficult to find competent help these days, isn't it?" Nell said sympathetically. "Little wonder you'd like our Carrie back. Make sure you tell her how valuable she was to you. I'm sure that will make an impression."

Seemingly resigned to following Nell's suggestion, Reynolds asked, "Where's this inn you mentioned?"

Mick gave him directions, then watched him leave before turning his gaze on his mother.

"You're a lot sneakier than I gave you credit for being. You know if he starts listing all the little menial tasks he wants her to do, Carrie will throw his offer back in his face."

"I think she's smart enough to see that he's looking for one of those gofer people," Nell agreed. "He's not interested in the kind of relationship Carrie thought she wanted with him. I also think she's smart enough to recognize that Sam is twice the man Marc Reynolds is, that she'll have a real partnership with him. And that her work here—a business she's building on her own from the ground up—will fulfill her in ways that job with Marc Reynolds never did."

"It's a big risk," Mick said. "Letting him dangle money and a fancy lifestyle in front of her."

"She had all that once and she still came home," Nell reminded him.

"Because that jerk broke her heart," Mick countered.

"No, because she knew it was where she belonged. If she'd only come to lick her wounds for a bit, would she be opening a day-care center? No, she'd have been on a plane back to Europe within a month. There were other designers she could have worked for, if that's what she truly wanted."

"I hope you're right," Mick said.

"Other than you, do you know of a single person in this family who knows what's in the hearts of our young ones better than I do?"

Mick smiled. "Now that you mention it, no."

"Then trust me. Carrie will send him on his way, that is if she shows up for that meeting at all."

"You going to tell her he's at the inn waiting to hear from her?"

Nell seemed to give the question a surprising amount of thought, then shrugged. "Could be I'll just leave it to fate. You do the same. We can consider it a test of that grapevine this town is reputed to have."

With that she walked down the steps and headed across the lawn toward her own cottage.

Fate? Mick stared after her. Or the Chesapeake Shores grapevine? Ma's sneakiness quotient just ticked up another notch.

"So, have you made your decision? Are you leaving?" Sam asked Carrie when he saw her in front of her house as he was heading home from work. She was on her knees pulling weeds, a streak of dirt on her face. He wanted to drag her into his arms and beg her to stay. Instead, he waited for her reply.

She regarded him curiously. "Leaving? I have no idea what you're talking about. I'm not planning a trip."

"I meant for good. That's why Marc Reynolds was here today, wasn't it? To lure you into coming back to him?"

She sat back on her heels and stared, clearly startled. "Sam, I never saw Marc, and even if I had, I certainly wouldn't be going anywhere with him. That part of my life is over and done with. I'm exactly where I want to be." Her gaze narrowed. "I thought you understood how important you and Bobby are becoming in my life, how determined I am to make this day-care center a success."

Relief washed over Sam, but he still had this tiny, niggling doubt tormenting him. "How can you say that with such certainty, if you don't know what he was offering?" he asked, though it did strike him as odd that the designer apparently hadn't even spoken to her. Was that Mick's doing?

"I can say it because it doesn't matter what he offers. I'm not going anywhere." She studied him curiously. "Sam, how do you even know that Marc was in town? Did you run into him? Did he say something to make you think I'd be jetting off with him?"

Regretting that he'd opened a whole can of worms that had somehow been left on the shelf by everyone else involved, Sam explained about Marc's visit to Sally's and the ensuing excitement.

"That's when I walked in. I never set eyes on

him myself. Sally said she pointed him in your grandfather's direction."

Carrie appeared taken aback yet again, but then her lips curved. Next thing he knew, she was laughing. "I'll bet that meeting went well. No wonder I haven't seen Marc. I probably need to investigate to make sure he's still in one piece."

"You don't seem overly concerned about whether he is or not," Sam said. This time he was able to bask in the relief that washed over him.

"There's almost nothing my grandfather could do, short of murder, that Marc doesn't deserve," she said, a surprisingly bloodthirsty note in her voice. Then she sighed. "But I really should check to see what's going on."

Just then her cell phone rang. She glanced at caller ID, then took the call. "Hey, Jess. What's going on?"

She listened to her aunt, another smile spreading across her face. "Yes, you can short-sheet his bed, and no, I won't be in it."

She disconnected the call and grinned at Sam. "Mystery solved. Gram dispatched him to the inn to work on a proper presentation to make to me in the morning. Jess says he's expecting me at nine."

"You going to be there?"

She stepped closer, stripped off her gardening gloves and framed his face with both hands. "Yes," she said, causing his heart to sink.

"Okay, I guess you need to hear him out," Sam said, deflated.

"I'm not going to hear him out," Carrie corrected. "I'm going to tell him good-bye once and for all. Then I'm going to find you and kiss you senseless, till you realize you're the only man I want in my life now."

Sam smiled at last. Now there was a plan he could definitely get behind.

"Stick to your guns, okay? I'd hate to have to find him and beat the tar out of him for hurting you again."

"You'd probably have to get in line to do that," she said. "But I love that you're willing to go that far to protect me."

"I'll go as far as I have to," he promised her quietly. She and Bobby were his life. As much as it surprised him, he knew he'd do whatever it took to keep them both safe and happy.

❦ 22 ❦

Carrie stood in the doorway to the inn's dining room and studied the man she'd once thought she loved. The sight of Marc no longer moved her as it once had. It seemed she'd recently fallen for a guy whose shirt was rarely tucked in, whose idea of fashion was a formfitting T-shirt that these days was most often smeared with jelly and whose hair was usually in need of a trim. Sam was a man whose world had been shaken by loss, and then turned upside down by instant parenthood, and yet he'd found a way to cope. Marc couldn't cope with making his own airline reservations.

In fact, Sam was quite a contrast to the man sitting at a table by the window, his attention focused on his tablet, rather than the spectacular view outside. Marc apparently couldn't even deal with the loss of an assistant with public-relations skills, though Carrie had to wonder if it was those skills he missed or her all-around adoration and twenty-four-hour availability for any and all tasks that made his life easier.

Now he was tapping impatiently on the tablet screen, his brow knit with a frown. He was too absorbed to notice her approach.

"I heard you wanted to see me," she said, pulling out a chair and sitting across from him.

He glanced up at that, delight spreading across his face. She had no doubt that much at least was genuine. If he needed her, which was the only explanation for his arrival in Chesapeake Shores, then he'd be all but certain she'd respond to his distress call and turn her life inside out to accommodate him. He'd no doubt dismissed her continued avoidance of his calls, considering that to be no more than an insignificant fit of pique.

"You look great!" he said, his gaze intent. "I

don't recognize the designer, though. Whose line are you wearing?"

"No idea," she said with a disinterested shrug. "I bought the clothes because they're practical for work."

He looked startled. "You have another job? I hadn't heard."

"I'm not surprised. News of my opening a day-care center wouldn't likely be on your radar."

He frowned at that. "A day-care center? You mean for children?"

"That's usually who they're meant for," she said, smiling at his reaction.

"Hold on, *you're* going to be a paid *baby-sitter?*" he asked incredulously.

She didn't bother taking offense. "It's a little more meaningful than that, but basically, yes. I should thank you. Had it not been for the whole fiasco with you, I never would have recognized what I was meant to do."

"Taking care of other people's children is not your calling," he scoffed. "If you think that, you're just settling. You were meant for much more."

"Such as making your airline reservations, dealing with the media, planting little items in the gossip columns to keep your name out there?"

"Of course. All of that is almost as essential in the fashion industry as the designs themselves."

"And no one's been able to fill that niche for

you the way I did? I assume that's why you're here. You discovered I'm indispensable? Or were my replacements too demanding? Maybe they expected time off? Or weren't willing to go along with the bedroom perks?"

He looked startled by her sarcastic tone. "I thought you loved your job."

"I loved you, you idiot! And I did the job exceedingly well to try to get your attention."

"Well, you have it now. I want you to come back to work for me, Carrie. I need you. There, I said it. Does that make you happy, knowing I can't function without you? I was foolish to let you leave, especially over some schoolgirl crush you thought you had on me."

She regarded him with shock. "That's what you think it was, a schoolgirl crush?" She sighed and shook her head. "That certainly explains a lot."

"Meaning?"

"It tells me the kind of man you are. You took advantage of a woman you thought had a silly, meaningless crush simply to make your life easier." She shook her head. "How could I possibly have been so blind?"

He winced at the scathing note in her voice. He finally seemed to realize she wasn't going to fall into line quite so readily and changed tactics. "Okay, I admit it. I didn't treat you well. I was careless with your feelings. It won't happen again, Carrie."

She sighed at his pitiful attempt to appear contrite. "As apologies go, that one lacked a certain amount of sincerity," she said. "But you are right about one thing. It won't happen again, because I'm not coming back, Marc."

He waved off the statement. "Of course you are. I'm prepared to make a very generous offer, much more than you were making before. It's certainly more than you'll ever make as a babysitter."

"Marc, there's not enough money in the world to persuade me to come back and be one of the minor planets orbiting around you," she said, standing. "I hope you take the time to look around town while you're here. It's a great place and it's filled with people who know what's important in life. Good-bye, Marc."

She turned on her heel and walked away. This time she didn't look back. Nor did she have a single regret. She could hardly wait to find Sam and make good on her promise. Kissing him senseless would wipe this depressing encounter right out of her head.

"Thanks for meeting me here," Connor told Mack as they sat on the deck at Brady's. The first crisp hint of fall was in the air and the warmth of the sun felt good.

"Why are we here instead of in your office?" Mack asked. "Or at the pub or Sally's?"

"Because I wanted this conversation to be

private. If you'd stopped by the office, someone might have gotten wind of it, and if we'd met at the pub or the café, word would have spread in a nanosecond. Even more likely, someone in the family would have joined us."

Mack studied him intently. "You're sounding awfully mysterious. What's going on?"

"I have news," Connor said. "And I'm not sure how you're going to feel about it, much less how Susie will react."

Mack saw exactly where this was heading. "Another adoption? Susie's definitely not ready to consider that, Connor. She's better, but she's still reeling from last time."

"It's not exactly another adoption," Connor said. He drew in a deep breath. "Let me just get this out. The mother changed her mind again. Things didn't work out with the boyfriend, and once again, she's decided she's not cut out for motherhood. She called my former law office and said she wanted to go through with the adoption."

Jaw dropping, Mack simply stared at him. When he could finally gather his thoughts, his temper kicked in. "Are you kidding me? Why in heaven's name would we take another chance with her? She clearly has no idea what she wants. I can't ask Susie to agree to this, maybe even to bring that baby girl home, and have this woman change her mind yet again. Having that baby literally ripped out of her arms this time would be the final straw for Susie."

"I know," Connor agreed, his tone quietly reasonable, a sharp contrast to Mack's incensed reaction. "It's a terrible risk, and there are no guarantees. There could very well be maneuvering room in the law for her to decide again that she wants to keep her baby." He leveled a look into Mack's eyes. "But here's the thing—this baby is real. It's available. It needs the sort of loving home you and Susie could provide."

"For the moment," Mack said direly.

"Yes, for the moment," Connor agreed.

"Let somebody else face the prospect of heartbreak," Mack said heatedly. "We can't do that to Susie again."

"Are you sure? Are you 100 percent certain the risk isn't worth it?" Connor sighed. "I'm really not trying to sell you on this. It has to be your decision, Mack. You know Susie better than any of us."

Mack raked a hand through his hair and regarded Connor with dismay. "What am I supposed to do? I can't bear the thought of Susie hurting like this ever again."

"Or this could be the best thing that ever happened," Connor said and reached into his pocket. He pushed a small square of paper in Mack's direction.

Mack flipped it over and saw a sweet little face

with a tiny bow of a mouth, huge brown eyes and a fluff of dark hair with a pink bow on an elastic ribbon. He drew in a sharp breath and something in his heart turned over.

"This is her?"

Connor nodded.

"She's beautiful," Mack whispered, awed by the possibility that she could be his daughter. If he was this taken with her after only a glimpse, how would Susie feel? Could he deny her the right to make this decision for herself, even though it came fraught with peril? "Connor, what am I supposed to do?"

"Take that picture home and talk to your wife," Connor said quietly. "You know that's the only real choice you have."

"Is there any way we can protect ourselves this time?" Mack asked. "Any way to make this decision binding and scrap the waiting period when the mom can suddenly take her from us?"

"I can try, given the circumstances. I can make a strong case for not allowing you to get burned twice, but the law really does give the birth mother a fair amount of protection."

"Even after she's proved her immaturity?" Mack said.

"Like I said, I can try."

Mack touched a finger to that tiny, precious face, then picked up the photo and tucked it into his pocket. He stood up. "I'll let you know."

"Don't wait too long," Connor warned. "Her attorney wants to move on this, get the baby settled into a good home."

Mack couldn't seem to prevent a hint of bitterness from creeping into his voice. "Any home would have to be better than where she is right now."

"Before you judge the mom too harshly, think about this. She really is trying to do right by her baby. And you and Susie could be the beneficiary of that."

Mack sighed. "You're right. I'll try to keep that in mind."

At home, while he waited for Susie to get there, Mack opened the door to the nursery Susie had decorated with so much joy and hope just a few months earlier. Unless she'd gone in there when he wasn't around, it had stood empty ever since she'd slammed the door shut on the day they'd gotten the news that the baby wouldn't be coming home with them.

And now he was about to ask her to get back onto that emotional roller coaster, even knowing how fragile her recovery was.

He heard the front door open and close, then heard her calling his name.

"Back here," he called out.

He heard Susie's footsteps getting closer, then nothing. He turned and saw her at the end of the hall, unable or unwilling to come into the room they'd decorated as a nursery.

"Why are you there?" she asked. "Please do not tell me it's time to dismantle the nursery, Mack. I know I've been struggling, but I'm doing the best I can. I can't face that room yet."

"Please," he said, and held out his hand. "Please, Suze. That's not what I'm asking, but we do need to talk. I think we need to do it here."

She hesitated for what seemed like an eternity before finally approaching. Even after she joined him, she kept her back to the room.

"I spoke to Connor earlier," he said, holding her gaze. "The mom has decided to give her baby up for adoption, after all."

Susie stared at him, clearly not comprehending. "What does that mean?"

"The baby could be ours, Susie." He let the thought hang in the air, tried to gauge her reaction, but her expression gave away nothing. "But we have to be willing to take another chance. It doesn't come with guarantees, though Connor says he'll try to make it as solid as he can." He drew the picture out of his pocket and handed it to her.

She reacted then. Tears filled her eyes and spilled down her cheeks. "Oh, my God," she whispered, then lifted her eyes to look into his. "She really could be ours, after all? When?"

"As soon as we agree, I think. Connor and I

didn't talk about that. I wasn't even 100 percent sure I should tell you. I don't think I could bear it if you got your heart broken again."

She studied the picture intently, then asked, "How can we say no, Mack?" When she looked up from the picture, her eyes were shining. "This little girl could be ours. Fate's giving us a second chance."

He studied her face and saw the Susie he'd fallen in love with, the one who almost always let hope and optimism outshine despair. "Are you sure this is what you want, even after what you've been through? I know I've been encouraging you to consider adoption again, but this mom, you know she could be a bad risk when it comes to sticking with her decision."

"Mack, I want so badly to hold a baby in my arms. I want us to have a family and this is our chance. I think this was meant to be. I have to believe that."

"And you're strong enough to deal with it, if it turns out you're wrong?" He pulled her close, rested his chin on her head. "Because I can't lose you over this, Suze. You're my world."

"And you're mine. You always have been. I think we can make room in it for one more."

Mack saw no way around it. As terrified as he was of a repeat of the last time, if this baby was what Susie needed, he'd put his own fears aside and move heaven and earth to see that it happened. He thought of the face in that tiny photograph and the powerful pull he'd felt as he'd stared into those solemn brown eyes.

"I'll call Connor," he said. "Why don't you open the windows and get a little fresh air into this room?"

While he made the call, he watched as Susie opened windows, then moved around the room, touching the mobile over the crib to set the little bunnies into motion, then taking a ruffled pink dress from the rack inside a white wardrobe and holding it to her face. She picked up a pale yellow onesie next, then a stuffed bunny, all the while with tears streaming.

Mack disconnected the call and went to his wife. "Connor thinks he can make the arrangements for tomorrow."

Her gaze shot up. "That soon?"

"Soon?" he said. "It feels as if we've been waiting forever."

"You're right, but an hour ago we didn't think it was possible. Now we have to be ready by tomorrow."

Mack looked around the perfect nursery. "I think we have pretty much everything we need."

"But I need to call everyone. We'll want to have the family here to meet her," she said excitedly. Then her face fell. "Or maybe not."

Mack knew exactly what she was thinking. "It won't be like last time, Suze." No matter what he had to do, he would make sure of that. This time they would bring a baby home.

"Still I think we'd better wait before planning anything," she said, her apprehension plain.

Her expression had lost a little of its spark. Mack could understand that. His own stomach was in turmoil. If it was possible for hope and dread to coexist, that's what was going on inside him right now. And if he felt this way, it would be quadrupled for Susie.

Please, God, let it work out this time, he prayed silently. Since his communications with God were pretty rare, he was tempted to call Nell and get her on the case, but they'd just agreed to keep this news to themselves a little longer. Hopefully his heartfelt plea would be enough just this once.

Sam watched warily as Carrie wandered around his living room, straightening this, examining that. She was clearly on edge, though he had no idea why. She'd already told him she'd sent Marc Reynolds on his way a couple hours earlier, so that was behind her. Was she having second thoughts already?

"Bobby's in school?" she asked eventually.

"He left a couple of hours ago," Sam said. Surely she already knew that, given it was midmorning.

"Then we're alone?"

Suddenly he understood her nerves. They were

430

alone with no likely interruptions. "We are alone," he said, walking across the room to join her.

"And you don't have to be at work right away?"

"Not till much, much later," he confirmed. "You?"

"If I spend another minute going over the same papers for the hundredth time or checking the supplies, I might lose my mind," she admitted. "I'm as ready to open as I'm going to be."

"Interesting," he said, running his finger along the curve of her jaw. "Here we both are, all alone, at loose ends. What do you suppose we should do?"

Her gaze held his. "If you don't come up with an idea pretty darn quickly, you're not the man I thought you were."

Sam laughed and scooped her into his arms, but instead of heading for a bedroom, he sat on the sofa, Carrie snuggled in his lap.

She regarded him with obvious disappointment. "Seriously?"

"I am not going to drag you off to my room to make love for the very first time just because we both have some time to kill," he said. "That's no way to treat a lady."

"Are you sure? The idea holds a lot of appeal to me. I thought you were as frustrated as I am."

"Believe me, I'm plenty frustrated," Sam said with heartfelt emotion. In fact, if she kept wiggling around, she was going to discover just how ready he was to take the next step. "I'm trying to play fair. You're not the kind of woman a man just ravishes without thinking of the consequences."

Her eyes narrowed. "Are we talking about condoms?"

This time her expression was so filled with disbelief that Sam resisted the desire to laugh. "No, we're okay on the condom front."

"Then what consequences?"

"Carrie, what does sleeping with me mean to you?"

"It means what it would to any woman," she said impatiently, "that we're getting closer, as close as two people can be. And, believe me, I'm aware that it doesn't always mean the same thing to men. I learned that the hard way from the very man who tried to entice me back into his life earlier this morning."

"And that's why I want to be sure you and I are on the same page before we take that step. It would kill me to think that I'd hurt you the way Marc Reynolds did."

"You couldn't possibly do that, unless you've been secretly seeing some model I don't know about."

"You're the only woman I'm seeing, the only woman I want in my life," he said with complete sincerity.

"Then you're making this a lot more complicated than it needs to be," she said.

Sam knew what he was about to say was likely going to get this sexy, wonderful woman not only out of his arms, but likely out the door. Still, he had to be honest with her. Cards on the table, and all that.

"If I were remotely ready to take the next step," he said.

"You mean sex?"

"I mean marriage."

Her eyes widened. "When did marriage enter into this?"

"Right now, or at least it should have. You're the kind of woman who deserves to walk down the aisle in a gorgeous white gown with your whole family looking on. I want that for you."

"Okay," she said slowly. "But?"

"I'm not sure I can be the guy who's waiting for you at the front of the chapel."

She was on her feet in a heartbeat, just as he'd predicted, looking glorious in her anger.

"Have I said one single word about marriage? Have I hinted that I need a ring on my finger? Or that you'd be the man I want to put it there? No, I have not! I'm no more ready for that than you are."

She started to pace. "How could I have done this twice?" she asked of no one in particular.

"Done what twice?" Sam asked, confused.

"Fallen in love with a complete idiot."

When he stared at her in shock, she waved him off with an impatient gesture. "Oh, don't go getting yourself all worked up. I might love you, but I'm not some clinging vine who needs hearts and flowers and romance every minute of every day. I need a partner who values me. I need a man who wants what I want, who knows the importance of family. I thought that might be you. Maybe you're not the one who's an idiot. Maybe it's me, after all."

"You are not an idiot," Sam said forcefully. "The jury's probably still out on me. I'm just trying to do the right thing."

"Yeah, you want to be fair. You don't want to take advantage of me under false pretenses. I get it. You're noble."

She made it sound as if that was the worst thing in the world he could possibly be. Since, at the moment, it was keeping her out of his bed, where they both wanted to be, maybe she was right.

Chin held high, she leveled a look at him. "Call me when you decide you're ready to take the next step. If you're very, very lucky, maybe I'll still be available."

And then she was gone, just as Sam had also predicted. He'd done the right thing just now. He knew in his heart that he had. He'd been honest.

So why did it feel as if it had cost him everything he'd ever wanted?

434

❧ 23 ❧

Carrie opened her kitchen cupboards, which were filled with family castoffs, and tried to choose a dish she wasn't overly fond of, something dispensable, something she wouldn't regret smashing into a thousand pieces.

Her gaze fell on a gravy boat. Who needed a gravy boat? Not her, since she hadn't cooked a meal requiring gravy even once in her entire life. Gravy was Nell's domain, as were the mashed potatoes and everything else that tasted better when covered with rich, flavorful gravy. Her attempt to make gravy under Nell's tutelage hadn't gone all that well. She doubted she'd repeat it.

She yanked the piece off the shelf and tested the weight in her hand, delighted to discover it wasn't some kind of delicate porcelain, but rather something substantial that would make a satisfying crash against the wall. Too bad she couldn't toss it straight at Sam's hard head.

Wasn't it enough that she'd had to deal with Marc again first thing this morning and send him on his way? Had she really needed Sam going all noble on her and refusing to sleep with her because he wasn't ready for marriage, wasn't sure he ever would be?

Really? What man refused when a willing woman was stretched across his lap? It wasn't as if he'd been immune to her, either. That would have opened a whole other kettle of fish, but she knew he wanted her just as badly as she'd wanted him. There'd been no mistaking the evidence of that.

So, he was an idiot or a saint. Because it suited her mood, she was going with idiot! Saying a mental good-bye to the gravy boat, she hurled it at the wall, where it shattered so thoroughly, gave her such satisfaction that she grabbed blindly for something else, anything else that might get this fit of temper out of her system.

She pulled back her arm to throw a silly souvenir mug from Paris—two birds with one mug, so to speak, since Marc had bought the stupid thing for her—when she heard her mom's voice.

"So this is why you didn't answer the door when I knocked," Abby said, looking at the shards of pottery on the floor and the mug still gripped tightly in Carrie's hand. "Having a bad day?"

Abby plucked the mug out of danger, then walked to the pot of coffee that was still warm on the kitchen counter and filled the mug. "Think of this as giving it one last useful moment before you destroy it," she said.

Carrie studied her mother with a suspicious

gaze. "Mom, what are you doing here? I don't imagine you came to rescue my dishes."

"I heard Marc was in town. Jess said you had quite the meeting at the inn. I thought you might need to talk."

Carrie waved off the entire confrontation with Marc. "It doesn't matter. *He* doesn't matter."

"Good to know," Abby said with satisfaction, studying Carrie over the rim of the mug as she took a leisurely sip of coffee. "So," she asked eventually, "the shattered pottery has nothing to do with Marc?"

"Nope."

"No more unresolved feelings, no more longing for what you once had?"

Carrie actually shuddered. "Not even a tiny bit."

"I'm glad to hear it," Abby said. "He wasn't worthy of you." She studied Carrie for another minute, then said oh-so-innocently, "So, this must be about Sam."

Carrie frowned. "Why must it be about Sam? Why does it have to be about any man? Maybe I'm just having a lousy day. Maybe I failed an inspection at the day-care center. Maybe Grandpa Mick made me crazier than usual."

Her mother made a valiant effort to hide a smile, but failed miserably. "Okay, that's fair enough. I jumped to a conclusion. I'll rephrase. What brought on this mood?"

Carrie didn't appreciate the oh-so-patient, patronizing tone, especially since they both knew what her response was going to be. "Sam, of course." Before her mom could gloat, she added, "But I don't want it to be about Sam. I don't want it to be about me falling for yet another man I've apparently been reading all wrong. Marc accused me of having a little schoolgirl crush on him, something of no consequence. Maybe that's all it is with Sam, too. He certainly doesn't see it going anywhere."

"Have you stopped to consider the possibility that he's scared? This is a man who, by his own admission, never really thought much about settling down, much less having a family. Now, out of the blue, he's a dad. And, also out of the blue, he discovers he has feelings for you. That's a lot for a carefree guy to try to absorb in a matter of a few months."

"I'm not trying to rush him down the aisle, for heaven's sake. I just want to sleep with him."

Abby didn't even try to contain her laugh at that. "Too much information, sweetie. Not that I'm easily shocked. We've all seen this coming. And we all know that you have very little patience. You want what you want when you want it. I blame your grandfather for that. He always saw that you and your sister got everything you ever asked for. I'm sure if you were to tell him you want to jump into bed with Sam, he'd do his level best to make that happen, too."

"Mom!" Carrie protested, though she, too, laughed. "He probably would, wouldn't he?"

"It might make him a little crazy, because you are one of his innocent little angels, but yes, he probably would. Do you want that?"

"Heavens, no!" she said fervently. "If Grandpa Mick interferes, it would probably send Sam packing."

"And you don't want that?"

"No, of course not. I don't want marriage, either. Not right away, anyway."

"But you are in love with Sam? And you see marriage to him in your future?"

Carrie sighed. "I'm scared to," she admitted. "He might never change his mind."

"Oh, I think he will, once his nerves have a chance to settle."

"So we're back to patience," Carrie said, resigned.

"And that open heart Nell talks about so much." Abby set her mug in the sink and pulled Carrie into an embrace. "Focus on the day-care center for now. We're going to celebrate that at Sunday dinner. Nell has all your favorites on the menu. Enjoy your big moment. Focus on the grand opening that's coming up in just a few more weeks. Everything else will fall into place."

"Promise?" Carrie said wistfully. O'Brien promises were always kept.

"As much as it's in my power," Abby said, then smiled. "And we always have your grandfather in reserve for backup."

Carrie chuckled, just as her mom had intended. She had to wonder, though—if it came right down to it, she'd resort to whatever devious means were necessary to convince Sam the future wasn't as scary as he was imagining it to be . . . as long as they faced it together.

Sam spent the rest of the morning after Carrie's departure pacing around his house and trying to convince himself he'd done the right thing. Somehow, though, he couldn't shake the look on her face as she'd left, as if he'd turned his back on something important. Not just sex, but on the two of them.

Since the house wasn't big enough to contain his frustrated pacing, he stepped outside just in time for the arrival of the mail carrier, who handed him an express envelope. Glancing at the return address, he saw it was from Robert's parents.

Inside there was a sealed envelope he recognized at once as being Laurel's favorite lavender stationary. A note from Robert's mother had been paper-clipped to it.

Dear Sam, I found this addressed to you when we were cleaning out the house. I'm sorry I didn't spot it sooner, but I wanted to get it to you as quickly as I could. I hope you and Bobby are doing well and that we can all get together soon. We loved the pictures from the birthday party. Thanks so much for doing that. Sincerely, Delores

Sam's hand trembled as he held the envelope from his sister. Why had she tucked it away somewhere and never mailed it? He sighed. Only one way to find out.

He tore open the envelope and removed two sheets of faintly scented stationary.

My dearest Sam,

As I write this, I'm hoping you'll never read it, but if you are, then something has happened to me and Robert. I know it must be hard for you to imagine that I had enough foresight to prepare for the worst, but that's what maturity and having a family does to a carefree spirit like mine.

I suspect you're pretty angry with Robert and me for picking you as Bobby's guardian, but he and I agreed that you're the absolute best choice. I think I know you even better than you know yourself. For years you've been running from the past—our past—but that's no way to find what you truly need. To do that you need to fall deeply in love and create the kind of family we never had. I've done that with Robert and our boy. I think Bobby will be that blessing in your life, too.

You can do this, Sam. You're a better man than our dad. You're a forever guy. If I didn't believe that with my whole heart, I'd have let Robert's parents take Bobby. But our son needs exactly what you can provide if you believe in yourself. You'll give him a home and stability—I'll bet you already have, haven't you?—and you'll give him the taste of adventure every little boy needs to thrive, too.

We love you, Sam. We're trusting you with the most valuable part of us. I know you won't let us down. Don't let yourself down, either, and grab every ounce of happiness that's out there for yourself.

Love, Laurel and Robert

The pages, dampened with Sam's tears, fluttered to the ground. He thought of his sister and the faith she had in him, of Carrie and the trust she'd placed in him. And he thought of Bobby, who believed that Sam could make everything in his life okay.

"Carrie was right," he murmured. "I am an idiot."

And at the very first opportunity, he was going to claim the happiness that just a few short hours ago he hadn't felt he deserved. He just prayed he wasn't too late.

● ● ●

Susie was clinging so tightly to Mack's hand, she'd almost cut off the circulation.

"What's taking so long?" she asked for what had to be the tenth time.

"It's not as if we're picking up produce at a farm stand," Mack soothed. "I'm sure there's a lot of paperwork and Connor's probably doing everything he can to make sure we're protected."

They were sitting in a conference room at Connor's old law offices in Baltimore, waiting for the moment when they would finally hold their baby.

"Do you suppose we'll have to see the mom?" Susie asked.

"Do you want to?"

"I do and I don't. I want to thank her for doing this, for giving us this amazing gift. Then I think about all the heartache and I want to snatch the hair right off her head."

Mack knew she wasn't entirely joking. He was pretty much filled with mixed emotions, too. "Let's just focus on the gratitude," he suggested.

Just then the door opened and Connor walked in, a baby girl—*their* baby girl—cradled in his arms.

"Susie, Mack, I'd like you to meet your daughter. Her mom's given her a name, but you're free to change it. I'm thinking you might not want to."

Mack watched as his wife took a hesitant step forward, then reached out and gently brushed a finger along the baby's cheek. Tears were streaming down Susie's face. His own eyes were welling up—at this incredible, long-awaited moment and at the joy shining in Susie's eyes right along with those tears.

Susie held out her arms and Connor carefully placed the baby into them. "I'm shaking," Susie whispered.

"You're doing fine," Connor assured her. His eyes looked a little damp, too.

"What did the mom name her?" Susie asked.

"Josephine," Connor said. "She's been calling her Jo."

Susie's gaze lifted in shock. "My mom's name?" Connor nodded.

"I think it's perfect," Mack said. "What do you think, Suze?"

Blinking back tears, she looked into his eyes. "I think this was meant to be, don't you?"

His throat tightened at the pure joy on her face. "I think it's the miracle we've all been praying for." He cast a quick look in Connor's direction. "It is, isn't it?"

"It's as airtight as I can possibly make it," Connor promised. "She's yours."

Mack moved to his wife's side and gazed down into that sweet, precious little face that had captivated him from the instant he'd set eyes on her tiny picture. He put an arm around his wife, then tucked his other hand beneath the baby, feeling the weight of her, close enough now to draw in that baby smell that women always grew so nostalgic about. Susie looked up into his eyes, then down into the face of their daughter.

"Jo, I'm your mom and this is your dad. We're going to love you so much it'll probably make you crazy, but you are our gift from God, and we'll never forget that."

"Never," Mack said, his heart suddenly so full he couldn't help wondering how he'd ever thought their life would be complete without this tiny little princess in his wife's arms.

Now, at long last, they had their family.

On Sunday, Sam once again found himself at the big family dinner at Mick O'Brien's, though this time it was Mack who'd insisted he come.

"We're celebrating the opening of Carrie's day-care center. You should be there," Mack had said. "I don't care what sort of disagreement the two of you had. Today's a day for showing that we support her."

"Shouldn't the focus be on you and Susie and your new baby?" Sam had asked. Though he was eager to make things right with Carrie, he wasn't sure this was the occasion for it. "This will be her introduction to the family, right?"

The bemused look of a new dad passed across

Mack's face. "Believe me, everybody in the family has been by the house at least once to get a peek at her. The christening is coming up in a couple of months, once we're certain the adoption is going to be finalized. I imagine she's going to get passed around to every female present on Sunday, but the day is really about Carrie. I know you care about her. Be there to share this with her."

Sam had been just desperate enough for a glimpse of Carrie to agree. She'd been surprisingly elusive ever since she'd walked out of his house a few days earlier. No question that she'd been deliberately avoiding him. What else had he expected since he'd all but told her that he didn't intend to get involved in anything serious.

Now that he'd come to his senses, in part because of his sister's reassurances from beyond the grave, he was ready to take it all back. He wanted Carrie to know that he was crazy in love with her.

Bobby clearly adored her, too. In fact, the second they'd arrived at Mick's and he'd spotted Carrie in the yard, he'd gone running off to throw his arms around her. She'd glanced Sam's way, then, just as quickly, looked away. With her cheeks pink, her hair tousled and kids swarming around her, she was everything the perfect mother should be, not a thing in the world like the sad, broken woman with whom he'd grown up.

How had he ever thought he could turn away from that, he asked himself. Even a six-year-old had sense enough to gravitate straight to her. As his sister had essentially told him, it was time for him to start running toward something, rather than away from it. People who loved deeply got hurt. They suffered terrible losses. It was unavoidable. But loving deeply was the only way to truly live.

Gathering up his courage and all the strength that came from knowing this was the right thing to do—for him and for Bobby—Sam walked slowly across the yard. He was halfway to Carrie, when she noticed his approach. Gazes locked, she extricated herself from the kids and took a half step in his direction, then stopped and waited. Clearly, she was leaving whatever happened next up to him. He got that. He'd rebuffed her too many times before.

"Hi," he said inanely when he reached her.

A smile tugged at her lips. "Hi."

"I'm sorry."

"For?"

"Being an idiot."

"I have it on good authority, you're not the first man to excel at it."

"How are you at forgiving it and moving on?"

"I'm not sure," she said. "I haven't been tested that often."

"I love you, Carrie."

Shock registered in her eyes. Clearly she hadn't expected the words to come out here, maybe ever. "Seriously?"

"Don't tell me I've finally surprised you."

"You said something about moving on. The love thing is pretty much out of the blue."

He held her gaze. "Is it?"

"For you, I meant. Not for me. I saw the handwriting on the wall for us weeks ago."

"Yeah, about that handwriting. It took me a while to translate it into a language I could understand."

"English?"

"No, the language of the heart. I'll admit I had a little help."

"From?" A horrified look crossed her face. "Please tell me my grandfather didn't have anything to do with this?"

"No. I had a letter from my sister."

Her eyes widened. "Seriously?"

"Apparently Robert's parents found it as they were cleaning out the house. She told me why she wanted Bobby to be with me. She had so much faith that I could get this right, and she encouraged me to take a chance on happiness when I found it, so that's what I'm doing. I'm going for broke here. I'm willing to choose love over fear."

"Fear?"

"That I could lose you."

She tucked her hand into his. "I'm not going anywhere, Sam."

He nodded, choosing to have faith. He swallowed hard. "Okay, then. If you're not afraid to take a chance on a guy who never imagined he'd settle down in one place with a wife and a houseful of kids, then I'm not afraid of that anymore, either."

She searched his face. "You're sure, Sam? Really sure? Because once we go inside and people find out we're together, there will be hell to pay if you decide later to bail on me."

"No bailing," he swore. "Not on my side."

A full-fledged smile broke across her face then. "Not on mine, either."

"Then I guess it's safe to tell Bobby, your parents and your grandfather," he said, pulling her into his arms, then murmuring against her lips, "Maybe not right this minute, though."

But by the time he'd kissed her thoroughly in front of what grew to be a cheering throng of O'Briens, he figured there was no need to make any sort of announcement. The news that he'd come to his senses was clearly out!

Bobby danced around them, his excitement contagious. "We're getting married," he announced to anyone who'd listen.

"Hey, pal, that news is supposed to come from me and Carrie," Sam told him, though he couldn't help being grateful for the help in making that final leap.

Abby and Trace were quick to offer their congratulations, then Mick O'Brien headed their way. He hugged his granddaughter, then gave Sam a hearty slap on the back. "Welcome to the family, son!"

"Thank you, sir. You've set the bar for this family pretty high. I'll do my best to deserve to be a part of it."

"You just love my girl here with your whole heart and you'll have done everything I've ever asked of anyone." Mick looked around, a beaming smile on his face. "Ma sent me out here to get all you hooligans inside and around the table. Dinner's ready. Wait till she hears this news. I imagine she'll be raiding my fancy wine cellar for my best champagne." He cast a meaningful look toward Mack, Susie and their baby girl. "O'Briens have a lot to celebrate today and more blessings than any man has a right to ask for."

"Amen to that," Megan said, linking her arm through his.

As Sam, Carrie and Bobby joined the others heading inside, Sam stopped for a moment to look into Carrie's eyes. He needed to be sure she understood exactly how he was feeling.

"Just so you know, marriage was part of that whole speech of mine a while ago, even if

Bobby kind of stole my thunder by getting the actual words out before I could. I love you, Carrie."

"I love you, too, with all my heart." She reached for Bobby's hand, too, and winked at him. "We're getting married!"

"Awesome!" Bobby declared.

Sam caught Carrie's gaze and held it. "It is pretty darn awesome."

In fact, he couldn't think of a single thing to top it. Then he glanced at Susie and Mack staring down into the face of their daughter, their expressions filled with awe. *Except, perhaps, that,* Sam thought. A baby would complete things.

Even as the thought struck, he waited for panic to follow. When it didn't come, when the only thing stirring inside him was anticipation, he knew all the adventures he'd ever need were right here.

❧ EPILOGUE ☙

Mick sat at the head of the massive table in his dining room for Sunday dinner and looked around with satisfaction. Smaller tables had been added here and there, squeezed into corners, for his grandchildren. So many leaves had been added to the main table, it actually stuck out of the room and into the foyer. Even so, he could see everyone who mattered to him in this life.

Megan was right next to him. When it came to his greatest blessings, she was right up there. He was thankful every day that they'd made their peace. Their marriage was on a more solid foundation today than it had been at any time since they'd first wed so many years ago.

Ma was at the opposite end of the table, reunited with Dillon, the Irishman who'd been her first love and who'd come back into her life just a few years ago, a timely if unexpected reunion that allowed them to live out their days together.

In between, his brothers and their spouses and their grown children, all married now. His own children were there, too, most of them parents themselves now. Abby's twins were the first of his grandchildren to marry and Caitlyn had even given him his first great-grandchild, little Jackson McIlroy. Too bad about that Scottish heritage, but Mick could live with it as long as his girl was happy. He had a feeling it wouldn't be long before Caitlyn's sister, Carrie, added yet another baby to the mix. She and Sam had the look of two people who couldn't wait to get started on adding to their family.

He was blessed, to be sure! Everyone always thought that this town that he'd designed and built from scratch, butting heads with his brothers all the way, was his pride and joy. To be sure, Chesapeake Shores was the crowning achievement of his career. It was a community the way a community was meant to be, filled with good people who cared about one another.

But the crowning achievement of his life was right here in this room, a strong family with a solid foundation of values and love. They'd made their share of mistakes, him most of all—not that he'd ever admit it aloud—but they'd learned from those mistakes. They were stronger for having weathered tough times. They were stronger for having each other.

As if she sensed his thoughts, Megan reached over and took his hand in hers. He lifted their clasped hands and brushed a kiss across her knuckles.

"It's a little overwhelming sometimes, isn't it?" she said quietly. "Looking around and seeing this family gathered together, thinking of everything we've been through."

"It is, indeed," Mick said.

For most men the sight would have been satisfaction enough, evidence of a life well-lived, but his glance strayed to the little ones at those tables Ma had tucked into corners of the room. They were the future of the O'Briens, and until they were grown and settled, his work here was far from done.

Megan smiled. "You know, Mick, there are

always going to be more O'Brien babies in this world," she said, as if once more she'd been reading his mind. "We can't stick around to guide them all. Sooner or later we'll just have to trust that the lessons you've passed on, the values your mother taught you and your brothers are in their hands."

Mick nodded, suddenly aware of his own mortality. He squeezed his wife's hand. "But not just yet," he said softly. "Not just yet."

Center Point Large Print
600 Brooks Road / PO Box 1
Thorndike, ME 04986-0001 USA

(207) 568-3717

US & Canada:
1 800 929-9108
www.centerpointlargeprint.com